本书为广州市哲学社会科学发展"十三五"规划2019年度一般课题（编号：2019GZYB51）最终成果

陈津津 著

英语诗歌创意写作研究

南京大学出版社

图书在版编目(CIP)数据

英语诗歌创意写作研究/陈津津著. —南京：南京大学出版社，2024.5
ISBN 978-7-305-28027-6

Ⅰ.①英… Ⅱ.①陈… Ⅲ.①英语诗歌—诗歌创作—研究 Ⅳ.①I052

中国国家版本馆 CIP 数据核字(2024)第 055810 号

出版发行	南京大学出版社
社　　址	南京市汉口路 22 号　　邮　编　210093
书　　名	英语诗歌创意写作研究 YINGYU SHIGE CHUANGYI XIEZUO YANJIU
著　　者	陈津津
责任编辑	官欣欣　　　　　　　编辑热线　025-83593947
照　　排	南京开卷文化传媒有限公司
印　　刷	南京人文印务有限公司
开　　本	787 mm×1092 mm　1/16　印张 18　字数 373 千
版　　次	2024 年 5 月第 1 版　2024 年 5 月第 1 次印刷
ISBN	978-7-305-28027-6
定　　价	98.00 元

网　　址：http://www.njupco.com
官方微博：http://weibo.com/njupco
微信服务号：njuyuexue
销售咨询热线：(025)83594756

* 版权所有，侵权必究
* 凡购买南大版图书，如有印装质量问题，请与所购图书销售部门联系调换

前　言

诗　歌

　　诗歌是古老的文学体裁，人类社会很早就使用诗歌形式进行记录或者交流活动。比如，古希腊神谕是用诗歌形式说出来的；古希伯来先知们使用诗歌形式做出预言；美索不达米亚和埃及的古代文献是用诗歌形式写成的；印度最古老的宗教文献《吠陀》也是诗歌文献；中国最早的诗歌集《诗经》中收集的最早诗歌距今已有三千年左右；前穆斯林时期的阿拉伯预言家也是用诗歌传达预言。不管是在古代西方还是古代东方，诗作者即诗人的两个主要职责都是：一、预言；二、赞美[1]。

　　在古代社会，诗人还常常同时扮演其他角色，如萨满巫师、部落首领、教师、史官，等等。据公元前一世纪的文献记载，高卢人把抒情诗人称为吟游诗人(bard)，这些诗人使用里拉琴(lyre)伴奏吟唱诗歌。吟游诗人同时记录部落历史。不管是和平时期还是战争时期，吟游诗人和德鲁伊祭司(druid)一样都得到高卢人的尊敬。在战时，对吟游诗人和德鲁伊祭司的尊敬不仅适用于己方也适用于敌方。在古代中国，很多诗人同时也是政府官员，而在古爱尔兰人中，教士诗人(fili)的地位相当于国王或者主教。在古爱尔兰和古印度，诗人是某些家族的世袭职业，需要经过长达数年甚至二十几年的专门训练。当然，世袭的诗人与宫廷联系紧密，收入不菲[2]。

　　千百年来，诗歌曾经占据西方社会文化生活的中心地位。但是，随着社会中神性信仰(Mythos)逐渐被理性罗各斯(Logos)取代，情况开始发生改变。到十九世纪部分因为工业革命，部分因为抒情诗(lyric)代替诗剧(drama)和叙事诗(narrative)成为诗歌的主要形式，诗歌在西方社会生活中的功能发生了变化。前现代主义和现代主义诗人如查尔斯·波德莱尔(Charles Baudelaire)和亚瑟·兰波(Arthur Rimbaud)等使用各种前所未有的实验手法创作诗歌，挑战传统诗歌功能与诗人形象。此外，精神病学家和心理

---

[1] 参见 Dobyns, Stephen. *Next Word, Better Word: The Craft of Writing Poetry*. New York: Palgrave Macmillan (a division of St. Martin's Press LLC), 2011(e-book), chap.13。

[2] 参见 Dobyns, chap.13。

学家如西格蒙·弗洛伊德(Sigmund Freud)等则试图勾画无意识版图,使主观自我可以量化研究,于是诗歌逐渐被社会边缘化,失去往日的文化中心地位①。不过,虽然诗歌在二十世纪西方文化舞台上虽未占据中心地位,但不同时期的诗歌运动和流派却一直活跃在社会文化生活当中。

诗歌是创造语言新用法的文学体裁。与散文相比,诗歌语言主要有两个特点:一、诗歌语言集中、精准。如果说散文是均匀挥洒、让人看到大地万象的阳光,诗歌则更像是黑夜中的火炬,集中照亮某个事物的细节。好的诗歌不用一个冗词,不说一句废话。二、与语言的所指相比,诗歌更关注语言本身,尤其重视语言的声音。抒情诗既是一种诗歌体裁也是一种诗歌观念,常常使用第一人称,主观、感性。在西方诗学中,基于诗歌与抒情诗都具有的主观、感性和形式集中的特点而把所有诗歌都叫做抒情诗的倾向至今依然存在②。这样的诗歌在很大意义上是人类的一种精神和情感旅程。读者读诗可以了解人类的情感历史,而诗人写诗就是记录和创造自己的情感历史。

诗人、创作、读者

诗人至少有两种才能,一是精通语言,二是有丰富的想象力。真正的诗人不一定是好诗人,但一定是一位充满激情、充满写作欲望的诗人。诗人比较敏感,能够比常人看到更多的颜色,对同一事物有着比常人更为独特的阐释和更为丰富的反应。诗人的心中总有一种单纯的天真浪漫,总有一种精神冲动想把看到的、听到的、想到的东西转化为诗。正如诗人威廉·华兹华斯(William Wordsworth)在"我心跳加速"("My Heart Leaps Up")一诗中看到天空中的彩虹就会心跳加速一样,真正的诗人天真、浪漫,至老都童心未泯:

My Heart Leaps Up
By William Wordsworth

My heart leaps up when I behold
    A rainbow in the sky:
So was it when my life began;
So is it now I am a man;
So be it when I shall grow old,
    Or let me die!

---

① 参见 Dobyns, chap.13。
② 参见 Greene, Roland. ed. *The Princeton Encyclopedia of Poetry and Poetics*. 4th edition. New Jersey: Princeton University Press, 2012, p.826. 本书对此文献的参考或引用标注为 *The Princeton Encyclopedia*。

The Child is father of the Man;
And I could wish my days to be
Bound each to each by natural piety.①

  诗人写诗可能出于不同的动机。有的诗人创作是为了对自己进行心理疗伤和宣泄;有的是为了认识自我和发展自我;有的是为了以诗的形式保留自己的生命历史痕迹,记录并与读者分享自己的经历,在读者脑中激活诗人看到、听到、想到的意象、声音、思想;有的是为了在世界上获得一席之地、获得承认。不过,诗人写诗的最根本动机是为了获得快感,因为写诗可以创造美,可以进行语言游戏,可以享受语言游戏带来的纯粹快乐。写诗的快感只有诗人才能感受得到,与作品质量无关,与读者是否欣赏无关。诗人可能会用傻气、荒谬、疯狂、无用这样的词来形容自己的诗歌创作,但同时又会享受到巨大的成就感。这种成就感的主要来源之一就是写作的快感。

  诗人写诗可以傻气,可以游戏,甚至自以为是,但却不可以心胸狭隘。诗人,应该视野开阔、胸怀悲悯,有共情力和同理心。诗人不可以虚伪。但这并不是说诗歌不可以想象、创造故事和细节,而是说诗人不可以对情感和认知虚伪。诗人应该人格完整、情感真挚。诗人的创作可能与其本人的阅读和学习紧密相关。能够激发想象力的、有趣的阅读与学习对进行创作的诗人意义重大。不过,诗人需要在写作过程中学会创作。学习创作中的诗人要注意避免四个误区:一、为杂事困扰,找不到时间写作;二、写作练习做得太少,无法取得实质性进步;三、无法接受写作过程的挫折,坚持不下去;四、敝帚自珍,对自己的作品失去批判能力与意愿,拒绝修改重写②。

  一首诗的创作可能始于诗歌灵感的突然降临,也可能始于诗人对诗歌灵感的有意识激发,包括对自动写作过程的有意识模仿和对某些诗歌理念规则的实践,等等。诗歌创作灵感有时激昂澎湃,有时蛰伏静守,这是一个自然过程和现象。诗人不能错过激情澎湃的创作高光时机,也不必过于忧虑灵感的暂时匮乏。不过,真正的诗人在灵感相对干涸的时间里,也会坚持练习和书写,在练笔中静待高光时刻的来临,因为缪斯不会垂青于无准备的人。初学英语诗歌创作的中国诗人更加需要坚持练笔。

  诗歌创作既可以学,也可以教。英语诗歌创意写作教学发源于美国爱荷华大学,其教学目标是培养诗人。诗歌工作坊(poetry workshop)是英美高校诗歌创意写作教学的典型模式。在诗歌工作坊课程教学中,每个学生既是诗人,又是读者,既研究熟悉经典诗作和诗歌术语理念、丰富诗歌创作技巧、提高诗歌写作能力,也从诗人教师和同学诗人那里获得读者阅读反应和评论意见,研究自己作品的优点与不足,找到最好的诗歌

---

  ① 转引自 Vendler, Hellen. *Poems, Poets, Poetry: An Introduction and Anthology*. Boston: Bedford Books of St. Martin's Press, 1997, p.577。
  ② 参见 Kowit, Steve. *In the Palm of Your Hand: The Poet's Portable Workshop*, Gardiner Maine: Tilbury House Publishers, 1995, p. v。

表现形式，进而发展出自己的诗歌风格和特色。因为诗人可能遇到的最大写作障碍（writing block）是没有灵感，所以诗人教师会采用各种方式激发学生诗人的诗歌灵感和创作热情。

英语诗歌创意写作教学在各个过程中激发学生的创作灵感。首先，让学生熟悉各种诗歌术语、运动、传统和形式并研究经典、成功诗作，目的是为了使学生获得创作灵感，并将真正引起心灵共鸣的观点、形式、技巧运用于自己的创作实践中。其次，要求学生对任何诗歌创作可能性保持开放态度，并采用各种方法，比如设计各种诗歌题材要求、设计各种实验技巧形式或语言游戏规则、鼓励学生根据各种规则合作写诗、运用课堂物理环境激发学生不同情感体验进行创作、把诗歌工作坊与其他艺术课堂结合起来、运用通艺作诗法（ekphrasis）等各种方法激发学生的创作灵感。再次，在工作坊环节中让学生阅读和评论同学诗作，使学生在与同行诗人的思想撞击中进一步触发创作灵感。

在诗歌初稿写作中，诗人可以不考虑读者因素，但在修改甚至重写过程中，诗人就应该考虑读者反应，判断作品中哪些是有效表达，能够准确激起理想的读者情感反应，让读者获得期待的读诗效果。因为即使诗人不是为了发表出版而创作诗歌，其写作也是为了跟某些目标读者比如百年之后的未来读者进行交流，而读者读诗主要是期待从读诗中得到愉悦，感受自己的生命，从诗中找到自己。因为诗人经常难以判断自己作品中哪些是有效表达，所以很多严肃诗人在诗稿修改甚至重写过程中会仔细倾听读者意见。英语诗歌创意写作教学的工作坊环节中一个公认原则是在同学评论过程中诗作者要保持沉默，因为征求和倾听读者意见有一个普遍规则就是诗人不能向读者揭示写作目的，不能做辩解，以此获得最真诚的读者反应。

诗人应该对读者反应持辩证态度，对读者意见保有采用与否的自由。诗歌的价值不在于是否得到读者的承认，也不在于是否发表、出版。诗歌发表出版有时是一个社会条件问题，有时也是一个个人选择的问题。事实上很多诗人写作并非为了发表、出版。比如，十八世纪英国为数众多的女诗人创作了体量可观的诗歌，但因为社会历史原因很多无法及时出版，而十九世纪美国女诗人艾米莉·狄金森（Emily Dickinson）的作品丰富，但诗人自己却选择了不出版。诗歌创作是涉及抓住灵感、激发灵感、发现真正题材、找到合适形式、写成初稿、关注读者反应、修改重写、出版传播等系列行为的系统过程。对于诗人来说，这很可能是一个孤独的、煎熬的、通常不能带来物质利益的过程，但同时也是一个不可抗拒的、能够带来精神满足感的过程。诗歌创作对诗人来说更多的是精神上的快乐和享受。

中国人写英语诗

2021年，22岁的诗人阿曼达·戈尔曼（Amanda Gorman）成为美国史上首位在总统就职典礼上朗诵诗歌的"青年桂冠诗人"(Young People's Poet Laureate)。"青年桂冠诗人"的选拔是美国著名的"诗歌基金会"(The Poetry Foundation)对面向年轻诗歌读者有突出写作成就的诗人的承认。当前美国英语诗歌创作与阅读具有明显的年轻化特点,而这离不开美国高校和各种文化组织对年轻诗人和年轻诗歌读者的培育。比如,美国高校的诗歌创意写作教学不仅培养了大批聪明、热情的年轻诗人,也培育了大批忠诚的年轻诗歌读者。此外,"诗歌基金会"于2005年和美国"国家艺术赞助基金会"(The National Endowment for the Arts,简称NEA)联合启动的全美中学生"诗歌朗诵比赛"(Poetry Out Loud)项目则与美国高校诗歌创意写作教学一起促进了年轻诗歌读者数量的增长。

年轻化的英语诗歌创作者与诗歌读者在数字媒体技术的支持下共同推动了表演化、口头化、听觉化的美国新诗歌文化的发展。这种新诗歌文化促进了英语诗歌的网络传播,并且进一步触发读者对诗歌文本阅读的兴趣。数字媒体技术在客观上促进了英语诗歌的国际传播,也推动了英语诗歌创作的进一步国际化。虽然长期以来不乏来自不同英语国家的诗人,但是在当代数字媒体技术支持下,英语诗歌创作国际化有了新的发展。目前,从各种线上诗歌写作群组、线上诗歌工作坊、各种权威组织如"诗歌基金会"和"美国诗人学会"(Academy of American Poets)等的诗歌网站,到表演诗歌(performance poetry)的网络直播,英语诗歌创作正通过数字网络媒体渠道向世界上越来越多不同国家的人开放。

当今世界,各地不同民族在接受欣赏英语诗歌之时,也在反向影响英语诗歌创作的内容,甚至形式。不同国家与地区的诗人写的英语诗歌在内容上不可避免都会带上其地方特点。中国人写英语诗歌,自然会反映中国社会、生活、历史、文化,带上中国文化特有的意象。中国人进行英语诗歌创意写作,不仅能够丰富英语诗歌,而且能够以诗歌形式向世界呈现中国情感态度,在国际社会发出中国新声音,为国际英语诗歌读者提供了解中国的崭新视角,在中外文化交流中发挥独特作用。

中国人写英语诗,当然要遵循英语诗歌形式传统,借鉴现当代英语诗歌创作方法方式。中国人写英语诗,更要结合中国元素,积极从题材和形式上探索英语诗歌中国化的可行方案。中国人写英语诗,应该通过各种途径线下或线上参与国际英语诗歌创作活动。这既有利于中国的英语诗人与当前国际诗坛建立联系,接触并实践国际最新诗歌创作理念,也有利于扩大中国英语诗歌的国际知名度,使更多国际受众了解中国,理解中国,达到中外文化、思想、感情方面的更充分有效沟通。中国人充当英语诗歌读者的时间久矣,是时候尝试做一做英语诗歌的创作者了!

本书将从英语诗歌创意写作实践需要出发,研究相关的英语诗歌形式、技巧、传统,重点研究将相关形式、技巧、传统甚至读者意见应用于英语诗歌创意写作实践特别是灵感激发及诗歌形式发现创造中的具体方法方式,最后探讨将英语诗歌创意写作与中国元素相结合的可能途径。与其他伟大艺术一样,诗歌致力于在琐碎、日常、平凡中发现庄重、神圣、超越。诗人不需要阅遍山河才能创作。诗人只需有写作的强烈愿望,只需关注生活和环境,并进行反应、吸收、转化、利用、借用,就可以创作。诗人歌德(J. W. Goethe)曾说诗人莎士比亚(William Shakespeare)"用银盘子给了我们金苹果"①。作为谦卑的诗歌学生,即使现在还没有金苹果可以装在银盘子上,也可以先把银盘子准备好,也许诗神眷顾,哪一天金苹果突然就降临在银盘子上了呢!

陈津津
二〇二三年春天
广东技术师范大学

---

① 据 Dobyns(2011)书中前言写道:"Goethe, as quoted by Walter Jackson Bate, said that Shakespeare 'gives us golden apples in silver dishes.'" 详见 Walter Jackson Bate, *The Burden of the Past and the English Poet*, New York: W. W. Norton, 1972, p.5。

目　　录

第一章　英语诗歌中的声音 ……………………………………………… 1

 第一节　音节(syllable) ………………………………………………… 1

 第二节　节奏(rhythm)和格律(meter) ……………………………… 4

 第三节　格律和句法节奏的旋律对比(counterpoint)与跳跃律(sprung rhythm)
……………………………………………………………………… 9

 第四节　押韵(rhyme)：行尾韵(end rhyme)、行内韵(internal rhyme) ……… 12

 第五节　重复的声音美与意义建构：叠句(refrain)、排比(parallel) ……… 22

 第六节　诗歌的断行(line break)：与散文最明显的视觉区别 ……… 29

 第七节　停顿断行(end stop)与跨行连续(enjambment) ……… 34

第二章　英语诗歌中的修辞、意象、面具 ……………………………… 40

 第一节　隐喻(metaphor)与象征(symbol) ……………………… 40

 第二节　意象(image)与客观对应物(objective correlative) ……… 49

 第三节　意象派(Imagism) ……………………………………… 54

 第四节　说话者与人格面具(persona/mask) ……………………… 56

 第五节　叙事诗(narrative)与抒情诗(lyric) ……………………… 59

第三章　传统英语诗歌形式 ……………………………………………… 65

 第一节　离合诗(acrostic) ………………………………………… 65

 第二节　歌谣(ballad) ……………………………………………… 66

 第三节　素体诗(blank verse) ……………………………………… 69

 第四节　打油诗(limerick) ………………………………………… 71

 第五节　十四行诗(sonnet) ………………………………………… 73

 第六节　维拉纳诗(villanelle) ……………………………………… 75

第四章　现当代英语诗歌形式 79

第一节　自由诗(free verse) 79
第二节　俳句(haiku) 82
第三节　"潘图"诗(pantoum/pantun) 84
第四节　散文诗(prose poem) 85
第五节　现成发现诗(found poem) 86
第六节　偶然诗(chance poem)：拼贴(collage)、擦涂(erasure) 88
第七节　视觉诗(visual poem) 91

第五章　英语诗歌题材 95

第一节　爱情(晨曲)、身体、欲望、失落、悲伤、死亡(挽歌) 95
第二节　时间、历史、地方、身份 106
第三节　社会：见证诗(witness poem) 112
第四节　自　然 124

第六章　英语诗歌意义建构中的权衡取舍 135

第一节　诗歌的意义建构在于题材更在于形式 135
第二节　声音与事实的取舍：服从声音要求 138
第三节　诗节(stanza)与标题(title)：题材与形式的点睛结合 140

第七章　英语诗歌创意写作 148

第一节　灵感降临与自动写作 148
第二节　英语诗歌创意写作中的灵感激发(trigger) 152
第三节　英语诗歌修改和读者因素：一些诗歌创作和修改建议 161
第四节　英语诗歌创意写作中的工作坊(workshop) 169
第五节　诗歌朗读会(open mic & poetry slam)、表演诗歌(performance poetry) 173
第六节　英语诗歌的发表与出版 177

第八章　中国人写英语诗 180

第一节　年轻化、国际化的英语诗歌读者和诗人 180
第二节　中国人的英语诗歌创意写作 182

第三节　一个中国人的英语诗歌选录 ·· 190

参考文献 ··· 238

附录1：英语诗歌写作刍议 ··· 243

附录2：创意写作可借鉴英语诗歌集 ······································ 246

索　引 ·· 248

后　记 ·· 273

第一章
英语诗歌中的声音

诗歌与散文的一个重大区别就是其对语言声音(sound)的重视程度一点也不逊于其对语言意义(sense)的重视程度。对于一些诗人来说,创作时语言声音的重要性甚至远超语言意义的重要性。这也是诗歌成为创造语言新用法的文学体裁的原因之一。英国浪漫主义诗人格勒律治(Samuel Taylor Coleridge)说过"诗歌是以最佳的顺序说出来的最好的话"①。这句话中的"最佳顺序"就包括诗歌中的语言声音组织顺序。在英语诗歌中,不管是传统律诗(accentual-syllabic verse,使用格律写成,可以押韵可以不押韵)还是现当代自由诗(free verse,不使用格律,不以规则方式押韵),诗歌的形式工具建构起来的声音都具有自己的美感和价值。

第一节 音节(syllable)

英语诗歌语言声音的一个基本单位是音节(syllable)。音节是一个在元音(vowel)、辅音(consonant)上一级,在单词(word)下一级的语言单位。在英语中,根据读音,一个音节的构成可以有四种情况,或只包括一个元音,或一个辅音(组)加一个元音,或一个元音加一个辅音(组),或一个辅音(组)加一个元音加一个辅音(组)。前面两种可以称为开音节(open syllable),后边两种可以称为闭音节(close syllable)。一个音节必须包括一个元音,这是音节构成的必要条件。音节对英语律诗的格律和押韵等声音要素的构成具有重要意义,这个将在后边的三节中探讨。本节主要探讨音节本身的声音效果。

影响人对音节的感觉有四个因素:重音(stress,即重读非重读)、音长(duration,即声音长短)、音高(pitch,即声音高低,主要指音频)、音色或音质(timbre/quality,即声音粗糙或圆润)。音节四因素影响诗行的声音效果。如果一行诗的多数音节是重音,那么

---

① "Poetry is the best words in the best order",转引自 Vendler, p.151。

该行诗读起来的声音效果就比较淤塞,令人呼吸不畅;如果一行诗的多数音节是非重音,那么该诗行读起来就软弱无力。诗歌中多音节词出现的频率不高,一个原因就是多数多音节词是一个重音带两个以上的非重音,而几个多音节词紧接着出现就会使诗句软弱无力,变得像散文一样①。

音长影响诗行速度。诗行速度不是由诗行书写长度决定的,而是由其音节的长度和辅音的具体发音决定的。长音节和软辅音(如 w、th、ch、n、fl)会使诗行速度变慢,因此虽然其书写看起来短,其实读起来长,从而使诗行读起来显得比较休闲或者松散。注意以元音结尾(开音节)的词在声音上是开放的,该词的发音可以持续不断;以辅音结尾(闭音节)的词在声音上是闭合的,该词的发音不能持续不断。不过,l、wn、ts、ng 等结尾辅音的发音持续时间比一般辅音长,比元音短②。

音长较长的音节和音高较低的音节都会产生低沉、缓慢、严肃、阴郁的声音效果。元音中音高最高的为 ee,最低的为 oo。处于这两类之间的元音是 u,如 mud、blunder、bungle、chump、clumsy、crummy、runt、pus、repugnant 等词中的 u。元音具有心理暗示效果,比如低音词 cool、calm、soothe 与高音词 scream、shriek 所起的心理暗示作用是不一样的。音质的作用通过对比能够凸显出来③。音节四因素影响诗行的声音效果,从而影响诗歌的意义建构。对于没有格律帮助建构意义的自由诗而言,诗人更应该注意用词的音节四因素对意义建构的影响,以免引起过分误读,使读者读诗得到的意义与诗人的本意背离太远。

做为音节构成的必要条件,元音对诗行的声音乐感影响明显。相对于元音来说,辅音似乎是"杂音"。不过,在音乐性明显的诗行中,不仅元音读起来流动和谐,元音之间的辅音过渡效果也是自然流畅的。在乐感明显的诗行中,音节与音节之间、词与词之间的声音过渡(主要是辅音过渡)没有强迫的停顿或者阻塞。试比较诗人阿尔弗雷德·丁尼生(Alfred, Lord Tennyson)的"食莲人"("The Lotus-Eaters")中合唱(Choric Song)部分的第一、二行诗和诗人托马斯·哈代(Thomas Hardy)的"灰色调"("Neutral Tones")中最后两行诗的声音效果有何不同:

There is sweet music here that softer falls
Than petals from blown roses on the grass,
　　　　　　——from "The Lotus-Eaters" by Alfred, Lord Tennyson

Your face, and the God-curst sun, and a tree,

---

① 参见 Dobyns, chap.9。
② 参见 Dobyns, chap.4。
③ 参见 Dobyns, chap.4。

And a pond edged with grayish leaves.

——from"Neutral Tones"by Thomas Hardy

丁尼生的诗行与哈代的诗行读起来声音效果是完全不同的,这从朗读时口腔与舌头等发音器官的位置和感觉可以体验出来。丁尼生的诗行中 sweet 与 music、softer 与 falls、Than 与 petals、blown 与 roses 等词与词之间的声音过渡和谐流畅。哈代的诗行中,God-curst 两个音节之间、God-curst 与 sun 两个词之间的辅音过渡(d-c、st-s)比较困难,必须停顿才能正确发音;而 pond 与 edged、grayish 与 leaves 之间为避免连读引起误解也必须停顿。这些停顿都带有强迫性,使这两行诗读起来淤塞不畅,没有悦耳的乐感[①]。当然,诗行读起来是否悦耳充满乐感并不是评价其是否成功的依据。

单音节词只包含一个音节。单音节词简洁明快,铿锵有力,诚实粗犷。单音节并以清辅音结尾的英语单词是力量的象征,如诗人叶芝(W. B Yeats)有一行诗:Stumbling upon the blood dark track once more,其中的 blood、dark、track 三个词连在一起,制造了类似哒哒哒的枪声音响效果。多音节词则舒缓语言速度,软化语言力量。多音节词适合表达柔情与安宁,也显得更加优雅有教养[②]。但,如前所述,诗行中几个多音节词紧接着出现会使诗行软弱无力,变得像散文一样。

为了制造某种诗歌节奏或韵律,诗人有时需要使用包含不同音节数的同义词或近义词来替代原来想用的单词,比如用双音节词代替单音节词,或者用单音节词代替双音节词。常见的音节数不同但意思基本可以互相替代的单词有:someone—somebody、just—only、start—begin、seem—appear、out of—from、another—each other,等等。现今使用的英语主要由九世纪国王阿尔弗雷德(King Alfred)王宫使用的方言西撒克逊语(West Saxon)演化而来。该方言主要使用地区是伦敦,是 1066 年诺曼征服之后伦敦下层人民使用的语言。经过诺曼征服,属日耳曼语系(Germanic language)的古英语原本包含性别、数、格、时态和人称等信息的曲折现象(inflections)开始消失,发展成为诗人杰弗里·乔叟(Geoffrey Chaucer)使用的中古英语(Middle English)。曲折现象的消失使得英语单词的词尾变化多样,这使其不像法语、西班牙语和意大利语那样容易押韵。不过,诺曼征服后,因为法语等外来语的加入,英语中同义词和近义词增多[③]。在当今西方语言中,英语拥有最多的近义词[④]。这一点对于需要制造诗歌节奏韵律的英语诗人来说是一个有利条件。

---

① 参见 Brooks, Cleanth & Robert Penn Warren, *Understanding Poetry*, the 4th edition, Beijing: Foreign Language Teaching and Research Press & Thomson Learning, 2004, pp.520 – 522 & pp.542 – 543。本书对此文献的参考或引用标注为 Brooks & Warren。

② 参见 Hugo, Richard. *The Triggering Town: Lectures and Essays on Poetry and Writing*, New York & London: W.W.Norton & Company, Inc., first published in 1982, reissued in 2010, chap.4。

③ 参见 Dobyns, chap.4 & chap.11。

④ 参见 Dobyns, chap.13。

第二节　节奏(rhythm)和格律(meter)

日常生活中充满各种节奏(rhythm)，或称节拍(beat)。人的心脏以某种节奏有规律地跳动；人们以某种有节奏的模式走路、跑步、跳绳、跳舞；漏水的水龙头有节奏地滴水；电话铃以某种节奏响着；沙滩上的海浪以某种节奏涨潮退潮，等等。节奏，是某种可感模式在时间或空间上的重复①，也可以说是声音或运动的规律性、模式化的流动②。有规律的节奏能够带来安宁和美感；规律性的节奏如果出现了变化或者受到干扰会引起人们特别的注意；不断重复、毫无变化的节奏则会给人带来疲劳和厌倦。本书主要关注诗歌中的声音节奏。英语律诗组织声音顺序的一个重要形式工具是格律(meter/metrics/measure)。格律是高度组织化、结构化的节奏(organized rhythm)。英语律诗的诗行是用格律写成的。

英语律诗的格律同时提示了诗行的节奏和长度，一般由音步(foot)和音步数两方面构成。常见的格律音步包含一个重读音节和若干非重读音节，一个重读音节在节奏上称为一拍(a beat)。常见的格律音步有抑扬格(iamb)、扬抑格(trochee)、抑抑扬格(anapest)、扬抑抑格(dactyl)。抑扬格由一个轻读音节(unstressed or unaccented syllable)和一个重读音节(stress or accent syllable)构成。以此类推，扬抑格就是由一个重读音节和一个轻读音节构成；抑抑扬格由两个轻读音节和一个重读音节构成；扬抑抑格由一个重读音节和两个轻读音节构成。若用符号、来代表重读音节，用符号－来代表轻读音节，那么以上几个常见格律音步可以用以下符号排列来表示：

抑扬格：－、

扬抑格：、－

抑抑扬格：－－、

扬抑抑格：、－－

抑扬格是英语传统律诗最常见的格律音步，十四行诗(sonnet)、素体诗(blank verse)以及其他多种律诗形式都是用抑扬格写成。抑抑扬格经常用于打油诗(limerick)中，用来制造轻松滑稽幽默的气氛。严格统一的抑抑扬格律诗乐感强烈，但也显得矫揉造作③，因而这种诗作易引起幽默诗戏仿(parody)。英语律诗中以扬抑格为主导音步的作品不多见，并且使用扬抑格写成的诗行常以一个重音节结尾。诗人亨

---

① 参见 Brooks & Warren, pp.1–2。
② 参见 Brooks & Warren, p.493。
③ 参见 Brooks & Warren, pp.506–507。

利·华兹华斯·朗费罗(Henry Wadsworth Longfellow)比较常用扬抑格写诗,他的《海华沙之歌》(*The Song of Hiawatha*)和"人生颂"("Psalm of Life")主要使用扬抑格写成①。一首诗很难完全用扬抑抑格写成,连续不变的扬抑抑格读起来沉重且乏味。一般来说,比较常见的作诗法是抑扬格和抑抑扬格组合使用或者扬抑格和扬抑抑格组合使用。将上升的抑扬格或抑抑扬格与下降的扬抑格或扬抑抑格组合使用,从音律上听起来比较怪。诗人罗伯特·路易斯·斯蒂文森(Robert Louis Stevenson)在"火车上"("From a Railway Carriage")中就结合使用扬抑抑格与扬抑格制造一种急促的速度感:

Faster than | fairies, | faster than | witches,
Bridges and | houses, | hedges and | ditches... ②

当然,还有一些不太常见的格律音步如扬扬格(spondee)和四音节格(Paeon),等等。四音节格,顾名思义,含四个音节,其中一个为重音。如果四音节格的重音在第一个音节,后边三个为轻音,叫首重四音节格(first paeon)。以此类推,如果重音在第四个音节,前边三个为轻音,叫四重四音节格(fourth paeon)③。四音节格在普通英语律诗中很少使用,但在诗人杰拉德·曼利·霍普金斯(Gerard Manley Hopkins)使用的跳跃律(sprung rhythm)中很受青睐。一般情况下,整行诗用扬扬格写成的也比较少见,除非是一行单音节词的排列,如诗人詹姆森(E. D. Jameson)写的下边两行诗的第一行:

Cheese, grapes, pears, nuts, beans
combined in a salad with lots of fresh greens.④

英语律诗的格律音步数决定了诗行的长度。根据每个诗行的音步数,可以把诗行分为单音步(monometer)、双音步(dimeter)、三音步(trimeter)、四音步(tetrameter)、五音步(pentameter)、六音步(hexameter)、七音步(heptameter)、八音步(octameter),等等。大部分的英语传统律诗使用三音步、四音步或者五音步写成,比如,诗人戏剧家莎士比亚(William Shakespeare)的所有诗剧都使用五音步,虽然有时会插入少量散文(prose)和短歌(short song)⑤。下边是包含不同音步数的诗行例子⑥:

---

① 参见 Livingston, Myra Cohn. *POEM-MAKING: Ways to Begin Writing Poetry*. New York: Harper Collins Publishers, 1991, p.76。也可参见 Brooks & Warren, p.507。
② 转引自 Livingston, p.78。
③ 参见 Kowit, p.167。也可参见 *The Princeton Encyclopedia*, p.386 & p.990。
④ 转引自 Kowit, p.166。
⑤ 参见 Vendler, p.594。
⑥ 转引自 Vendler, pp.594 – 595。

单音步：Adam
　　　　Had'em.
　　　　　　　　　　　　　　　　　　　　——from "Fleas"

双音步：Take her up tenderly,
　　　　Lift her with care,
　　　　Fashioned so slenderly,
　　　　Young and so fair.
　　　　　　　　　　　——from "The Bridge of Sighs" by Thomas Hood

三音步：It is time that I wrote my will;
　　　　I choose upstanding men
　　　　That climb the streams until
　　　　The fountain leap, and at dawn
　　　　Drop their cast at the side
　　　　Of dripping stone; I declare
　　　　They shall inherit my pride.
　　　　　　　　　　　　　——from "The Tower" by W. B. Yeats

四音步：Whose woods there are I think I know
　　　　His house is in the village though,
　　　　He will not see me stopping here
　　　　To watch his woods fill up with snow.
　　　　　　　　　　　——from "Stopping by Woods" by Robert Frost

五音步：The woods decay, the woods decay and fall,
　　　　The vapours weep their burthens to the ground,
　　　　Man comes and tills the soil and lies beneath,
　　　　And, after many a summer dies the swan.
　　　　　　　　　　——from "Tithonus" by Alfred, Lord Tennyson

六音步：I will arise and go now, and go to Innisfree,
　　　　And a small cabin build there, of clay and wattles made.
　　　　　　　　　　——from "The Lake Isle of Innisfree" by W. B. Yeats

英语律诗的诗行可以由不同的格律音步（节奏）和音步数（长度，也即行宽）组成，从而形成多样化的格律。比如三音步可以与抑扬格构成三音步抑扬格（iambic trimeter），与扬抑格一起构成三音步扬抑格（trochaic trimeter），与抑抑扬格一起构成三音步抑抑扬格（anapestic trimeter），等等。五音步抑扬格（iambic pentameter）是很多英语律诗的默认格律，比如十四行诗、素体诗、英雄体双行诗（heroic couplet）等基本都是用五音步抑扬格写成。对诗行的格律节奏和长度进行识别的技术叫音步划分(scan or scansion)。诗人克里斯蒂娜·罗萨蒂(Christina Rossetti)以下的十四行诗行基本是用五音步抑扬格写成,如果进行音步划分则可以表示如下:

```
 -  `  -  `  -  `  -  `  -  `
Remember me when I am gone away,
 -  `  -  `  -  `  -  `  -  `
Gone far away into the silent land;

When you can no more hold me by the hand,
 -  `  -  `  -  `  -  `  -  `
Nor I half turn to go yet turning stay.
```

——from "Remember" by Christina Rossetti

英语律诗的不同格律可以制造不同的节奏,表达不同的感情、情绪、语气、态度,从而达到不同的意义建构。然而,如果一首诗的格律一直相同,完全可预见,毫无变化意外(surprise),那么这首诗就会变得像贺卡祝词一样无聊无趣。进行诗行的音步划分能够揭示诗歌的总体格律节奏,但同时也要注意到,诗人会在总体整齐的格律节奏中采用多种方式比如音步替换、音步变异等进行节奏变异,这些节奏变异往往指向特定的诗歌意义构建。比如莎士比亚的十四行诗基本采用五音步抑扬格,但是他也会使用一些音步变异来增加诗行的活力。比如下边其第 76 号十四行诗("Sonnet 76")的开头就使用了一个出人意料的扬抑格强调了一种意外的提问语气,而其后该行的四个音步则使用了正常的抑扬格:

```
 `  -  -  `  -  `  -  `  -  `
Why is my verse so barren of new pride?
```

除了上述如莎士比亚那样使用格律音步变异来改变诗行节奏外,行内停顿(caesura)和跨行连续(enjambment)也是诗人改变诗歌格律节奏整齐划一的有用工具。跨行连续将在本章第七节进行详述。诗歌的行内停顿可以用来变换诗行节奏,使诗行读起来更加自然不僵硬,是影响诗行节奏的一个重要因素。诗人克里斯蒂娜·罗萨蒂(Christina Rossetti)下边这首诗的第七、第十行都有标点符号指示的行内停顿,而第八行的 then 则是没有符号指示的弱停顿(weak caesura)。这三个停顿都对各自诗行的节奏产生了影响,这种影响在大声朗读时比较明显[①]。

---

① 参见 Kowit, p.149。

Remember
By Christina Rossetti

Remember me when I am gone away,
 Gone far away into the silent land;
 When you can no more hold me by the hand,
Nor I half turn to go yet turning stay.
Remember me when no more day by day
 You tell me of our future that you plann'd:
 Only remember me; you understand
It will be late to counsel then or pray.
Yet if you should forget me for a while
 And afterwards remember, do not grieve:
 For if the darkness and corruption leave
 A vestige of the thoughts that once I had,
Better by far you should forget and smile
 Than that you should remember and be sad.①

  英语律诗使用格律写成，格律由音步和音步数两方面构成。音步数决定了诗行的长度，而重读音节与非重读音节的不同结合方式构成了不同的格律音步。不同的音步数和不同的格律音步相结合构成了传统英语律诗多样化的格律。不同格律制造不同的诗行节奏，表达不同的感情、情绪、语气、态度，达到不同的诗歌意义建构。一直相同、完全可预见、毫无变化意外的格律会使一首诗变得无聊无趣。学习传统格律的意义在于，先掌握好基本模式要领，再进行适时的变异以取得需要的表达效果。
  现当代英语诗歌不再坚持使用严格格律进行创作，其断行依据更加多样化，因此能够制造更加丰富的诗歌节奏。关于诗歌断行将在本章第六、七节详述。现当代英语诗歌创作除了可以使用传统格律（同时包含重音数元素和音节数元素）来制造诗行节奏外，有时也会单独强调重音数或者音节数来制造诗行节奏。只计算诗行中的重音数的诗，叫重音诗（accentual verse），而只计算诗行中的音节数的诗，则叫音节诗（syllabic verse）。重音诗和音节诗并非现当代英语诗人的发明，尤其是重音诗，但现当代英语诗人将写作异于传统律诗的重音诗和音节诗作为一种对诗歌形式的革新②。

---

① 转引自 https://www.poetryfoundation.org/poems/45000/remember-56d224509b7ae。
② 参见 Brooks & Warren, p.559。

第三节 格律和句法节奏的旋律对比(counterpoint)与跳跃律(sprung rhythm)

诗行的格律节奏(轻重音定位)和句法节奏(轻重音定位)所指是不同的。一个使用五音步抑扬格的英语律诗诗行其格律节奏(轻重音定位)是十个音节在轻读和重读之间轮流替换;而其句法节奏(轻重音定位)指的是该诗行所属句子在正常说话中轻重读音的自然定位①。一个自然的英语句子,不同的人朗读,因为理解不同,其选择强调重读的音节也可能不同。另外,在英语中,因为地域口音不同同一单词的轻重发音位置也可能有所不同。比如 detail 一词,有的地域人们把重音放在第一个音节,有的地域人们把重音放在第二个音节。因此,理论上,一个句子的句法节奏,即其轻重音定位可以是多样的。

如前所述,对传统律诗诗行的格律节奏进行识别的技术叫音步划分。如果按照句法节奏对一行诗进行重读音节定位,则其音步划分可能出现多种情况。在英语律诗中,对一行诗的音步划分主要根据其在整首诗中对应诗行的格律节奏采用"规律趋同"的原则进行。例如,如果一行诗可以做四音步划分,也可以做五音步划分,而此诗的其他对应诗行均是五音步,一般这行诗就划分为五音步②。这样的音步划分原则使得一些普通情况下不重读的音节得到重读。这也与1900年丹麦语言学家奥托·叶斯柏森(Otto Jesperson)提出的"相对重读原则"相呼应。"相对重读原则"即音节重读程度受语境影响的原则。奥托·叶斯柏森认为,一个音节的重读程度应根据它前后音节来判断。一些重读音节放在两个更重的音节中间,会变成轻读;一些轻读音节放在两个更轻读音节中间,会变成重读③。一般来说,英语律诗中包含一个以上重读音节的单词在诗行中会得到强调,比如诗人弥尔顿(John Milton)的《失乐园》(*Paradise Lost*)第一行中的 disobedience 一词就是这样:

Of man's first disobedience, and the fruit
Brought death into the world, and all our woe④

一个句子作为诗行时的格律节奏(趋同原则)与作为自然句时的句法节奏(多种

---

① 参见 Dobyns, chap.4。
② 参见 Vendler, p.598。
③ 参见 Dobyns, chap.4。
④ 参见 Brooks & Warren, pp.498–499。

可能)有可能重合。比如上一节举例说明音步划分时提到的诗人克里斯蒂娜·罗萨蒂的十四行诗行"Remember me when I am gone away",如果完全按照其句法节奏,则有一种可能就是只重读 remember 的第二个音节和 away 的第二个音节。但是因为抑扬格在整首诗规整明显,该诗行的格律五音步抑扬格的重音模式也就凸显出来,并且与其自然句法节奏允许的重音模式并不相悖。同理,同一首诗中"When you can no more hold me by the hand"这个诗行,如果完全按照其句法节奏,有一种可能就是只重读 you、hold 和 hand 三个单词,但是因为抑扬格在整首诗规整明显,该诗行的格律五音步抑扬格的重音模式也凸显出来,并且与其自然句法节奏允许的重音模式不相悖①。再比如,在诗人弥尔顿关于眼睛失明的十四行诗首行"When I consider how my light spent"中,格律节奏与句法节奏是一致的;在诗人菲利普·拉金(Philip Larkin)的"Aubade"首行"I work all day and get half drunk at night"中,格律节奏与句法节奏也是一致的②。

但是,诗行的格律节奏与句法节奏也可能存在差异。对于英语律诗来说,格律节奏与句法节奏明显不同但又共存于一首诗的现象可称为节奏对比或旋律对比(counterpoint)。旋律对比既对诗歌声音有影响,也对意义表达与理解有影响③。比如,诗人唐纳德·贾斯提斯(Donald Justice)的十四行诗"七岁的诗人"("The Poet at Seven")的第一、二行"And on the porch across the upturned chair, /The boy would spread a dingy counterpane…"应更侧重句法节奏,按照句法节奏来读诗,如果按照格律节奏来读会显得矫揉造作。又如菲利普·拉金的"爆炸"("Explosion")的第一、二、三行"On the day of the explosion/ Shadows pointed from the pithead. /In the sun the slagheap slept"就更应该侧重句法节奏。拉金的这首诗是用四音步扬抑格写成,这前三行诗就是严格的扬抑格。但是如果真的按照格律节奏来读这三行诗的话,则不仅显得矫揉造作,而且会很滑稽④。旋律对比现象在非格律诗中也存在,不过没那么明显。

与旋律对比现象密切相关的是因诗人杰拉德·曼利·霍普金斯(Gerard Manley Hopkins)而著名的跳跃律(sprung rhythm)。为了说明跳跃律,霍普金斯举了诗人弥尔顿的三部史诗《失乐园》、《复乐园》(*Paradise Regain'd*)和《力士参孙》(*Samson Agonistes*)为例。霍普金斯认为这三部史诗中的旋律对比现象非常明显,特别是《力士参孙》中的合唱,更是始终具有旋律对比的特征,即每个诗行都可以进行两种完全不同但又彼此共存的音步划分。但是弥尔顿诗中的这种旋律对比到了某些地方,原来共存的两种节奏中非传统的那种(弥尔顿的史诗为素体诗,格律为传统的五音步抑扬格)明

---

① 参见 Kowit, pp.147-148。
② 参见 Dobyns, chap.4。
③ 参见 Dobyns, chap.5 & chap.12。
④ 参见 Dobyns, chap.4。

显压制住了传统的格律节奏。霍普金斯把弥尔顿诗中这种压制了传统格律节奏的非传统节奏称为跳跃律。在他看来,跳跃律非常活跃强烈,具有排斥性,其他格律节奏无法与之共存形成旋律对比[①]。

跳跃律做音步划分时以重音为依据,一个音步可能只是包含一个重读音节,也可能包含一个重读音节和若干轻读音节。跳跃律音步一般包括四种情况:一个重读音节、一个重读加一个轻读的扬抑格、一个重读加两个轻读的扬抑抑格、一个重读加三个轻读的首重四音节格。例如,霍普金斯把自己的诗"茶隼"("The Windhover")中的跳跃律音步称为降调四音节格(falling paeon)。霍普金斯使用跳跃律是为了使诗歌语言更加原始自然,接近口语节奏,使诗行同时具有重音的强调作用和口语表达的自然性。跳跃律诗行中不同音步自由结合,因此同一诗行两个重音之间的距离可能短,也可能长。四音节格在普通英语律诗中很少使用,但在霍普金斯的跳跃律诗歌中很受青睐。重音及其构成的节奏是跳跃律的生命,它不仅把跳跃律与传统英语诗歌格律区别开来,也把跳跃律诗行与普通自然语言区别开来。霍普金斯关于跳跃律的创作理念在一定程度上影响了二十世纪早期自由诗(free verse)的兴起[②]。霍普金斯的诗歌实践了其跳跃律的理念,以下两首"上帝的荣耀"("God's Grandeur")和"斑斓之美"("Pied Beauty")是其使用跳跃律写成的著名短诗:

跳跃律短诗 1:
God's Grandeur
By Gerard Manley Hopkins

The world is charged with the grandeur of God.
 It will flame out, like shining from shook foil;
 It gathers to a greatness, like the ooze of oil
Crushed. Why do men then now not reck his rod?
Generations have trod, have trod, have trod;
 And all is seared with trade; bleared, smeared with toil;
 And wears man's smudge and shares man's smell: the soil
Is bare now, nor can foot feel, being shod.

And for all this, nature is never spent;
 There lives the dearest freshness deep down things;

---

① 参见 *The Princeton Encyclopedia*, p.1354。
② 参见 *The Princeton Encyclopedia*, p.1354。

And though the last lights off the black West went
　　Oh, morning, at the brown brink eastward, springs—
Because the Holy Ghost over the bent
　　World broods with warm breast and with ah! bright wings.①

跳跃律短诗 2：
Pied Beauty
By Gerard Manley Hopkins

Glory be to God for dappled things-
　For skies of couple-colour as a brinded cow;
　　For rose-moles all in stipple upon trout that swim;
Fresh-firecoal chestnut-falls; finches' wings;
　Landscape plotted and pieced-fold, fallow, and plough;
　　And áll trádes, their gear and tackle and trim.

All things counter, original, spare, strange;
　Whatever is fickle, freckled (who knows how?)
　　With swift, slow; sweet, sour; adazzle, dim;
He fathers-forth whose beauty is past change:
　　　　　　Praise him.②

第四节　押韵(rhyme)：行尾韵(end rhyme)、行内韵(internal rhyme)

　　除了格律，英语律诗组织声音顺序的另一个重要形式工具是押韵。如果说音乐性是诗歌的必要部分，那么押韵是一个制造诗歌乐感的很好工具。有人认为押韵是一种使用神奇的催眠法术把语言声音交织起来的魔法，而英国诗人奥斯卡·王尔德

---

　　① 转引自 https://www.poetryfoundation.org/poems/44395/gods-grandeur。
　　② 转引自 https://www.poetryfoundation.org/poems/44399/pied-beauty。

(Oscar Wilde)则把押韵比喻成人们在希腊里拉琴上加的一条琴弦①。英语诗歌中的押韵,一般指尾韵(end rhyme),既指词尾韵也指行尾韵,常指行尾韵。严格说来,在英语诗歌中押韵(行尾韵)的定义是:不同诗行末尾的两个(或多个)音节,如果重读元音及其后的音素相同,其前的辅音(如果有的话)不同,这两个(或多个)音节就押韵。不过后来也有不考虑重读因素,只需词尾元音及其后音素相同就看做押韵的。简单地说,押韵就是两个音节开始不同,结尾相同②。

从其定义,押韵派生出来的一个意思是不同的单词中声音的重复(repetition)、回声(echo)或者共鸣(resonance),故此广义的押韵还包括头韵(alliteration,有时也称为front rhyme③)、谐音(assonance,有时也称为 interior rhyme④)、和音(consonance)等韵音现象⑤。两个或多个押韵的词称为韵词(rhyme-mate)。最简单的押韵是韵词均为单音节词(单音节词只含一个音节,是自然重读)并且韵音(相同的元音及其后音素)拼写相同、词性相同。比较成功的押韵是韵词在语义上有相关性⑥。诗人威廉·华兹华斯(William Wordsworth)下边这个诗节中的两对韵词 seal-feel、fears-years 就是既简单又成功的押韵:

  A slumber did my spirit seal;
  I had no human fears;
  She seemed a thing that could not feel
  The touch of earthly years.

上述诗行中的两对韵词 seal-feel、fears-years 结尾的元音与辅音完全相同,这样的押韵也称完全韵(perfect or complete or full or true or exact or pure or strict rhyme)。在完全韵中,如果韵音落在韵词的最后一个音节且为重读则为阳韵(masculine rhyme)。阳韵多为单音节词,如 seal-feel、fear-year 押的就是阳韵。如果韵音落在倒数第二个音节,后边跟随一个非重读音节,如 better-letter、carried-married,则称为阴韵(feminine rhyme)。Immutable-irrefutable、longevity-brevity 等则可称为双阴韵(double feminine rhyme)。此外还有三阴韵(triple feminine rhyme)的,不过,双阴韵和三阴韵一般也均统称为阴韵。

除了完全韵,一些诗行末尾有时也押不完全韵(off or slant or half or near or

---

① 参见 The Princeton Encyclopedia, p.1184。
② 参见 The Princeton Encyclopedia, pp.1184–1185。
③ 参见 Brooks & Warren, p.524。
④ 同上。
⑤ 参见 The Princeton Encyclopedia, pp.1184–1185。
⑥ 参见 Vendler, pp.72–74。

imperfect or partial rhyme)。顾名思义,不完全韵就是韵词的韵音不完全相同,但在声音上接近,具有回声效果,比如 face-dress、fear-care、blend-stand、here-chair、open-broken 就是一些押不完全韵的例子。押不完全韵有时客观上是因为诗人没找到合适的完全韵词,但很多时候是诗人为了某种表达效果故意为之。比如诗人格温多琳·布鲁克斯(Gwendolyn Brooks)在其诗"查尔斯"("Charles")中为了显示病中 Charles 的不舒服、不快乐,特意为 away 押了一个不完全韵 by:

Sick-times, you go inside yourself,
And scarce can come away.
You sit and look outside yourself
At people passing by.①

诗人威廉·布莱克(William Blake)在其"迷失的小男孩"("The Little Boy Lost")的如下四行诗中也特意使用了一对不完全韵词 fast-lost。对于布莱克来说,要找到 fast 的完全韵词并不难,如 blast、cast、mast、past、passed 等很多词都是,但是不完全韵 fast-lost 却能够很好地表现迷路男孩的无助和迷茫。在这对不完全韵词中,fast 和 lost 的词尾辅音组合 st 相同,这是和音在不完全韵中的使用:

"Father! father! where are you going?
"O do not walk so fast.
"Speak, father, speak to your little boy,
"Or else I shall be lost."②

和音即韵词词尾辅音相同但其他音素不同,如 fallen-open、fast-lost。像这种只是词尾辅音相同的韵词,有人也称之为部分和音(partial consonance),而像 golden-garden、root-right-rat-rate-wrote-rout 这样既有头韵效果,也有和音效果的韵词,有人也称之为完全和音(full or rich consonance),但这种叫法比较少见③。诗人艾米莉·狄金森下边的这首诗也使用和音即 up-step、Swoon-Bone 来押不完全韵:

There is a pain—so utter—
It swallows substance up—

---

① 转引自 Livingston, p.65。
② 转引自 Livingston, p.67。
③ 参见 Kowit, p.58。

Then covers the Abyss with Trance—
So Memory can step
Around—across—upon it—
As one within a Swoon—
Goes safely—where an open eye—
would drop Him—Bone by Bone.①

和音除了作为不完全韵用于押行尾韵之外,更多的是用于行内韵(internal rhyme)中。行内韵与行尾韵相对,指在一行诗中除行末以外位置出现的韵音现象,既包括词尾韵(韵音为相同的词尾元音及其辅音),也包括头韵(韵词词首辅音相同,其它不同)、谐音(韵词词中元音相同,其它不同)、和音(韵词词尾辅音相同,其它不同)等②。与行尾韵的限制相比,行内韵是一种广义的押韵。行内韵一般出现在一行诗内,但有人把一行诗中的词与该诗行末词、一行诗中的词与相邻诗行中的词出现的上述韵音现象也称为行内韵③。韵词之间的距离对韵音现象的构成是有影响的。太近的韵词回声效果太密集,不一定是好的韵音;而太远的韵词回声效果太微弱,则构不成韵音。

头韵,严格来说,是指位置足够相近、能够引起听觉效果的重读词首辅音或辅音组的声音重复。头韵有时也包括非重读词首辅音的情况。一些头韵辅音重复现象可能跨越多个诗行。古英语史诗 *Beowulf* 是用头韵写作的典型例子④。诗人弥尔顿描写夜莺歌声的诗行使用了头韵制造美妙的乐感:Sweet Bird that shunn'st the noise of folly, / Most musical, most melancholy⑤。歌曲"她在海边卖海贝"("She sells seashells by the seashore")和下边的童谣也是使用头韵的典型例子。据说如果可以一口气把下边这个童谣读三遍,就可以治好打嗝的毛病:

Peter Piper picked a peck of pickled pepper;
A peck of pickled pepper Peter Piper picked;
If Peter Piper picked a peck of pickled pepper,

---

① 详见 Dickinson, Emily. *The Complete Poems of Emily Dickinson*. Thomas H. Johnson ed., New York, Boston, London: Back Bay Books, 1960, p.294。
② 参见 Kowit, pp.57–67。
③ 参见 Addonizio, Kim & Dorianne Laux, *The Poet's Companion: A Guide to the Pleasures of Writing Poetry*, New York & London: W. W. Norton & Company, 1997, p.144. 本书对此文献的参考或引用标注为 Addonizio&Laux。
④ 参见 *The Princeton Encyclopedia*, pp.40–41。
⑤ 转引自 https://www.poetryfoundation.org/poems/44732/il-penseroso。

Where's the peck of pickled pepper Peter Piper picked?①

注意头韵是声音的重复,因此即便两个词的词首字母拼写不同,只要发音相同,也可以构成头韵,如:quick-cat、never-know、keep-care、city-sleep,等等。头韵是一种效果明显、引人注目的声音工具,但如果使用过度,有时反而会伤害诗歌表达。自然的甚至是看似无意的头韵使用,却能为诗歌表达增添魅力。"可怜的老佩内洛普"("Poor Old Penelope")的以下开头几行中字母 p 的头韵重复充满了滑稽感:

Poor old Penelope,
great are her woes,
a pumpkin has started
to grow from her nose.
"My goodness," she warbles,
"this makes me *so* glum,
I'm perfectly certain
I planted a plum."②

谐音是指位置足够相近、音响效果能够被感知的若干非尾韵词的重读音节中的元音重复,比如 seek-feat、rose-float、shine-bride、proud-cowl,等等③。谐音通常能够产生舒缓的音响效果。谐音不仅可以作为行内韵为诗歌制造音响效果,有时也可以成为不完全韵用于行末押韵。比如,诗人戏剧家莎士比亚的 第 66 号十四行诗("Sonnet 61")中就使用谐音制造了不完全韵的效果。在下面的第二和第四行末的 open 和 broken 两词尾因为 p 和 k 而成为不完全韵,在这两个韵词中,由 o 引起的谐音起了非常重要的作用④:

Is it thy will thy image should keep open
My heavy eyelids to the weary night?
Dost thou desire my slumbers should be broken
While shadows like to thee do mock my sight?

---

① 转引自 Livingston, p.58。
② 转引自 Livingston, p.60。
③ 参见 *The Princeton Encyclopedia*, p.94。
④ 参见 Hewitt, Geof. "Assonance", Padgett, Ron, ed. in *The Teachers & Writers Handbook of Poetic Forms*. Second Edition. New York: T&W books, 2000, p.16.

英语律诗一定的行尾押韵模式叫做韵式(rhyme scheme),一定的律诗韵式可以形成诗节(stanza)。有时一节诗就是一首诗,这首诗可叫单节诗。律诗的诗节按照其诗行数量各有名称:双行诗(couplet)、三行诗(tercet)、四行诗(quatrain)、五行诗(quintet)、六行诗(sestet)、七行诗(septet)、八行诗(octave)、九行诗(nine-line stanza)、十行诗(ten-line stanza)……。长诗节经常是由双行诗、三行诗和四行诗的各种变体构成,因此,这三种诗节也成为律诗的"基础原件"(building block)。下边是几种诗节的例子①:

双行诗1:
One, two,
Buckle my shoe.

(童谣)

双行诗2:
Rain, rain, go away,
Come again another day.

(童谣)

三行诗1:
I don't mind eels
Except as meals
And the way they feels.

——from "The Eel" by Ogden Nash

三行诗2:
A little light is going by,
Is going up to see the sky,
A little light with wings.
I never could have thought of it,
To have a little bug all lit
And made to go on wings.

——from "Firefly" by Elizabeth Madox Roberts

三行诗3:
This is my rock,
And here I run
To steal the secret of the sun;

---

① 转引自 Livingston, pp.35-48。

This is my rock

And here come I

Before the night has swept the sky;

This is my rock,

This is the place

I meet the evening face to face.

——from"This Is My Rock" by David McCord

四行诗 1:

Everett Anderson thinks he'll make

America a birthday cake

Only the sugar's almost gone

and payday's not till later on.

——from "July" by Lucille Clifton

四行诗 2:

"You are old, Father William," the young man said,

"And your hair has become very white;

And yet you incessantly stand on your head—

Do you think, at your age, it is right?"

"In my youth," Father William replied to his son,

"I feared it might injure the brain;

But now that I'm perfectly sure I have none,

Why, I do it again and again."

——from "Father William" by Lewis Carroll

四行诗 3:

Cock a doodle do!

My dame has lost her shoe,

My master's lost his fiddlestick

And knows not what to do.

(童谣)

四行诗 4:

About his shadowy sides: above him swell

Huge sponges of millennial growth and height;

And far away into the sickly light

From many a wondrous grot and secret cell.

——from "The Kraken" by Alfred, Lord Tennyson

英雄体双行诗(heroic couplet)是用五音步抑扬格写成的双行诗,通常在押韵的第二行诗结尾处停顿断行(end-stopped)①。但丁三行体(terza rima)是意大利诗人但丁·阿利吉耶里(Dante Alighieri)在《神曲》(*The Divine Comedy*)全诗中使用的五音步三行诗节,押交织韵,即每节的第二行押与下一节第一、第三行同样的韵。后来英国诗人珀西·比希·雪莱(Percy Bysshe Shelley)的"西风颂"("Ode to the West Wind")、美国诗人华莱士·斯蒂文斯(Wallace Stevens)、爱尔兰诗人谢莫斯·希尼(Seamus Heaney)也常使用这种诗节韵式。一般来说,在诗歌创作中,如果诗人使用韵式严格或者不太严格的五音步三行诗节时,都有提醒该诗与但丁相联系的作用②。但丁三行体可以包含数量不限的诗节,在最后的诗节常常会多出一行,多出来的这一行与最后诗节的中间一行押韵,构成 yzy z 韵式③。

四行诗是英语律诗中最常见的诗节。上边诗人阿尔弗雷德·丁尼生(Alfred, Lord Tennyson)的"怪物克兰肯"("The Kraken")四行诗节中第一和第四行押韵,第二和第三行押韵,这种 abba 韵式像信封被封口一样,可以叫"封口诗"(envelop verse)④。英雄体四行诗为五音步抑扬格,韵式为 abab,经常用于哲学思考或者其他比较庄严的主题⑤。前边第二节曾经提到,连续不变的扬抑抑格读起来沉重而且乏味,一首诗一般很难完全用扬抑抑格写成。不过,有一种包含两个四行诗节的"双扬抑抑格"诗,其格律节奏有点傻气,可以表达幽默讽刺的效果,比如下边这首无名作者的无名诗就是写给爱猫人士的⑥:

Hestimus-festimus
Felix Domesticus
Regal as princes and
lazy as bums.

Partial to canned food and
ultra-magnanimous
folks who have got those op-
posable thumbs.

---

① 参见 Vendler, p.599。
② 参见 Vendler, p.600。
③ 参见 Mayer, Bernadette. "Terza rima", Padgett. Ron, ed. in *The Teachers & Writers Handbook of Poetic Forms*. Second Edition. New York: T&W books, 2000, p.192.
④ 参见 Livingston, pp.35-48。
⑤ 参见 Vendler, p.601。
⑥ 参见 Kowit, pp.156-158。

"双扬抑抑格"诗包含两节四行诗,每节的前三行都是两个扬抑抑格,每节的最后一行包含一个扬抑抑格再加一个重音节。第一节诗的第一行和第二行要押韵,两节诗的最后一行要押韵。第一节的第一行诗为了与第二行诗押韵可以是废话性质的词语。第一节诗的第二行必须是专有名词,如 Bank of America、Blind Lemon Jefferson、Eleanor Roosevelt、Hans Christian Andersen、Jacqueline Kennedy、Statue of Liberty、Tess of the D'Urbervilles,等等,而第二节诗的第二行必须是一个词,即一个六音节词,并且其重音在第一和第四个音节,如 antediluvian、bisexuality、extraterrestrial、multidimensional、phantasmagorical、permeability、uncomplimentary、veterinarian、等等。Higgledy piggledy 就是两个扬抑抑格①。

二十世纪初美国女诗人阿德莱德·克莱普茜(Adelaide Crapsey)发明了一种音节诗形式叫五行诗节(cinquain or quintet)。这种音节诗的第一行2个音节,第二行4个音节,第三行6个音节,第四行8个音节,第五行2个音节,共22个音节。第一行和最后一行的两个音节一般都是重读音节,有时使用抑扬音步。五行诗节是一种比较严肃的诗歌形式(form),主要使用意象(image)呈现意义。诗中可能使用一到两句话,但并不过分关注句子成分。五行诗节一般不押韵,如果押韵一般有幽默效果。写作五行诗时不可以为了满足诗行的音节数要求而把一个多音节词拆分到不同的诗行②。

写作五行诗还有几点要注意:第一,多数写得好的五行诗坚持使用命名物体的名词,不要为了满足音节数形式要求而滥用形容词。第二,避免每行都断得很整齐,比如避免每行都是一个很完整的短语。五行诗的诗行很简短,如果每行都断得很整齐的话,整首诗从每个行末跳到下一个行末,读起来会太颠簸跌宕。第三,五行诗应该构建高潮,比如下边克莱普茜最有名的一首五行诗"三位无声"("Triad")中,诗人在倒数第二行制造了一个悬念(suspense),而最后一行又提供了一个意外(surprise)③:

Triad
By Adelaide Crapsey

These be
Three silent things:
The falling snow... the hour
Before the dawn... the mouth of one

---

① 参见 Kowit, pp.156 – 158。
② 参见 Livingston, pp.111 – 116。
③ 参见 Higginson, William J. "Cinquain", Padgett. Ron, ed. in *The Teachers & Writers Handbook of Poetic Forms*. Second Edition. New York: T&W books, 2000, pp.49 – 50。

Just dead.

传统英语律诗中的五行诗节可以由一个双行诗和一个三行诗构成。六行诗节的韵式组合是多样的,可以是三个双行诗,或者是一个双行诗和一个四行诗,或者两个三行诗,或者其他韵式组合,比如下边的六行诗节例子用的是封口诗韵式。七行诗节可以由一个四行诗和一个三行诗构成。八行诗节的韵式组合可以是四个双行诗,或者是两个三行诗和一个双行诗,或者是两个四行诗,或者是开头和结尾各一个双行诗中间一个四行诗。长诗节的韵式灵活多变,创作时诗人可以视需要选择合适的韵式组合。下边是传统英语律诗五行诗节和六行诗节的例子①:

五行诗1:
The little caterpillar creeps
Awhile before in silk it sleeps.
It sleeps awhile before it flies,
And flies awhile before it dies,
And that's the end of three good tries.

——from "Cocoon" by David McCord

五行诗2:
To make a prairie it takes a clover and one bee,
One clover and one bee,
And revery.
The revery alone will do
If bees are few.

——by Emily Dickinson

六行诗:
We found him down at Turtle Creek,
Reached in the water and pulled him out,
His back all sticky with muck and slime.
We didn't take him home that time
But Saturday he was still about
So we brought him home. It's been a week.

一种常见的七行诗节叫君王体(rime royal/rhyme royal),为五音步抑扬格,韵式为

---

① 转引自 Livingston, pp.35-48。

ababbcc，因为英国国王詹姆斯一世（King James I）的使用而得名。最有名的八行诗节叫八行体（ottava rima），五音步抑扬格，韵式为abababcc，诗人乔治·戈登·拜伦（George Gordon, Lord Byron）在其长诗 *Don Juan* 中使用了这种诗节。最有名的九行诗节叫斯宾塞诗节（Spenserian stanza），因为诗人埃德蒙·斯宾塞（Edmund Spenser）在《仙后》（*The Faerie Queene*）中使用而出名，前八行为五音步格，第九行为六音步格，韵式为 ababbcbcc①。诗人通常不会在写作之前决定采用哪种韵式，对韵式的选择常常是在写作过程中基于写作内容做出选择，通过不断试验而确定的②。

押韵，是一种声音的重复，是一种回声，所以具有回归、呼应的功能以及闭合、总结、结束的意义。写得好的押韵能够增加诗歌的平衡感，使诗歌表达有序、悦耳动人，可以帮助人记忆诗句。诗人创作韵诗时寻找并从一系列韵词中进行选择的过程，其实也是对其诗歌写作方向的一个选择过程。不同的韵词为写作提供了不同的可能性；韵词的最终选择也影响了写作的方向。因此，创作韵诗是诗人寻找创作可能性、获得创作灵感的有效方式。不过，押韵也可能使人写出句法颠倒或者虽精致但不真诚的诗句，这样的诗句不仅使作品听起来矫揉造作，甚至使作品的实际表达效果与诗人的期望相去甚远。诗歌的格律和韵音使用的最高境界是不显山露水，是润物无声。诗人要让读者读到诗，而不只是读到诗中的格律与韵式。这也使格律与押韵变异成为一种必要。

第五节　重复的声音美与意义建构：
叠句（refrain）、排比（parallel）

传统英语律诗中的格律与押韵是相对规整的节奏和音响重复。除了格律与押韵，英语诗歌中的重复还包括单词重复、短语重复和诗行重复。单词重复和短语重复叫做循环节（repetend）。连续几行诗的首词或开始短语相同的重复叫首语重复（anaphora）。一整行诗的重复叫做叠句（refrain）③。莎士比亚在其第66号十四行诗中使用首语重复排列了诸多不公平：

Sonnet 66
By William Shakespeare
Tired with all these, for restful death I cry:

---

① 参见 Vendler, p.601。
② 参见 Livingston, pp.35-48。
③ 参见 Kowit, pp.57-59。

As, to behold desert a beggar born,
And needy nothing trimmed in jollity,
And purest faith unhappily forsworn,
And gilded honour shamefully misplaced,
And maiden virtue rudely strumpeted,
And right perfection wrongfully disgraced,
And strength by limping sway disabled,
And art made tongue-tied by authority,
And folly, doctor-like, controlling skill,
And simple truth miscalled simplicity,
And captive good attending captain ill.
Tired with all these, from these would I be gone,
Save that, to die, I leave my love alone.①

诗人沃尔特·惠特曼年轻时在纽约常听牧师布道。受《圣经》(*Bible*)诗句风格影响，惠特曼也很喜欢首语重复②，并在其诗作"自我之歌"("Song of Myself")中多次使用这种重复工具。首语重复使惠特曼的诗行形成排山倒海之势，加上谐音、头韵等的运用，诗行的音乐感非常强烈，比如下边的诗行：

Where the mocking-bird sounds his delicious gurgles, cackles, screams, weeps,
Where the hay-rick stands in the barn-yard, where the dry-stalks are scatter'd, where the brood-cow waits in the hovel,
Where the bull advances to do his masculine work, where the stud to the mare, where the cock is treading the hen,
Where the heifers browse, where geese nip their food with short jerks,
Where sun-down shadows lengthen over the limitless and lonesome prairie,
Where herds of buffalo make a crawling spread of the square miles far and near,
Where the humming-bird shimmers, where the neck of the long-lived swan is curving and winding,

---

① 转引自 https://www.poetryfoundation.org/poems/45097/sonnet-66-tird-with-all-these-for-restful-death-i-cry。

② 参见 Dobyns, Chap.1 & Kowit, pp.57-59。

Where the laughing-gull scoots by the shore, where she laughs her near-human laugh,
Where bee-hives range on a gray bench in the garden half hid by the high weeds,
Where band-neck'd partridges roost in a ring on the ground with their heads out,
Where burial coaches enter the arch'd gates of a cemetery,
Where winter wolves bark amid wastes of snow and icicled trees,
Where the yellow-crown'd heron comes to the edge of the marsh at night and feeds upon small crabs,
Where the splash of swimmers and divers cools the warm noon,
Where the katy-did works her chromatic reed on the walnut-tree over the well,
... ①

受沃尔特·惠特曼影响,诗人艾伦·金斯伯格(Allen Ginsberg)也喜欢使用首语重复。在他著名的诗作"嚎"("Howl")中,就有很多首语重复的使用②。除了首语重复,二十世纪诗人如路易斯·麦克尼斯(Louis MacNeice)、艾德温·摩根(Edwin Morgan)、查尔斯·考斯利(Charles Causley)等则更喜欢在诗歌中使用叠句。叠句即同一行诗的重复。维拉纳诗(villanelle)是一种既有规则的押韵要求,也有规则的叠句要求的传统十九行诗体,深受现当代诗人的青睐。北美印第安诗歌也使用很多叠句,如下边这首"提防我!"("Beware of Me!")四次使用相同的叠句来体现诗歌的节奏和幽默滑稽感:

Beware of Me

i stand on the rock
ho, bear!
beware of me!

i stand on the tree
ho, eagle!

---

① 转引自 https://www.poetryfoundation.org/poems/45477/song-of-myself-1892-version。
② 参见 Addonizio&Laux, p.152。

beware of me!

i stand on the mountain
ho, enemy!
beware of me!

i stand in the camp
ho, chiefs!
beware of me!

here comes a bee!
i run and hide!
he would sting me! ①

叠句的位置可以是一首诗的开头行和结尾行,也可以是一首诗各诗节的第一行或最后一行。有些叠句则可能是在诗中某些不规则位置上出现若干次(一般二到三次)诗行重复。不规则重复的叠句不能太多,否则失去意义。被重复的诗行中某些词出现变化的叫增量叠句(incremental refrain)。下边诗作"华尔兹玛蒂尔达"(Waltzing Matilda)开头几个诗节中相同的几个诗行"You'll come a-waltzing, Matilda, with me"是普通叠句,而诗行"And he sang as he watched and waited till his billy boiled"在后边的诗节中变成了"And he sang as he stowed that jumbuck in his tucker bag",这两个诗行就是增量叠句。诗人克里斯蒂娜·罗萨蒂著名的抒情诗"歌"中两个诗节的最后一个双行诗也是增量叠句。

叠句诗例1:
Once a jolly swagman camped by a billabong
Under the shade of a coolibah tree.
And he sang as he watched and waited till his billy boiled:
"You'll come a-waltzing, Matilda, with me!"

Chorus:
Waltzing, Matilda, waltzing, Matilda,
You'll come a-waltzing, Matilda, with me.

---

① 转引自 Livingston, p.54。

And he sang as he watched and waited till his billy boiled,
"You'll come a-waltzing, Matilda, with me!"

Down came a jumbuck to drink at the billabong,
Up jumped the swagman and grabbed him with glee,
And he sang as he stowed that jumbuck in his tucker bag:
"You'll come a-waltzing, Matilda, with me!"

——From "Waltzing Matilda" ①

叠句诗例2：

Song

By Christina Rossetti

When I am dead, my dearest,
Sing no sad songs for me;
Plant thou no roses at my head,
Nor shady cypress tree:
Be the green grass above me
With showers and dewdrops wet;
And if thou wilt, remember,
And if thou wilt, forget.

I shall not see the shadows,
I shall not feel the rain;
I shall not hear the nightingale
Sing on, as if in pain:
And dreaming through the twilight
That doth not rise nor set,
Haply I may remember,
And haply may forget. ②

排比(parallel)也是英语诗歌中的一种重复。排比是《圣经》的国王(King James)

---

① 转引自 Livingston, p.56-57。
② 转引自 Kowit, p.137。

版本经常使用的重复方式①。沃尔特·惠特曼受《圣经》影响也很喜欢在其诗歌中使用排比。排比包括结构排比（parallel structure）和句子排比（parallel sentence）。结构排比即结构的重复，比如名词、动词、同位语（appositive）、动词分词（verbal）、分句（clause）等等都可以列举成为排比结构。上面举例的惠特曼使用首语重复的诗行其实也使用了结构排比。

英语诗歌中的格律、押韵、首语重复、叠句、排比等等重复工具能够制造不同的声音效果。杰出的诗人会综合使用多种声音重复工具制造诗歌的音乐美感。比如诗人威廉·布莱克著名的"老虎"（"The Tyger"）整首诗读起来音乐感特别强，就是因为该诗大量使用了尾韵、头韵（包括 what、when 等词中的 w 音）、单词重复（如 tiger，what 等）、诗行重复，甚至诗节重复等各种手段，使整首诗读起来节奏感特别强烈，而扬扬格的重复使用又使其诗行读起来铿锵有力：

The Tyger
By William Blake

Tyger! Tyger! burning bright
In the forests of the night,
What immortal hand or eye
Could frame thy fearful symmetry?

In what distant deeps or skies
Burnt the fire of thine eyes?
On what wings dare he aspire?
What the hand, dare seize the fire?

And what shoulder, & what art,
Could twist the sinews of thy heart?
And when thy heart began to beat,
What dread hand? & what dread feet?

What the hammer? what the chain?
In what furnace was thy brain?
What the anvil? what dread grasp

---

① 参见 Addonizo & Laux, p.181。

Dare its deadly terrors clasp?

When the stars threw down their spears,
And water'd heaven with their tears,
Did he smile his work to see?
Did he who made the Lamb make thee?

Tyger! Tyger! burning bright
In the forests of the night,
What immortal hand or eye,
Dare frame thy fearful symmetry?①

诗人阿尔弗雷德·丁尼生（Alfred, Lord Tennyson）下边三个诗节的诗行中也综合使用了多种声音重复工具，包括行尾韵、行内韵和叠句等来制造回环往复的诗歌乐音。三个诗节中，每个诗节的第二和第四行押行尾韵，即：story-glory、going-blowing、river-ever；每个诗节的第一和第三行又各自与本行的一个词押行内韵，即：falls-walls、shakes-lakes、hear-clear、far-scar、die-sky、roll-soul。三个诗节结尾的三个双行诗是叠句，其中后两个双行诗中各含第一个双行诗的一个增量叠句和一个普通叠句：

The splendor falls on castle walls
And snowy summits old in story;
The long light shakes across the lakes,
And the wild cataract leaps in glory.
Blow, bugle, blow, set the wild echoes flying,
Blow, bugle; answer, echoes, dying, dying, dying.

O, hark, O, hear! how thin and clear,
And thinner, clearer, farther going!
O, sweet and far from cliff and scar
The horns of Elfland faintly blowing!
Blow, let us hear the purple glens replying,
Blow, bugle; answer, echoes, dying, dying, dying.

---

① 转引自 Vendler, p.343。

O love, they die in yon rich sky,
They faint on hill or field or river;
Our echoes roll from soul to soul,
And grow for ever and for ever.
Blow, bugle, blow, set the wild echoes flying,
And answer, echoes, answer, dying, dying, dying. ①

英语诗歌中的格律、押韵、首语重复、叠句、排比等重复工具能够制造不同的声音效果和音乐美感。诗歌中的重复不仅能使诗歌声音悦耳动人、表达有序、有助于记忆诗句,而且这些重复的节奏和音响效果及其变异对诗歌的意义建构作用也显而易见。进行诗歌创作的时候,诗人可以尝试这样使用重复:在首行和末行重复同一句话;用同一句话作为每节诗的首行;在诗中重复两三次想要读者记住的词。但要注意:重复的诗行或者词语应该是对诗作的声音效果和意义建构有作用的,否则就不值得重复。

第六节 诗歌的断行(line break):
与散文最明显的视觉区别

每行诗与下一行诗的断开即断行(line break)。在传统英语律诗中,断行是格律节奏要求的结果,因此,一首英语律诗,其每行的长度基本是一定的。但在十九世纪中自由诗开始出现以后,同一首诗的诗行长短就变得复杂多样。自由诗先锋诗人沃尔特·惠特曼的同一首诗中诗行时长时短,其写于 1865 年的"骑兵过滩"("The Cavalry Crossing the Ford")总共 7 行,诗行最短为 8 音节,最长为 23 音节。不仅如此,同时期其他诗人的律诗诗行长度也开始多样化。诗人马修·阿诺德(Matthew Arnold)发表于 1867 年的诗"多佛海滩"("Dover Beach")共 37 行,其中诗行长度一半为五音步,另外几乎一半的诗行要么是二音步,要么是三音步,要么是四音步,而且二音步、三音步、四音步诗行的出现并无明显规律。同样于十九世纪中写作的诗人艾米莉·狄金森的"在他们的石膏房安然无恙"("Safe in their Alabaster Chambers")共 13 行,诗行长度从 4 音节到 11 音节不一,其诗行长度变化也没有明显规律②。

断行,是除散文诗(prose poem)之外的诗歌与散文在视觉上最明显的区别。一句很普通的散文句子"So much depends upon a red wheelbarrow glazed with rainwater

---

① 转引自 Livingston, p.69。
② 参见 Dobyns, Chap.5。

beside the white chickens.",经过诗人威廉·卡洛斯·威廉斯(William Carlos Williams)的断行,就成为一首著名的意象派诗作"红色手推车"("The Red Wheelbarrow")。这个散文句子之所以成为著名诗歌,一个重要的原因就在于诗人巧妙的断行艺术。首先,这个句子被断为四个诗节,每个诗节只含两行,第一行都是三个单词,第二行只有一个单词两个音节。其次,第一和第四诗节的第一行各含四个音节,而中间第二和第三诗节的第一行各含三个音节。所以不管是从视觉上还是从听觉上,这首诗断行的结果就是使它的结构很有对称感,而对称总能给人一种和谐的美感享受①。

The Red Wheelbarrow
By William Carlos Williams

So much depends
upon

a red wheel
barrow

glazed with rain
water

beside the white
chickens ②

在上述这首诗的第一节,depends upon 本是一个短语,却被断开放在两行。这除了产生前述视觉和听觉效应外,在意思表达上也有通过拖延造成悬念,使读者对 upon 后面可能出现的事物充满期待的效果。第二和第三诗节中把两个本应连起来的单词 wheelbarrow 和 rainwater 分别拆开放在两行,除了前述视觉和听觉上的效果外,也使 barrow 和 water 两个词与第四诗节第二行的 chickens 一起得到强调。正是这三样动静结合、闪闪发光的东西吸引了诗人的注意力,而 barrow 的 red 与 chickens 的 white 在颜色上的强烈对比与和谐对称更加激起了诗人的诗情,引起了读者的感动③!

下边诗行摘自诗人查尔斯·布考斯基(Charles Bukowski)的"明眸男子"("The

---

① 参见 Vendler, p.607。
② 转引自 https://www.poetryfoundation.org/poems/45502/the-red-wheelbarrow。
③ 参见 Vendler, p.607。

Man with the Beautiful Eyes")。试试比较将所有句子都变成不断行的散文后效果有何不同？变成散文句后是这样的："he was holding a fifth of whiskey in his right hand. he was about 30. he had a cigar in his mouth, needed a shave. his hair was wild and uncombed and he was barefoot in undershirt and pants. but his eyes were bright. they *blazed* with brightness."。诗人布考斯基的原诗行是这样的：

> he was holding a
> fifth of whiskey
> in his right
> hand.
> he was about
> 30.
> he had a cigar
> in his
> mouth,
> needed a
> shave.
> his hair was
> wild and
> uncombed
> and he was
> barefoot
> in undershirt
> and pants.
> but his eyes
> were
> bright.
> they *blazed*
> with
> brightness... ①

在英语律诗的创作中，断行受格律节奏形式规定的影响，相对比较容易决定。在自由诗的创作中，因为没有格律节奏的形式要求，断行相对灵活。但是，一首自由诗如果

---

① 转引自 Kowit, p.172。

断行毫无目的就毫无意义，不能称其为"诗"①。诗人在具体诗歌创作中进行断行时会考虑很多因素。视觉效果(visual effect)、节奏、意义(meaning)是自由诗断行的三个主要根据②。下边摘自诗人特利·赫茨勒(Terry Hertzler)的"越南字母表"("A Vietnam Alphabet")的开头诗行就是意义逻辑的自然断行：

A is for America. It's funny the things we do for love.
B is for bombs. B-52s dropped thousands of bombs on Vietnam—they tore
    up a lot of ground. Bouncing Betties were small, anti-personnel bombs
    used in ambushes. One blew the legs off a friend of mine.
C is for Charlie; the Viet Cong. They thought we were invading their
    country.
D is for dead.
E is for E-1, E-2, E-3, etc. Those are Army ranks. The higher the number,
    the less chance you'd fall under "D".③

一般来说，在视觉效应上，一行诗的行尾词最显眼突出，因此具有最大的强调作用，而一行诗的行首词在视觉上具有第二显眼的突出效应，因此具有第二位的强调作用④。下边摘自诗人金·阿多尼兹奥(Kim Addonizio)的"夜哺"("Night Feeding")一诗的片段将一个充满张力的动词 tugging 和两个具有反向意思的动词短语即 put out 和 go in 都放在了行末，突出了夜色中室外风声的诗情召唤与室内女儿酣睡的温馨日常之间的诗歌张力：

Darker now. I put out
the wet laundry. In the wind
the pulley creaks and shifts.
My dresses lift, tugging
at the pins. I go in
to where my daughter sleeps.⑤

当诗歌下一行的行首词或短语完全改变了上一诗行营造的意义时，断行能够制造

---

① 参见 Vendler, p.608。
② 参见 Dobyns, chap.5。
③ 转引自 Kowit, p.178。
④ 参见 Addonizio & Laux, p.110。
⑤ 转引自 Kowit, pp.172-173。

意外惊喜或者讽刺效果①。比如前面第四节提到的诗人阿德莱德·克莱普茜最有名的五行诗"三位无声"("Triad")最后两行的断行就具有这种意外效果。在断行中,有时诗人为了节奏会故意把韵词放在行中而不是行末以弱化韵音(如诗人格温多琳·布鲁克斯的"我们真的酷"——"We Real Cool"),也可能把韵词放在行末以示强调。下边保罗·布雷克伯恩(Paul Blackburn)的诗"致电卢瑟福"("Phone Call to Rutherford")记录了其与诗人威廉·卡洛斯·威廉斯的最后一次通话。威廉斯在生命的最后几年因为生病说话困难。布雷克伯恩的诗行排列方式和标点符号的奇怪标示在视觉和声音节奏效果上真实再现了威廉斯说话过程的艰难和迟疑：

```
Phone Call to Rutherford
By Paul Blackburn

"It would be—
            a mercy if
you did not come see me...
"I have dif-fi / culty
            speak-ing, I
cannot count on it, I
am afraid it would be too em-
            ba
            rass-ing
for me    ."
            —Bill, can you still
            answer letters?
"No . my hands
are tongue-tied . You have... made
a record in my heart.
            Goodbye."②
```

创作自由诗,除了上述视觉效果、节奏和意义等方面的断行考量之外,诗人还可能基于以下考虑做出断行决定:第一,使用短诗行可以制造言简意赅、充满活力的效果;第二,视野开阔、眼界恢弘的诗歌更可能需要成分较多的长诗行,比如诗人威廉·布莱

---

① 参见 Kowit,pp.170-178。
② 转引自 Kowit, p.176。

克、沃尔特·惠特曼、卡尔·桑德堡（Carl Sandburg）、艾伦·金斯伯格等的诗作就经常使用长诗行。当一行诗的长度超过纸张的右边而不得不跨行时，要缩进，以与新诗行区别开来。不过，断行有时仅仅就是基于诗人说不出来但与声音乐感相关的无意识直觉。有些现当代诗人也可能不再奉行新诗行必须从页面的左手边缘开始的规则，而采用开放性或者即兴的排行法，比如在视觉上模仿海浪形状或者锯齿形状排列诗行，等等①。

第七节 停顿断行（end stop）与跨行连续（enjambment）

　　诗歌的断行能起到标点符号的作用，使诗行的句法与意思更加清晰，尤其在没有或者只有极少标点符号的诗作中。如果诗行在句子、从句、短语的结尾断开，因此在诗行末尾有一个自然的句法停顿，这行诗就是停顿断行（end stop）。以标点符号结尾的诗行都是停顿断行，但是停顿断行不一定需要在行末使用标点符号。使用首语重复手法的诗歌经常使用停顿断行。如果诗行在短语的中间断开，则会迫使读者要么相对忽视行末，要么只是在行末稍作停顿，这样就制造了诗行之间语音语义不间断流动的紧张效果，这种断行可称为跨行连续（enjambment）。使用跨行连续的诗行也叫连续诗行（run-on lines）。下边的三行诗是停顿断行②：

　　I said I was sorry
　　but wasn't qualified,
　　neither nurse nor masseuse.

　　除了律诗之外，自由诗的停顿断行效果自然，不会引起特别的注意。如果诗歌以跨行连续形式断行，则会因人为停顿痕迹明显而引人注意。从强调的角度来说，任何一行诗的行尾词和行首词都是得到明显强调的位置。停顿断行诗行（end-stopped line）是如此，跨行连续诗行（enjambed line）也是如此③。诗人兰斯顿·休斯（Langston Hughes）的"二战"（"World War II"）前面合唱部分是停顿断行，而后边回声部分则是跨行连续。不仅如此，回声句子只包括了三个单词，但三个单词每个各占一行，强烈突出了每个词的重要性。读这首诗时需要注意的是，因为第二次世界大战给美国经济带来了极大的

---

① 参见 Kowit, pp.170-178。
② 同上。
③ 参见 Dobyns, chap.5&9。

机遇,所以才有开头的那个欢乐大合唱①:

World War II

By Langston Hughes

What a grand time was the war!
  Oh, my, my!
What a grand time was the war!
  My, my, my!
In wartime we had fun,
Sorry that old war is done!
What a grand time was the war,
  My, my!
Echo:
  Did
  Somebody
  Die? ②

  诗人格温多琳·布鲁克斯(Gwendolyn Brooks)著名的"我们真的酷"("We Real Cool")典型地说明了跨行连续和停顿断行的区别。诗标题"We real cool"的语法问题首先反映了 We 的身份应是黑人,因其口语习惯性地省略动词 be。下面左边是布鲁克斯的原诗③。可以看到,诗人特意使用了跨行连续把单词 We 放在诗行末端进行强调,同时把每个双行诗节可能的尾韵放在了行中从而弱化了韵音。与右边改编了的去掉跨行连续的停顿断行诗节相比,布鲁克斯原诗中的跨行连续把单词 We 置于行末,这对 We 的强调作用显而易见。同时,将单词 We 与其所属句子的其他成分割断分成两行,也使得 We 与主流社会文化的割裂而形成的尴尬得到凸显。

We Real Cool	We Real Cool
By Gwendolyn Brooks	
The Pool Players.	The Pool Players.

---

① 参见 Vendler, p.243。
② 转引自 Vendler, p.243。
③ 转引自 https://www.poetryfoundation.org/poetrymagazine/poems/28112/we-real-cool。

Seven at the Golden Shovel.	Seven at the Golden Shovel.
We real cool. We Left school. We	We real cool. We left school.
Lurk late. We Strike straight. We	We lurk late. We strike straight.
Sing sin. We Thin gin. We	We sing sin. We thin gin.
Jazz June. We Die soon.	We jazz June. We die soon.

与停顿断行相比,跨行连续对下一行诗的行首词的强调相对加强。格温多琳·布鲁克斯使用的跨行连续断行不仅突出强调了一个被割裂被孤立的 We,而且也强调了下一行行首的动词 left、lurk、strike、sing、thin、jazz、die 等,动态刻画了几个少年胡作非为、外强中干的形象。值得一提的是,这首诗除了跨行连续引人注目以外,其诗行音乐性效果也非常突出。头韵和多种行内韵的运用使这首诗成为朗朗上口、读过不忘的经典诗作,而诗行强烈的乐感与跨行连续形成的对 We 的孤立割裂和少年们的胡作非为的强调也形成了强烈对比。

英语诗歌的跨行连续现象早在十四世纪末杰弗里·乔叟的诗中已经出现,到十六世纪末的诗歌已经十分明显,在素体诗和诗人莎士比亚的十四行诗中跨行连续现象已经很常见。不过,十八世纪常见的英雄体双行诗是停顿断行。浪漫主义诗歌因为追求自然与逼真,跨行连续用得较多。到了非律诗时期,对诗歌跨行连续和行末人为停顿的使用出现了多样化:诗人沃尔特·惠特曼的诗大多是停顿断行;诗人华莱士·斯蒂文斯和一些其他现代诗人朗读自己的诗作时使用了跨行连续的读法,没有明显的行末停顿;诗人玛丽安·穆尔(Marianne Moore)常以音节数作为断行依据,而不是为了强调某个词而断行[①]。

不过,从整个二十世纪来说,许许多多律诗或者非律诗人,如詹姆斯·赖特(James Wright)、西尔维娅·普拉斯(Sylvia Plath)、亚兰·杜根(Alan Dugan)、唐纳德·贾斯提斯、高尔韦·金内尔(Galway Kinnell)、威廉·斯坦利·默温(W. S. Merwin)和艾德里安·里奇(Adrienne Rich),等等,使用跨行连续行末人为停顿来强调某些词以及制

[①] 参见 Dobyns, chap.5 或 *The Princeton Encyclopedia*, p.410。

造微妙诗意(nuance)。二十世纪五十年代末诗歌跨行连续问题受到了格外的关注。可惜的是,诗人罗伯特·洛威尔(Robert Lowell)之后的第四代美国诗人似乎因为没有经过严格的格律诗训练,其诗句断行稍显无力、随意、缺乏根据,这使他们的诗行有时读起来像散文,不知为何称其为诗歌①。

按照跨行连续造成的诗句流动在行尾的人为切断(也即诗行末尾词与前后紧接词的人为切断)痕迹明显程度可以分为温和跨行连续(light enjambment)与激进跨行连续(radical enjambment)。在名词或者动词后断行、在形容词与其修饰的名词或者副词与其修饰的动词的中间断行、在连词或者代词后断行、在介词或冠词后断行,这四种断行情况的人为切断痕迹依次增加,因而其跨行连续是从温和到激进的递增。越激进的跨行连续其断行越难以成功。不过,一旦成功,该跨行连续实现的人为意图效果也越明显②。

读者在读诗过程中会对作品逐渐形成一定的假设和期待。如果一行诗出现了与前文明显的差异,不符合读者的假设和期待,读者会停下来思考这个差异。通常这种明显差异是由语气(tone)的突然变化引起的。诗歌中的语气可以是热烈诚挚的,可以是轻描淡写的,可以是委婉幽默的,也可以是讽刺的,甚至是似非而是的。语气体现的是诗歌中的意思与态度③。语气变化可能体现在语义、句法、措辞、声音以及节奏上。突然的语气变化使读者质疑已经建立的对该诗的一些假设。如果读者无法为这种突然的变化找到合理解释,就会怀疑这种变化的合法性。这也是在诗作的第一行或者第一句出现奇怪元素时比较容易蒙混过关的原因,因为第一行或第一句中,读者还没有形成对诗作的语气假设④。

一般来说,一首诗有一个总体节奏。如果一首诗分为一定数量的诗节,那么不同诗节可能有不同的节奏并且其节奏差异还可能很大。最明显的比如诗人威斯坦·休·奥登(W. H. Auden)的"纪念叶芝"("In Memory of W. B. Yeats")。该诗的开头两节格律松散,诗行长度差别很大,而第三节却是格律严格并且都是七音节诗行。第三节在节奏上对第一、二节的偏离虽然让读者惊讶,但却有合法性,因为这种节奏差异显示了诗中说话者的情感思想变化,因此可以被读者接受。总的来说,读者如果能理解这种诗中说话者的情感思想变化,也就能理解和接受这种诗节之间的节奏变化⑤。

当然,读者对诗作形成的假设、期待或意外、怀疑既同诗作本身有关,也同读者的学识与经历有关,不一定是由诗人和诗作造成的。读者的阅读期待总是得到满足,则其阅读

---

① 参见 Dobyns,chap.5。
② 同上。
③ 语气(tone)反映了说话的态度和意思。讽刺(satire)语气类似反讽(irony),提示说话的表面意思与实际相反。轻描淡写(understatement)和似非而是(paradox)也具有接近反讽语气的效果,因为这三种语气都是表面所说与实际存在差异。轻描淡写即说话有所保留;似非而是即表面上说的是"非",实际上说的是"是"。可参见 Brooks & Warren, p.115。
④ 参见 Dobyns,chap.5。
⑤ 参见 Dobyns,chap.5。

过程会变得无聊;读者的阅读期待总是得不到满足,则读者会备受打击。因此,诗人要考虑读者的阅读期待,既适当打击读者阅读期待,提供阅读惊喜,又不过度晦涩,适当满足读者的阅读成就感。诗人可以从形式到内容制造一系列意外惊喜吸引读者。新内容或者旧内容新说法对读者来说都可能是意外。任何意想不到的观点、词语、声音、断行等,都能给读者带来意外或惊喜①。

一旦发现意外而至的明显差异,读者就会尝试把它放进诗作整体进行理解阐释。跨行连续总是能带来意外,因为它带来了诗行节奏上的人为停顿。停顿的人为痕迹越明显,其带来的意外就越强烈,该跨行连续就越激进。遇到跨行连续带来的意外,读者会努力从形式或者内容中找出造成这种差异的原因。如果读者无法找到原因,这种跨行连续的合法性就会受到质疑。如果只是小意外,跨行连续合法性受损不大,该断行的合法性也就相应受损不大;但如果是很大的意外,如以冠词断行的激进跨行连续,那么这种跨行的连续合法性就会受损很大,相应地该断行的合法性也就很微弱了。激进跨行连续难以成功的主要原因就是其人为停顿在诗歌节奏上,打破了读者期待,制造了悬念,带来了意外,但是又不能提供合理解释,因而不能为突兀的人为断行提供合法性②。

诗歌阅读总是在张力与安逸交替中进行。跨行连续带来张力,而停顿断行则带来安逸;建立一种模式后的偏移带来张力,而回归则带来安逸。假如诗人不断地进行跨行连续,则这种张力会持续增加,其结果可能是停顿断行的出现缓解了这种张力,也可能是读者直接中断阅读。像"when I saw an/ eagle disappear within a/ reddening cloud..."这样激进的跨行连续是很可能使作品完全失去作为诗歌的合法性而迫使读者中断阅读的。读者在读诗过程中,特别是读非律诗时,经常会思考诗作断行的理由。如果读者找不到解释的理由,那既可能是读者寻找力度不够,也可能是诗人本来就没有根据,而这后者当然就是诗人的问题了③。

诗歌形式工具的一个功能就是进行微妙的诗歌意义建构。对诗行中的音节长短、声音高低、重读或轻读音节、完全韵或不完全韵、和音、谐音、头韵、格律节奏、旋律对比、行宽、断行等等形式工具的操作,都可以制造微妙诗意。下边诗人詹姆斯·赖特(James Wright)的"逝"("Rip")体现了断行、跨行连续、叠句、行内停顿这些形式工具对制造微妙诗意的作用。该诗的第一和第二行的跨行连续分别强调了第二和第三行行首的"that"和"just"两个词的具体指向。第七行的跨行连续突出了第八行的行首意象"a bird",而这个白色猫头鹰意象与此诗开头和结尾的增量叠句中的白色影子意象构成了整首诗的主导象征(dominant symbol,意象和象征将于下一章详述)。第十一至第十四共四行诗中出现了十个行内停顿,真切表现了诗人念及年少往事时心中的思

---

① 参见 Dobyns, chap.5。
② 同上。
③ 同上。

潮起伏。这种起伏的思潮急需平复,于是第十五行出现了独立句子的停顿断行"It's best to keep still."。如果这首诗不进行断行而是排成普通散文体,则其语言平淡无奇,诗意几无。正是断行、跨行连续等形式工具的使用让它成其为诗[①]。

Rip
By James Wright

It can't be the passing of time that casts
That white shadow across the waters
Just off shore.
I shiver a little, with the evening.
I turn down the steep path to find
What's left of the river gold.
I whistle a dog lazily, and lazily
A bird whistles me.
Close by a big river, I am alive in my own country,
I am home again.
Yes; I lived here, and here, and my name
That I carved young, with a girl's, is healed over, now,
And lies sleeping beneath the inward sky
Of a tree's skin, close to the quick.
It's best to keep still.
But:
There goes that bird that whistled me down here
To the river a moment ago.
Who is he? A little white barn owl from Hudson's Bay,
Flown out of his range here, and lost?
Oh, let him be home here, and, if he wants to,
He can be the body that casts
That white shadow across the waters
Just off shore. [②]

[①] 参见 Dobyns, chap.5。
[②] 转引自 Dobyns, chap.5,详见 Wright, James. "Rip," *Above the River: The Complete Poems*, New York: Farrar, Straus and Giroux, 1990, p.162。

第二章
英语诗歌中的修辞、意象、面具

语言学中曾用象征(symbol)一词来定义指向事物的词语(words)。后来结构主义语言学家弗迪南·德·索绪尔(Ferdinand de Saussure)用符号(sign)代替象征来定义指向事物的词语,并为其加上能指(signifier)和所指(signified)两个属性。解构主义(deconstruction)语言学和文学理论批评则认为既然能指和所指之间的联系是任意的,那么语言本身就具有多种意思[①]。作为一种特殊语言,英语诗歌中的词语可能同时具有字面义(literal)和比喻义(figurative)等多种意思,从而具有多义性(ambiguity)。多义性既是英语诗歌追求的一种效果,也是英语诗歌中常用的语言技巧。双关(pun)和隐喻(metaphor)都是达到多义性的重要形式,也是重要的修辞手法(rhetorical figure/rhetorical device/figure of speech)。从这一点看来,多义性也是修辞手法的目的与效果之一。最常见的修辞手法包括类比(analogy)、拟人(personification)、呼语(apostrophe)、夸张(hyperbole)等。呼语、拟人、类比等如果达到了夸张的效果,则同时也是夸张修辞手法。前面章节介绍的英语诗歌声音重复手段如首语重复和排比等也是修辞手法[②]。

第一节 隐喻(metaphor)与象征(symbol)

呼语,是一种常见的修辞手法,其希腊语原意是"转开",即从听者处转开而对某些并不在听的对象直接说话,比如婴儿、动物、不在场的或已死的人、不能动的事物或者抽象物,等等。诗人威廉·布莱克 e 在"The Lamb"中的"Little lamb, who made thee?"就是呼语,直接对动物小绵羊说话。也有人把呼语等同于另一个动作"对…说话(address)"。这就使呼语的动作所指不仅包括不在听的对象,也包括在听的对象,

---

[①] 参见 *The Princeton Encyclopedia*, pp.1392 – 1393。
[②] 参见 Vendler, pp.615 – 616。

比如爱人、朋友、同时代的甚至是未来时代的读者,等等①。

传统英语诗歌形式颂歌(ode)和挽歌(elegy)中常见呼语修辞手法的使用。英语诗歌中,呼语常常以表达强烈感情的"O"开始。呼语最适合于表达强烈的感情、提出疑惑、给出建议。下边的诗行中,诗人正想近距离欣赏一朵正在盛开的玫瑰,一只蜜蜂嗡嗡叫着盘旋而下,似乎在挑战诗人,看看谁才有资格享受玫瑰的芳香。于是受到挑战的诗人直接质问蜜蜂:

> Who has the better
> right to smell the first summer
> rose, bee—you or I?②

拟人是与呼语相关联的另一种修辞手法。这种修辞手法把一些抽象的、集体性的、无生命的、死亡了的、非理性的、笼统的事物当做有生命的人来对待③。人在童年时期很容易把周围的事物当作是和自己一样能说话的生命。儿童常常会自言自语或者与没有生命的事物说话,而诗人则经常保留着这份童真。

在诗歌中使用拟人的修辞手法,赋予无生命的事物以声音,诉说它们各自拥有或者知道的故事,是诗人们常用的创作工具。比如,在下边"流转"("Taking Turns")的诗行中,诗人诺马·法伯(Norma Farber)把傍晚的太阳动感而形象地拟人化为一个归家的女子。女子回家关上了窗,天就黑了,于是拟人化了的星星就带着银色钥匙来打开了黑夜的门。这几个诗行中拟人手法的使用让太阳下山、星星出现等天体现象与人的日常行为紧紧相连,充满烟火味又不失灵性:

> When sun goes home
> behind the trees,
> and locks her shutters tight—
> then stars come out
> with silver keys
> to open up the night.④

明喻(simile)是日常生活中经常使用的修辞手法,它把一件事物与另一件事物做比较(comparison, analogy),比较明显的标志是使用关联词如"like、as、as though"等。在

---

① 参见 *The Princeton Encyclopedia*, p.61。
② 转引自 Livingston, p.16。
③ 参见 *The Princeton Encyclopedia*, p.1025。
④ 转引自 Livingston, p.99。

诗人罗伯特·伯恩斯的著名明喻"my love is like a red, red rose"中，比喻或者说比较的本体(tenor)是"我的爱人(my love)"，喻体(vehicle)是"红玫瑰(red rose)"。这个明喻将爱人比喻为红玫瑰，意即这位女子对于说话人来说就像春天之于世界，给他带来重生与欢乐。

因为日常生活中长期经常使用，有些明喻已经成为陈词滥调。诗人使用明喻进行诗歌创作就一定要能标新立异。下列诗行摘自题为"新笔记本"("New Notebook")的作品，诗人茱蒂丝·瑟曼(Judith Thurman)把新笔记本上精细水平的分行线比喻为雪原上平直延伸的电话线，把行间的黑色字母比作稳坐电话线上的乌鸦。这两个比喻首先从颜色和形状上对本体和喻体进行类比，非常形象。在这两个明喻的喻体中出现了三个意象：电话线、雪原、乌鸦。电话线具有连接沟通功能，雪原的白也代表了无限的可能性。然而，雪原的冷和乌鸦带来的不测感则激起一种消极感受。三个意象的同时出现使这两个明喻呈现了一种多义性，表现了对新笔记本既期待又不安的复杂感受，非常新颖：

> Lines
> in a new notebook
> run, even and fine,
> like telephone wires
> across a snowy landscape.
>
> With wet, black strokes
> the alphabet settles between them,
> comfortable as a flock of crows.①

隐喻(metaphor)的希腊语原意是"转换(transfer)、转移(carry across)"，即用一个事物来说明另一个事物②。语言通过隐喻扩大词汇意义。比如"山脚(the foot of a mountain)"与"河口(the mouth of a river)"就是通过消亡隐喻(dead metaphor)获得词意。"根(root)"一词，本意指植物的根部，但"问题的根源(the root of the problem)"或"萧条的根本原因(the root causes of depression)"等词语用的就是"根(root)"的隐喻义。语言通过隐喻机制从具体发展到抽象，从形象发展到观念③。通过隐喻，可以用具体事物或形象将抽象概念具体化。

---

① 转引自 Livingston, p.83。
② 参见 Dobyns, Introduction。
③ 参见 *The Princeton Encyclopedia*, p.663。

作为修辞手法的隐喻则把一件事物说成是另一件事物,明显标志是使用动词 be 的各种变形。在其作品"梦想"("Dreams")的下列诗行中,诗人兰斯顿·休斯使用隐喻手法把失去梦想的人生比喻为"断翼的鸟(a broken-winged bird)"和"贫瘠的田野(a barren field)",通过断翼而无法飞翔的鸟和被大雪冻僵的贫瘠田野这两个意象直接具体可感地把失去梦想以后的生命残缺与贫瘠呈现给读者:

Hold fast to dreams
For if dreams die
Life is a broken-winged bird
That cannot fly.

Hold fast to dreams
For if dreams go
Life is a barren field
Frozen with snow. ①

作为修辞手法的隐喻常常与其他修辞手法结合使用,以实现隐喻的魅力。比如,呼语和拟人就常常与隐喻结合使用。下边诗行来自题为"雾角"("Foghorns")的作品,诗人丽莲·穆尔通过隐喻的手法拟人化了港口的雾角,形象刻画了其声音的低沉伤感,接着又通过隐喻把这个声音拟人化为城市睡梦中的哭泣。在这个例子中,拟人可以说就是一种特殊的隐喻。

The foghorns moaned
in the bay last night
so sad
so deep
I thought I heard the city
crying in its sleep. ②

诗人洛温·布朗的"周六一晚后的周日清晨"("A Sunday Morning After a Saturday Night")则通过夸张手法充分实现了隐喻的魅力,即:热恋中的女孩两眼发光,可以为迷雾中的飞机照亮前路;额头发烫,可以烤黑吐司;手掌发热,可以融化手

---

① 转引自 Livingston, pp.90 - 91。
② 转引自 Livingston, p.96。

中所握的电话筒。而此诗拟人化的细节描写,即电话线在女孩手中弹跳而出,告知对方女孩说出的爱意等,也相当形象生动:

A Sunday Morning After a Saturday Night
By LoVerne Brown

She's so happy, this girl,
she's sending out sparks like a brush fire,
so lit with life
her eyes could beam airplanes through fog,
so warm with his loving
we could blacken our toast
on her forehead.

The phone rings
and she whispers to it
"I love you."
The cord uncoils
and leaps to tell him
she said it,
the receiver melts in her hand
as if done by Dali,
the whole room crackles

and we at the breakfast table
smile
but at safe distance
having learned by living
that love so without insulation
can immolate more than the toast. ①

在隐喻中,最核心关键的是本体与喻体的联系或者互动。新颖的隐喻可以让人用新视角认识事物,从而发现事物未被注意到的新特征。通过隐喻,可以用具体事物或形

---

① 转引自 Kowit, p.200。

象将抽象概念具体化,而抽象概念反过来也提升和拓展了具体事物和形象。隐喻的浅表意思可能立即为人所理解,但隐喻的深层意思却可能在后来的不同解读中不断出现①。诗歌是用隐喻方式说话的艺术,是让很多本身就是隐喻的语言、词汇变得更加隐喻性,就像诗人艾米莉·狄金森说的"Tell all the truth but tell it slant"。

诗人威廉·布莱克的"病玫瑰"("The Sick Rose")中从第二行开始直至最后一行是一个句子。这个句子陈述一个自然现象,即肉眼不可见的害虫因一己之私摧毁了玫瑰的生命。玫瑰和害虫表面上看是两个自然意象,但是诗中指称害虫时使用的拟人化代词"his"和第一行诗对玫瑰使用的呼语,又明显扩展了这两个自然意象的范畴,使它们成为两个有社会意义指向的隐喻。第一行对玫瑰的呼语是一种判断、诊断,甚至是警告,对全诗的理解和诠释具有决定性意义:

The Sick Rose
By William Blake

O Rose, thou art sick!
The invisible worm,
That flies in the night,
In the howling storm,

Has found out thy bed
Of crimson joy:
And his dark secret love
Does thy life destroy.②

一首诗既可以包含多个隐喻,也可以整首诗构成一个隐喻。诗人杰克·吉尔伯特(Jack Gilbert)的"米奇可已逝"("Michiko Dead")中的"盒子(box)"意象是一个隐喻,而整首诗也是一个隐喻。标题中的 Michiko 是诗人因病逝去的妻子。样如骨灰盒的盒子意象隐喻失去妻子之后诗人的悲伤,而整首诗所描述的诗人为应对这种背负盒子的沉重感所变换的各种行为姿势等细节则隐喻诗人失去妻子之后的悲痛及其逐渐对悲痛的适应和对失落的接受:

---

① 参见 Dobyns, Introduction。
② 转引自 https://www.poetryfoundation.org/poems/43682/the-sick-rose。

Michiko Dead
By Jack Gilbert

He manages like somebody carrying a box
that is too heavy, first with his arms
underneath. When their strength gives out,
he moves the hands forward, hooking them
on the corners, pulling the weight against
his chest. He moves his thumbs slightly
when the fingers begin to tire, and it makes
different muscles take over. Afterward,
he carries it on his shoulder, until the blood
drains out of the arm that is stretched up
to steady the box and the arm goes numb. But now
the man can hold underneath again, so that
he can go on without ever putting the box down.①

诗人 Ernesto Cardenal 的"鹦鹉"("The Parrots")整首诗也是一个隐喻。被抓起来意欲走私到美国强迫学讲英语的鹦鹉总共有 186 只,47 只已经死于囚笼中。截获该批走私鹦鹉的指挥官将它们运回故土平原放飞。囚笼打开时,所有幸存的鹦鹉激奋中振翼齐飞,像箭一样射归高山。囚笼、鹦鹉、放飞,三个意象组合起来一起隐喻了革命的解放作用,而死去的 47 只鹦鹉则隐喻了革命的代价:

The Parrots
By Ernesto Cardenal (Jonathan Cohen 译)

My friend Michel is a commanding officer in Somoto,
  near the border with Honduras,
and he told me about finding a shipment of parrots
that were going to be smuggled to the United States
  in order for them to learn to speak English.
There were 186 parrots, and 47 had already died in their cages.
And he took them back to the place from where they'd been taken,

---

① 转引自 https://www.poetryfoundation.org/poems/43407/michiko-dead。

and when the truck was getting close to a place called The Plains
near the mountains where those parrots came from
  (the mountains looked immense behind those plains)
the parrots began to get excited and beat their wings
  and press themselves against the walls of their cages.
And when the cages were opened
they all flew like arrows in the same direction to their mountains.
That's just what the Revolution did with us, I think:
it freed us from the cages
  in which we were being carried off to speak English.
It brought us back to the Homeland from which we'd been uprooted.
Comrades in fatigues green as parrots gave the parrots their green mountains.
  But there were 47 dead. ①

当整首诗构成一个隐喻的时候,这首诗可能成为一个寓言(allegory)、神话(fable/parable/myth)或者一个象征②。诗人特莉丝(Virginia R. Terris)的散文诗"不速之客"("The Uninvited")整首诗就相当于一个寓言或者神话。饥瘦如纸的一众儿童从紧闭的门窗细缝中滑入高官的晚宴大厅,张大着饥渴的嘴巴,瞪大着黑色的眼睛注视着政府高官们饱餐盛宴中翕合的大嘴。饱食的高官与饥饿的儿童两个群体形成了鲜明的对比,其寓意非常明显,而饥瘦如纸的儿童进入宴会厅的方式及厅外黑夜的氛围则使整首诗带上了神话色彩:

The Uninvited
By Virginia R. Terris

As the heads of state feast with one another, the tables in the gilded hall loaded with caviar, venison, exotic fruits and vegetables and gallons of champagne, there's a tapping on the windows. A child's face, then another, presses against the panes, the eyes in them black as the night the children stand in, their mouths open as if they were howling with the wind.

---

① 转引自 Kowit, p.185。
② 参见 Kowit, p.80。

"Who are they?" ask the guests uneasily. "Where did they come from?"

"Keep them out!" yells the host. "Get Security! Where's Security?"

But the children are so thin, they slip under the doors, around the edges of the windows. Noiselessly. In great numbers. They move forward to the tables. Their fingers grip the edges of the tables. Their eyes gaze upward into the enormous openings and closings of official mouths.①

寓言指的是文学作品中对抽象事物的拟人化。诗人埃德蒙·斯宾塞的《仙后》就是一则典型的寓言，其中拉克罗斯骑士（Recrosse Knight）代表基督精神，丢萨（Duessa）代表口是心非的诱惑，尤那（Una）代表真正的教会，等等。一部寓言性作品中不仅仅人物是寓言性的，环境和行为也可能是寓言性的。寓言与象征类似。寓言与象征的不同在于寓言从本体开始，喻体是为了本体而构建；而象征是从喻体开始，本体是从喻体中发现、引申，或者诱发的。寓言与象征的这一区别使象征在以诗人歌德（J. W. Goethe）和格勒律治（Samuel Taylor Coleridge）始的浪漫主义和现代主义批评中被赞美为自然有活力，寓言被批评为说教而做作②。

象征是一种隐喻性语言。象征可能从字面行为（literal action）或字面意象（literal image）开始，通过隐喻等修辞手法的运用，而获得字面行为和意象以外更多甚至完全不同的意义。因此，隐喻是象征的一个手段③。象征可以看做是倒装隐喻（metaphor in reverse）。象征同样有本体和喻体，并且其喻体即本体，即喻体得到扩展而代替了本体，而本体是从喻体的暗示中发现、引申或者诱发的④。诗人查尔斯·列兹尼克夫（Charles Reznikoff）以下的两行诗就使用时钟齿轮象征时间的流逝，而头发被时间齿轮撕扯剥离导致的秃顶则隐喻着时间流逝对人的无情剥削：

My hair was caught in the wheels of a clock
and torn from my head: see, I am bald!⑤

象征的喻体与本体之间的关联可以像隐喻一样基于相似性，也可以是基于其他方面，比如诗人艾略特（T. S. Eliot）的"荒原"（"The Waste Land"）中包含的贫瘠、不育

---

① 转引自 Kowit，pp.187 – 188。
② 参见 *The Princeton Encyclopedia*，pp.1392 – 1393。
③ 其他象征手段包括做梦（dream）、幻想（fantasy）等想象性行为。
④ 参见 *The Princeton Encyclopedia*，pp.1392 – 1393。
⑤ 转引自 Kowit，p.70。

(sterility)与肥沃、繁殖(fertility)的象征非常明显,这种象征不是基于相似性,而是基于神话或者仪式关联。隐喻经过不同时代或者不同诗人的不断重复以后喻体单独出现也可以引发对本体的关联从而成为象征。这种情况下,象征是因为不断重复而得到普遍认可的隐喻。诗人叶芝的作品"丽达与天鹅"("Leda and the Swan")和"学童中"("Among School Children")中的天鹅意象就是这样的象征①。某些象征因其在人类经验中的普遍性而成为原型(archetype)②,比如太阳、白色以及梦境中的水、老人等意象都是已经成为原型的象征。关于梦的解析文献中,不管是西方还是东方,人的梦境中出现的意象经常是一种象征语言,具有象征意义。

意象与包括隐喻与象征等在内的修辞紧密联系,所以也可以是一种修辞工具。诗人罗伯特·伯恩斯的著名明喻"my love is like a red, red rose"呈现了红玫瑰与我的爱人即一位女子这两个既相互独立又相互联系的意象。在这个明喻中,喻体红玫瑰的色彩、纹理、气味呈现的是本体女子脸红、皮嫩、体香的特点。红玫瑰和女子都是独立的意象,通过思考、感觉、写作和阅读而关联了起来。这些关联行为是这个明喻本体和喻体连接的基础。但是不管这种关联多么细致复杂且富有成效,红玫瑰与女子仍然是两个独立的并且彼此不能代替的意象③。这正像诗人格特鲁德·斯坦所说的:玫瑰就是玫瑰就是玫瑰④。

第二节 意象(image)与客观对应物(objective correlative)

诗歌创作应该进行描写呈现,而不是陈述告知。创作中的现当代英语诗人经常说的一句话就是:We do not tell in poetry, we show! 类似 He felt so happy; She felt very sad; That summer at camp he missed his mother; The letter confused her; He felt angry; She begged him to stay. 这样的陈述并不能像 He grinned despite himself and rushed to greet her. 这样的细节描写有效呈现诗歌中的感受情感态度。诗歌感受情感态度的呈现可以通过动作细节描写来实现,也可以通过意象来实现。意象可以是简单直接的,也可以是比喻性或象征性的。下边诗行来自诗人瓦莱丽·华斯(Valerie Worth)题为"太阳"("Sun")的诗,其中出现了多个意象,即跳跃的火、温暖的黄色广场、平坦的被子、猫,等等。这些意象生动地呈现了不同状态下太阳给人的感觉,特别是被子和猫意象的使用,让人真实感受到温和阳光下的那种慵懒与舒适:

---

① 参见 *The Princeton Encyclopedia*, pp.1392-1393。
② 参见 Brooks & Warren, pp.580-581。
③ 参见 *The Princeton Encyclopedia*, p.664。
④ "a rose is a rose is a rose",转引自 *The Princeton Encyclopedia*, p.664。

The sun
Is a leaping fire
Too hot
To go near,

But it will still
Lie down
In warm yellow squares
On the floor

Like a flat
Quilt, where
The cat can curl
And purr.①

诗歌中精彩的比喻常常从异乎寻常的角度使用巧妙精准的意象呈现事物的联系和特点。这样的比喻和意象，通常是诗歌最吸引人的地方。本章第一节所述诗人兰斯顿·休斯的"梦想"("Dreams")中使用了两个隐喻来说明没有梦想的生命的悲哀与贫瘠。这两个隐喻中分别出现了两个意象，即折翼的鸟儿和积雪覆盖的荒野。这两个意象非常直观地把这种悲哀与贫瘠呈现出来。假如不使用隐喻修辞手法，不引入意象，原来的诗行可能会变成下边的模样。这样的诗并不成功，因为它没有诗意，它只是在说教：

Hold fast to dreams
For if dreams die
It's going to be hard for you
To get by.

Hold fast to dreams
For when dreams go
You can be disappointed
You know.

---

① 转引自 Livingston, pp.91–92。

在诗歌中描写呈现某种情感情绪的时候，可以使用合适的意象来做这种情感情绪的"客观对应物"(objective correlative)。客观对应物是诗人艾略特引入的一个概念，指的是代表某种具体情感情绪的一系列物体、一种情形、一连串事件，这些物体、情形、事件出现在文学作品中就会引起这种特定的情感反应。充当情感客观对应物的可以是星辰大海，可以是历史事件，也可以是日常家什①。诗人尼卡诺尔·帕拉(Nicanor Parra)下边的"洋槐"("Acacias")就表现了客观对应物这种奇妙的情绪激发作用。在一条洋槐花盛开的街上，诗中说话人听到了曾经的爱人与别人结婚的消息。此后多年，说话人一看到洋槐花盛开，就心碎欲绝。

Acacias
By Nicanor Parra(David Unger 翻译)
Strolling many years ago
Down a street taken over by acacias in bloom
I found out from a friend who knows everything
That you had just gotten married.
I told him that I really
Had nothing to do with it.
I never loved you
—You know that better than I do—
Yet each time the acacias bloom
—Can you believe it? —
I get the very same feeling I had
When they hit me point-blank
With the heartbreaking news
That you had married someone else.②

诗人简·凯尼恩(Jane Kenyon)下边的"外套"("Coats")从第三者视觉描写一个男人失去或者即将失去其所爱的人时所感受到的凄凉。诗中大衣的意象出现了两次，第一次出现的是其爱人的大衣，爱人已经不再需要，但他需要，他带着它；第二次出现的是男人自己的大衣，在风和日丽的十二月大衣的拉链被紧紧拉起，以抵御心中的寒意。此诗虽然是从第三者视觉用平淡的语气进行外貌和行为描写，却能让读者真实体会感受到男人深深的失落和凄凉。这两个大衣意象就是男人心中失落凄凉的情感状态的客观

---

① 参见 Kowit, p.204。
② 转引自 Kowit, p.216。

对应物。

Coats
By Jane Kenyon

I saw him leaving the hospital
with a woman's coat over his arm.
Clearly she would not need it.
The sunglasses he wore could not
conceal his wet face, his bafflement.
As if in mockery the day was fair,
and the air mild for December. All the same
he had zipped his own coat and tied
the hood under his chin, preparing
for irremediable cold.①

意象一词对应的英语单词可以是 image,也可以是 imagery。意象,最狭义最直白的意思就是图形或者形象(即 image)。意象,在包括诗歌的文学中是指语言文字在人脑中制造形象(即 imagery),这些语言文字激起人的身体感觉:视觉(visual)、听觉(auditory)、味觉(taste)、触觉(tactile)、嗅觉(smell),等等。因此文学中的意象包括视觉意象、听觉意象、味觉意象、触觉意象、嗅觉意象、动觉意象,等等。诗歌中的意象(image or imagery)可以是隐喻,可以是象征,可以是重复出现的母题,可以是一种心理事件,也可以是诗歌本身。意象概念在中国文学传统中出现已经数千年,在中国诗学占据中心位置也已经数百上千年,但在西方诗学中得到重视的时间则相对晚得多,是相对现代的现象②。

古希腊哲学家柏拉图(Plato)不认为绘画和诗歌是知识,因此也否定意象的作用。虽然后来的哲学家亚里士多德(Aristotle)承认意象在思想形成过程中的作用,其他诗人或学者如贺拉斯(Horace)、郎吉那斯(Longinus)和昆提连(Quintilian)等也谈论过意象在诗歌和修辞中的作用,并且古希腊和罗马作者广泛使用通艺法(ekphrasis)来指那些使出现在诗歌中的事物栩栩如生恍若在眼前的意象,但是,西方文学理论和实践中把意象当做一个严肃范畴来思考是始于现代文学批评早期,即大约十六、七世纪。在此期间,诗人菲利普·西德尼(Sir Philip Sidney)于1595年在《诗辩》(*Defence of Poesy*)中

---

① 转引自 Kowit, p.215。
② 参见 The *Princeton Encyclopedia*, pp.660 – 666。

提出了一个观点,认为诗歌意象悦人的引导作用把抽象哲学和具体历史熔合了起来①。

十七世纪晚期十八世纪早期,随着怀疑论和经验论的发展人们开始关注意象的认知功能。哲学家托马斯·霍布斯(Thomas Hobbes)和约翰·洛克(John Locke)把诗歌中的意象看做是客观经验和主观知识的连接,即当人的身体感官产生了最初的感觉,人脑中就会复制一个相关意象。比如,当眼睛看到一种颜色,人脑中就会记录下这种颜色的意象。意象只是颜色这种客观现象在人的主观感官感觉中的复制品。当人回忆曾经感觉过但不再在场的东西,或者思考记忆中的经历,或者既感觉又想象,或者在睡梦和发烧中产生幻觉等时,脑中也会出现意象②。

十八世纪超验主义浪漫诗歌把意象提升到了象征的高度。十九世纪晚期科学和文学都很重视意象的作用。隐喻性意象被当做语言发展的有机部分而非装饰品。在思考非物质性事物时,因为人类语言无法满足概念性需求,人们不得不用物质性形象即意象来表达。语言是通过隐喻从形象到观点而发展的。比如 spirit 这个词,其本义是 breath。当人类需要一个表达灵魂或者神性的抽象词的时候,一个本来指称具体物质现象的现有词就被拿来代表那个抽象意义了③。

二十世纪初心理学家西格蒙·弗洛伊德(Sigmund Freud)和卡尔·古斯塔夫·荣格(Carl Gustav Jung)的理论关注意象在人格和文化层面的情结(complex)功能。二十世纪初的意象派(Imagism)诗人埃兹拉·庞德(Ezra Pound)把意象定义为"that which presents an intellectual and emotional complex in an instant of time"时就强调了意象瞬间呈现智性或感性情结的功能。在庞德的"在地铁站"("In a Station of the Metro")中,人群中的几张脸被看做树枝上的花瓣。庞德认为,这样的诗精确记录了外在客观事物转化为内在主观感觉的那一瞬间。因为意象派的巨大影响力,意象在二十世纪的诗学批评中成为了诗歌的常量。对于很多现代和当代诗人来说,每首诗都是一个意象④。

二十一世纪,随着视觉媒体的日益发展,对于意象的理解也继续发展变化着。机械和数字图像复制技术使意象或图像不再直接通向现实,而是不断指向别的意象或图像。正如语言文字一样,意象或图像也有了自己的语法和修辞,必须根据具体的规则进行解码阐释。后现代批评不再追求意象的像似性,转而强调意象和模仿(imitation)的词源关系,认为意象和文字都具有重现(representation)的共同特点⑤。

在实际的英语诗歌创作中,出现在同一首诗里的不同意象至少要在想象的空间里有所关联。当一首诗出现两个以上的意象的时候,第二个意象一般要对前面第一个意

---

① 参见 The *Princeton Encyclopedia*, pp.660-666。
② 同上。
③ 同上。
④ 同上。
⑤ 同上。

象有补充、纠正甚至代替作用。如果不是因为前面第一个意象有瑕疵,则不需要第二个意象①。智利著名诗人巴勃罗·聂鲁达(Pablo Neruda)的诗歌中经常出现"根(root)"意象,这个意象在其前期的诗中主要是追溯个人的根,在其后期的诗中主要是追溯民族的根。诗人叶芝三十岁前的诗歌中也经常出现"玫瑰(rose)"意象②。每个创作中的诗人都应该思考、寻找、确定属于自己的诗歌意象。

第三节 意象派(Imagism)

In a Station of the Metro
By Ezra Pound

The apparition of these faces in the crowd:
Petals on a wet, black bough. ③

诗人埃兹拉·庞德这首模仿俳句(haiku)写成的"在地铁站"("In a Station of the Metro")堪称意象派诗歌的标志性作品。这首诗通过具体生动的视觉意象(潮湿黑枝上的花瓣)的直接呈现记录了某个时刻某个外在客观事物(美丽的人脸)如何瞬间转化为内在主观感情、态度、想法、思想(震撼心灵的感动)。本书第一章第六节分析过的诗人威廉·卡洛斯·威廉斯的"红色手推车"("The Red Wheelbarrow")也是一首典型的意象派诗作。威廉斯的"红色手推车"除了断行之外,意象的作用也引人注目。该诗第二和第三诗节中把两个本应连起来的单词 wheelbarrow 和 rainwater 分别拆开放在两行,除了视觉和听觉上的效果外,也使 barrow 和 water 两个词与第四诗节第二行的 chickens 一起得到强调。而两个一静一动,颜色对比强烈的意象(红色手推车、白色的小鸡)的直接呈现瞬间就吸引了人的注意力,激起了诗情与感动。

意象派是发源于英国,于 1912—1917 年主要在美国发展并获得影响力的一个自由诗流派。意象派反对维多利亚时代诗歌的繁冗华丽辞藻,主张用词言简意赅,直接呈现诗歌意象。意象派的宣言文章与意象派诗歌作品一样具有历史意义。1913 年 1 月著名的美国诗刊 Poetry 刊登了诗人希尔达·杜丽特(Hilda Doolittle)用"H. D.,

---

① 参见 Vendler, pp.82-83。
② 参见 Dobyns, chap. 2。
③ 转引自 https://www.poetryfoundation.org/poetrymagazine/poems/12675/in-a-station-of-the-metro。

'Imagiste'"署名的三首小诗和埃兹拉·庞德关于伦敦"有勇气把自己称为一个流派的最年轻诗派"的一篇报告。在报告中,埃兹拉·庞德把这一派诗人称为英国诗人哲学家托马斯·厄内斯特·休姆(T. E. Hulme)领导的诗人俱乐部一派的传人[①]。

1913年3月诗刊 Poetry 发表了诗人弗兰克·斯图尔特·弗林特(F. S. Flint)题为"意象主义"("Imagisme")的文章和埃兹拉·庞德题为"意象主义者的几条禁律"("A Few Don'ts by an Imagiste")的文章。弗兰克·斯图尔特·弗林特(F. S. Flint)写道,意象派遵循的几条原则是:一、直接处理写作对象,不管是客观的还是主观的;二、与呈现对象无关的词一律不用;三、格律上,按乐句作诗,不按节拍器作诗(即注重诗句内部节奏,不关注格律或押韵);四、某种程度上信奉意象(不过其时并未付诸写作实践,故暂与读者无关)。弗林特和庞德的这两篇文章都强调意象派的视觉倾向。庞德在"几条禁律"("A Few Don'ts")中一开始就把意象定义为"在一瞬间呈现智性或者感性情结"的形象[②]。

1914年意象派的第一部诗集《意象主义者》(Des Imagistes)收入了弗兰克·斯图尔特·弗林特、埃兹拉·庞德、理查·奥尔丁顿(Richard Aldington)、艾米·洛威尔(Amy Lowell)、威廉·卡洛斯·威廉斯、詹姆斯·乔伊斯(James Joyce)等人的诗。埃兹拉·庞德后来因为领导权问题与艾米·洛威尔发生了严重分歧,离开了意象派运动。艾米·洛威尔在1915、1916、1917三年中每年出版一期名为 Some Imagist Poets 的诗集。艾米·洛威尔领导下的意象派淡化了在运动初期休姆和庞德对唯物的具体视觉意象和唯心的心理情结的强调。

虽然意象派被称为是英语文学中的第一个先锋派,有学者却认为虽然它在欧洲先锋派运动中得到宣传推广,其实却是第一个反欧洲先锋派运动的流派。这首先表现在欧洲先锋派运动中的未来派号召要破坏过去和传统,而弗兰克·斯图尔特·弗林特却声称意象派是要根据最优秀的诗歌传统来写作。意象派的第一部诗集《意象主义者》(Des Imagistes)则再次体现了意象派在现代与传统之间的摇摆。一方面,这本诗集潜在的专利商业利益是先锋派所追求的,并且后来在某种形式上被实现了;另一方面,这本诗集又保留了意象派中坚力量所追溯的古代传统。在其中,理查·奥尔丁顿(Richard Aldington)和希尔达·杜丽特的诗追溯至希腊传统,而庞德等人的诗则追溯至经由孔子和屈原传承下来的中国传统[③]。

---

① 参见 The Princeton Encyclopedia, pp.674-675。
② "which presents an intellectual and emotional complex in an instant of time",参见 The Princeton Encyclopedia, p.660 & pp.674-675。
③ 参见 The Princeton Encyclopedia, pp.674-675。

第四节　说话者与人格面具(persona/mask)

与修辞相关的一个问题是诗歌中的说话者和听话者的身份问题。诗歌中的说话者有时会对"你/你们(you)"说话,这可能是对读者说话,也可能是对包括读者在内的任一人说话,或者是对某一特定人或物说话。这其实就是拓展了的呼语修辞手法的使用。诗歌中的说话者有时使用"我们(We)"自称。这种自称具有包含性,说话者是一个集体,而不是个人。诗歌中的说话者,如果直接用"我(I)"自称,并且经研究该诗是高度自传性的,那么这个说话者可以直接用"诗人"指称。诗人艾米莉·狄金森下边的这首诗中,"You"既可能是指读者,也可能是诗人假设的某一特定人物,而"I"则可以当做指称诗人本人:

I'm Nobody! Who are you?
Are you—Nobody—Too?
Then there's a pair of us!
Don't tell! they'd advertise—you know!

How dreary—to be—Somebody!
How public—like a Frog—
To tell one's name—the livelong June—
To an admiring Bog!①

但是,即便是高度自传性的诗歌,其中的"I"也未必完全与诗人相同,毕竟诗歌是想象性的创意作品。诗歌创作需要传递真诚的情感与观念,但可以想象与创造物理性事实与细节。有时候诗歌中的说话者明显不是诗人本身,而是很确定的另一个人或者物的身份,这时诗人采用了人格面具(persona/ mask)进行写作。人格面具(persona)来源于拉丁语的动词 personare,意思是通过一个面具(mask)说话②。在一首使用人格面具的诗中,诗人假装是另一个人或者物在说话。诗人丽莲·穆尔在写"毛毛虫的信息"("Message from a Caterpillar")的时候就使用了人格面具。诗中的说话者"I"的身份其实是一条羽化前的毛毛虫:

---

① 详见 Dickinson, p.133。
② 参见 Vendler, p.185。

Don't shake this
bough.
Don't try
to wake me
now.

In this cocoon
I've work to
do.
Inside this silk
I'm changing
things.

I'm worm-like now
but in this
dark
I'm growing
wings. ①

上述这首诗中的人格面具既使用了拟人化的修辞手法,也使用了隐喻的修辞手法。可见,使用人格面具写作的诗歌因为其说话者明显不是诗人,所以使得诗歌创作内容和视角等等更加自由。事实上,很多名诗人在创作时喜欢使用人格面具,比如诗人艾略特的"个性逃离"说、约翰·济慈(John Keats)的"赋形并填充另一主体"说、叶芝的"面具"说、威斯坦·休·奥登(W. H. Auden)的"在诗中变成他者"说②,等等,其实都是诗人创作时不同程度使用人格面具的说法。

诗歌选择从哪个视角切入,说话者采用第一人称视角如"我们(We)"或"我(I)",还是采用第三人称视角,包括是否使用人格面具,等等,都是诗人需要认真思考的问题。第一人称视角的诗歌可能忽略的细节可能在第三人称视角的诗歌中得到强调③。如果诗人顾忌写出来的作品暴露太多的个人信息和历史,可以考虑使用人格面具来写作,让诗中说话者变成第三人称,这样的说话者身份在性别、名字、族裔、国籍、星球籍上都比较自由。

---

① 转引自 Livingston,pp.20 - 21。
② 参见 Hugo,chap.7。
③ 参见 Dobyns,chap.9。

一些诗歌作品可能同时出现两个以上的对话者声音,这种对话诗中没有直接点明对话者身份,对话者身份需要通过阅读进行诠释理解。比如诗人艾德里安·里奇(Adrienne Rich)的"婆母"("Mother-in-Law")就是采用对话形式写成。诗中婆婆的话用斜体书写,而儿媳的话则正体书写,除了标题及说话内容提示为婆媳对话之外,诗中并没有在说话内容前后直接表明说话者身份是婆婆还是儿媳①。有些采用诗歌体裁的神话、传说(legend)和寓言中使用万能作者角度直接点明对话者身份,这种对话与本处讨论的对话诗形式不同。诗人约翰·德林克沃特(John Drinkwater)如下的"蜗牛"("Snail")是用对话诗的形式写成,同时使用了呼语和拟人的修辞手法:

Snail
By John Drinkwater

Snail upon the wall,
Have you got at all
Anything to tell
About your shell?

Only this, my child—
When the wind is wild,
Or when the sun is hot,
It's all I've got. ②

在因诗人罗伯特·勃朗宁(Robert Browning)而著名的戏剧独白(dramatic monologue)中,诗歌说话者明显不是诗人,而说话者直接对着说话的听话者也不是读者,而是一个与说话者一同在场的、不出声的、具体的人。在戏剧独白中,读者更像是一个路过顺便听到对话的人③。在其他诗歌比如抒情诗中,说话者也可能直接对"你/你们(you)"说话,但这个"你/你们(you)"并不出现在说话场景的现场,并且有时其角色可能在同一首诗中有变化,比如可能是某个或某些特定身份特征的人,也可能是读者。很多时候,抒情诗的读者也像一个路过时顺便听到诗歌说话者声音的人。

在诗歌创作中,要使诗歌中的说话者声音具有可信度,诗人需要在大约 150 个词的空间内说服读者,诗中说话者说话必须有事有因有感而发,说话语气应该反映起因和反

---

① 参见 Vendler, p.212。
② 转引自 Livingston, p.27。
③ 参见 Kowit, p.159。

应,语言表达要多样有变化以形成故事活力①。诗歌中说话者语气是直接诚恳还是委婉幽默,是轻描淡写还是讽刺,甚至似非而是,使用抒情还是叙事,这些都是诗人应该考虑的问题。诗歌并不需要忠于叙事的真实性,而应忠于诗人的思想感情。为了表达诗人的思想感情,有时想象的叙事可能会比真实的叙事更有效。诗歌的叙事无需连贯,可以通过细节、意象激发读者的感觉和想象。

第五节 叙事诗(narrative)与抒情诗(lyric)

与说话者视角相关的一个问题是英语诗歌中关于叙事诗(narrative)和抒情诗(lyric)的区分和选择。叙事诗以讲述故事为主,着重情节发展,比如史诗(epic)、歌谣(ballad)和前述采用诗歌体裁的神话、传说、寓言等。十七世纪,抒情诗尚未成为现代意义上的诗歌体裁(genre),而叙事诗中的史诗却是已经需要革新的老体裁了②。在叙事诗中,为了增加叙事的戏剧效果,诗人会使用悬念和冲突(conflict)等技巧。冲突即故事中的问题和矛盾,冲突会制造悬念,而悬念会吸引读者③。叙事诗常常以第三者视角(万能作者视角)直接点明说话者身份。

英语诗歌中的抒情诗一般不以第三者视角(万能作者视角)点明说话者身份,而常常使用"I"及其相关词如"me、my、mine、we、us、our、ours"等等来说话。抒情诗虽然可能带有一点叙事的胚芽,但着重的是表达个人的主观感情感受。诗人约翰·斯图尔特·密尔(John Stuart Mill)在1833年的文章"什么是诗歌"中写道,"诗歌是孤独时刻的情感自白"④。这里的"诗歌"实际上说的就是抒情诗。下边摘选自诗人安德鲁·马维尔(Andrew Marvell)的"花园"("The Garden")的诗节最后一行是经典的抒情诗行:

The Garden
...
Meanwhile the mind, from pleasure less,
Withdraws into its happiness;
The mind, that ocean where each kind
Does straight its own resemblance find,
Yet it creates, transcending these,

---

① 参见 Vendler, p.171。
② 参见 *The Princeton Encyclopedia*, pp.826–834。
③ 参见 Dobyns, chap.3。
④ 参见 Dobyns, chap.11。

Far other worlds, and other seas;
Annihilating all that's made
To a green thought in a green shade.
… ①

叙事诗和抒情诗很多时候可能会重叠,因为叙事诗中除了情节发展,还会包含人物的感情感受等抒情成分,而抒情诗中也在某种程度上含有情节等叙事成分。诗人威廉·华兹华斯提出的抒情歌谣(lyrical ballad)概念就是这种重叠的体现②。包含叙事元素的抒情诗中的动词常有时态的变化,而不含叙事成分的抒情诗中的动词常常只用一般现在时。比如,诗人菲利普·拉金的"床上谈话"("Talking in Bed")就是一首抒情诗,是对曾经的亲密关系逐渐变陌生的惋惜与反思,不含叙事成分,通篇使用一般现在时:

Talking in Bed
By Philip Larkin

Talking in bed ought to be easiest,
Lying together there goes back so far,
An emblem of two people being honest.

Yet more and more time passes silently.
Outside, the wind's incomplete unrest
Builds and disperses clouds about the sky,

And dark towns heap up on the horizon.
None of this cares for us. Nothing shows why
At this unique distance from isolation

It becomes still more difficult to find
Words at once true and kind,
Or not untrue and not unkind. ③

---

① 转引自 https://www.poetryfoundation.org/poems/44682/the-garden-56d223dec2ced。
② 参见 Vendler, p.102。
③ 转引自 Vendler, p.104。

在现当代,抒情诗通常被用来指一种面对私密读者以集中而和谐的形式表达诗人个人感情的一种诗歌体裁。这种诗歌常常与简短、主观、热情、感性、非叙事性等特点相联系,并常常以第一人称"我(I)"及其相关词来说话。抒情诗一词,从词源学来看,来自希腊语 lyra,即英语 lyre,是指为诗人唱诗伴奏的希腊乐器里拉琴,其样似小竖琴(small harp)。文艺复兴时欧洲诗人唱诗使用的则是鲁特琴(lute),而现代类似的乐器叫吉他(guitar)①。诗人萨福(Sappho)、阿勒凯奥斯(Alcaeus)、阿那克里翁(Anacreon)和品达(Pindar)等被称为最早的抒情诗人,但其实在他们的时代还未有抒情诗这个名称。只是到了亚历山大大帝(Alexander the Great)(公元前336—323年在位)时期,希腊诗人唱的歌词(即诗)被收集起来并称为 lyrikos/lyrics。可见,抒情诗一开始是指一种已经听不到的音乐,也是指一种失落的诗歌集体体验②。

十六和十七世纪经常被认为是抒情诗创作在欧洲盛行的时期。但在那时候,抒情诗只是多种诗歌类型(variety)之一,其他类型还包括英雄诗(heroic)、挽歌诗(elegiac)、警句诗(epigrammatic),等等。抒情诗在当时被认为是最不重要、最随意和最不经岁月打磨的诗歌类型。十六世纪末英国诗人菲利普·西德尼在其 *Defence of Poesy* 为抒情诗做出了强有力的辩护。西方学者倾向于把文艺复兴时期从诗人彼得拉克(Petrarch)开始的十四行诗(sonnet),尤其是莎士比亚的十四行诗作为现代意义上的抒情诗的开始,也就是说,十六世纪抒情诗的典型形式是十四行诗。十七世纪至十八世纪初的新古典主义(neoclassicism)推崇理性(reason)故而是压抑抒情诗的。十七世纪和十八世纪抒情诗的典型体裁是颂歌③。

自十八世纪以来,"lyric"一词慢慢从主要为形容词性的观念转为名词性的体裁。有十八世纪的西方学者认为,抒情诗在所有诗歌类型(kind)中最具有诗意。这些学者认为抒情诗与其他诗歌类型在文体(style)与思想(thought)上的区别就如诗歌与散文的区别。十八世纪中,随着颂歌的抒情诗化、诗歌来源于情感和想象的理论的出现、对东方民族原始诗歌的抒情形式的强调(某种程度上推翻了阿里士多德的"诗歌模仿论"),抒情诗成为诗歌最基本的类型(category)。东方民族类似歌谣的原始诗歌也是应景抒发情感的想象性诗歌,对这种诗歌的抒情形式的强调为诗人威廉·华兹华斯和格勒律治命名诗集《抒情歌谣》(*Lyrical Ballads*,1798)提供了理论合法性背景④。十八世纪末开始的浪漫主义(romanticism)推崇感性(sensibility),这对抒情诗的兴盛起了主要推动作用。十八世纪末,随着科学与经济学科知识生产的逐渐系统化和更多特

---

① 参见 Lenhart, Gary. "Lyric", Padgett, Ron, ed. in *The Teachers & Writers Handbook of Poetic Forms*. Second Edition. New York: T&W books, 2000, p.105。
② 参见 *The Princeton Encyclopedia*, pp.826-834。
③ 同上。
④ 参见 *The Princeton Encyclopedia*, pp.826-834。

点规律特征的辨认总结引起文学的逐渐类型化,抒情诗也逐渐体裁化①。

十九世纪,作为个人情感表达工具的抒情诗既是一种诗歌体裁,也是一个超越体裁的诗歌观念。诗人歌德(J. W. Goethe)在1819的《西东合集》(*West-östlicher Divan*)中把诗歌分成的三种形式(form):抒情诗、史诗和诗剧(drama)。歌德认为诗歌的这三种形式可以组合成无限的体裁。至十九世纪中,理想化的西方抒情诗人要同时具有像诗人珀西·比希·雪莱(Percy Bysshe Shelley)那样的独创天才和像诗人威廉·华兹华斯那样的习得素养。诗人哲学家拉尔夫·沃尔多·爱默生(R. W. Emerson)在其"诗人"("The Poet",1844)中叹惜这样二合一的诗人尚未出现。诗人沃尔特·惠特曼则向着成为这样的人而努力。十九世纪下半叶,抒情诗一词几成诗歌的同义词。十九世纪九十年代诗人艾米莉·狄金森的作品第一次出版,使狄金森成为十九世纪抒情诗自我表达、不以发表为目的的诗人代表。十九世纪末的象征主义(Symbolism)诗歌也被称为是从以物质为中心转向以精神为中心的抒情诗②。

二十世纪,诗人艾略特把抒情诗定义为"诗人自言自语的声音"。这种定义对二十世纪中的自白诗(Confessional Poetry)影响比较大。至二十世纪中,抒情诗已被用来指称所有以第一人称写作的诗歌。从十六世纪末抒情诗作为一种诗歌观念开始发挥体裁作用开始,到二十世纪诗歌完全成为抒情化的文学体裁,用了四百年时间。需要注意的是,并不存在"浪漫主义抒情诗"(romantic lyric)或者"现代抒情诗"(modern lyric)等说法,因为在这些阶段,抒情诗都既是诗歌体裁也是超越体裁的诗歌观念③。

在现代西方诗学,有一种基于诗歌与抒情诗都具有主观、感性和形式集中的特点把所有诗歌都叫做抒情诗的倾向。新批评(New Criticism)是用抒情诗观念来解读所有诗歌的典型。美国批评家如 克林斯·布鲁克斯(Cleanth Brooks)和罗伯特·佩恩·沃伦(Robert Penn Warren)在二十世纪三十年代、维姆萨特(W. K. Wimsatt)和比尔兹利(M. C. Beardsley)在四十年代、鲁本·布劳尔(Reuben Brower)在五十年代以各自的方式均采用诗人艾略特关于个人抒情诗(personal lyric)的定义以及理论家理查兹(I. A. Richards)关于个人诗歌(individual poem)的观点来构建一种把所有诗歌解读为抒情诗的模式。这种模式主要是在教学上使用,但它逐渐成为一种影响诗歌创作的解读方式④。

在当代,把所有诗歌解读为抒情诗的比较有影响力的代表是诗歌学者海伦·文德勒(Helen Vendler)。从其著作《诗、诗人、诗歌:概述与诗集》(*POEMS,POETS,POETRY:An Introduction and Anthology*)的引子"关于诗人和诗歌"("About Poets

---

① 参见 *The Princeton Encyclopedia*,pp.826-834。
② 同上。
③ 同上。
④ 参见 *The Princeton Encyclopedia*,pp.826-834。

and Poetry")中可以看出,海伦·文德勒基本用抒情诗代替诗歌了①。海伦·文德勒主张把抒情诗定义为一个虚构的说话人的个人表达,是一种模仿孤独言语时思维运作的体裁②。新批评的这种解读模式现在还存在于许多诗歌教学中,但是也受到了与海伦·文德勒同为鲁本·布劳尔学生的理论家保罗·德·曼(Paul de Man)的后结构主义(post-structuralist)、后现代主义(postmodernism)以及先锋派诗学(avant-garde poetics)的挑战③。

二十一世纪,诗人和批评家不再坚信所有后浪漫主义(post-romantic)个人诗歌都是抒情诗。另外,还有人提出要防止抒情诗概念的狭隘化,同时避免使用叙事模式处理抒情诗的倾向。因为使用叙事模式处理抒情诗会使戏剧独白成为抒情诗的模板,而这不是诗歌界愿意看到的现象。直至现在,关于抒情诗的定义仍未有定论,仍会随着诗歌和诗学观念的发展而发展④。

抒情诗组(lyric sequence)是一组抒情诗,这组诗中的每一首都是独立自足的抒情诗,但又与整组诗存在某种联系⑤。从诗人彼得拉克(Petrarch)的《歌本》(或可称《松散韵诗》,*Rime sparse*,即 Scattered Rhymes)开始,到莎士比亚的十四行诗,到诗人艾米莉·狄金森的诗,到诗人沃尔特·惠特曼的《草叶集》(*Leaves of Grass*,1855),等等,都是抒情诗组。诗人埃兹拉·庞德的《诗章》(*The Cantos*)也是组诗(poetic sequence),不过不是抒情诗组,而是史诗组。贯穿起组诗的整体性连续性的方式可以有多种,可以是内容上的,可以是形式上的,甚至可以只是写作时间,比如诗人约翰·贝里曼的《梦之歌》组诗的关联点在于诗中人物 Henry,而诗人弗兰克·奥哈拉(Frank O'Hara)的《午餐诗歌》(*Lunch Poems*)组诗的关联点则是诗人每天午休时间穿越曼哈顿时的随想⑥。

如前所述,十七世纪和十八世纪抒情诗的典型体裁是颂歌。颂歌由古希腊诗人品达(Pindar)开始创作,其创作的颂歌一般包括六个部分:形式开头(formal beginning)——乞灵(invocation)——祈祷(prayer)——神话(   )——道德剧(moral)——结尾(conclusion)。品达颂歌(Pindar ode)有复杂的格律和诗节模式。后来的罗马诗人贺拉斯(Horace)的颂歌也有复杂的格律和诗节模式。一般的不规则颂歌(irregular ode)没有特定格律韵式和行宽。颂歌主要书写典雅高尚的题材,感情强烈,经常使用呼语修辞⑦。

在关于抒情诗的历史与定义发展的研究讨论中,西方学者用了形式(form)、风格

---

① 参见 Vendler, pp. ix – xiii。
② 参见 Vendler, p. x。
③ 参见 *The Princeton Encyclopedia*, pp.826 – 834。
④ 同上。
⑤ 参见 *The Princeton Encyclopedia*, p.835。
⑥ 参见 *The Princeton Encyclopedia*, pp.834 – 835。
⑦ 参见 *The Princeton Encyclopedia*, pp.826 – 834。

(style)、体裁(genre)、类型(category/variety/kind)等词。在浪漫主义时期,抒情诗既是诗歌体裁也是超越体裁的诗歌观念,传统上的叙事诗歌谣和信札(epistle)等也被放到了抒情诗的名下。同理,田园诗(idyll)、牧歌(pastoral)等体裁也可算为抒情诗①。一种诗歌形式要成为一种体裁,不仅要有形式上的特点,还要有内容和语言风格上的特点,比如俳句就是这样的一种体裁②。赞美诗即圣歌(hymn)、挽歌、警句诗(epigram)等诗歌体裁在内容上可归于产生于希腊的抒情诗范畴,但在诗歌格律韵式上有自己产生于拉丁罗马时代的形式规则③。本书接下来的两章主要基于诗歌的形式而非体裁,来探讨一些传统和现当代英语诗歌的特点和写作技巧。

---

① 参见 The Princeton Encyclopedia, pp.826 – 834。
② 参见 Higginson, William J. "Haiku", Padgett. Ron, ed. in The Teachers & Writers Handbook of Poetic Forms. Second Edition. New York: T&W books, 2000, p.86。
③ 参见 The Princeton Encyclopedia, pp.826 – 834。

第三章
传统英语诗歌形式

英语律诗(accentual-syllabic verse)使用格律写成,常常押韵,是最受熟知的传统英语诗歌。英语律诗诗行既考虑重音因素也考虑音节因素。传统英语诗歌的诗行也有只考虑重音因素写成的。只考虑诗行重音数的诗叫重音诗(accentual verse)。重音诗自古英语诗歌以来就一直存在,古英语史诗《贝奥武夫》和很多民谣、童谣都是重音诗。《贝奥武夫》(*Beowulf*)每行诗四个重音,四重音诗行被一个明显的行中停顿一分为二,四个重音节中一般有三个使用头韵[①]。现当代英语诗人将写作异于传统律诗的重音诗作为一种对诗歌形式的革新,因此本书将主要在第四章"现当代英语诗歌形式"中讨论重音诗。本章主要研讨一些比较受现当代英语诗人重视和喜爱的传统英语诗歌形式,包括一些英语律诗形式和一些并不要求使用格律的传统诗歌形式。

英语律诗的格律和用韵传统可以追溯至 1400 年去世的杰弗里·乔叟及其同时期诗人。这些英国诗人参考同时期法国和意大利的作诗法,不再使用古英语(Old English or Anglo-Saxon)的头韵传统写诗,而用格律和押韵写诗[②]。格律由音步和音步数两方面构成。重读音节与非重读音节的不同结合方式构成了传统英语律诗的格律音步,而音步数决定了诗行的长度,不同的音步数和不同的格律音步相结合构成了英语律诗多样化的格律。英语律诗常押行尾韵,一定的行尾押韵模式叫做韵式。英语律诗的韵式也是多样化的。

第一节 离合诗(acrostic)

古老的字母表离合诗(alphabetic acrostic),顾名思义,就是诗中每一行或者每一节的首字母按照字母表顺序排列。字母表离合诗在古代西方社会经常用于祈祷、颂歌、预

---

① 参见 Brooks & Warren, p.553。
② 参见 Kowit, p.138。

言中,既是一种精神冥思的工具,也是一种儿童语言教学的工具。最基本类型的离合诗(acrostic)即诗中每一行或者每一节的首字母从上往下看,要么构成一个单词,如诗作者、赞助人、爱人、圣人等的名字,要么构成一个短语,要么在极少情况下拼出一个完整句子①。基本类型的离合诗类似于中国的"藏头诗"。离合诗的特点和意义需要在页面上才能体现。

离合诗不仅可以在行首字母拼出名字,也可以在诗行的中位字母拼出名字,或者在行尾字母拼出名字。在诗行的中位字母拼出名字的离合诗叫中位离合诗(mesostich)。在行尾字母拼出名字的离合诗叫末位离合诗(telestich)。末位离合诗也可以从末行向首行反向拼写名字。如果行首字母和行尾字母同时使用,叫做双位离合诗(double acrostic)。如果行首字母、中位字母和行尾字母同时使用,叫做三重离合诗(triple acrostic)②。复杂的离合诗与中国的"回环诗"或叫"回文诗"相类似。

写作离合诗并不难。首先,垂直写出一个英语单词、短语或者句子,每个字母一行。然后,用每个字母作为那一行的首字母,写出那一行诗,每行诗长度不限。可以从诗人自己的名字开始练写,然后拓展至复杂的短语甚至句子。先写首位离合诗,然后试写中位或末位离合诗,甚至双位离合诗、三重离合诗等。诗人荣·帕德哥特(Ron Padgett)下边的这首诗是连续双位离合诗(run-on double acrostic),每行诗的首字母及行末字母从上往下读构成一个短句"My name is Mary."

Many times I
Yelled across the cosmoS
Not knowing to whoM
And/or what everlasting top bananA
Men had sought in faR
EternitY. ③

第二节 歌谣(ballad)

民间歌谣(folk ballad)是一种古老的诗歌形式,在世界各地,包括亚洲、非洲、欧洲、

---

① 参见 *The Princeton Encyclopedia*, p.1 & p.6。
② 参见 *The Princeton Encyclopedia*, p.6。
③ 详见 Padgett, Ron. ed. *The Teachers & Writers Handbook of Poetic Forms*. Second Edition. New York: T&W books, 2000, p. 4。

美洲、澳洲普遍存在。在古代西方社会，歌谣经常配乐而唱，吟游诗人通过口头吟唱传统把故事传唱到各地，传播给后代。"兰德尔勋爵"("Lord Randall")是欧洲很多语言文学中都有的歌谣。歌谣（ballad）一词在英语中的使用始于十六世纪。自十八世纪以来，歌谣成为涉及文学、音乐学、语言学以及民族学的跨学科概念，指按照乐章式曲调唱的叙事歌或者以这种歌曲模式写的诗。结构上分诗节是歌谣与史诗的最大区别；歌谣呈现人物的行为，这是其与抒情诗的最大区别①。

源自口头吟唱歌谣（oral ballad）的传统歌谣（traditional ballad）具有以下形式特点：叙述的事件涉及人物数量不多；事件的情节发展戏剧化，结局常常是灾难性的、致命性的；人物的动作行为很重要，用语简单、直白；不描述细节或者环境；以对话为主；语言上的重复很多；一般使用第三人称；一般为四行诗节：第一、第三行各含四个音步，不押韵，第二、四行各含三个音步，押韵；在四行诗节后常有一到两个叠句②。

在英语国家，一些古老的传统歌谣来自于家庭宗族（clan）聚居地彼此相隔甚远的英格兰和苏格兰边境地区。十八世纪苏格兰诗人罗伯特·伯恩斯（Robert Burns）和十九世纪小说家沃尔特·司各特（Sir Walter Scott）都是传统歌谣的著名收集者。十八世纪的诗人和学者重新发现了古老的苏格兰和英格兰歌谣之后，诗人们开始创作文学歌谣（literary ballad）。浪漫主义诗人威廉·华兹华斯的"露西·格雷"("Lucy Gray")、"七姐妹"("Seven Sisters")和格勒律治的"古舟子咏"("The Rime of the Ancient Mariner")、"三墓穴"("The Three Graves")等都是在某种程度上模仿传统歌谣写成的文学歌谣。文学歌谣适合阅读，不适合吟唱③。

歌谣对欧洲包括英国在内的浪漫主义诗学影响很大。诗人威廉·华兹华斯在《抒情歌谣》(*Lyrical Ballads*，第二版，1800 年)的前言中声称采用诸如歌谣等平民化形式是为了使诗歌表达更加接近真实生活语言。诗人罗伯特·伯恩斯（Robert Burns）的"五个老妇人"("The Five Carlins")、威廉·布莱克的"玛丽"("Mary")和"高个子约翰·布朗和小玛丽·贝尔"("Long John Brown and Little Mary Bell")、约翰·济慈的"无情的妖女"("La Belle Dame sans Merci")、克里斯蒂娜·罗萨蒂（Christina Rossetti)的"茅黛·克莱尔"("Maude Clare")和"托马斯勋爵与美人玛格丽特"("Lord Thomas and Fair Margaret")、托马斯·哈代（Thomas Hardy）的"第二夜"("The Second Night")和"钟声未响"("No Bell-Ringing")、奥斯卡·王尔德的"雷丁监狱之歌"("The Ballad of Reading Gaol")等都是歌谣体诗④。

---

① 参见 *The Princeton Encyclopedia*, pp.114-118。
② 参见 *The Princeton Encyclopedia*, pp.114-118；或 Livingston, pp.49-52；或 Vendler, pp.600-602。
③ 参见 Bye, Reed. "Ballad", Padgett, Ron, ed. in *The Teachers & Writers Handbook of Poetic Forms*. Second Edition. New York: T&W books, 2000, pp.18-21。
④ 参见 *The Princeton Encyclopedia*, pp.114-118。

二十世纪，诗学家克林斯·布鲁克斯和罗伯特·佩恩·沃伦（Robert Penn Warren）的新批评诗学把歌谣看做易读的集体声音诗学的样板，这种观点在诗人伊丽莎白·毕晓普（Elizabeth Bishop）的作品"巴比伦盗贼之歌"（"The Ballad of the Burglar of Babylon"）中有所体现。诗人兰斯顿·休斯的"西尔维斯特的亡床"（"Sylvester's Dying Bed"）、"地主之歌"（"Ballad of the Landlord"）和诗人格温多琳·布鲁克斯（Gwendolyn Brooks）的"德·威特·威廉斯前往林肯墓地路上"（"of De Witt Williams on his way to Lincoln Cemetery"）、"已故安妮之歌"（"The Ballad of Late Annie"）等作品则受布鲁斯歌谣（blues ballad）的影响①。下边的"狐狸"（"The Fox"）是一首作者不明的美国歌谣：

The Fox

The fox went out on a chilly night,
Prayed to the moon for to give him light,
For he'd many a mile to go that night
Afore he reached the town-o.

He ran till he came to a great big bin;
The ducks and the geese were put therein.
"A couple of you will grease my chin,
Afore I leave this town-o."

He grabbed the gray goose by the neck,
Throwed a duck across his back;
He didn't mind the "quack, quack, quack"
And the legs a-dangling down-o.

Then old mother Flipper-Flopper jumped out of bed,
Out of the window she stuck her head,
Crying "John! John! The gray goose is *gone*
And the fox is on the town-o!"

Then John, he went to the top of the hill,

---

① 参见 *The Princeton Encyclopedia*，pp.114-118。

Blowed his horn both loud and shrill;
The fox, he said, "I better flee with my kill
Or they'll soon be on my trail-o."

He ran till he came to his cozy den,
There were the little ones, eight, nine, ten.
They said, "Daddy, better go back again,
'Cause it must be a mighty fine town-o."

Then the fox and his wife without any strife,
Cut up the goose with a fork and a knife;
They never had such a supper in their life
And the little ones chewed on the bones-o.①

第三节　素体诗(blank verse)

　　从传统来看,素体诗(blank verse)多与讲故事有关,因此常用于戏剧或者史诗。素体诗这一名称来源于其不押韵机制。十六世纪晚期当英国诗人受意大利不押韵诗歌影响开始写作十音节诗时,他们使用一个非押韵词(blank word)来结束每个诗行。这种诗行通常包含十个音节,其中五个音节重读,即使用五音步抑扬格的不押韵诗歌,后来就叫素体诗②。

　　诗人亨利·霍华德(Henry Howard,即萨里伯爵 Earl of Surrey)是第一个写作素体诗的英语诗人。诗人戏剧家克里斯托弗·马洛(Christopher Marlowe)是使素体诗成为一流诗歌形式的诗人,其作品《浮士德博士》(*Doctor Faustus*)使用素体诗写成。诗人戏剧家莎士比亚的戏剧则使素体诗艺术达到高峰。诗人弥尔顿的史诗《失乐园》、威廉·华兹华斯的自传诗《序曲》(*The Prelude*)、罗伯特·勃朗宁的部分戏剧独白也是用素体诗写成③。

　　写作素体诗可以从练写十音节诗行开始。先用自然的声音学习写作,一开始可能

---

① 转引自 Livingston, pp.50 – 51。
② 参见 Zavatsky, Bill. "Blank Verse", Padgett. Ron, ed. in *The Teachers & Writers Handbook of Poetic Forms*. Second Edition. New York: T&W books, 2000, pp.25 – 28。
③ 同上。

有不少诗行没有五个重读音节，或者不是十音节，而是八、九、十一、十二音节等等，但没关系。可以通过换词，特别是同义词或近义词，把诗行变成五音步抑扬格。素体诗也可用于写作抒情诗，其格律节奏适合于沉思性言语和内心辩论，比如下边节选自诗人戏剧家莎士比亚的《哈姆雷特》(*Hamlet*)中的独白(soliloquy)[①]：

Hamlet：
　　To be, or not to be, that is the question：
　　Whether 'tis nobler in the mind to suffer
　　The slings and arrows of outrageous fortune,
　　Or to take arms against a sea of troubles
　　And by opposing end them. To die, to sleep—
　　No more—and by a sleep to say we end
　　The heartache and the thousand natural shocks
　　That flesh is heir to. 'Tis a consummation
　　Devoutly to be wished. To die, to sleep;
　　To sleep, perchance to dream. Ay, there's the rub,
　　For in the sleep of death what dreams may come,
　　When we have shuffled off this mortal coil,
　　Must give us pause. There's the respect
　　That makes calamity of so long life.
　　For who would bear the whips and scorns of time,
　　Th' oppressor's wrong, the proud man's contumely,
　　The pangs of disprized love, the law's delay,
　　The insolence of office, and the spurns
　　That patient merit of th'unworthy takes,
　　When he himself might his quietus make
　　With a bare bodkin? Who would fardels bear,
　　To grunt and sweat under a weary life,
　　But that the dread of something after death,
　　The undiscovered country from whose bourn
　　No traveler returns, puzzles the will,
　　And makes us rather bear those ills we have

[①] 参见 Zavatsky, Bill. "Blank Verse", Padgett. Ron, ed. in *The Teachers & Writers Handbook of Poetic Forms*. Second Edition. New York: T&W books, 2000, pp.25-28.

Than fly to others that we know not of?
Thus conscience does make cowards of us all;
And thus the native hue of resolution
Is sicklied o'er with the pale cast of thought,
And enterprises of great pitch and moment
With this regard their currents turn awry
And lose the name of action. —Soft you now,
The fair Ophelia. —Nymph, in thy orisons
Be all my sins remembered. ①

第四节 打油诗(limerick)

There was a young woman named Bright,
Who traveled much faster than light,
She set off one day
In a relative way
And returned on the previous night.②

这是一首无名诗人写的打油诗(limerick)，内容幽默搞笑。打油诗是英语中最流行的喜剧或者活泼诗歌形式，有些打油诗包含无厘头甚至下流的内容。打油诗形式上包括五个诗行，第一、二、五行各三个音步，押同一韵脚，第三、四行各两个音步，押同一韵脚，韵式为 aabba。打油诗的格律音步一般为听起来轻松幽默的抑抑扬格。不过，打油诗中的格律音步允许有变异。

打油诗格律音步的一个变异在于第一、二、五行的第三个音步。这个音步以抑抑扬格开始，但可以在其后加多一个甚至两个非重读音节以调节音韵。另一个更常见的变异是用一个抑扬格代替任意一行的第一个抑抑扬格。比如上边无名诗人的打油诗第一个音步就是抑扬格。不过，这样的变异使得作品没有原来的幽默喜感。例如，试比较左

---

① 详见 Shakespeare, William. *Four Tragedies*: *Hamlet*, *Prince of Denmark* &*Othello*, *the Moor of Venice* & *King Lear* & *Macbeth*, David Bevington & David Scott Kastan, ed., New York: Bantam Dell, A Division of Random House, Inc., 2005, pp.122 - 124。

② 转引自 Livingston, p.121。

边的打油诗和变形后右边的形式①：

There was once a young fellow of Wall	There was a young fellow of Wall
Who grew up so amazingly tall	Who grew so amazingly tall
That his friends dug a pit	His friends dug a pit
Where he'd happily sit	And urged him to sit
When he wished to converse with them all②	To talk and converse with them all.

　　打油诗这种诗歌形式很早就存在，但直到十九世纪末才获得了现在的名字。在十九世纪末之前，打油诗的第五行一般只是简单重复第一行，如1744年的童谣"滴答滴答"（"Hickere, Dickere Dock"）就使用这种早期形式，不过内容不下流。第一位著名打油诗人爱德华·李尔（Edward Lear）的《胡诌诗集》（*A Book of Nonsense*, 1846）对打油诗形式的各种成功变异使这种形式广泛而持久地流行开来。二十世纪初，写打油诗成为一种时尚。从二十世纪初开始，打油诗的第五行不再简单重复第一行，而经常是充满机智的反转或者意外③。

　　打油诗是一种轻松幽默搞笑的诗歌形式，写打油诗可以编造幽默场景，可以编造搞笑名字，写得越幽默越搞笑越好。要写好打油诗，当然要用好抑抑扬格④。除此之外，还可以使用其他音韵工具来制造幽默效果。比如，著名打油诗人爱德华·李尔下边的这首诗中既使用头韵，也使用了拟声词。拟声词 buzz 的使用既是为了与 does 押韵，也是为了制造一种滑稽、幽默感：

There was an Old Man in a tree,
Who was horribly bored by a Bee;
When they said, "Does it buzz?"
He replied, "Yes, it does!
It's a regular brute of a Bee." ⑤

---

① 参见 *The Princeton Encyclopedia*, p.800。
② 参见 Livingston, pp.117-120。
③ 参见 *The Princeton Encyclopedia*, p.800。
④ 参见 Livingston, pp.117-120。
⑤ 转引自 Livingston, p.62。

第五节 十四行诗(sonnet)

十四行诗(sonnet)发源于意大利,其意大利文为 sonetto,意为小歌(little song),顾名思义,包含十四个诗行。十四行诗的格律基本都是五音步抑扬格。十六世纪抒情诗的典型形式是十四行诗,传统十四行诗的内容经常跟爱情有关。不过,后来也有诗人用这个形式写作各种各样的题材,包括政治、宗教,等等。自古以来,十四行诗在欧洲各国流行并且在形式上有各种变异。最有名的三种十四行诗是意大利十四行诗(Italian sonnet)或称彼得拉克十四行诗(Petrarchan sonnet)、英国十四行诗(English sonnet)或称莎士比亚十四行诗(Shakespearean sonnet)、斯宾塞十四行诗(Spenserian sonnet)[①]。

彼得拉克十四行诗的前八行(octave)的韵式是 abba abba,后六行(sestet)的韵式是 cde cde 或者 cd cd cd 或者其他类似的变异,这些变异一般避免最后以一个双行诗(couplet)结束。彼得拉克十四行诗的前八行与后六行常常在意思上有明显不同甚至转折。后六行因为韵式上的不可预测性增强而在思想或者情感表达强度上有所增加[②]。彼得拉克体韵式要求比较高,适应于同韵词比较多的意大利语。诗人克里斯蒂娜·罗萨蒂下边这首十四行诗使用了彼得拉克体的前八行韵式 abba abba,后六行诗的韵式则做了封口韵式(envelop scheme)变异,即 cde edc:

After Death

By Christina Rossetti

The curtains were half drawn, the floor was swept
And strewn with rushes, rosemary and may
Lay thick upon the bed on which I lay,
Where through the lattice ivy-shadows crept.
He leaned above me, thinking that I slept
And could not hear him; but I heard him say,
'Poor child, poor child': and as he turned away
Came a deep silence, and I knew he wept.
He did not touch the shroud, or raise the fold

[①] 参见 *The Princeton Encyclopedia*, pp.1318-1320。
[②] 参见 *The Princeton Encyclopedia*, p.1318。

> That hid my face, or take my hand in his,
> Or ruffle the smooth pillows for my head:
> He did not love me living; but once dead
> He pitied me; and very sweet it is
> To know he still is warm though I am cold.①

十四行诗由英国诗人托马斯·怀亚特(Thomas Wyatt)从意大利介绍进英国。托马斯·怀亚特沿用彼得拉克体的前八行韵式，但是他更喜欢在后六行的最后两行使用一个双行诗。第一个写作素体诗的英语诗人亨利·霍华德（即萨里伯爵 Earl of Surrey），开创了英国十四行诗的韵式，即 abab cdcd efef gg，而将这种韵式使用到极致的是诗人莎士比亚，故而这种韵式也被称为莎士比亚体。与彼得拉克体相比，莎士比亚体的韵式要求稍低，适应于同韵词较少的英语。

如本书第一章第一节所述，经过诺曼征服，古英语原本包含性别、数、格、时态和人称等信息的曲折现象开始消失，这使得英语单词的词尾变化多样，不像法语、西班牙语和意大利语那样容易押韵。这是十四行诗从意大利传入英国之后，韵式从彼得拉克体转变为莎士比亚体的原因之一，因其需要适应英语词汇同韵词少的现实而适当增加诗中尾韵。斯宾塞体的韵式要求难度介于彼得拉克体和莎士比亚体的中间，是彼得拉克体与莎士比亚体的妥协。斯宾塞体的韵式是：abab bcbc cdcd ee。斯宾塞体十四行诗的前九行韵式 abab bcbc c 也称为斯宾塞诗节(Spenserian stanza)②。斯宾塞诗节前八行为五音步格，第九行为六音步格。

英国文艺复兴时期出现了很多十四行诗组(sonnet sequence)，最著名的有诗人莎士比亚的十四行诗组、诗人菲利普·西德尼(Sir Philip Sidney)的《爱星者与星》(*Astrophil and Stella*)、诗人埃德蒙·斯宾塞的《爱情小唱》(*Amoretti*)，等等。不过，将真正的意大利彼得拉克体十四行诗韵式引入英国、将十四行诗组的创作导向随机十四行诗(occasional sonnet)的创作、在十四行诗中使用跨行连续的是诗人弥尔顿③。

十四行诗，不管是意大利彼得拉克体，还是英国莎士比亚体，还是斯宾塞体，其诗歌内容都常常随着诗中韵式的重大变化而发生明显不同的改变甚至是转折。一般来说，彼得拉克体中的前八行诗和后六行诗之间在内容上有一个转折。莎士比亚体的前三个四行诗在内容上常有递进或者顺承关系。莎士比亚体和斯宾塞体中的前十二行和后面的双行诗在内容上也有一个铺排与总结的关系④。这是形式与内容相统一的体现，形式与内容紧密结合，形式的改变引起了内容的改变。

---

① 转引自 https://www.poetryfoundation.org/poems/50497/after-death。
② 参见 *The Princeton Encyclopedia*, p.1320。
③ 同上。
④ 参见 *The Princeton Encyclopedia*, pp.1318–1320。

包括诗歌在内的文学创作,很大程度上是对已有的、经典的、传统的既定形式或成果的借用、延伸、偷窃,或反抗。古今以来的西方诗人对十四行诗的韵式甚至行长等各方面都进行过各种创新变异。他们有时不遵守十四行诗的传统韵式,或按四行诗—三行诗—四行诗—三行诗的韵式轮流排列,或按四行诗—三行诗—三行诗—四行诗的韵式排列,或将六行诗置于八行诗之前;他们有时在第14行后边加多一对韵句,有时写作28行的十四行诗;他们有时完全不遵守形式规则,只在诗作短小方面与"小歌"含义有联系,等等。

十四行诗在当代国际诗歌界仍是备受欢迎、创新不断的诗歌形式。如果一个当代诗人只愿意选择一种传统英语律诗形式来写作的话,这种形式应该就是十四行诗。十四行诗的写作可以从写十四行押韵的素体诗开始练习。在写作莎士比亚体或斯宾塞体十四行诗时,虽然其最后的双行诗常常有总结作用,但写作时应注意避免平铺直述,应注意通过适当的形式工具比如描写、意象、隐喻甚至格律等的使用让读者感受体验后做出结论[1]。此外,也可将颇受欢迎的彼得拉克体前八行韵式与各种后六行韵式搭配起来写作十四行诗。

第六节 维拉纳诗(villanelle)

维拉纳诗(villanelle)是既有规则的押韵要求,也有规则的叠句要求的传统诗体,是一种从意大利民歌演变而来的法国诗歌形式。十六世纪晚期法国诗人冉·帕斯莱特写了一首诗"维拉纳",自此这首诗的形式成为所有维拉纳诗的标准[2]。维拉纳诗全诗十九行,由五个三行诗和最后一个四行诗组成,其中有两个诗行在全诗中按照特定顺序进行重复构成叠句。五个三行诗的韵式为 aba,而最后的四行诗的韵式为 abaa。下边是维拉纳诗的韵式图示:

a1(第一个叠句)
b
a2(第二个叠句)

---

[1] 参见 Brooks & Warren, p.10。
[2] 参见 Logue, Mary & Anne Waldman. "Villanelle", Padgett. Ron, ed. in *The Teachers & Writers Handbook of Poetic Forms*. Second Edition. New York: T&W books, 2000, p.197。

a
b
a1

a
b
a2

a
b
a1

a
b
a2

a
b
a1
a2

如上所示，第一个三行诗中的第一和第三行在后边四个三行诗节的最后一行轮流得到重复，然后在四行诗节中又一起得到重复。a(含 a1 和 a2)诗行同尾韵，而 b 诗行也同尾韵。维拉纳诗经常用五音步抑扬格写成，不过，这个不是硬性的形式要求。注意两个叠句并不是简单的重复，而应该随着诗歌的行文内容而发展，因此，每次重复允许有一定的变异。世界上第一首维拉纳诗，即诗人冉·帕斯莱特的"维拉纳"如下：

Villanelle
By Jean Passerat

I have lost my dove：
Is there nothing I can do?
I want to go after my love.

Do you miss the one you love?
Alas! I really do：
I have lost my dove.

If your love you prove
Then my faith is true；
I want to go after my love.

Haven't you cried enough?
I will never be through：
I have lost my dove.

When I can't see her above
Nothing else seems to do：
I want to go after my love.

Death，I've called long enough，
Take what is given to you：
I have lost my dove，
I want to go after my love.①

创作维拉纳诗的时候，两行叠句最好长度相当，既互相独立又彼此兼容，但看起来又是漫不经心地说出来的。写作维拉纳诗的一个吸引人之处就是一旦确定下经得起重复并且押韵的两个有趣的好叠句，整首诗就已经初具雏形，后边要做的就类似于做填空题了。不过，要记住每个诗节的首行要与两个叠句押韵，而每个诗节的第二行押另外一个韵。维拉纳诗是深受现当代英语诗人青睐的传统诗歌形式。许多现当代诗人都钟情维拉纳诗的创作，比如诗人威斯坦·休·奥登（W. H. Auden）的"如果我能告诉你"（"If I Could Tell You"）、伊丽莎白·毕晓普（Elizabeth Bishop）的"一种艺术"（"One Art"）、西奥多·罗特克（Theodore Roethke）的"苏醒"（"The Waking"）、迪伦·托马斯（Dylan Thomas）的"不要温和地走进那良夜"（"Do not go gentle into that good night"）等都是维拉纳诗。

传统英语诗歌形式，是把习惯了写作自由诗的当代诗人从普遍的无力感中解放出

---

① 转引自 Logue, Mary & Anne Waldman. "Villanelle", Padgett. Ron, ed. in *The Teachers & Writers Handbook of Poetic Forms*. Second Edition. New York：T&W books, 2000, pp.197-198。

来从而释放创造力的美丽工具。诗人罗伯特·弗罗斯特(Robert Frost)曾经说过写自由诗就像打网球而没有网[①]。不懂作诗的人可能认为写作传统形式诗歌让人受制于形式约束,而真正写作的诗人却知道传统诗歌形式规则可解决的具体要求往往反而能带给诗人以创造的喜悦。对诗歌形式与技巧要求的关注可能间接导致意想不到的重大写作题材的出现,成为激发诗歌创作灵感的方式之一。传统英语诗歌形式包括格律和韵式的使用会强迫习惯用自由诗写作的当代诗人的创作思维进入陌生轨道,从而激发诗歌创意,开拓想象空间。

---

① 参见 Livingston,p.127。

第四章
现当代英语诗歌形式

　　1855年诗人沃尔特·惠特曼自费出版的《草叶集》为二十世纪初美国自由诗(free verse)的兴起打下了地基。本书第二章第三节讨论过的意象派(Imagism)是发源于英国,于1912年到1917年主要在美国发展并获得影响力的一个自由诗流派。1916年诗人埃兹拉·庞德在《一些意象派诗人》(*Some Imagist Poets*)的序言中公开摒弃格律的使用。至此,英语诗歌的主流诗人开始放弃使用维持了六百多年的传统英语格律韵诗形式,转而主要采用非律诗形式进行创作[①]。重音诗(accentual verse)、音节诗(syllabic verse)、俳句(haiku)、"潘图"诗(pantoum/pantun)、散文诗(prose poem)等诗歌形式虽然不是传统律诗形式,但也不是现当代英语诗人的发明。现当代英语诗人希望通过对这些诗歌形式的借用或变异实现对诗歌风格和形式的发展和创新。某些传统诗歌形式,包括前面第三章涉及的一些传统形式,至今还是深受创作中的现当代英语诗人的喜爱。创新是现当代英语诗歌创作的普遍信条,为了实现创新,现当代英语诗人进行各种诗歌实验,创作各种实验题材或者实验形式的诗歌。

第一节　自由诗(free verse)

　　自由诗由精通传统英语律诗写作的诗人发明,如沃尔特·惠特曼、埃兹拉·庞德、艾略特、华莱士·斯蒂文斯、威廉·卡洛斯·威廉斯、罗伯特·洛威尔、伊丽莎白·毕晓普(Elizabeth Bishop)等。这些诗人转向自由诗形式的个人原因有所不同:沃尔特·惠特曼喜欢原始粗犷,接近吟游诗风格的诗歌形式;艾略特是模仿诗人乔乐斯·拉法格(Jules Laforgue)而写自由诗;庞德为追求汉字表意效果而写自由诗;威廉·卡洛斯·威廉斯和华莱士·斯蒂文斯则是为了摆脱像约翰·济慈那样的诗人的

[①] 参见 Kowit, p.138。

影响而写作自由诗①。不过，虽然个人原因有所不同，传统律诗形式限制性太强，束缚了英语诗歌的发展动力，无法表现现代生活的特点，是主流英语诗人转向自由诗写作的共同原因。

自由诗的"自由"在于其不受严格的格律和规则的韵式限制。自由诗不以任何规则方式押韵，其断行不受格律束缚，因此其诗行长度也不规则。总的来说，自由诗比律诗提供更多的偶然性和可能性②。然而，自由诗其实并不自由，并不是随便想写什么就写什么。比如自由诗先驱沃尔特·惠特曼诗歌的自由之处在于他舍弃了行尾韵，但是他的诗歌节奏却是深受其在纽约时所听牧师布道的圣经赞美诗影响，起伏节奏感很强。此外，他还经常使用排比、行内韵、和音技巧等制造诗歌节奏③。进行自由诗创作的诗人们会适当选择使用诸如传统格律（不严格）、重音、音节、押韵（不规则）、修辞、意象等诗歌形式工具，以达到最好的诗歌意义建构。

事实上，要写出一首好的自由诗远比写出一首好的传统英语律诗要难得多。比如说，虽然自由诗的断行不受格律束缚，但必须有合法性理由，否则就不必断行，不能称之为诗④。关于自由诗的断行，除了前面第一章中所述各种理由之外，诗人们还各有其他见解。有的诗人比如查尔斯·奥尔森（Charles Olson）认为诗的断行要呈现一次呼吸能够说的东西，而诗人沃尔特·惠特曼和艾伦·金斯伯格的长诗行能够达到的最大长度就是一次呼吸能读完的长度⑤。有的诗人把自己写的一行诗叫做一个音步。有的诗人写作重音诗，写诗时只计算每行诗的重读音节数量。有的诗人写作音节诗，写诗时只计算每行诗的音节数量⑥。诗人菲利普·莱文（Philip Levine）常写重音诗和音节诗，比如其"周六打扫"（"Saturday Sweeping"）是一首重音诗，而"工作是什么"（"What Work Is"）是一首音节诗。"周六打扫"（"Saturday Sweeping"）的每行两个重音，每行音节数不同，而"工作是什么"（"What Work Is"）的大多数诗行都是九个音节⑦。以下为"周六打扫"（"Saturday Sweeping"）的部分节选：

> Everybody's
> had this room
> one time or another
> and never thought
> to sweep. Outside

---

① 参见 Vendler, pp.606–607。
② 同上。
③ 参见 Dobyns, chap. 1。
④ 参见 Vendler, pp.606–607。
⑤ 参见 Vendler, p.607。
⑥ 参见 Livingston, pp.127–130。
⑦ 参见 Kowit, pp.169–170。

the snows stiffen,

the roofs loosen

their last teeth

into the streets. ①

音节诗可以是每行音节数相同,也可以是每行音节数不同,但有一定的变化规律。英语诗歌中音节诗数量不多。注意本书第一章第四节中介绍的二十世纪初美国女诗人阿德莱德·克莱普茜(Adelaide Crapsey)发明的五行诗节就是一种音节诗,而下一节将探讨的俳句(haiku)在某种意义上也是一种音节诗。诗人玛丽安·穆尔(Marianne Moore)和西尔维娅·普拉斯(Sylvia Plath)也喜欢写音节诗。普拉斯(Sylvia Plath)的"蘑菇"("Mushrooms")中每行诗都有五个音节,每个诗节的音节是十五个②。普拉斯下边的"隐喻"("Metaphors")既是一首音节诗,也是一个谜语。这首诗的标题有九个字母,每行有九个音节,整首诗是九行。这些都是猜谜底(一个孕妇)的线索。

Metaphors

By Sylvia Plath

I'm a riddle in nine syllables,
An elephant, a ponderous house,
A melon strolling on two tendrils.
O red fruit, ivory, fine timbers!
This loaf's big with its yeasty rising.
Money's new-minted in this fat purse.
I'm a means, a stage, a cow in calf.
I've eaten a bag of green apples,
Boarded the train there's no getting off. ③

当代英语诗人重新审视传统韵律,认为选择使用传统英语律诗形式还是自由诗形式,应该由作品本身决定,关键是要使诗歌形式和内容相统一。当代英语诗歌因为形式选择上的自由,有些诗人会创作包含多个不同说话者声音的诗歌,其意义诠释困难而不

---

① 转引自 Kowit, pp.169-170。
② 参见 Livingston, pp.127-130。
③ 转引自 Kowit, p.170。

确定;有些诗人在诗中频繁快速变换语气、主题、文体风格等等;有些诗人会通过借用已有文本操作产生偶然诗(chance poem);有些诗人放弃清晰的创作主题或题材;一些诗人认为诗歌的真正题材就应该是语言本身。

　　认为诗歌的真正题材应该是语言本身的著名现代诗人有格特鲁德·斯坦(Gertrude Stein),"Rose is a rose is a rose is a rose."是她最著名的一句诗。她曾经写道:我挑中个别词语,对其进行思考,直到我完全掌握了这些词语的重量与容量,然后把它们与其他词排列在一起,这样我马上就发现,没有一次这样的词语排列是没有意义的①。格特鲁德·斯坦或者通过词语的各种形式变异,或者让词语与不同修饰成分组合,或者将词语放在不同语境,通过多样方式对普通词语进行重复,使普通词语获得不同寻常、超越其普通所指的意义。

第二节　俳句(haiku)

old pond...
a frog leaps in
water's sound ②

　　这是俳句大师松尾芭蕉(Matsuo Basho)写的最著名的日本俳句。俳句在日本流传了几百年,该词由癸句(hokku)发展而来,意思是"扉首句",即"开始的诗行",是日本古代一种长诗的开始诗节,后来发展成为独立的诗歌形式。到 1900 年日本诗人开始使用"俳句(haiku)"来称呼这种独立的诗歌形式。俳句不仅是一种诗歌形式,也是一种诗歌体裁,其在内容、语言和形式上都有自己的特点。俳句的最基本特点是内容与自然相关,语言表达简单,直接呈现生动具体的意象,包含三个短诗行③。

　　日本俳句一般都涉及自然与季节,记录关于人性和自然关系的瞬间顿悟。俳句一般不使用隐喻或明喻,很少使用形容词,只集中描写突出一个意象或者几个意象构建起来的一种关系。俳句常常使用现在时态使意象生动形象地呈现在读者面前。上边松尾芭蕉(Matsuo Basho)的诗中就是使用现在时态呈现青蛙跳水的动作,使古老池塘和跳

---

　　① 转引自 Kowit, p.124;笔者译。
　　② 转引自 Higginson, William J. "Haiku", Padgett, Ron, ed. in *The Teachers & Writers Handbook of Poetic Forms*. Second Edition. New York: T&W books, 2000, p.86,译者不详。
　　③ 参见 Higginson, William J. "Haiku", Padgett, Ron, ed. in *The Teachers & Writers Handbook of Poetic Forms*. Second Edition. New York: T&W books, 2000, pp.86-88。

水青蛙的意象如在读者眼前①。

俳句不押韵,形式上包括三个短诗行,第一和第三行长度相似,第二行比较长。历史上,俳句形式有多种变异。一种最常见的俳句形式包括十七个音节,分三行,第一第三行五个音节,第二行七个音节。虽然有一些俳句是句法完整的句子,但是不少俳句整首诗在句法上并不完整。上述松尾芭蕉写的诗就不是完整句子,而下边日本诗人三浦(Sanpu)使用最常见的 5—7—5 十七音节三诗行形式写的俳句(译者不详)也不都是完整句子②:

Perfect moon for love!
You and I, O my sweet quilt—
against the night's frost. ③

二十世纪初,诗人埃兹拉·庞德、艾米·洛威尔、华莱士·斯蒂文斯、威廉·卡洛斯·威廉斯等受日本俳句的简约与直接风格启发,希望借此开创英语诗歌新风格。与此同时也有日本俳句诗人受英语诗歌的影响放弃传统日本俳句的题材与形式。后来的英语诗人包括艾伦·金斯伯格等对俳句进行了美国化改造:保留十七个音节,以生活意象表现顿悟式主题,但用词和意象都充满美国特色。这种俳句的美国化改造包括形式上分三行的美国俳句(American Haiku)和不分行的美国句子(American Sentence)④。诗人特利·赫茨勒(Terry Hertzler)写的一个美国句子是这样的:The phone, coiled like an ancient serpent, whispers vague threats and promises.⑤诗人杰克·凯鲁亚克(Jack Kerouac)写的一首美国俳句如下:

In my medicine cabinet,
the winter fly
has died of old age. ⑥

当今世界很多诗人写作俳句。当代俳句不一定是十七个音节,可能少于十七个音节,只要是三个短诗行,第一和第三行较短,第二行较长就可以。在当代,城市景观越来

---

① 同上;或参见 Livingston, p.104 – 107;或参见 Kowit, p.71。
② 同上。
③ 转引自 Kowit, p.72。
④ 参见 Kowit, pp.71 – 74。
⑤ 转引自 Kowit, p.74。
⑥ 同上。

越成为俳句中的意象①。写作俳句的挑战性在于只用十七个甚至更少的音节就通过普通生活意象来表达永恒的主题或者诠释不同维度的存在。因此写作俳句用词要非常精炼,不能有冗词。写作俳句,即便是记忆中的场景,最好也用现在时态写成,将场景和意象以现在时呈现在读者眼前,比如日本诗人小林一茶(Issa)下边的这首俳句(译者不详):

Six feet above Hell
I walk through this world gazing
at lovely flowers.②

第三节 "潘图"诗(pantoum/pantun)

"潘图"诗(pantoum/pantun)来源于十五世纪的马来诗歌,它的根是中国和波斯诗歌。"潘图"诗每节诗四行,诗节数不限。每节诗的第二和第四行成为下一节诗的第一和第三行。一般来说,整首诗的第一节的第一行和第三行分别成为最后一节的最后一行和倒数第三行(也即最后一节的第二行)。"潘图"诗可以押韵,也可以不押韵。押韵的话,可以是每节的第一、第三行同韵,第二、第四行同韵,也可以采用其他韵式③。

"潘图"诗的写作看起来复杂,其实掌握了规律,写起来比较有趣。首先要确定好第一节诗。因为第一节的第一和第三行需要在最后一节进行重复,所以这两行诗在意思上要经得起进一步发展,可以是顺承性发展,也可以是转折性发展。一旦有了第一节诗,就可以将其第二和第四行"复制"成为下一节的第一和第三行,这样一来,写作就可以妥妥地进行下去。最后一节的第一和第三行是倒数第二节的第二和第四行,最后一节的第二行和第四行(即全诗最后一行)则是全诗第一节的第三和第一行。最后的结果就是全诗所有诗行都重复了一次④。

当然,各诗行按规则进行的重复并不是完全相同的复制,可以根据诗歌的发展进行一些有关联的词法、句法变异以避免单调,而最后一节对第一节的诗行重复的位置也可以稍有调整。"潘图"诗是突出重复技巧的一种诗歌形式,其重复具有意义强调和声音

---

① 参见 Higginson, William J. "Haiku", Padgett. Ron, ed. in *The Teachers & Writers Handbook of Poetic Forms*. Second Edition. New York: T&W books, 2000, pp.86–88。
② 转引自 Kowit, p.73。
③ 参见 Addonizio&Laux, pp.163–166。
④ 同上。

回环等优点,而其重复规则又允许作品内容根据需要不断推进,是一种可能让人上瘾的诗歌形式①。"潘图"诗行的重复模式如下所示:

..........第1行
..........第2行
..........第3行
..........第4行
..........第5行(重复第2行)
..........第6行
..........第7行(重复第4行)
..........第8行
..........第9行(重复第6行)
..........第10行
..........第11行(重复第8行)
..........第12行
....
....
....
....
..........倒数第4行(重复上一节的第2行)
..........倒数第3行(重复全诗第3行)
..........倒数第2行(重复上一节的第4行)
..........最后1行(重复全诗第1行)

第四节 散文诗(prose poem)

诗人查尔斯·波德莱尔(Charles Baudelaire,1867已辞世)于1869年被发表的诗集《巴黎的忧郁:一些散文诗》(*Paris Spleen: Little Poems in Prose*)使散文诗形式开始流传开来。波德莱尔(Charles Baudelaire)的作品影响了诗人亚瑟·兰波(Arthur Rimbaud)。散文诗跨越散文和诗歌,看起来是散文(即不断行),读起来是诗歌,具有诗歌的节奏、意象、强度、敏锐和新颖,一般比较短。不过,一首散文诗可能是几句话也可能是几页纸。在诗人格特鲁德·斯坦的作品中,有时难以区分哪些是诗性散文

---

① 参见 Addonizio & Laux, pp.163 – 166。

(poetic prose),哪些是散文诗①。前面第二章中涉及的诗人特莉丝(Virginia R. Terris)的寓言诗"不速之客"("The Uninvited")也是散文诗。下边是诗人阿尔·左立纳斯(Al Zolynas)的散文诗"想想手风琴"("Considering the Accordion"),最后两句充满抒情诗意。

Considering the Accordion
By Al Zolynas

　　The idea of it is distasteful at best. Awkward box of wind, diminutive, misplaced piano on one side, raised braille buttons on the other. The bellows, like some parody of breathing, like some medical apparatus from a Victorian sick-ward. A grotesque poem in three dimensions, a rococo thing-am-a-bob. I once strapped an accordion on my chest and right away I had to lean back on my heels, my chin in the air, my back arched like a bullfighter or flamenco dancer. I became an unheard-of contradiction: a gypsy in graduate school. Ah, but for all that, we find evidence of the soul in the most unlikely places. Once in a Czech restaurant in Long Beach, an ancient accordionist came to our table and played the old favorites: "Lady of Spain," "The Sabre Dance," "Dark Eyes," and through all the cliches his spirit sang clearly. It seemed like the accordion floated in air, and he swayed weighdessly behind it, eyes closed, back in Prague or some lost village of his childhood. For a moment we all floated—the whole restaurant: the patrons, the knives and forks, the wine, the sacrificed fish on plates. Everything was pure and eternal, fragiley suspended like a stained-glass window in the one remaining wall of a bombed-out church.②

第五节　现成发现诗(found poem)

在已有非诗歌文本中发现的某些非常诗性的段落,不经编辑或稍经编辑,比如通过

---

① 参见 Ziegler, Alan. "Prose Poem", Padgett. Ron, ed. in *The Teachers & Writers Handbook of Poetic Forms*. Second Edition. New York: T&W books, 2000, p.142;或参见 Kowit, p.21。
② 转引自 Kowit, p.23。

断行、首字母大写等非常简单的加工,即成为一首诗,这种诗叫现成发现诗(found poem)。诗人查尔斯·列兹尼克夫(Charles Reznikoff)的《证词》(Testimony)中有很多最早的、非常有趣的现成发现诗,这些诗主要是在法庭审判过程中发现的。另外一个很可能找到或者创造发现诗的来源是一些自然科普读物。现成发现诗的神奇之处在于当文本脱离了原来的语境单独存在时反而获得了更多的表现力。下面左边的诗[1]是母亲把儿子贴在冰箱上的留言经过断行和首字母大写后发现的,右边的诗[2]则是诗人从报纸文章中发现的:

Dear Mom

Dear Mom,
I ate all my lunch
And went back to school.
I am all washed up.
Astronaut Jim Lovell
flying in Gemini 7
high over Hawaii,
today spotted
a tiny pinpoint
of greenish—blue brilliance
far below.
He successfully "locked on"
for 40 seconds
and sent
the world's first communication
down a laser beam
to earth.

"I've got it," Lovell cried.

——By John Giorno

---

[1] 转引自 Hewitt, Geof. "Found Poem", Padgett. Ron, ed. in *The Teachers & Writers Handbook of Poetic Forms*. Second Edition. New York: T&W books, 2000, p.79。

[2] 转引 Hewitt, Geof. "Found Poem", Padgett. Ron, ed. in *The Teachers & Writers Handbook of Poetic Forms*. Second Edition. New York: T&W books, 2000, pp.80 - 81。

第六节　偶然诗(chance poem)：
　　　　拼贴(collage)、擦涂(erasure)

与现成文本的诗性段落不经编辑或只经简单编辑就产生的发现诗类似，偶然诗(chance or aleatory poem)也是通过借用已有文本产生，但需经过相对复杂的加工操作。比如，可以本人的生日数字为基准，按照自定的规则排列数字，按排好的数字翻开一本书或词典的相应页码，找到该页的第一个和/或者最后一个词语作为原始文字素材，允许改变词语形式，然后使用这些文字素材作诗。这样产生的诗就是一种偶然诗。诗人杰克森·麦克·娄(Jackson Mac Low)就会先通读一篇文本，找出一些"种子"单词或者短语，然后用这些单词和短语建构自己的诗歌。下边这首偶然诗是他从诗人路易斯·朱可夫斯基(Louis Zukofsky)的五首诗里抽出一些句子成分创作的，是其系列诗"5首诗——纪念或者来自路易斯·朱科夫斯基1963年5月1日"("5 Poems for & from Louis Zukofsky 1 May 1963")之一①：

Z3

By Jackson Mac Low

GETS DOWN FOR A MOMENT ON ONE KNEE.
WHAT'S TROUBLING YOU?
AREN'T YOU DEAD?
LISTEN.
WE WERE GOING SOMEWHERE,
STEPPING OFF SOMEWHERE.
REMEMBER? FROM ANOTHER WORLD.
SAD RECOGNITION.
WE'RE GOING TO A WEDDING.
AFTER THE DREAM CURTAIN FALLS. ②

诗人也可以设定如下规则来写偶然诗：拿起任意一本英语诗歌书籍，闭上眼睛打开

---

① 参见 Kowit, p.114。
② 转引自 Kowit, p.114。

书,手指放在打开的页面上,睁开眼睛,记下手指所指的单词及其前三个单词和后三个单词,这样就获得了一个含七个单词的短语。接下来把这个短语写在纸上,然后连续快速写作五分钟,在这五分钟的类自动写作(auto writing)中,手不要停,脑子不要想。五分钟连续快速写作结束后,先正向读一遍所写乱七八糟的东西,再从结尾反向读回到开始的地方,认认真真一个词一个词地读,并划出一个有某种意义并具有如下特点之一的短语:有活力、让人意外、以前从没写过。这个短语可以是一整个句子,也可以是一个句子的结尾及其下一句的开头。然后写一首自然出现这个划出的短语的诗。写成的这首诗,也是一首偶然诗①。

事实上,偶然诗的写作规则可以无限设计。诗人之间也可以使用对方设计的规则来写作偶然诗。有两种创作偶然诗的方法比较特别,第一种方法是拼贴(collage)或剪贴(cut up),第二种方法是擦涂(erasure)。相应的,使用这两种方法创作的偶然诗也称为拼贴诗(collage or cut-up poem)和擦涂诗(erasure poem)。创作擦涂诗需要的工具是一页文本和一支宽黑芯或宽白芯笔。创作方法就是用笔在文本上擦涂废弃的文字,留下的文字就是一首诗。下边是诗人马克·梅尔尼科夫(Mark Melnicove)创作的一首擦涂诗②。

```
Each                              soul
Is a glowing spark of
           light

       learning to
                                 pulsate
On the wings of        the
                              unequivocal

                              mother
```

创作拼贴诗的一个具体过程可以如下:选择四张内容风格完全不同的纸质报纸、杂志、书籍、宣传单等等。分别在每张纸上随意地、不做停顿地圈出二十、三十个词语。圈词时只考虑词语的声音,而不考虑词语的意思。从四张纸圈出大约一百个词语后,再从随意一本诗集的三首不同诗作中各圈出一个词。现在可以用句法工具(如连词)把这一百多个词连成句子,必要的时候可以改变原有词语的词性或者形式,使句子句法正常。连词成句的时候不必使用所有词语,并且可以使用突然在脑中冒出来的其他词语。这样连成的句子大部分在意义上不会有什么指向,因为这种连词成句的目标只是把词语和语音游戏性地结合起来。连成的句子就构成了拼贴诗的初稿。经过若干次修改,去掉初稿中毫无联系的句子,变换没有表现力的词语,特别是动词、名词等之后,很可能得到一首想象性极强但又无法阐释的独特作品。当然在修改中,如果诗句呈现出一种意

---

① 参见 Morley, pp.5-6。
② 转引自 Kowit, p.110。

义走向，诗人也可以顺着那种走向改成一首意义明了的诗作①。诗人狄波拉·哈丁(Deborah Harding)下边的"想象着红"("Imagining Red")是一首拼贴诗，并且是一首具有逻辑意义的爱情诗。

Imagining Red
By Deborah Harding

In our room, a picture of farmland—
   blue inside white groves of almonds.
     Through the tops of trees,

Fluttering like a cotton sash over our heads,
   hundreds of butterflies,
     gold wings folded like cloth.

Under the flames, someone is trimming a hedge
     as the sun, amber wheel, sparks the orchard
       drops stars on jagged trunks—

Beneath the frame, this man I cannot get over
   is combing my hair, burning rope tangled
     beside me, turning to copper—

he is humming to himself
   lost in the soft mud of this room,
     that kind of weightlessness,
       just before going to bed together.

He has carried me upstairs
   like a sleeping child, spread me like warm
     linen on the forest floor—

The red hood of his sweatshirt

---

① 参见 Kowit, pp.103–108。

propped under my head, as if protected

　　from the rough earth. ①

有一种叫"勒索信"(ransom note)的拼贴诗可以通过如下操作产生:准备任意一页文本、一把剪刀、一支胶水、一张白纸,然后就发挥视觉和文字创造力进行创作。"勒索信"也不必使用所有剪出来的词语,可以使用没有剪出来但突然在脑中冒出来的词语。"勒索信"与后边将介绍的视觉诗的区别在于"勒索信"通过在现成文本上随意裁剪出词语作为文字材料进行视觉和语义的同时创作。这样,现有文本对之后的视觉和语义的双重创作具有一定的限制或者导向作用②。下边是诗人马克·梅尔尼科夫(Mark Melnicove)创作的一个"勒索信"③:

用拼贴方法作诗,诗人先搁置自己对作品的批判审查以及连续性和逻辑性发展的要求,专注于语言的声音音乐性,不考虑作品的题材与意义,让无意识深处的材料产生诗歌。创作拼贴诗或者擦涂诗,所用现有文本来源越多越不同越有趣。如果不舍得文本原件,可以复印后使用。拼贴诗和擦涂诗的创作过程直接从已有文本圈、剪、涂、擦文字材料,因此其创作内容可能受已有文本材料的限制或导向影响,其成形具有偶然因素,所以也是偶然诗。上一章介绍的离合诗的写作规则其实也含有偶然诗的成分。

第七节　视觉诗(visual poem)

视觉诗(visual or concrete or shaped or pattern poem)不是现当代诗人的发明创造。在西方,视觉诗的创作传统至少可以追溯至古希腊诗歌。写作视觉诗,可能需要先

---

① 转引自 Kowit, pp.107–108。
② 参见 Kowit, p.108。
③ 转引自 Kowit, p.108。

想好一个有清楚外围的图形,比如一个球或者一个窗,然后用图形激发起来的灵感进行创作,将相关的诗歌语言填进图形。可以对图形中语言的字体、字号、颜色等等进行视觉设计,等等①。上一节介绍的"勒索信"是一种受已有文本材料限制或者导向影响具有偶然因素的视觉诗,本节所说视觉诗的创作过程不直接从已有文本圈、剪、涂、擦文字材料,因此不受已有文本限制或影响。十七世纪诗人乔治·赫伯特(George Herbert)的"复活节翅膀"("Easter Wings")是一首视觉诗。

Easter Wings
By George Herbert

Lord, who createdst man in wealth and store,
　Though foolishly he lost the same,
　　Decaying more and more,
　　　Till he became
　　　　Most poor:
　　　　With thee
　　　O let me rise
　　As larks, harmoniously,
　And sing this day thy victories:
Then shall the fall further the flight in me.

My tender age in sorrow did begin:
　And still with sicknesses and shame
　　Thou didst so punish sin,
　　　That I became
　　　　Most thin.
　　　　With thee
　　　Let me combine,
　　And feel thy victory:
　For, if I imp my wing on thine,
Affliction shall advance the flight in me.②

---

① 参见 Padgett, pp.34–37。
② 转引自 https://www.poetryfoundation.org/poems/44361/easter-wings。

诗人艾德温·摩根（Edwin Morgan）的"午睡的匈牙利蛇"（"Siesta of a Hungarian Snake"）是一首视觉诗：s sz sz SZ sz SZ sz ZS zs ZS zs zs z①。这首诗只用字母 s 和 z，通过其正反、大小写的有规律组合排列，不仅从视觉上呈现了蜿蜒躺着睡午觉的爬行动物蛇的形状与纹理，而且从字母 s 和 z 的音响效果上也呈现了蛇午间的酣睡，尤其是从 s 到 z 的排列顺序变化呈现了酣睡中的蛇的吸气与呼气的规律性。诗人诺曼·亨利·普理查德二世（Norman Henry Pritchard II）标题为"♯"的视觉诗②则用一个字母 Z 通过图形视觉排列直接涵盖了从 A 到 Z 的所有字母表字母：

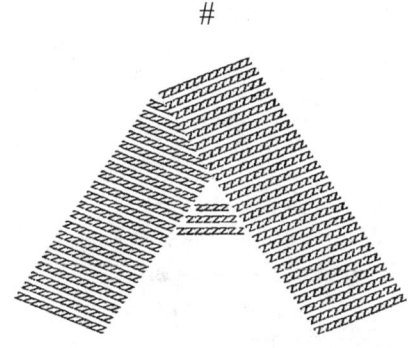

——By Norman Henry Pritchard II

诗人莱因哈德（Reinhard Döhl）的"视觉诗——藏匿的入侵者"（"Pattern Poem with an Elusive Intruder"）也是视觉诗③。首先，这首诗的形状在视觉上就是一个苹果。Apfel 是德文的"苹果"，这个词被排列成为一个苹果形状。所以，苹果的意象不仅通过视觉呈现，也通过该词的重复得到强调。而在诸多的 Apfel 中，经过仔细检查，可以看到 Wurm 一词，这在德文中是"虫子"的意思。这条虫子如果不仔细找，是很难察觉的，这也在视觉与语义上呈现了该诗标题 elusive intruder 的所指。

Pattern Poem with an Elusive Intruder
By Reinhard Döhl

---

① 转引自 Livingston，p.138。
② 转引自 Kowit，p.113。
③ 转引自 Livingston，p.137。

诗人多希·查尔斯(Dorthi Charles)的"具象猫"("Concrete Cat")① 不仅用文字呈现了猫的形状,而且将每个单词或其中字母的表义作用发挥到极致。比如,诗中使用大写字母 A、Y、U 模拟猫的耳朵、眼睛和嘴巴的形状;单词 tail 中的字母被特意拉开间距以呈现猫的长尾巴。诗中其余单词的使用也从语义上帮助加强猫的身体各部位的形象感,而右下角 mouse 一词被刻意倒置,则呈现了猫的战利品:一只死了的老鼠。难怪猫猫如此开心惬意地趴着!

Concrete Cat
By Dorthi Charles

```
          A           A
          e           e
          r           r

        eYe         eYe      stripestripestripestripe    t
                                                          a i l t
   whisker      whisker      stripestripestripe               a i l
                                                                  
   whisker    m    h         stripestripestripestripes
              o         whisker   stripestripestripe
              U                   stripestripestripestripe

                     paw paw      paw paw          ǝsnoɯ

          dishdish                    litterbox
                                      litterbox
```

视觉诗,是适合用眼睛看,用心阅读,但不适合用嘴巴朗读的诗。写作视觉诗,可能是语言灵感早于画面出现,也可能是画面灵感早于语言出现。对于一些诗人来说,语言因素比画面更重要,而某些词或者思想素材确实也适合用视觉诗的形式来表达。从诗歌是语言艺术的意义上来说,语言,确实应该比画面更重要。

---

① 转引自 Livingston,pp.139 - 140。

第五章
英语诗歌题材

诗歌题材(subject/content/theme)既可以是充满时代感的话题(topic)也可以是人类永恒的母题(motif)。诗人威廉·华兹华斯和格勒律治在诗集《抒情歌谣》的出版告示中宣称普通人的日常语言也能制造诗性愉悦,诗歌的魅力在于任何感人的素材都可以成为诗歌题材①。也就是说,每个人生命中的所见、所听、所想、所做、所爱、所望、所知和未知的一切都可以变成诗歌。个人或社会群体的生活、工作、学习、友谊、爱情等经历经验,或者关于死亡等未知世界的想象,甚至包括语言和诗歌本身,都可以入诗。如果生活中状况百出,当然是写诗的好素材,但是人不需要浪迹天涯,也不需要经历惊涛骇浪,就可以写出好诗。诗人不需要等待什么惊天动地的大事发生,只需要关注身边当下发生的一切,就可以开始写诗了。

第一节　爱情(晨曲)、身体、欲望、失落、悲伤、死亡(挽歌)

诗歌从自我开始。人的记忆、阅读、观察、思考、想象等都是诗歌题材的来源,而其中人的回忆和做梦的内容则几乎无所不包。写作大题材或者抽象题材,比如爱情、死亡等,应该从小、从细、从具体着手。诗人理查·雨果(Richard Hugo)说过:"从小处想,思绪会自己扩张"②,前面第二章第一节中诗人洛温·布朗的"周六一晚后的周日清晨"("A Sunday Morning After a Saturday Night")就是以家中长辈的第三者视觉通过细节描写并结合使用隐喻、夸张等修辞手法表现热恋中的少女情态。

爱情是人的一种感情,爱情诗歌是最常见的抒情诗,因此关于爱情的诗歌最常见的便是使用第一人称来书写。诗人托马斯·卢克斯(Thomas Lux)的"我觉得你很棒"("I Think You're Wonderful")就是一首以第一人称书写的爱情狂想曲。这首诗在诗题、

---

① 参见 *The Princeton Encyclopedia*, pp.826–834.
② "Think small, the mind will expand",详见 Hugo, chap. 1.

首行和末行重复使用了同一叠句。叠句在诗中关键的三个位置的重复使得本来很普通甚至有点儿俗套的句子获得了非同寻常的重要性。诗中使用独特的意象即燃烧的女用内衣和撒哈拉沙漠上的一滴雨来表现爱情的热烈与滋润。诗中还使用夸张(驱车途中见到沿途各家邮箱上都有爱人的名字)与隐喻(多年前已经丢进河里的生命在菲律宾重新找回)等修辞手法来表现说话者对爱人的热望与感激之情。

I Think You're Wonderful
By Thomas Lux

I think you're wonderful.
I'm driving my car
and your name is on every mailbox.
I'm kissing you
and my shoes crawl away
in darkness, sweet gadgets
sing in my wrists, the life
I dumped into the river years ago
is reported found in the Philippines...
Why do I tell you this?
Because your lingerie
is burning, because a lone drop
of rain is falling somewhere
above the Sahara, because
I think you're wonderful.①

英语诗歌中有一种特殊的爱情题材诗叫"晨曲"(aubade)。传统的晨曲常常是关于不为世俗接受的爱情,表达了一夜欢爱之后黎明来临时爱人不得不分离的遗憾。在传统晨曲中,黑夜隐喻密闭空间中非世俗之爱,白天隐喻礼仪道德社会。诗中常有第三个声音,一般是守夜人的声音,会宣布黎明的来临,催促恋人们分开。守夜人是黑夜与白天代表的两个不同世界的调停人。晨曲可能包含恋人间或者恋人与守夜人的对话或者系列独白,有时可能包含独白与简单叙事。晨曲没有固定的格律形式。诗人杰弗里·乔叟的《特洛伊罗斯与克瑞西达》(*Troilus and Criseyde*)和"长官的传说"("Reeve's Tale")、莎士比亚的《罗密欧与朱丽叶》(*Romeo and Juliet*)中的片段、约翰·邓恩(John

---

① 转引自 Kowit,p.197。

Donne)的"初升的太阳"("The Sun Rising")和"早安"("The Good Morrow")、罗伯特·勃朗宁(Robert Browning)的"晨别"("Parting at Morning")等,都是晨曲[①]。下边是诗人戏剧家莎士比亚 的《罗密欧与朱丽叶》中的晨曲片段:

Juliet: Wilt thou be gone? It is not yet near day:
It was the nightingale and not the lark,
That pierced the fearful hollow of thine ear;
Nightly she sings on yon pomegranate tree:
believe me, love, it was the nightingale.

Romeo: It was the lark, the herald of the morn,
No nightingale: look, love, what envious streaks
Do lace the severing clouds in yonder east:
Night's candles are burnt out, and jocund day
Stands tiptoe on the misty mountain tops.
I must be gone and live, or stay and die.

Juliet: Yon light is not daylight, I know it, I:
It is some meteor that the sun exhales,
To be to thee this night a torch-bearer,
And light thee on thy way to Mantua:
Therefore stay yet, thou need'st not to be gone.

Romeo: Let me be ta'en, let me be put to death;
I am content, so thou wilt have it so.
I'll say yon grey is not the morning's eye.
Tis but the pale reflex of Cynthia's brow;
Nor that is not the lark whose notes do beat
The vaulty heaven so high above our heads:
I have more care to stay than will to go. —
Come, death, and welcome! Juliet wills it so. —
How is't my soul? let's talk, —it is not day.

---

① 参见 The Princeton Encyclopedia, p.29。

Juliet: It is, it is, —hie hence, be gone away!
It is the lark that sings so out of tune,
Straining harsh discords and unpleasing sharps.
Some say the lark makes sweet division:
This doth not so, for she divideth us:
Some say the lark and loathed toad change eyes;
O, now I would they had changed voices too!
Since arm from arm that voice doth us affray,
Hunting thee hence with hunt's up to the day.
O, now be gone; more light and light it grows.

Romeo: More light and light, —more dark and dark our woes!
(Act III, Scene V)①

在上边片段中，两个恋人罗密欧（Romeo）和朱丽叶（Juliet）从唯一的一次共度良宵中醒来。罗密欧必须马上离开去流放地，两个恋人在朱丽叶俯视花园的闺房中依依不舍②。罗密欧和朱丽叶的这首著名的晨曲使用素体诗写成，偶尔使用尾韵。诗中使用大量的头韵和谐音制造了诗行内部的乐感。这段诗歌句法平衡、用词雄辩、有效比喻、情感温柔悲伤炽热，令人难忘。从上边的片段也可以看出，传统晨曲中经常出现两个鸟意象，一个是代表夜晚的夜莺（nightingale），一个是代表黎明的云雀（lark）。

现当代诗人写作晨曲，当然可以采用现代语言、现代意象以及现代借口以挽留即将离去的情人。现当代晨曲比较有名的有诗人埃兹拉·庞德的"晨曲"（"Alba"）、威斯坦·休·奥登的"晨曲"（"Aubade"）、菲利普·拉金（Philip Larkin）的"晨曲"（"Aubade"）、罗伯特·克里利（Robert Creeley）的"晨曲"（"Alba"）等等③。与表现爱人依依不舍的晨曲相似的另一类诗歌的主题是及时行乐（carpe diem）。Carpe diem 是拉丁语，"及时行乐（seize the day）!"的意思。十一世纪日本诗人和泉式部（Izumi Shikibu）的一首诗仅用了五个短诗行就表达了生命短促、及时行乐的必要性：

  Come quickly—as soon as
  these blossoms open,

---

① 转引自 Kowit, p.195。
② 参见 Kowit, pp.194-196。
③ 参见 The Princeton Encyclopedia, p.29。

they fall.
This world exists
as a sheen of dew on flowers. ①

关于爱情的诗歌有时会涉及感官激情与身体欲望的表现。Bible 里边有一个部分叫"雅歌"("Song of songs"),是关于感官激情的诗歌。关于身体或者欲望的诗歌创作不管在哪种文化中都是比较有难度的,有时候甚至是禁忌。这种诗歌既要表现出激情,又不能变成黄色下流写作。诗人昆西·楚佩(Quincy Troupe)下边的这首"那一晚"("The Other Night"),既表现了欲望与激情,同时也用一种喜剧性的幽默使作品不致成为色情描写。

The Other Night
By Quincy Troupe

the other brandysweetened
night, eye dreamed we
was kissing so hard & good, you
sucked my tongue right on out
my trembling mouth
& eye had to sew it back in
in order to tell you about it ②

诗人杰克·吉尔伯特(Jack Gilbert)的"新汉普郡大理石雕像"("New Hampshire Marble")主要是一首叙事诗,没有直接的激情描写,但从两个旧日情人见面的持续时间、两人在屋舍间的草地到处寻找即将与别人结婚的情人的订婚戒指的戏剧性细节已经侧面暗示两人的旧情复燃。最后的冬夜月光下发光的人体意象配上诗歌的标题,充满诗意地影射了旧情复燃的情人见面后发生的行为。

New Hampshire Marble
By Jack Gilbert

I called Sue the week I moved back from Rome.

---

① 转引自 Kowit,p.196,Jane Hirshfield 与 Mariko Aratani 翻译。
② 转引自 Kowit,p.210。

She was getting married on Sunday she said,
but would drive over after lunch to say goodbye.
Later, in the tall grass between some homes,
we were searching around in the torn dirt,
frantic and laughing. Trying to find
the huge diamond engagement ring.
Our bodies flaring in the winter moonlight. ①

爱情与欲望,既可能带来激情满足,也可能带来失落悲伤,而因死亡造成的失落悲伤则常常是不易逾越的创伤,因此也是诗歌中经常出现的母题。比如前面第二章第一节中讨论过的诗歌"米奇可已逝"("Michiko Dead")表现的就是失去爱人之后的悲痛。这首诗通过诗人为应对背负重盒(骨灰盒)的沉重感所变换的各种行为姿势等等细节隐喻诗人失去妻子之后的悲痛及对悲痛的逐渐适应和对失落的最终接受。再比如第二章第二节提到诗歌"外套"("Coats")。这首诗两次使用大衣意象作为男人心中失落凄凉的情感状态的客观对应物,从第三者视觉描写一个男人失去或者即将失去爱人时所感受到的凄凉。诗人雷蒙德·卡佛(Raymond Carver)的"余晖"("After-Glow")也是关于死亡与失落的诗。

After-Glow
By Raymond Carver

The dusk of evening comes on. Earlier a little rain
had fallen. You open a drawer and find inside
the man's photograph, knowing he has only two years
to live. He doesn't know this, of course,
that's why he can mug for the camera.
How could he know what's taking root in his head
at that moment? If one looks to the right
through boughs and tree trunks, there can be seen
crimson patches of the after-glow. No shadows, no
half-shadows. It is still and damp...
The man goes on mugging. I put the picture back
in its place along with the others and give

---

① 转引自 Kowit, p.210。

my attention instead to the after-glow along the far ridge,
light golden on the roses in the garden.
Then, I can't help myself, I glance once more
at the picture. The wink, the broad smile,
the jaunty slant of the cigarette. ①

正如"爱"并不仅仅局限于情人、夫妻之间,失落感也不仅仅限于情人、夫妻之间,它也可能存在于其他关系中。并且,失落可能是死亡造成的,也可能是其他原因比如分离造成的。诗人露易丝·格丽克(Louise Glück)的"学童"("The School Children")表现的就是母亲在与孩子分离之时感受到的失落。母亲们在果园里摘下来准备送给老师的苹果这一意象,其实是她们自己苦心培育的孩子的隐喻,而教室里巨大的讲台和整齐的衣帽钉意象则是学校权威的隐喻。最后一个诗节描写母亲们在果园中收拢果实所剩无几的树枝时使用的形容词 gray 和名词 so little ammunition 形象刻画了母亲们在把自己的孩子交到学校教师手里时的失落感及对孩子们在学校权威下的处境的担忧。

The School Children
By Louise Glück

The children go forward with their little satchels.
And all morning the mothers have labored
to gather the late apples, red and gold,
like words of another language.

And on the other shore
are those who wait behind great desks
to receive these offerings.
How orderly they are—the nails
on which the children hang
their overcoats of blue or yellow wool.

And the teachers shall instruct them in silence
and the mothers shall scour the orchards for a way out,

---

① 转引自 Kowit, p.56。

drawing to themselves the gray limbs of the fruit trees
bearing so little ammunition.①

诗人菲利普·拉金的诗歌中有一个反复出现的母题是死亡,其诗"晨曲"("Aubade")也是关于死亡母题的作品②,因此在内容上与传统晨曲有所不同。拉金的"晨曲"包含五个诗节,每节十行,整齐使用 ababccdeed 的韵式,每节除了第九行外,每行基本包含十个音节,大体为五音步抑扬格。借用传统晨曲中对于催人离别的白天来临造成的不舍和悲伤,"晨曲"标题的使用凸显了诗人对于生命的不舍以及对于必将到来的死亡和虚无的无奈与悲伤。此诗最后一节中白日来临时如棺材般的房间、灰色的天空、如收尸医生般的邮递员等意象加强了全诗的悲剧色彩。

Aubade
By Philip Larkin

I work all day, and get half-drunk at night.
Waking at four to soundless dark, I stare.
In time the curtain-edges will grow light.
Till then I see what's really always there:
Unresting death, a whole day nearer now,
Making all thought impossible but how
And where and when I shall myself die.
Arid interrogation: yet the dread
Of dying, and being dead,
Flashes afresh to hold and horrify.

The mind blanks at the glare. Not in remorse
—The good not done, the love not given, time
Torn off unused—nor wretchedly because
An only life can take so long to climb
Clear of its wrong beginnings, and may never;
But at the total emptiness for ever,
The sure extinction that we travel to

---

① 转引自 Vendler, pp.4-5。
② 参见陈津津,"为了不朽而创作——菲利普·拉金新解",《译林》,2012 年 6 月号:总第 167 期,p.58-73。

And shall be lost in always. Not to be here,
Not to be anywhere,
And soon; nothing more terrible, nothing more true.

This is a special way of being afraid
No trick dispels. Religion used to try,
That vast moth-eaten musical brocade
Created to pretend we never die,
And specious stuff that says No rational being
Can fear a thing it will not feel, not seeing
That this is what we fear—no sight, no sound,
No touch or taste or smell, nothing to think with,
Nothing to love or link with,
The anaesthetic from which none come round.

And so it stays just on the edge of vision,
A small unfocused blur, a standing chill
That slows each impulse down to indecision.
Most things may never happen: this one will,
And realisation of it rages out
In furnace-fear when we are caught without
People or drink. Courage is no good:
It means not scaring others. Being brave
Lets no one off the grave.
Death is no different whined at than withstood.

Slowly light strengthens, and the room takes shape.
It stands plain as a wardrobe, what we know,
Have always known, know that we can't escape,
Yet can't accept. One side will have to go.
Meanwhile telephones crouch, getting ready to ring
In locked-up offices, and all the uncaring
Intricate rented world begins to rouse.
The sky is white as clay, with no sun.
Work has to be done.

Postmen like doctors go from house to house.①

与诗人菲利普·拉金借用晨曲来命名书写死亡母题不同,在西方诗歌中,与死亡题材更为密切相关的诗歌形式是田园诗、颂歌、挽歌,特别是挽歌。在西方诗歌中,挽歌原指用格律形式复杂的挽歌双行体(elegiac couplet)写成的诗,这种诗题材广泛,包括墓志铭(epitaph),也包括非哀悼性的非世俗爱情。后来,挽歌发展成为主要关于死亡或者哀悼的诗。挽歌中也经常出现田园诗式的非人类元素,如仙女、萨梯、山水风景等。诗人弥尔顿的"利西达斯"("Lycidas")、斯宾塞(Edmund Spenser)的"达芙娜伊达"("Daphnaida")、珀西·比希·雪莱的"阿多尼斯"("Adonais")、沃尔特·惠特曼的"当紫丁香最近在庭院中开放"("When Lilacs Last in the Dooryard Bloom'd")和"走出摇摆不停的摇篮"("Out of the Cradle Endlessly Rocking")、奥登的"纪念西格蒙·弗洛伊德"("In Memory of Sigmund Freud")等,都是挽歌②。

挽歌诗节(elegiac stanza)也叫挽歌四行诗(elegiac quatrain),是韵式为 abab 的五音步抑扬格四行诗节,也即传统英语诗歌中经常用于哲学思考或者其他庄严主题的英雄体四行诗(heroic quatrain),因为诗人托马斯·格雷(Thomas Gray)在"墓畔挽歌"("Elegy Written in a Country Churchyard",1750)中的使用而得名,之后一百年间英语挽歌几乎都使用这种格律韵式③。虽然有所谓的挽歌诗节,挽歌本身并没有特定的形式。从最广义的角度来说,关于任何事物包括时间、爱情、生命的结束的诗都可以叫挽歌④。从这个意义上看,诗人珀西·比希·雪莱的"奥西曼迭斯"("Ozymandias",埃及国王 Ramses II 的希腊名字)也是一首关于生命、权势结束湮灭的挽歌。

Ozymandias
By P. B. Shelley

I met a traveller from an antique land,
Who said: "Two vast and trunkless legs of stone
Stand in the desert... Near them, on the sand,
Half sunk, a shattered visage lies, whose frown,

---

① Larkin, Philip. "Aubade", *Collected Poems*. Ed. Anthony Thwaite. London: The Marvell Press & Faber and Faber Limited, 1988.或可详见 https://www.poetryfoundation.org/poems/48422/aubade-56d229a6e2f07。
② 参见 *The Princeton Encyclopedia*, pp.397-398。
③ 同上。
④ 参见 Logue, Mary. "Elegy", Padgett. Ron, ed. in *The Teachers & Writers Handbook of Poetic Forms*. Second Edition. New York: T&W books, 2000, pp.62-64。

And wrinkled lip, and sneer of cold command,
Tell that its sculptor well those passions read
Which yet survive, stamped on these lifeless things,
The hand that mocked them, and the heart that fed:
And on the pedestal, these words appear:
"My name is Ozymandias, king of kings;
Look on my works, ye Mighty, and despair!"
Nothing beside remains. Round the decay
Of that colossal wreck, boundless and bare
The lone and level sands stretch far away.[①]

挽歌通常是哀悼死者的诗,可以侧写死者,也可以使用呼语修辞直接对死者说话。直接对死者说话是一种亲密话语,诗人应该让读者获得这种亲密话语与感情的语境[②]。不过,并非所有人面对死亡时都是哀伤的,并非所有关于死亡的诗歌都是哀悼性质的。当此生已经没有意义没有价值,死亡就是归途。诗人叶芝的"一个爱尔兰飞行员预见自己的死亡"("An Irish Airman foresees his Death")是来自中立国爱尔兰而正在保卫英国的空军士兵对自己的生命价值和死亡的思考,颇有视死如归的从容和淡定,甚至喜悦。

An Irish Airman foresees his Death
By William Butler Yeats

I know that I shall meet my fate
Somewhere among the clouds above;
Those that I fight I do not hate,
Those that I guard I do not love;
My country is Kiltartan Cross,
My countrymen Kiltartan's poor,
No likely end could bring them loss
Or leave them happier than before.
Nor law, nor duty bade me fight,
Nor public men, nor cheering crowds,

---

① 转引自 https://www.poetryfoundation.org/poems/46565/ozymandias 或 Vendler, pp.524–525。
② 参见 Addonizio & Laux, p.42。

A lonely impulse of delight
Drove to this tumult in the clouds;
I balanced all, brought all to mind,
The years to come seemed waste of breath,
A waste of breath the years behind
In balance with this life, this death.①

第二节　时间、历史、地方、身份

　　时间是诗歌创作的常见题材。诗人莎士比亚在其第 60 号十四行诗("Sonnet 60")中综合运用明喻、隐喻、拟人等手法生动描述了时间的流逝、人生的短暂、诗歌书写的永恒：时间流逝像拍击沙滩的海浪一样不断后浪推前浪；人的生命流逝，就是像太阳的升起、当空和落幕一样的悲剧；时间就像死神的镰刀，收割着人的青春美貌和自然的奇珍异宝；只有诗歌书写才能抵御时间和死神的侵蚀，在后世称颂人的价值②。

Sonnet 60
By William Shakespeare

Like as the waves make towards the pebbled shore,
So do our minutes hasten to their end;
Each changing place with that which goes before,
In sequent toil all forwards do contend.
Nativity, once in the main of light,
Crawls to maturity, wherewith being crowned,
Crooked eclipses' gainst his glory fight,
And Time that gave doth now his gift confound.
Time doth transfix the flourish set on youth
And delves the parallels in beauty's brow,
Feeds on the rarities of nature's truth,

---

① 转引自 https://www.poetryfoundation.org/poems/57311/an-irish-airman-foresees-his-death。
② 参见 Vendler, p.13 & pp.52-53。

And nothing stands but for his scythe to mow:
And yet to times in hope my verse shall stand,
Praising thy worth, despite his cruel hand.①

时间流逝就像死神的镰刀，从不停止其收割生命、抹去人生痕迹的暴行。镰刀是英语诗歌中象征死神的经典意象。然而，人是智慧生物，总会想办法留下自己的生命证据和历史。如果说诗歌写作是古代诗人莎士比亚留下人的生命痕迹，在后世彰显人的存在价值的方式选择，照片则为现代诗人记录生命历史多提供了一种方式选择。诗人桑德拉·希斯内罗丝（Sandra Cisneros）的"我的恶劣行径"（"My Wicked Wicked Ways"）通过描述一张家庭照片回忆过去的时间和父母婚姻、孩子发展的历史：

My Wicked Wicked Ways
By Sandra Cisneros

This is my father.
See? He is young.
He looks like Errol Flynn.
He is wearing a hat
that tips over one eye,
a suit that fits him good,
and baggy pants.
He is also wearing
those awful shoes,
the two-toned ones
my mother hates.
Here is my mother.
She is not crying.
She cannot look into the lens
because the sun is bright.
The woman,
the one my father knows,
is not here.

---

① 转引自 https://www.poetryfoundation.org/poems/45095/sonnet-60-like-as-the-waves-make-towards-the-pebbld-shore。

She does not come till later.

My mother will get very mad.
Her face will turn red
and she will throw one shoe.
My father will say nothing.
After a while everyone
will forget it.
Years and years will pass.
My mother will stop mentioning it.

This is me she is carrying.
I am a baby.
She does not know
I will turn out bad. ①

照片是关于时间和历史题材诗歌很好的载体。写作照片题材的时候,可以表现照片中的人、物、事,也可以涉及照片中没有的人、物、事;可以让照片中的人、物、事动起来,就像视频一样,也可以变换诗歌说话者的身份,等等。写作家庭成员、历史、事件的诗歌,一个可能遇到的难题就是隐私曝光。诗人要学会采用各种方式保护自己及家庭不致过度曝光,比如可以使用第三人称或使用人格面具进行写作,可以隐去或者修改不想曝光的细节,等等。只要采用适当的方式,这种隐私顾忌就不会妨碍诗人的创作。

与时间涉及人的历史和生命过程类似,地方也可能涉及诗人的身份认同。地方,是诗歌创作的重要题材,有时甚至是诗歌创作灵感的来源。诗人理查·雨果就常常通过想象其路过的城镇的人、事、物来进行诗歌创作。他称这样的城镇为灵感启动镇(triggering town)。诗人出生、成长、居住的地方,以及诗人具有强烈意识认同或者感悟的其他地方,都是诗人身份的组成元素。在诗人菲利普·莱文(Philip Levine)的诗中就经常涉及一个地方——底特律(Detroit)。某种程度上,底特律是诗人菲利普·莱文(Philip Levine)自我身份认同的一个元素。

菲利普·莱文的"你可以拥有它"("You Can Have It")中,1948 作为一个失落的年份和底特律作为一个汽车制造中心被单独提出来书写,突出了工业社会中维持和标识个人身份的困境。该诗以书写兄弟开始,到了第四诗节,兄弟与"I"已经合二为

---

① 转引自 Kowit, pp.95 – 96。

一,共同面对工业流水线的机械性非人生活之困。兄弟俩转瞬即逝的二十岁、失落的 1948 年、诗末"give back my young brother"等等似乎都暗示这首诗是一首对蓝领工人兄弟的挽歌。该诗通过对一个家庭成员——兄弟的书写,同时达到身份认同和历史记载的目的。

You Can Have It
By Philip Levine

My brother comes home from work
and climbs the stairs to our room.
I can hear the bed groan and his shoes drop
one by one. You can have it, he says.

The moonlight streams in the window
and his unshaven face is whitened
like the face of the moon. He will sleep
long after noon and waken to find me gone.

Thirty years will pass before I remember
that moment when suddenly I knew each man
has one brother who dies when he sleeps
and sleeps when he rises to face this life,

and that together they are only one man
sharing a heart that always labors, hands
yellowed and cracked, a mouth that gasps
for breath and asks, Am I gonna make it?

All night at the ice plant he had fed
the chute its silvery blocks, and then I
stacked cases of orange soda for the children
of Kentucky, one gray boxcar at a time

with always two more waiting. We were twenty
for such a short time and always in

the wrong clothes, crusted with dirt
and sweat. I think now we were never twenty.

In 1948 in the city of Detroit, founded
by de la Mothe Cadillac for the distant purposes
of Henry Ford, no one wakened or died,
no one walked the streets or stoked a furnace,

for there was no such year, and now
that year has fallen off all the old newspapers,
calendars, doctors' appointments, bonds,
wedding certificates, drivers licenses.

The city slept. The snow turned to ice.
The ice to standing pools or rivers
racing in the gutters. Then bright grass rose
between the thousands of cracked squares,

and that grass died. I give you back 1948.
I give you all the years from then
to the coming one. Give me back the moon
with its frail light falling across a face.

Give me back my young brother, hard
and furious, with wide shoulders and a curse
for God and burning eyes that look upon
all creation and say, You can have it.①

  人的社会身份既有与生俱来继承的成分,也有后天习得养成的成分。诗歌是建构性、想象性的作品,好的诗作在构建身份时,要对社会身份可能的刻板印象进行批判或者重建。如前所述,诗人艾德里安·里奇(Adrienne Rich)的"婆母"("Mother-in-Law")②写的是一对婆媳的对话,探讨了中外家庭关系中最纠结最尴尬的婆媳关系的破

---

① 转引自 https://www.poetryfoundation.org/poems/49118/you-can-have-it。
② 原诗详见 Vendler, pp.212-213。

冰之道:双方相向的好意与不懈的沟通。同时,这首诗还探索了时间流逝与身份变化的关系:年轻的儿媳变成年长丧偶的同性恋;年幼的孩童变成独立的成人;曾经疏远的婆媳关系和未来可能的亲如母女,等等。

注重思考的诗人总会对自己的社会身份有深入思索。有些诗歌对说话者的身份特征进行了非常具体化的塑造,从而使说话者成为一个有独特身份的个体。比如,只有诗人弗兰克·奥哈拉(Frank O'Hara)这个个体才能写出下边的这首诗"女士去世那天"("The Day Lady Died"),因为诗中给出了非常具体的只属于诗人本人的行为细节和社会关系。只有诗人本人在那年那天那个时间在纽约曼哈顿做了那些事情,然后看到著名爵士歌手比莉·哈乐黛(Billie Holiday)的死讯[①]。

The Day Lady Died
By Frank O'Hara

It is 12:20 in New York a Friday
three days after Bastille day, yes
it is 1959 and I go get a shoeshine
because I will get off the 4:19 in Easthampton
at 7:15 and then go straight to dinner
and I don't know the people who will feed me

I walk up the muggy street beginning to sun
and have a hamburger and a malted and buy
an ugly NEW WORLD WRITING to see what the poets
in Ghana are doing these days

         I go on to the bank
and Miss Stillwagon (first name Linda I once heard)
doesn't even look up my balance for once in her life
and in the GOLDEN GRIFFIN I get a little Verlaine
for Patsy with drawings by Bonnard although I do
think of Hesiod, trans. Richmond Lattimore or
Brendan Behan's new play or Le Balcon or Les Nègres
of Genet, but I don't, I stick with Verlaine

---

① 参见 Vendler, pp.222 - 224。

after practically going to sleep with quandariness

and for Mike I just stroll into the PARK LANE
Liquor Store and ask for a bottle of Strega and
then I go back where I came from to 6th Avenue
and the tobacconist in the Ziegfeld Theatre and
casually ask for a carton of Gauloises and a carton
of Picayunes, and a NEW YORK POST with her face on it

and I am sweating a lot by now and thinking of
leaning on the john door in the 5 SPOT
while she whispered a song along the keyboard
to Mal Waldron and everyone and I stopped breathing①

第三节 社会:见证诗(witness poem)

  诗歌既是记录个人历史构建个人身份的方式,也是记录社会事件书写社会历史的方式。诗歌中的多样体裁和不同的说话者视角决定了其记录的社会事件社会历史既有荷马史诗那样波澜壮阔的画卷,也有华兹华斯抒情歌谣中乡间少女边收割边哼曲的孤独画面。诗人对生命生活的热情和真诚决定了诗歌中既有对辉煌史绩的歌颂,也有对黑恶劣行的揭露。

  1655年意大利西北部一支新教徒因为拒绝接受罗马天主教而遭到血腥迫害。英国诗人弥尔顿用一首十四行诗("Sonnet 18")记录了这桩宗教迫害。在诗中,诗人直接对上帝说话,呼吁上帝为遭迫害的信徒报仇,并为信徒忠心护教却遭受迫害的经历做好记录,使其免受后世遗忘。诗中的 triple tyrant 是指被赋予天上、地上、地狱三重权威的罗马教皇;诗末的 Babylon 是指新教徒口中的罗马天主教堂②。诗中多次使用行内停顿和跨行连续调节诗行节奏并突出某些词如"bones、groans、moans"等,强调了宗教迫害的恶劣。

---

① 转引自 https://www.poetryfoundation.org/poems/42657/the-day-lady-died。
② 参见 Vendler, p.16。

Sonnet 18
On the Late Massacre in Piedmont
By Jonh Milton

Avenge, O Lord, thy slaughter'd saints, whose bones
    Lie scatter'd on the Alpine mountains cold,
    Ev'n them who kept thy truth so pure of old,
    When all our fathers worshipp'd stocks and stones;
Forget not: in thy book record their groans
    Who were thy sheep and in their ancient fold
    Slain by the bloody Piemontese that roll'd
    Mother with infant down the rocks. Their moans
The vales redoubl'd to the hills, and they
    To Heav'n. Their martyr'd blood and ashes sow
    O'er all th' Italian fields where still doth sway
The triple tyrant; that from these may grow
    A hundred-fold, who having learnt thy way
Early may fly the Babylonian woe.[①]

诗人叶芝的"复活节1916"("Easter, 1916")为历史保留了爱尔兰1916年4月24日都柏林复活节起义的几位参加者的面貌。叶芝的几位朋友是起义的参加者或者组织者。其中帕特里克·皮尔斯(Patrick Pearse)除了是起义领导人,还是一位诗人,而托马斯·麦克布莱德(Thomas MacBride)则娶了叶芝心中的爱人茅德·冈(Maud Gonne)。起义者在4月29日前被捕或被杀,其领导人在5月被执行死刑[②]。诗中的意象wingèd horse是诗歌灵感的象征,而第一、二、四诗节末尾两行的增量叠句则强调了起义者的英雄主义气概。

Easter, 1916
By William Butler Yeats

I have met them at close of day

---

① 转引自 https://www.poetryfoundation.org/poems/44747/sonnet-18-avenge-o-lord-thy-slaughterd-saints-whose-bones。

② 参见 Vendler, pp.268–270。

Coming with vivid faces
From counter or desk among grey
Eighteenth-century houses.
I have passed with a nod of the head
Or polite meaningless words,
Or have lingered awhile and said
Polite meaningless words,
And thought before I had done
Of a mocking tale or a gibe
To please a companion
Around the fire at the club,
Being certain that they and I
But lived where motley is worn:
All changed, changed utterly:
A terrible beauty is born.

That woman's days were spent
In ignorant good-will,
Her nights in argument
Until her voice grew shrill.
What voice more sweet than hers
When, young and beautiful,
She rode to harriers?
This man had kept a school
And rode our wingèd horse;
This other his helper and friend
Was coming into his force;
He might have won fame in the end,
So sensitive his nature seemed,
So daring and sweet his thought.
This other man I had dreamed
A drunken, vainglorious lout.
He had done most bitter wrong
To some who are near my heart,
Yet I number him in the song;

He, too, has resigned his part
In the casual comedy;
He, too, has been changed in his turn,
Transformed utterly:
A terrible beauty is born.

Hearts with one purpose alone
Through summer and winter seem
Enchanted to a stone
To trouble the living stream.
The horse that comes from the road,
The rider, the birds that range
From cloud to tumbling cloud,
Minute by minute they change;
A shadow of cloud on the stream
Changes minute by minute;
A horse-hoof slides on the brim,
And a horse plashes within it;
The long-legged moor-hens dive,
And hens to moor-cocks call;
Minute by minute they live:
The stone's in the midst of all.

Too long a sacrifice
Can make a stone of the heart.
O when may it suffice?
That is Heaven's part, our part
To murmur name upon name,
As a mother names her child
When sleep at last has come
On limbs that had run wild.
What is it but nightfall?
No, no, not night but death;
Was it needless death after all?
For England may keep faith

For all that is done and said.
We know their dream; enough
To know they dreamed and are dead;
And what if excess of love
Bewildered them till they died?
I write it out in a verse—
MacDonagh and MacBride
And Connolly and Pearse
Now and in time to be,
Wherever green is worn,
Are changed, changed utterly:
A terrible beauty is born.①

关于"复活节 1916"("Easter, 1916")这首诗,一个值得注意的历史背景是事件发生前,英国已经许诺爱尔兰自治②,故诗中有关于牺牲的必要性的思考。社会历史问题,特别是政治或伦理问题,常常是存在争议的,而争议各方的观点或陈述都可能存在宣传成分。然而,如果诗人在呈现这些事件或问题时也陷入简单化单方面的宣传,不真实呈现社会事实,包括其争议、灰色地带,甚至痛苦和灾难,是有悖于诗歌追求的真诚原则的。不能社会喜欢听什么就说什么,而应该什么是真的就说什么。

诗人对于诗歌艺术及诗人身份应保有的原则底线在于"真诚"二字。然而,不同的社会对艺术家保持真诚原则的容忍度不同。在容忍度低的社会,诗人如何做到保持真诚真实原则?人格面具、寓言、讽刺或反讽、幽默甚至黑色幽默等,都是一些可用的工具。诗人乔治·赫伯特(George Herbert)的十四行诗"救赎"("Redemption")使用人格面具通过幽默的寓言手法表现了富贵者需对其剥削行为做出的救赎:

Redemption
By George Herbert

Having been tenant long to a rich lord,
　　Not thriving, I resolvèd to be bold,
　　And make a suit unto him, to afford
A new small-rented lease, and cancel the old.

---

① 转引自 Vendler, pp.268-270。
② 参见 Vendler, pp.268-270。

In heaven at his manor I him sought;
    They told me there that he was lately gone
        About some land, which he had dearly bought
Long since on earth, to take possession.

I straight returned, and knowing his great birth,
    Sought him accordingly in great resorts;
        In cities, theaters, gardens, parks, and courts;
At length I heard a ragged noise and mirth

    Of thieves and murderers; there I him espied,
    Who straight, *Your suit is granted*, said, and died. ①

寓言是写作政治诗的常用工具。本书第二章第一节中诗人特莉丝的散文诗"不速之客"也是一首讽喻政治现实的寓言诗。讽刺同样是政治诗的常用工具，文学家乔纳森·斯威夫特(Jonathan Swift)的"一个温和的建议"("A Modest Proposal")是讽刺作品中的典范。讽刺的极致形式就是黑色幽默。诗人贝托尔特·布莱希特(Bertolt Brecht)也是二十世纪德国剧作家，先后反对希特勒和战后东德统治集团，其"焚书"("The Burning of the Books")使用了讽刺的手法对统治集团的思想钳制和出版审查进行了控诉。

The Burning of the Books
By Bertolt Brecht

When the Regime ordered that books with dangerous teachings
Should be publicly burnt and everywhere
Oxen were forced to draw carts full of books
To the funeral pyre, an exiled poet,
One of the best, discovered with fury, when he studied the list
Of the burned, that his books
Had been forgotten. He rushed to his writing table
On wings of anger and wrote a letter to those in power.

---

① 转引自 https://www.poetryfoundation.org/poems/50694/redemption-56d22df62943a。

Burn me, he wrote with hurrying pen, burn me!
Do not treat me in this fashion. Don't leave me out. Have I not
Always spoken the truth in my books? And now
You treat me like a liar! I order you:
Burn me! ①

古罗马诗人贺拉斯（Horace）有一个鼓励战士为国捐躯的经典句子：Dulce et decorum est pro patria mori，意思是"为国战死心甘情愿，无上光荣"，用英语可以这样说：It's sweet and fitting to die for one's country。然而，一战中毒气弹的使用及其恐怖后果颠覆了对战争的美化。诗人威尔弗雷德·欧文（Wilfred Owen）在1918年死于一战战场。作为在战壕里亲身经历了毒气袭击的见证者，威尔弗雷德·欧文（Wilfred Owen）在其诗"无上荣光"（"Dulce et Decorum Est"）中细细描述了战争的恐怖。诗中基本采用了庄严的英雄四行诗体，也即挽歌诗节：五音步抑扬格，abab韵式。不过"无上荣光"（"Dulce et Decorum Est"）的诗节没有严格按照四行诗形式传统划分，而是按照内容需要划分。第三节只包含了两行，突出了毒气袭击的惨状给诗人带来的后续梦魇和心理后遗症之强烈②。

Dulce et Decorum Est
By Wilfred Owen

Bent double, like old beggars under sacks,
Knock-kneed, coughing like hags, we cursed through sludge,
Till on the haunting flares we turned our backs,
And towards our distant rest began to trudge.
Men marched asleep. Many had lost their boots,
But limped on, blood-shod. All went lame; all blind;
Drunk with fatigue; deaf even to the hoots
Of gas-shells dropping softly behind.

Gas! GAS! Quick, boys! —An ecstasy of fumbling
Fitting the clumsy helmets just in time,
But someone still was yelling out and stumbling

---

① 转引自 Kowit, p.182, H.R. Hays 翻译。
② 参见 Vendler, pp.245-246。

And flound'ring like a man in fire or lime. —
Dim through the misty panes and thick green light,
As under a green sea, I saw him drowning.
In all my dreams before my helpless sight,
He plunges at me, guttering, choking, drowning.

If in some smothering dreams, you too could pace
Behind the wagon that we flung him in,
And watch the white eyes writhing in his face,
His hanging face, like a devil's sick of sin;
If you could hear, at every jolt, the blood
Come gargling from the froth-corrupted lungs,
Obscene as cancer, bitter as the cud
Of vile, incurable sores on innocent tongues, —
My friend, you would not tell with such high zest
To children ardent for some desperate glory,
The old Lie: *Dulce et decorum est*
Pro patria mori. ①

除了前述的人格面具、寓言、讽刺、黑色幽默等可作为写作社会政治诗歌的工具外，现代西方诗坛还出现了另一种客观描述社会事件的诗歌类型：见证诗（witness poem）。见证诗观察现实、命名现实、打破对现实的沉默。它通常不向内观照自我，而是向外考察自我和世界的联系，考察社会和历史。诗人布鲁斯·韦戈（Bruce Weigl）的"汽油弹之歌"（"Song of Napalm"）见证了越战中美国汽油凝固炸弹对越南小女孩的残酷伤害：

Song of Napalm
By Bruce Weigl
for my wife
After the storm, after the rain stopped pounding,
We stood in the doorway watching horses
Walk off lazily across the pasture's hill.
We stared through the black screen,

---

① 转引自 https://www.poetryfoundation.org/poems/46560/dulce-et-decorum-est。

Our vision altered by the distance
So I thought I saw a mist
Kicked up around their hooves when they faded
Like cut-out horses
Away from us.
The grass was never more blue in that light, more
Scarlet; beyond the pasture
Trees scraped their voices into the wind, branches
Crisscrossed the sky like barbed wire
But you said they were only branches.
Okay. The storm stopped pounding.
I am trying to say this straight: for once
I was sane enough to pause and breathe
Outside my wild plans and after the hard rain
I turned my back on the old curses. I believed
They swung finally away from me...

But still the branches are wire
And thunder is the pounding mortar,
Still I close my eyes and see the girl
Running from her village, napalm
Stuck to her dress like jelly,
Her hands reaching for the no one
Who waits in waves of heat before her.

So I can keep on living,
So I can stay here beside you,
I try to imagine she runs down the road and wings
Beat inside her until she rises
Above the stinking jungle and her pain
Eases, and your pain, and mine.

But the lie swings back again.
The lie works only as long as it takes to speak
And the girl runs only as far

As the napalm allows
Until her burning tendons and crackling
Muscles draw her up
into that final position

Burning bodies so perfectly assume. Nothing
Can change that; she is burned behind my eyes
And not your good love and not the rain-swept air
And not the jungle green
Pasture unfolding before us can deny it.①

诗人泰德·库瑟(Ted Kooser)的"罗宾逊堡"("Fort Robinson")通过对捣毁喜鹊巢和杀戮喜鹊幼雏场面的见证描述,侧面影射了美国历史上对印第安土著如夏安族人(Cheyenne)的屠杀事实。不过,这首诗中对杀戮喜鹊鸟的见证不仅仅是对杀戮印第安土著的影射,其本身也具有见证记录价值,即对人类滥杀与灭绝大自然物种的见证。

Fort Robinson
By Ted Kooser

When I visited Fort Robinson,
Where Dull Knife and his Northern Cheyenne
were held captive that terrible winter,
the grounds crew was killing the magpies.

Two men were going from tree to tree
with sticks and ladders, poking the young birds
down from their nests and beating them to death
as they hopped about in the grass.

Under each tree where the men had worked
were twisted clots of matted feathers,
and above each tree a magpie circled,

---

① 转引自 https://www.poetryfoundation.org/poems/42752/song-of-napalm。

crazily calling in all her voices.

We didn't get out of the car.
My little boy hid in the back and cried
as we drove away, into those ragged buttes
the Cheyenne climbed that winter, fleeing.①

诗歌使用语言精确描绘人的经历和观察,讲述真话,这既是诗歌的力量也是诗歌对世界的影响力所在。对艰难事实的真诚呈现有时会置诗人本人于危险境地。诗歌是想象性文学体裁,真诚原则不是要求诗人对某一事件的具体细节或者全过程做事实性记录,而是要求诗人对基本社会事实有一个真诚真实的情感认知与价值判断。诗歌是允许对社会事件的具体细节进行想象性加工的,这是由诗歌的文学体裁性质所决定的。

写作见证诗要注意客观性和具体性,要防止落入概括笼统的陷阱,不能陷入空洞的宣教。写作见证诗时,特别是描述人间苦痛的见证诗时,有效打动读者的方法是具体描述一两个个体,把感情和观点揉进具体的故事和人物,使用一种谨慎的客观方式,抓住细节,少用明显的评论②。诗人罗伯特·平斯基(Robert Pinsky)的"衬衫"("Shirt")见证了制衣厂火灾的惨烈以及工人试图互助逃生的场景,其中男工人将一个个女工托出九楼厂房的窗口,然后该女工掉下摔死以及最后男工人自己从窗口跳下时衣裤逆风膨胀等细节描写真实再现了危境中人的无可选择和孤注一掷。

Shirt
By Robert Pinsky

The back, the yoke, the yardage. Lapped seams,
The nearly invisible stitches along the collar
Turned in a sweatshop by Koreans or Malaysians

Gossiping over tea and noodles on their break
Or talking money or politics while one fitted
This armpiece with its overseam to the band

---

① 转引自 Kowit, p.184。
② 参见 Kowit, pp.182-187。

Of cuff I button at my wrist. The presser, the cutter,
The wringer, the mangle. The needle, the union,
The treadle, the bobbin. The code. The infamous blaze

At the Triangle Factory in nineteen-eleven.
One hundred and forty-six died in the flames
On the ninth floor, no hydrants, no fire escapes—

The witness in a building across the street
Who watched how a young man helped a girl to step
Up to the windowsill, then held her out

Away from the masonry wall and let her drop.
And then another. As if he were helping them up
To enter a streetcar, and not eternity.

A third before he dropped her put her arms
Around his neck and kissed him. Then he held
Her into space, and dropped her. Almost at once

He stepped to the sill himself, his jacket flared
And fluttered up from his shirt as he came down,
Air filling up the legs of his gray trousers—

Like Hart Crane's Bedlamite, "shrill shirt ballooning."
Wonderful how the pattern matches perfectly
Across the placket and over the twin bar-tacked

Corners of both pockets, like a strict rhyme
Or a major chord. Prints, plaids, checks,
Houndstooth, Tattersall, Madras. The clan tartans

Invented by mill-owners inspired by the hoax of Ossian,
To control their savage Scottish workers, tamed
By a fabricated heraldry: MacGregor,

Bailey, MacMartin. The kilt, devised for workers
To wear among the dusty clattering looms.
Weavers, carders, spinners. The loader,

The docker, the navvy. The planter, the picker, the sorter
Sweating at her machine in a litter of cotton
As slaves in calico headrags sweated in fields:

George Herbert, your descendant is a Black
Lady in South Carolina, her name is Irma
And she inspected my shirt. Its color and fit

And feel and its clean smell have satisfied
Both her and me. We have culled its cost and quality
Down to the buttons of simulated bone,

The buttonholes, the sizing, the facing, the characters
Printed in black on neckband and tail. The shape,
The label, the labor, the color, the shade. The shirt.①

见证诗的叙事视角可以多样化。诗人写作见证诗，可以从自己的真实经历或者记忆出发来写，也可以使用人格面具通过代入式想象来写。比如，以居住在中国的中国人视角描述评论美国人的生活，或者以居住在美国的美国人视角描述评论中国人的生活，这是写作见证诗的一个有趣视角。再比如，在描述某一著名历史事件发生的同时描述某个具体个人可能正在做的事，将社会大事和个体事件并列穿插起来写，也是写作见证诗的一个有趣角度。

第四节 自 然

在诗人罗伯特·洛威尔的"臭鼬时光"("Skunk Hour")中，诗人个人身份的多重性

---

① 转引自 https://www.poetryfoundation.org/poems/47696/shirt。

在诗中化身为多个角色。根据对该诗原诗稿的有关研究,富有的女隐士、主教、百万富翁、装修商等等角色其实都与诗中说话者一样,是诗人个人身份的一个方面①。"臭鼬时光"既涉及诗中说话者的个体生活,也涉及女隐士、主教、百万富翁、装修商、小镇其他居民等的群体生活,还涉及自然。个体和群体人的文明没落并且最后被自然的活力所代替。

Skunk Hour
By Robert Lowell
For Elizabeth Bishop
Nautilus Island's hermit
heiress still lives through winter in her Spartan cottage;
her sheep still graze above the sea.
Her son's a bishop. Her farmer
is first selectman in our village;
she's in her dotage.

Thirsting for
the hierarchic privacy
of Queen Victoria's century,
she buys up all
the eyesores facing her shore,
and lets them fall.

The season's ill—
we've lost our summer millionaire,
who seemed to leap from an L. L. Bean
catalogue. His nine-knot yawl
was auctioned off to lobstermen.
A red fox stain covers Blue Hill.

And now our fairy
decorator brightens his shop for fall;
his fishnet's filled with orange cork,

---

① 参见 Vendler, p.46。

orange, his cobbler's bench and awl;
there is no money in his work,
he'd rather marry.

One dark night,
my Tudor Ford climbed the hill's skull;
I watched for love-cars. Lights turned down,
they lay together, hull to hull,
where the graveyard shelves on the town...
My mind's not right.

A car radio bleats,
"Love, O careless Love..." I hear
my ill-spirit sob in each blood cell,
as if my hand were at its throat...
I myself am hell;
nobody's here—

only skunks, that search
in the moonlight for a bite to eat.
They march on their soles up Main Street:
white stripes, moonstruck eyes' red fire
under the chalk-dry and spar spire
of the Trinitarian Church.

I stand on top
of our back steps and breathe the rich air—
a mother skunk with her column of kittens swills the garbage pail.
She jabs her wedge-head in a cup
of sour cream, drops her ostrich tail,
and will not scare.①

"臭鼬时光"是模仿诗人伊丽莎白·毕晓普（Elizabeth Bishop）的"犰狳"（"The

---

① 转引自 https://www.poetryfoundation.org/poems/47694/skunk-hour。

Armadillo")写的,这是诗题中出现"*For Elizabeth Bishop*"的原因①。"臭鼬时光"的诗中说话者乐见自然占了上风。事实上,人的一切都是有限的、不自由的,只有自然是无限的、自由的。诗人叶芝的"库尔的野天鹅"("The Wild Swans at Coole")就表现了这样的事实。"库尔的野天鹅"包含五个六行诗节,每个诗节采用二、四行押韵,五、六行押韵的韵式。数字的使用在这首诗中有特殊的意义。59只野天鹅19年来定期来到库尔湖(Coole)游弋。野天鹅自由来往,彼此忠诚,又规律迁徙,这是令人羡慕的自然生态。而十九年间,人的时间生命已经流逝,世事也多有变幻。当某一天诗中说话者再次醒来时,自由的、永恒的自然之道和自然之美可能就在它处愉悦他人。

The Wild Swans at Coole
By William Butler Yeats

The trees are in their autumn beauty,
The woodland paths are dry,
Under the October twilight the water
Mirrors a still sky;
Upon the brimming water among the stones
Are nine-and-fifty swans.

The nineteenth autumn has come upon me
Since I first made my count;
I saw, before I had well finished,
All suddenly mount
And scatter wheeling in great broken rings
Upon their clamorous wings.

I have looked upon those brilliant creatures,
And now my heart is sore.
All's changed since I, hearing at twilight,
The first time on this shore,
The bell-beat of their wings above my head,
Trod with a lighter tread.

---

① 参见 Vendler, p.46。

Unwearied still, lover by lover,
They paddle in the cold
Companionable streams or climb the air;
Their hearts have not grown old;
Passion or conquest, wander where they will,
Attend upon them still.

But now they drift on the still water,
Mysterious, beautiful;
Among what rushes will they build,
By what lake's edge or pool
Delight men's eyes when I awake some day
To find they have flown away?①

  自然不仅能够通过当下的存在给人带来快乐,还能够通过回忆给人带来穿越时空的愉悦。诗人威廉·华兹华斯著名的"我孤独地漫游像朵云"("I Wandered Lonely as a Cloud")就描写了大自然给人带来的即时的和长久的愉悦。这首诗的前三个诗节描写说话者在漫游中偶遇波光粼粼的湖边连绵不断、随风舞蹈的黄色水仙花时深受吸引、满心喜悦。最后一个诗节描写偶遇过后很久,黄色水仙花随风舞蹈的喜乐画面仍不时给独处中或者忧思中的说话者带来内心的欢愉。

I Wandered Lonely as a Cloud
By William Wordsworth

I wandered lonely as a cloud
That floats on high o'er vales and hills,
When all at once I saw a crowd,
A host, of golden daffodils;
Beside the lake, beneath the trees,
Fluttering and dancing in the breeze.

Continuous as the stars that shine
And twinkle on the milky way,

---

① 转引自 https://www.poetryfoundation.org/poems/43288/the-wild-swans-at-coole。

They stretched in never-ending line
Along the margin of a bay:
Ten thousand saw I at a glance,
Tossing their heads in sprightly dance.

The waves beside them danced; but they
Out-did the sparkling waves in glee:
A poet could not but be gay,
In such a jocund company:
I gazed—and gazed—but little thought
What wealth the show to me had brought:

For oft, when on my couch I lie
In vacant or in pensive mood,
They flash upon that inward eye
Which is the bliss of solitude;
And then my heart with pleasure fills,
And dances with the daffodils. ①

"我孤独地漫游像朵云"("I Wandered Lonely as a Cloud")包含四个整齐的六行诗节,每个诗节由一个交叉韵的四行诗和一个双行诗组成,韵式为 ababcc。这是一种常见的英语律诗韵式,因为诗人莎士比亚在其叙事诗"维纳斯与阿东尼斯"("Venus and Adonis")中的使用而被称为维纳斯与安东尼斯诗节(Venus and Adonis stanza)②。在前述涉及自然的诗歌中,时间和地方是经常出现的元素,"臭鼬时光"和"库尔的野天鹅"甚至直接以时间或地方命题。包含时间或地方元素的诗歌,既可能涉及人的生命、历史和身份认同,也可能涉及包括晨昏四季在内的自然时间和地方的自然环境。

在诗人约翰·济慈的莎士比亚体十四行诗"人生四季"("The Human Seasons")中,一年四季的运转与变化成为人生命过程中的不同思维和情绪反应的隐喻。这首诗的前三个四行诗分别是春季、夏季、秋季,最后一个双行诗是冬季。这首诗将四季与人的思维进行关联,而不是与人的肉体关联,这给读者提供了一个意外。除了四季之外,诗中还使用了其它诸多与自然相关的词汇,比如动词:chew、folded up;名词:cud、tired

---

① 转引自 https://www.poetryfoundation.org/poems/45521/i-wandered-lonely-as-a-cloud。
② 参见 Vendler, p.73。

wings、ports、havens、brook，等等。

The Human Seasons
By John Keats

Four seasons fill the measure of the year;
　　Four seasons are there in the mind of man.
He hath his lusty spring, when fancy clear
　　Takes in all beauty with an easy span:
He hath his summer, when luxuriously
　　He chews the honied cud of fair spring thoughts,
Till, in his soul dissolv'd, they come to be
　　Part of himself. He hath his autumn ports
And havens of repose, when his tired wings
　　Are folded up, and he content to look
On mists in idleness: to let fair things
　　Pass by unheeded as a threshold brook.
He hath his winter too of pale misfeature,
Or else he would forget his mortal nature.①

时间和地方是涉及自然题材诗歌中经常出现的元素，自然界中的动植物比如前述诗歌中的臭鼬、天鹅和黄色水仙花等等更是自然题材诗歌中的主要元素或者意象。诗人艾米莉·狄金森的"细长的家伙"（"A narrow Fellow in the Grass"）中的主要自然意象是草地上的一条蛇。诗中对蛇的指称前后有变化，当说话者能够明确蛇的身份时，使用拟人化的 He 或者 Him 对蛇进行指称，对其表现了平等化的尊重；而当说话者不能明确蛇的身份时，则采用了自然化的 it 对蛇进行指称。诗中的呼语 you 的所指也有变化，在第三行，它指的可能是读者，也可能是某个假定的听众；但在第二诗节的第三行，your 则更可能是指与蛇遭遇的说话者本人。

　　A narrow Fellow in the Grass
　　Occasionally rides—
　　You may have met Him-Did you not
　　His notice instant is—

---

① 转引自 Vendler, pp.12-13。

The Grass divides as with a Comb,
A spotted Shaft is seen,
And then it closes at your Feet
And opens further on—

He likes a Boggy Acre—
A Floor too cool for Corn—
But when a Boy and Barefoot
I more than once at Noon

Have passed I thought a Whip Lash
Unbraiding in the Sun
When stooping to secure it
It wrinkled, and was gone—

Several of Nature's People
I know, and they know me—
I feel for them a transport
Of Cordiality—

But never met this Fellow
Attended, or alone
Without a tighter Breathing
And Zero at the Bone- ①

——By Emily Dickinson

在艾米莉·狄金森上边这首诗中，说话者以一个男孩的形象出现。这是一个明显的人格面具，体现了面对大蛇时说话者虽心中紧张但仍保持沉着与勇敢的坚强品质。当然也可能是因为在艾米莉·狄金森的时代，家教良好的女孩子不被允许赤脚在田野里出没，因此诗中使用男孩作为人格面具。不过，不是所有的诗人都需要在大自然的环境中才能创作关于自然的诗。诗人威廉·卡洛斯·威廉斯的"完美"("Perfection")写的是住房门廊上放了一月丝毫未动的一个正在老去腐朽的苹果：

---

① 转引自 https://www.poetryfoundation.org/poems/49909/a-narrow-fellow-in-the-grass-1096。

Perfection
By William Carlos Williams

        O lovely apple!
beautifully and completely
               rotten,
hardly a contour marred—

        perhaps a little
shrivelled at the top but that
        aside perfect
in every detail! O lovely

        apple! what a
deep and suffusing brown
        mantles that
unspoiled surface! No one

        has moved you
since I placed you on the porch
        rail a month ago
to ripen.
        No one. No one! [①]

  要写好自然题材的诗，首先就要热爱自然，平等对待自然中的一切事物，要能敏锐感受自然事物的形态性质，特别是色、形、味、声等等。其次，可以适当做一些沉浸于自然的观察冥思练习，即完全沉浸在大自然事物的色、形、味、声中，不做其他思维活动。比如，可以找一天在太阳出来之前起床，去离得最近的一块开阔的绿地或者树林，仔细观察晨光出来的过程对自然万物的影响。可以观察动物、树木、花儿等等对晨光及其变化过程的各种反应。观察晨光变化对水的作用，或者光影在一面墙、一块石头的表面的作用，等等。认真观察，客观记录，然后用观察结果写一首诗[②]。
  据说沉浸自然的冥思到了极致，人就会出现一种超越世间烦事俗念的感觉，能够在

[①] 转引自 Kowit, p.240。
[②] 参见 Morley, p.137。

平凡中发现神性,写出欣赏平凡超越平凡的诗歌。日本俳句就是这样一种关于自然以及人与自然关系的诗。当然,可以使用任何合适的诗歌形式来写作自然题材的诗歌。一首诗的形式与题材能否完美结合决定了其能否给读者留下深刻印象。诗人伊娃·梅里亚姆(Eve Merriam)的"来自日本"("From the Japanese")在题材上涉及了类似日本俳句的自然意象,在形式上使用了俳句中一般不用的隐喻手法,把夏夜这个时间出其不意地具象化、空间化。

From the Japanese
By Eve Merriam

The summer night
is a dark blue hammock
slung between the white pillars of day.

I lie there
cooling myself
with the straw-colored
flat round fan
of the full moon.①

关于某一诗歌题材或者母题,历史上的诗人已经写尽了各种诗篇,甚至将绝大部分诗歌语言的可能性发挥到了极致。比如关于希腊神话中主神宙斯化身天鹅强暴女孩丽达(Leda)而后生下美人海伦(Helen)这一神话事件,诗人叶芝、赖内·马丽亚·里尔克(Rainer Maria Rilke)和希尔达·杜丽特(Hilda Doolittle,即 H.D.)写出来的诗歌就完全不同②。那么写作同一题材时,后来的诗人如何才能超越前人?这对后来的诗人是一个历史重负。诗人歌德(J. W. Goethe)对诗人莎士比亚推崇备至,但他也说过,如果他出生为英国人,在他还是诗歌学徒时就面临莎士比亚经典名作的威压,那么他就很可能被压垮而不知所措③。

为了解决同一题材的经典诗歌作品带来的历史重压,后来的诗人努力提出自己的

---

① 转引自 Livingston, p.92。
② 参见 Dobyns, chap.6。
③ 转引自 Dobyns 书中第二章:"Had I been born an Englishman and had those manifold masterworks pressed in upon me with all their power from my first youthful awakening, it would have overwhelmed me, and I would not have known what I wanted to do!"详见 Walter Jackson Bate, *The Burden of the Past and the English Poet*, Cambridge, MA: Belknap Press, 1970, p. 5.

新观点新理念来进行诗歌创新。除此之外,他们也会通过找经典诗歌的茬来获得自己的发展空间。找茬的方式其实是在批判中逃避甚至藐视。但是,创新的勇气和动力不能用对经典的无知、无视甚至怨恨来换取。一些诗人或学者都表达了这样的一种担忧:当经典的茬已经找完,又没有新模式出现的时候,不断寻求与前不同的动力可能会使诗歌最终走向反诗歌形式①。

---

① 参见 Dobyns, chap.2。

第六章
英语诗歌意义建构中的权衡取舍

诗歌是一种特殊的文学体裁,其意义建构离不开诗歌的内容或者题材,更离不开诗歌特殊的写作方式或者形式。诗人格勒律治说的"诗歌是以最佳的顺序说出来的最好的话"中的"最佳的顺序"主要指的就是包括语言声音组织顺序在内的诗歌形式。诗歌通过系列的形式工具比如格律、押韵、修辞、意象、断行等实现了对普通语言的组织化偏离。诗歌这种对普通语言的组织化偏离增强了语言的力量,使诗歌成为"最好的话"。诗歌的意义是由诗歌的形式帮助构建的,诗歌的形式是诗歌的意义建构不可分割的一部分。没有形式就没有诗歌。

第一节 诗歌的意义建构在于题材更在于形式

诗歌的意义建构离不开其内容或题材。诗歌的意义建构首先在内容上就是源于感动诗人,引起诗人持续关注的题材。如本书第五章所述,诗歌题材既可以是充满时代感的话题也可以是人类永恒的母题。诗人生命中的所见、所听、所想、所做、所爱、所望、所知和未知的一切都可以变成诗歌。记忆、阅读、观察、思考、想象等都是诗歌题材的来源。生活、工作、学习、友谊、爱情等或个人或群体的社会经历经验,或者关于死亡等未知世界的想象,甚至包括诗歌和语言等题材,都可以入诗。诗歌题材对诗歌意义建构的必要性是显而易见的。

诗歌既是记录个人历史构建个人身份的方式,也是记录社会事件书写社会历史的方式。诗歌使用语言精确描绘人的经历和观察,讲述真话,构建诗歌意义,这既是诗歌的力量也是诗歌对世界的影响力所在。但是,诗歌是想象性文学体裁,讲述真话并不是要求诗人对某一事件的具体细节或者全过程做事实性记录,而是要求诗人对基本社会事实有一个真诚真实的情感认知与价值判断。然而,不同的社会对艺术家保持真诚原则的容忍度不同。在容忍度低的社会,诗人如何做到保持真诚真实原则?人格面具、寓言、讽刺、黑色幽默等是一些可用的形式工具。

诗歌的意义建构离不开必要的形式工具。本书第一章、第二章探讨了诸多的诗歌形式工具和技巧。诗歌形式工具和技巧的一个功能就是制造微妙诗意。对诗行中的节奏、格律、旋律对比、尾韵、和音、谐音、头韵、断行等形式工具和技巧的操作，都可以制造微妙诗意。比如，断行是诗歌（除散文诗和一些视觉诗外）与散文在形式上最明显的视觉区别。除了视觉和听觉效果之外，断行在语义与诗歌结构上的微妙诗意制造功能使其成为诗歌意义建构的有效工具。

再比如，传统英语律诗的不同格律可以表达不同的节奏、情绪、感情和语气，从而影响诗歌的意义建构。有规律的节奏能够带来安宁和美感，但不断重复、毫无变化的节奏则会带来疲劳和厌倦。规律的节奏如果出现了变化或者受到干扰会引起人们特别的注意。在格律整体统一的某些诗行的某些位置使用格律音步变异，或者使用行内停顿，或者使用跨行连续，都是改变诗歌格律节奏整齐划一的有用工具。成熟的诗人在建立起基本规整的格律之后，会适时进行音步替换或者音步变异，打破单调重复的节奏，取得令人惊喜的表现效果，构建理想的诗歌意义。

另外，在传统英语格律诗里边，句子的自然句法节奏与诗行的格律节奏之间的旋律对比既对诗歌声音有影响，也对诗歌的意义建构有影响。一个句子作为自然句时的句法节奏与其作为诗行时的格律节奏可能重合也可能有差异。如果有差异，即出现了旋律对比。同理，诗歌的韵音现象对诗歌的意义建构作用显而易见。行中韵与行尾韵等诗歌韵音现象是一种声音的重复和回声。这种声音形式上的重复具有意义上的回归、呼应功能以及闭合、总结、结束的作用。与诗行的格律音步变异一样，规整押韵之外的变异对诗歌的意义建构作用也很明显。

同样，音节的四因素即重音、音长、音高与音色也会影响诗歌的意义构建。诗行重读音节的多寡决定了诗行朗读的淤塞或顺畅，诗行音节的音长与音高有心理暗示作用，而单音节词语多音节词表现出来的语言力量是不同的，所有这些因素都会影响诗歌的意义构建。对于没有格律帮助建构意义的自由诗而言，诗人更应该注意用词的音节四因素对意义建构的影响，以免引起过分误读，使读者读诗得到的意义与诗人本意背离太远。

诗歌的意义建构成功与否在某种程度上取决于题材与形式的结合是否成功。对诗歌形式工具的操作运用是否得当，是否制造了与诗歌题材相适应的微妙诗意，很大程度上决定了诗歌意义建构的成功与否。诗人梯奇波恩（Chidiock Tichborne）为自己写的下边这首"梯奇波恩挽歌"（Tichborne's Elegy）的题材与形式就不是很适配，故其意义建构的效果就令人存疑。这首诗的内容与诗行的声音节奏并不和谐：内容读起来比较悲戚，但是诗行节奏却显得有点轻佻，甚至有戏谑的感觉，尤其是各诗节最后的叠句。需要注意的是，这首诗使用的是维纳斯与安东尼斯诗节的韵式（ababcc），而不是挽歌诗节的韵式（abab）。

Tichborne's Elegy
By Chidiock Tichborne

Written with his own hand in the Tower before his execution

My prime of youth is but a frost of cares,
My feast of joy is but a dish of pain,
My crop of corn is but a field of tares,
And all my good is but vain hope of gain.
The day is gone and yet I saw no sun,
And now I live, and now my life is done.

The spring is past, and yet it hath not sprung,
The fruit is dead, and yet the leaves are green,
My youth is gone, and yet I am but young,
I saw the world, and yet I was not seen,
My thread is cut, and yet it was not spun,
And now I live, and now my life is done.

I sought my death and found it in my womb,
I looked for life and saw it was a shade,
I trod the earth and knew it was my tomb,
And now I die, and now I am but made.
The glass is full, and now the glass is run,
And now I live, and now my life is done.①

  诸多的或传统或现当代的英语诗歌形式分别强调使用不同的形式工具，而这决定了这些诗歌形式的意义建构各具特点，且各有不同效果。比如，"潘图"诗是突出重复技巧的一种诗歌形式。"潘图"诗中的重复具有意义强调和声音回环等特点，而其重复规则又允许作品内容根据需要不断推进发展。十四行诗是形式与内容紧密结合、形式改变引起内容改变的典型诗歌形式。不管是彼得拉克体，还是莎士比亚体，还是斯宾塞体，其诗歌内容都常常随着诗中韵式的重大变化而发生明显不同的改变，甚至是转折。一般来说，彼得拉克体韵式中的前八行诗和后六行诗之间在内容上有一个转折。莎士比亚体韵式的前三个四行诗在内容上常有递进或者顺承关系。莎士比亚体和斯宾塞体韵式中的前十二行和后面的双行诗在内容上也都有一个铺排与总结的关系。

---

① 转引自 https://www.poetryfoundation.org/poems/47443/my-prime-of-youth-is-but-a-frost-of-cares。

第二节 声音与事实的取舍:服从声音要求

诗歌是创造语言新用法的文学体裁。诗歌通过节奏、格律、旋律对比、押韵、和音、谐音、头韵、断行等等声音形式工具实现对普通语言的组织化偏离,构建诗歌意义。诗人格勒律治说的"诗歌是以最佳的顺序说出来的最好的话"中的"最佳顺序"当然包括了诗歌声音和声音重复的组织顺序。诗歌使用多种声音重复工具如格律、韵音、首语重复、叠句、排比等来制造不同的声音效果甚至音乐美感。诗人阿尔弗雷德·丁尼生(Alfred, Lord Tennyson)、埃德加·爱伦·坡(Edgar Allan Poe)、叶芝、奥登、斯坦利·库尼茨(Stanley Kunitz)、西奥多·罗特克(Theodore Roethke)、露易丝·博根(Louise Bogan)等的作品很多都充满音乐美感。

拟声法(onomatopoeia)也是英语诗歌制造声音效果的一种工具。英语单词如bam、bang、buzz、clunk、crackle、crunch、ding-dong、hiss、moan、murmur、roar、scratch、thwack、tick-tock、whisper、zoom等都有拟声作用[①]。但是这种本身具有拟声作用的英语单词很少,所以英语诗歌中的拟声主要通过使用头韵、和音、谐音、格律节奏甚至押韵来实现。诗人阿尔弗雷德·丁尼生在其"下来,噢,妞"("Come Down, O Maid")一诗中就使用了拟声法来表现众多蜜蜂发出的隐隐的嗡嗡声:And murmuring of innumerable bees[②]。诗人沃尔特·德·拉·梅尔(Walter de la Mare)在其诗"蜜蜂之歌"("The Bees' Song")中的多个诗行则用了字母 z 来模拟蜜蜂嗡嗡叫的声音:

> Thousandz of thornz there be
> On the Rozez where gozez
> The Zebra of Zee...
> Heavy with blossomz be
> The Rozez that growzez
> In the thickets of Zee.
> Where grazez the Zebra...
> And he nozez the poziez

---

① 参见 Brooks & Warren, p.534。
② 转引自 Livingston, pp.62-63。

Of the Rozez that growzez...①

　　元音对诗行的声音乐感影响明显。在音乐性明显的诗行中，不仅元音读起来流动和谐，音节与音节之间、词与词之间的声音过渡（主要是辅音过渡）效果也是自然流畅的，没有被迫的停顿或者阻塞。本书第一章第一节讨论的诗人阿尔弗雷德·丁尼生的"食莲人"（"The Lotus-Eaters"）中的两行诗和托马斯·哈代（Thomas Hardy）的"灰色调"（"Neutral Tones"）中的两行诗读起来声音效果完全不同。丁尼生的诗行读起来和谐流畅，音乐性强烈。哈代的诗行读起来淤塞不畅，没有悦耳的乐感。然而，不管是丁尼生诗行的乐感强烈还是哈代诗行的气郁不畅，两种声音效果都完美契合其所在整首诗作的意义建构。丁尼生的两行诗表现了其所在合唱（Choric Song）部分的乐感要求，而哈代的两行诗则表现了回忆中爱情的幻灭感。

　　诗歌语言的声音与意思是同等重要的两个元素。对于一些诗人来说，诗歌声音不仅仅是构建意义的形式工具，其本身具有的音乐美感也使其成为诗歌的内在价值之一。诗歌的声音也是诗歌的意义。对于一些创作中的诗人来说，诗歌语言的声音有时比诗歌语言的内容更为重要。比如，诗人埃德加·爱伦·坡（Edgar Allan Poe）的诗歌非常强调音乐性②，而诗人艾略特声称自己写作的时候有意识考虑的是那些"准音乐性质"的东西，比如格律、模式的设计安排等，而不是什么"思想"的说明表达③。

　　诗人理查·雨果也非常重视诗歌语言的声音，特别是声音的音乐美感。他主张当诗歌语言的事实元素与诗歌语言的声音元素相冲突的时候，应该优先服从声音的要求④。开始动笔写诗之际，诗人可能存在两种原则选择：声音决定事实还是事实决定声音。按照理查·雨果的看法，只有像威斯坦·休·奥登那样机智聪明的诗人才能在让事实决定声音的同时还能写出好诗。让声音决定事实的原则则能使一般诗人，特别是对生活（即事实）的意义感到困惑的诗人，还能够根据自己对声音的沉迷而不断创作。这就像小说家佛斯特作品中的一个女人所说："只有说出来的时候我才知道我在想什么"⑤。有时候声音确实决定了事实。

　　按照理查·雨果的看法，诗人从一个起始题材动笔写作，如果始终绕不开起始题材则可能思绪枯竭。解决这个问题的有效方法就是听从内心直觉与声音的引导，不惜绕开起始题材继续写下去。最好是在起始题材的相关材料枯竭之前就先绕开它写下去。不要担心离题万里，因为在想象的世界里，什么都不会离题。诗人的写作方式本身具有连贯统一作用，如此写下去最后一定能够到达诗歌要探索的真正题材或

---

① 转引自 Livingston，pp.62-63。
② 参见 Brooks & Warren，pp.544-546。
③ 参见 Brooks & Warren，p.475。
④ 参见 Hugo，chap.1。
⑤ 同上。

主题。在此过程,诗人应该暂时忘却读者①。

按照理查·雨果的看法,诗人对起始题材相关的事实材料知道得越多,反而可能对想象力和诗歌创作产生限制。这会对诗人听从声音直觉写诗产生一定的阻碍作用。对起始题材相关的事实材料的无知反而能更好发挥诗人的自由想象。创作中,诗人应该服从语言,服从声音,而不是起始题材的事实因素。在创作过程中,诗人应该遵守的规则是:语言(声音)不为起始题材(事实)服务,起始题材(事实)应该为语言(声音)服务;诗人不需为事实负责,只需为自己的真实情感负责②。

从起始题材开始,然后听从声音(特别是乐感)直觉的引导有意识甩开起始题材走向生成主题或真正题材的过程,其实就是理查·雨果说的"从小事想起,思维自己会扩展"③的具体化。这既是一个由语言声音通向语言意思、由诗歌形式通向诗歌题材的过程,也是诗人进行积极想象探索、发现、创造自我的过程。诗人的写作方式本身具有的连贯统一作用,能够使这个过程不致信马由缰。不过,诗人也可以通过设置某些稳定元素,使想象既可以自由高飞又不致于脱缰,比如特定时间、特定地点、特定读者,等等。这些元素可以帮助诗人选择诗歌中要呈现的事件细节④。诗歌用来呈现情感的事件细节可以是真实的,也可以是想象的,甚至可以是一个抽象概念。比如诗人叶芝的"丽达与天鹅"("Leda and the Swan")就使用了想象的事件,即宙斯强暴丽达生了海伦、上帝使圣母怀孕生了耶稣等,来呈现诗人对暴力和性能力的情感反应⑤。诗歌中的事件只是呈现情感的工具。

第三节 诗节(stanza)与标题(title):题材与形式的点睛结合

诗节(stanza /strophe)是诗歌的一个段落,与一首诗的其它段落(如果有的话)隔行断开⑥。有时一首诗只有一个诗节,这样的诗可叫单节诗。英语律诗一定的韵式可以形成诗节。英语律诗的诗节按照其诗行数量各有名称:双行诗、三行诗、四行诗、五行诗、六行诗、七行诗、八行诗、九行诗、十行诗(如济慈的"夜莺颂")……。长诗节经常是由双行诗、三行诗和四行诗的各种变体构成,因此,这三种诗节也成为传统英语律诗的

---

① 参见 Hugo, chap.1。
② 参见 Hugo, chap.1。
③ "Think small, the mind will expand",详见 Hugo, chap. 1。
④ 参见 Hugo, chap.2。
⑤ 参见 Dobyns, chap. 6。
⑥ 参见 Vendler, p.599。

"基础原件"。

在传统英语诗歌中,诗歌分节一般以一定的韵式为基础。因为英语诗歌开始于口头吟唱传统,所以韵式比较简单的歌谣和赞美诗较早成为重要的诗节形式。当诗歌从口头传唱转为主要是书写形式时,复杂的韵式诗节才发展起来①。长诗节的韵式灵活多变,诗人可以视需要选择合适的韵式组合。诗人通常不会在写作之前决定采用哪种韵式,对韵式的选择常常是在写作过程中基于写作内容做出选择,通过不断试验而确定的②。在现当代英语自由诗中,诗歌的分节则主要依靠诗人对形式结构和内容表达的判断③。

诗歌的分节是诗歌题材与形式最显眼的结合之一,每首诗的分节都应该契合诗歌的意义建构。页面上不同形状的诗节会产生不同的视觉效果与意义表达。没有中断的单一长诗节给人一种滔滔不绝、连绵不断的感觉;等长诗节能够制造一种整齐的秩序感;不等长诗节则会体现一种有机的自然发展。单诗节、等长诗节、不等长诗节,诗节中长诗行、短诗行、长短诗行混合等,都应该经得住推敲④。与诗行一样,诗节可以是常见的停顿分节(end-stopped),也可以是跨节连续(enjambed)。诗人玛丽安·穆尔的"致蒸汽压路机"("To a Steam Roller")的第二诗节的最后一行就是跨节连续。当然除此之外,这首诗的行首词位置也颇具特点⑤:

To a Steam Roller
By Marianne Moore

The illustration
is nothing to you without the application.
  You lack half wit. You crush all the particles down
   into close conformity, and then walk back and forth on them,

Sparkling chips of rock
are crushed down to the level of the parent block.
  Were not "impersonal judgment in aesthetic
   matters, a metaphysical impossibility," you

---

① 参见 Vendler, p.599。
② 参见 Livingston, pp.35 - 48。
③ 参见 Vendler, p.202。
④ 参见 Dobyns, chap.9。
⑤ 参见 Vendler, p.202。

        might fairly achieve
it. As for butterflies, I can hardly conceive
    of one's attending upon you, but to question
        the congruence of the complement is vain, if it exists.[①]

  诗歌的标题就像戴在诗歌头上的王冠,是一首诗的门或者窗,是读者对一首诗的第一印象[②]。如果一首诗以"诗(Poem/Poetry)"命名,那么诗中所述内容一定与诗或者作诗有关。诗人威廉·卡洛斯·威廉斯下边的这首"诗"("Poem")描写了一只试图爬过橱柜找到一个平稳落脚地的猫咪的冒险过程。全诗没有构成一个完整的句子,没有一个标点,几个句子成分被诗人分成了各自包含三个短诗行的四个短诗节,从诗行和诗节形状上模拟了猫咪一步一试探的过程。猫咪的冒险最后以一脚踩进花盆的尴尬局面而告终。

  Poem
  By William Carlos Williams

  As the cat
  climbed over
  the top of

  the jamcloset
  first the right
  forefoot

  carefully
  then the hind
  stepped down

  into the pit of
  the empty
  flowerpot [③]

---

① 转引自 Vendler, p.202。
② 参见 Morley, pp.132-133。
③ 转引自 Vendler, p.77。

猫咪的冒险过程虽然可笑甚至可爱,但是诗意何在?值得诗人用"诗"这么大的词命名?然而,此诗最精妙之处也就是在标题。猫咪一步步的冒险过程及最后陷入的尴尬境地,不正和诗人作诗的过程有异曲同工之妙吗?可以说,标题是本诗的点睛之笔①。当然,上述这首诗的标题从另一角度来看也可以说提示了一个事实,即就算是普通如猫咪探路这样的日常所见也是诗歌创作的题材来源。但这样的看法与将猫咪的笨拙探路过程与诗歌创作过程做类比的理解相比就魅力顿失。

诗歌的标题可以是如上述诗作那样以"诗"命名,也可以是一个能提示一定写作背景的标签(label/logo)。不过,虽然有时标签能够提供一些背景,但标签是最弱的标题,因为很多时候它们只是懒惰的一种体现②。当然,诗人也可以借用同样具有背景提示作用的某些名作的词语来做诗歌的标题,但这些词语必须与本诗形成共鸣③。有时候一首诗可能没有标题,这时,读者由于没有标题的引导就会更看重诗歌的首行。这种情况可能是诗人想要的效果,但也可能是诗人的一种懒惰或者逃避的体现④。

读者读一首诗有时候是为了寻找其标题的目的,因此诗歌标题的确定要求诗人具有读者眼光。不少诗作的标题是在作品写完很久之后当诗人可以用读者眼光来看待自己作品时定下来的。定题如果做不到很英明,至少也要做到准确。标题定得随意或者不准确,对一首诗来说是一个灾难⑤。一首诗的标题好不好,合不合适,很大程度上影响了读者是否读诗的决定。定题方式各有千秋,诗人要确定的就是哪种方式对具体的作品最有效。有些标题可能集中体现了整首诗作的意义建构,即所谓的点睛之笔,如上述诗人威廉·卡洛斯·威廉斯的"诗"。诗人科琳·黑斯(Corrine Hales)下边的"力量"("Power")的标题对该诗的整体意义建构也有类似的点睛作用。

Power
By Corrine Hales

No one we knew had ever stopped a train.
Hardly daring to breathe, I waited
Belly-down with my brother
In a dry ditch

---

① 参见 Vendler, p.77。
② 参见 Dobyns, chap.9。
③ 参见 Morley, pp.132-133。
④ 参见 Dobyns, chap.9。
⑤ 参见 Morley, pp.132-133。

Watching through the green thickness
Of grass and willows.
Stuffed with crumpled newspapers,
The shirt and pants looked real enough
Stretched out across the rails. I felt my heart
Beating against the cool ground
And the terrible long screech of the train's
Braking began. We had done it.
Then it was in front of us—
A hundred iron wheels tearing like time
Into red flannel and denim, shredding the child
We had made—until it finally stopped.
My brother jabbed at me,
Pointed down the tracks. A man
Had climbed out of the engine, was running
In our direction, waving his arms,
Screaming that he would kill us—
Whoever we were.
Then, very close to the spot
Where we hid, he stomped and cursed
At the rags and papers scattered
Over the gravel from our joke.
I tried to remember which of us
That red shirt had belonged to,
But morning seemed too long ago, and the man
Was falling, sobbing, to his knees.
I couldn't stop watching.
My brother lay next to me,
His hands covering his ears,
His face pressed tight to the ground. ①

这首诗的标题"Power"至少有三重含义:一、说话者与兄弟使火车停下来的恶作剧

---

① 转引自 Kowit, pp.9-10。

力量;二、火车车轮碾压撕碎人偶的力量;三、火车司机跪地啜泣对说话者的精神震慑力量①。第三种力量的作用通过诗句"I couldn't stop watching"得到了强化。通过对标题的三重含义的理解,读者基本可以接受该诗的意义建构。有些诗作的标题使用了作品中某些概括主要意思、精神、亮点的词语,这些词语可以是人物名字、环境背景、时代等。当读者在诗句中看到这些词时,这些词就有了特别重要的意义②。诗人菲利普·拉金下边的"高窗"("High Windows")以诗中最突出的意象高窗做标题,并在最后的诗节中再次强调了这个意象的重要性。

High Windows
By Philip Larkin

When I see a couple of kids
And guess he's fucking her and she's
Taking pills or wearing a diaphragm,
I know this is paradise

Everyone old has dreamed of all their lives—
Bonds and gestures pushed to one side
Like an outdated combine harvester,
And everyone young going down the long slide

To happiness, endlessly. I wonder if
Anyone looked at me, forty years back,
And thought, *That'll be the life*;
No God any more, or sweating in the dark

*About hell and that, or having to hide
What you think of the priest. He
And his lot will all go down the long slide
Like free bloody birds*. And immediately

Rather than words comes the thought of high windows:

---

① 参见 Kowit, pp.9-10。
② 参见 Morley, pp.132-133;或参见 Dobyns, chap.9。

The sun-comprehending glass,
And beyond it, the deep blue air, that shows
Nothing, and is nowhere, and is endless. ①

  包括标题和诗节在内的题材与形式的完美结合能够进行理想的诗歌意义建构。诗歌的意义建构首先在内容上源于感动诗人,引起诗人持续关注的题材。诗歌的形式是诗歌意义构建不可或缺的部分。诗歌意义建构的成功与否取决于对诗歌形式工具的操作运用是否得当,是否制造了与诗歌题材相适应的微妙诗意。当某一题材触发诗人的灵感,使诗人诗意充盈想象洋溢时,每首诗都有自己的形式与诗人的诗意灵感心灵韵律相对应。不过,在诗意灵感缺失时,诗人求助于形式要求也能写出诗歌,甚至好诗。

  诗歌形式的重要性还体现在其翻译时的不可复制性。这种不可复制性使得不同语言间的诗歌翻译只能在叙事、意象等方面仍有表现,但形式美感及其在意义建构上的功能则很难复现,因此翻译的诗歌一般只能分析内容题材,而很难分析其形式对诗歌意义建构的作用。诗人罗伯特·勃莱(Robert Bly)翻译的下边这首西班牙诗人安东尼奥·马查多(Antonio Machado)的"童年的记忆"("Memory from Childhood")就不得不牺牲原诗的尾韵而只保留原诗的具体细节和意象来表现童年课堂的无聊。

Memory from Childhood
By Antonio Machado (Robert Bly Trans)

A chilly and overcast afternoon
of winter. The students
are studying. Steady boredom
of raindrops across the windowpanes.

It is the schoolroom. In a poster
Cain is shown running
away, and Abel dead,
not far from a red spot.

The teacher, with a voice husky and hollow,
is thundering. He is an old man badly dressed,
withered and dried up,

---

① 转引自 https://www.poetryfoundation.org/poems/48417/high-windows。

who is holding a book in his hand.

And the whole child's choir
is singing its lesson:
one thousand times one hundred is one hundred thousand,
one thousand times one thousand is one million.

A chilly and overcast afternoon
of winter. The students
are studying. Steady boredom
of raindrops across the windowpanes. ①

---

① 转引自 Kowit, p.8。

第七章
英语诗歌创意写作

  英语诗歌创意写作是一个涉及抓住创作灵感、寻找创作灵感、发现真正题材、找到合适形式、写成初稿、修改、关注读者意见、出版与传播这一系列行为的系统过程。一首诗的创作可能始于灵感的突然降临，也可能始于诗人对灵感的有意识激发，包括对自动写作过程的有意识模仿和对某些诗歌理念规则的实践等。诗人应该在写作中学会创作。英语诗歌创作既可以学也可以教。以培养诗人为教学目标的英语诗歌工作坊课程在各个教学环节中运用多种方式激发学生的创作热情与诗歌灵感。

  在诗歌初稿写作中诗人可以不考虑读者因素，但在修改甚至重写过程中，诗人就应该考虑读者反应。诗人应该对读者反应持辩证态度，对读者意见保有采用与否的自由。诗歌的价值不在于是否得到读者的承认，也不在于是否发表出版。对于诗人来说，诗歌创作是一个孤独的、煎熬的、通常不能带来物质利益的过程，同时也是一个不可抗拒的、能够带来精神满足感的过程。诗歌创作对于诗人来说更多的是精神上的快乐和享受。

第一节　灵感降临与自动写作

  与其他文学创作一样，诗歌创作也会面对写作障碍的问题。诗人遇到的最大写作障碍是没有灵感。没有灵感，诗歌创作就无从开始。这也是为什么经常可见诗人在作品中祈求缪斯女神即诗歌灵感降临的原因。受到缪斯女神眷顾的诗人是幸运的。格勒律治无疑是最著名的幸运诗人。据记载，格勒律治某次因生病吃了一点止痛药沉睡了三个小时，睡前刚好看到有关忽必烈汗（Kubla Khan）命令建造宫殿和花园的句子，于是在睡梦中出现了相关意象和诗行。格勒律治醒来后记录下了梦中出现的大约两、三百个诗行，直到被一个人的到访打断，此诗即"忽必烈汗"（"Kubla Khan"）①。当灵感缪

---

① 参见 Brooks & Warren, p. 468-469。

斯降临的时候,幸运的诗人莫不受宠若惊,弹冠相迎。诗人加里·斯奈德(Gary Snyder)的"诗的光临"("How Poetry Comes to Me")是这样描述诗歌灵感的降临以及诗人的主动迎接的:

How Poetry Comes to Me
By Gary Snyder

It comes blundering over the
Boulders at night, it stays
Frightened outside the
Range of my campfire
I go to meet it at the
Edge of the light ①

正如诗人加里·斯奈德的缪斯在夜晚降临并且躲闪不定,惴惴如受惊的小动物(飞马?小鹿?)一样,某种突然降临、捉摸不定的灵感,比如让诗人无法安宁的感情、感受、记忆片段、不寻常意象、声音等等,常常触发诗歌创作。由莫名灵感触发创作的诗人通常并不知道诗作的走向,好像一种未知力量使正在写的诗产生了自己的动能。虽然诗人的写作经验会自动控制其诗行长度、韵音、诗节,但是诗人只能跟着直觉随着那个动能走。这种神秘的写作动能赋予诗作以情感真实,赋予诗歌以生命力。这正是所谓"不疯魔没好诗!"

由莫名灵感触发在神秘写作动能推动下跟随直觉进行的诗歌创作常常是诗人探索发现其本次写作原因的过程,是探索发现其无意识中深藏的意象和关切的过程,是探索发现其无意识自我的过程。在这个过程中,诗人应该抑制自己的内在理性审查。诗人理查·雨果坚称探索自我是诗歌创作的基本要义,他认为作诗必须服从自我的真实感觉②。即使在写作中发现的自我是丑陋的,或者政治不正确的,也应该让无意识自我完整释放出来,这是诗歌创作的真诚原则的要求。几乎每个诗人都有萦绕心底,经常是潜藏于无意识之中的持续关切,并在其写作生涯中不断找寻意象去表现这种关切。这种持续关切在无意识中潜藏得越深,诗人的创作灵感源泉就持续越久,越接近意识层面,则创作灵感源泉的持续时间就越短③。

捉摸不定的灵感降临是缪斯女神莫名的恩宠,但在灵感未现的时候,诗人如何创

---

① 转引自 Vendler, p.534。
② 参见 Hugo, chap. 4。
③ 参见 Dobyns, chap.2。

作?与格勒律治在睡梦中创作出"忽必烈汗"完全不同,诗人埃德加·爱伦·坡(Edgar Allan Poe)是根据自己的写作理念,事前设计了周密的写作规则,并严格按照规则创作出"渡鸦"("The Raven")的。据诗人自己介绍,写作"渡鸦"前,他设定了这样的原则,即:作品长度要能够保持读者的注意力,既不高于普通读者期待,又不低于批评家期待,大约100行;要制造美,带来快感;要带着忧郁语调或悲伤情绪;结构上要有可多次回归的中心(pivot),即要有重复多次的循环节,并且这个循环节必须是一个单词,这个单词结束每个诗节,声音响亮,基调忧郁。"渡鸦"("The Raven")的循环节最终使用单词"nevermore",整首诗最后包含108行,严格按照诗人设定的规则写作而成①。

诗歌创作可能开始于像格勒律治那样的灵感突然降临,也可能始于诗人对某些诗歌理念或规则的设计和实践,不过,像埃德加·爱伦·坡那样严格按照周密设计来创作理想作品的情况并不多见。在缪斯降临前,一些著名诗人是这样主动寻找灵感的:诗人沃尔特·惠特曼在平时就有记笔记的习惯,这些笔记常常为其诗歌创作提供题材甚至细节;诗人西奥多·罗特克(Theodore Roethke)平时会在笔记本上记下一些零散的诗句,然后把其中的一些诗句连起来加工成一首诗;诗人叶芝在诗歌创作之前会先用散文描述,在描述过程中有时就会出现诗歌的主导隐喻(controlling metaphor)或意象;诗人赖内·马丽亚·里尔克(Rainer Maria Rilke)在给雕塑家罗丹(Rodin)当秘书时学到捕捉灵感的方法:不等待灵感来临才开始写作,而是有时间坐下来就写,比如,描述一件东西或者事件等,然后灵感自然就会来临②。

如前所述,由莫名灵感触发创作的诗人通常并不知道诗作的走向,而是只能跟随直觉在神秘写作动能推动下进行创作。这种写作过程其实就是自由写作(free writing)或者说自动写作(auto writing)。受超现实主义(surrealism)影响的现当代诗人经常有意识地模仿这种直觉推动的自动写作。超现实主义是二十世纪二十年代由欧洲作家、诗人、画家发起的从梦境和无意识中获取灵感的文学、艺术运动。1900年,心理学家西格蒙·弗洛伊德出版的《释梦》(Interpretation of Dreams)部分引发了超现实主义运动。虽然画家萨尔瓦多·达利(Salvador Dali)和马塞尔·杜尚(Marcel Duchamp)等让超现实主义作为视觉艺术概念为大众所熟悉,但超现实主义运动首先是一个文学思潮,其文学先驱是象征主义③。

超现实主义遵从前理性、原逻辑和超现实法则,试图通过允许无意识的奇怪语言发出声音来探索和改变现实。超现实主义鼓励在诗歌创作中进行自动写作,即由精神的出神恍惚状态触发思维自由联系,允许无意识语言自由游戏而不被理性审查所抑制。

---

① 参见 Brooks & Warren, pp. 468-469。
② 参见 Dobyns, chap.2 & chap.6。
③ 参见 Kowit, pp.122-134 及 Addonizio & Laux, pp.130-131。

超现实主义作为一个运动结束后,其解放性的哲学和方法进入世界艺术主流,其思想观点长期影响着西方艺术。现当代世界的诗人、作家和画家在一定程度上都受其观点影响。不少诗人相信自动写作中无意识流出的意象才是最有意义的意象,鼓励通过搁置强加意义和联系来释放深层无意识意象①。自动写作产生的超现实主义诗歌作品充满狂野的想象和怪异的意象。诗人格雷高利·奥尔(Gregory Orr)下边的"房间"("The Room")是一首典型的超现实主义诗作:

The Room
By Gregory Orr

With crayons and pieces of paper, I entered the empty room.
I sat on the floor and drew pictures all day.
One day I held a picture against the bare wall:
it was a window. Climbing through,
I stood in a sloping field
at dusk. As I began walking, night settled.
Far ahead in the valley, I saw the lights
of a village, and always at my back, I felt
the white room swallowing what was passed. ②

诗人如何进行自动写作?首先要在心理上做好不让意识对写作过程进行审查评判的准备。然后,拿起笔,或者坐在电脑前,笔不停地写或者手不停地打字。当然,诗人需要从某个题材即理查·雨果所说的起始题材开始,然后就从这个题材开始写吧。一直写下去,写到什么是什么,不要停,即使写出来的不是诗而是散文也没关系。进行自动写作的时候应听从语言声音(包括其音乐性)直觉,由声音引导着写下去。实在卡住了,拿本词典随便找个词重新开始,继续写。一直不停地写至少两三页纸,这样写出来的文字就已经完全不受诗人的意识审查了。这时就进入真正的自动写作状态,无意识中的语言就会喷涌而出。进入真正的自动写作状态后,诗人应该让自己处于兴奋的精神状态。如果愤怒,就发狂吧!如果描写,就让描写异于寻常、脱离常规吧!让一直压抑的情感释放出来!让从不泄露的秘密说出来!撒谎吧!无中生有吧!如果最后筋疲力尽,或者精神混乱,累趴了,哭了,更好!照着这样写个六七页纸,如果

---

① 参见 Addonizio&Laux, pp.130-131。
② 转引自 Kowit, p.123。

能写二十页,更棒①!

上述类似迷狂状态的自动写作结束后,先把稿子放一放,休息一天,等第二天清醒的时候再读稿子,划出还能让人激动感兴趣的句子,特别是音乐性比较强的句子,把这些句子组合起来,不要管什么理性逻辑或者连续性。没有划出来的句子也不要随意丢弃,先留着,也许日后还能找到好句子。通常情况下,从一次自动写作留下的稿子中可以找到几首诗的种子②。跟随直觉由声音引导的自动写作以在独处中完成为宜。梦境,或者是类似做梦状态,比如醉酒未醉半醉半醒、清晨海边独自散步、长途列车旅行、看到老照片陷入回忆与联想,等等,常常是诗人进行自动写作探索无意识声音和深层意象的理想状态。

自动写作不是把语言当做意识的工具,而是把语言本身看成目的,关注诗歌语言声音,特别是其音乐性,让想象充分运作,通过语言游戏发现意想不到的深层意象,以接近神秘的自我无意识。一些现当代诗歌实验创作形式,比如第四章探讨过的拼贴和擦涂等偶然诗创作方法,也是诗人探索无意识深层意象的手段。这些实验创作游戏规则造成的语言陌生性也可能呈现意想不到的无意识意象,在意识思维无法到达的语言材料中产生诗篇。

受超现实主义影响的现当代诗人热衷于诗歌创作形式实验,不断创新语言游戏规则。他们在创作中制造意外和并置(juxtaposition),追求开放(openness)和运动(movement),强调留白(gap)与碎片化(fragmentation)③。但是,如果诗作者故作高深,在作品中过度使用省略、碎片、不命名、不完整等手法,而实际上作品中各元素真的毫无联系;或者要求读者像心理分析师一样,通过层层解码才能到达作品可能的主题,这样的实验手法的效果或者合法性就令人存疑。诗人理查·雨果认为,如果没有对自我的探索,所谓的形式技巧实验就只不过是不惜一切代价牺牲个人感情的精致方式④。

第二节 英语诗歌创意写作中的灵感激发(trigger)

诗歌创作灵感有时激昂澎湃,有时蛰伏静守,这是一个自然过程和现象。诗人不能错过激情澎湃的创作高光时期,也不必过于忧虑诗意和灵感的暂时缺乏。不过,真正的诗人在灵感相对干涸的时间里,也会坚持书写,在书写中静待高光时刻来临,因为缪斯

---

① 参见 Kowit, pp.134-136。
② 同上。
③ 参见 Addonizio&Laux, pp.130-131。
④ 参见 Hugo, chap. 4。

不会垂青无准备的人。当然,与其他诗人交流结伴写诗、参加诗歌朗读会、参加诗歌工作坊或者写作研讨会、阅读、旅游等,也能为诗人带来灵感。

初学英语诗歌创作的诗人更加需要坚持练笔。无论多忙,合理安排计划,每天至少挤出十分钟用英语诗歌形式写点儿什么,至少坚持十天!可以用这十分钟专门描写一个记忆中的意象,或者列举描写一系列记忆中的意象,或者描写那十分钟内目之所及的东西。如果控制不住一定要在十分钟内干点儿"实质性"的活儿的话,那就用英语诗歌形式回复电子邮件,或者用英语诗歌形式痛骂那些让你不能写作的事情。如果实在写不出来的话就拿着笔盯着纸发呆。至少坚持十天,每天至少十分钟,看看结果怎么样?

上面是进行英语诗歌创意写作教学的诗人给新手诗人的建议[1]。进行英语诗歌创意写作教学的诗人教师会采用各种方式激发学生诗人的创作热情和诗歌灵感。英语诗歌创意写作教学发源于美国爱荷华大学(University of Iowa)。美国爱荷华大学于1897年开设"诗歌写作"(Verse-Making)课程,于1936年成立包括诗歌工作坊和小说工作坊在内的"爱荷华作家工作坊"(Iowa Writers' Workshop)。以此为发端,美国高校英语诗歌创意写作教学迄今已经发展八十余年。据美国作家与写作项目协会(Association of Writers & Writing Programs,简称AWP)网站显示,截至2020年2月,在该协会正式注册的美国诗歌创意写作项目有370多个,这些诗歌创意写作项目绝大多数隶属于高校。

文学创意写作在美国高校作为一门课程首先是在硕士层次作为选修课开设,却意外受到学生的持续喜爱,很快在本科层次也得到开设并发展成为完整的学科专业。文学创意写作研究和师资也在学生对课程的热爱中得到驱动成长[2]。当创意写作成为高校课程时,很多人有一个疑惑:写作能教吗?事实证明:完全可以,写作既可以学也可以教。也许有人有一些写作的天分,但是即便是有天分的人,其写作才能也需要一定的训练才能真正创造出佳作。创意写作训练还能培养创意阅读能力。在数字媒体时代,人们阅读时注意力很容易开小差,而创意写作训练能够使人们关注每个词语、诗行格律音韵、句子结构、诗节段落节奏、全篇布局与留白,等等,从而获得更深层次的理解甚至创意。

诗歌创意写作作为一门专业学科,其教学目标就是培养诗人,实际就是帮助学生熟悉诗歌术语理念,学习创作技巧,进而发展出自己的诗歌风格和特色。诗歌工作坊是英美高校诗歌创意写作教学的典型模式,是实现诗歌创意写作教学目标的有效途径。在诗歌工作坊课程教学中,每个学生既是诗人,又是读者,既研究熟悉经典诗作和诗歌术语理念,丰富诗歌创作技巧,提高诗歌写作能力,也从诗人教师和同学诗人那里获得诗

---

[1] 参见 Addonizio & Laux, pp.200-202。

[2] 参见 Warner, Marina. "Foreword", Bell, Julia & Paul Magrs, ed. in *The Creative Writing Coursebook: Forty-four Authors Share Advice and Exercises for Fiction and Poetry*. London: Pan Macmillan, first published in 2001, electronic updated edition published in 2019, Foreword.

歌阅读反应和评论意见,研究自己作品的优点与不足,找到最好的诗歌表现形式。

在英美高校,本科层次的诗歌工作坊课程对学生是否已有作品要求不一。美国高校圣约翰大学(St. John's University)本科层次的诗歌工作坊课程不看选课学生专业,学生也不需要先提交作品,但是英国高校华威大学(Warwick University)本科层次的创意写作专业招生时要求学生提交创作稿件和个人陈述,还要面试①。本科层次的诗歌工作坊课程主要包括诗歌术语理念和写作技巧的讲授、诗歌写作练习、工作坊三个环节。硕士层次的诗歌工作坊则面对已经有很多作品的学生,课程教学主要是对学生作品进行评论的工作坊环节,比如一周用三个小时的课来讨论三篇作品②。本科层次的诗歌工作坊可以称为产出性的(generative)工作坊,而硕士层次的诗歌工作坊可以称为反应性的(responsive)工作坊③。

如何激发学生的诗歌创作热情与写作灵感?这是英美高校创意写作教学重点解决的问题。首先,创意写作教学强调研究经典诗作和诗歌术语理念的目的是为了获得诗歌创作灵感。这也是本书前面六章研究英语诗歌形式、题材、意义建构等方面相关诗歌术语与理念的目的所在。在诗歌工作坊中,诗人教师主要应用自己或者其他诗人有关诗歌创作的理论观点来解释经典诗作、成功诗作④。学生被要求熟悉各种诗歌术语、运动、传统和形式,研究经典、成功诗作,以此获得创作灵感,并将真正引起心灵共鸣的观点、形式、技巧运用于自己的创作实践中,并形成自己的"诗学宣言"(Poetic statement)。

个人"诗学宣言"一般要求约 800~1000 个单词,可以包括以下内容:为什么写作?怎样写作?是否存在不得不写作的原因?哪些诗人对本人的写作选择和方向有影响?什么因素驱动或者阻碍本人的写作?怎样尽量改善本人的写作条件?可以将这些问题设为标题,先不假思索地快速写出草稿,然后读给一位有见地的熟人听,让其指出其中的真实或者不实之处,然后进行修改⑤。个人"诗学宣言"写成之后,可于一年之后重读宣言,看看本人的诗歌创作实践是否对自己的诗学观念产生影响。

诗歌创意写作诗人教师要激发学生的创作热情与写作灵感,就要帮助学生诗人克服"写作障碍"。一个可以克服"写作障碍"的方法是描写身边某一个具体生活用具。先从五个感官细细观察体验这一生活用具。可以闭上眼睛仔细触摸该物体几分钟,记下

---

① 参见 Jones, Russell Celyn. "Standards in Creative Writing Teaching", Bell, Julia & Paul Magrs, ed. in *The Creative Writing Coursebook: Forty-four Authors Share Advice and Exercises for Fiction and Poetry*. London: Pan Macmillan, first published in 2001, electronic updated edition published in 2019。

② 参见 Bell, Julia. "Feeling the Burn", Bell, Julia & Paul Magrs, ed. in *The Creative Writing Coursebook: Forty-four Authors Share Advice and Exercises for Fiction and Poetry*. London: Pan Macmillan, first published in 2001, electronic updated edition published in 2019。

③ 参见 Morley, p.118。

④ 参见 Bizzaro, Patrick. "Workshop: an ontological study", Donnelly, Dianne. ed., in *Does the Writing Workshop still Work?*, Bristol & Buffalo & Torontao: Multiligual Matters, 2010, pp.40 – 41。

⑤ 参见 Morley, p.37。

触摸时的感觉,再睁开眼睛仔细观察,记下物体的外形、气味、味道和声音等等。然后再写出关于该用具的想法、记忆等等。这样写出来的用具已经不再只是物体,而经常成为一个意象或者象征。这个方法能够训练集中描写的能力①。

上述写作练习还可以做如下扩展,比如,将这个生活用具拟人化,用第一人称使其开口说话,叙述它的一天是在哪儿度过的?是怎样被使用的?这一天中它见证了哪些故事?可以为其配置人的外形、缺陷、性格,等等。诗人西尔维娅·普拉斯(Sylvia Plath)的"蘑菇"("Mushrooms")就是这样的一首诗,刚开始也是做为练习写出来的。进行物体写作还可以从这样的假设开始:假如不幸发生了火灾,诗人只能从火灾中抢救出来一个物件。思考自己最想从火中抢救出来的是什么?为什么?把它写出来②。

诗人还可以将自己身边的物件与一些时间、人物、情感、回忆相关联进行诗歌创作。具体方法可以如下:选一个非常熟悉了解的人,列出与那个人相关的一系列物件,具体描写这些物件,选出一个最相关的物件,再用十分钟时间写作有关这个物件的具体回忆。这样写出来的作品常常很感人③。诗人罗伯特·赫里克(Robert Herrick)的"朱丽叶的衣裙"("Upon Julia's Clothes")就是一首表面写一个物件即衣服,实际写人的诗。诗中写衣服的三个动词性名词"liquefaction"、"vibration"、"glittering"和两个形容词"brave"、"free"实际上都是在写穿衣服的人Julia的动作状态和精神面貌。

Upon Julia's Clothes
By Robert Herrick

Whenas in silks my Julia goes,
Then, then, methinks, how sweetly flows
That liquefaction of her clothes.

Next, when I cast mine eyes, and see
That brave vibration each way free,
O how that glittering taketh me! ④

---

① 参见 Morgan, Esther. "Articles of Faith: Using Objects in Poetry", Bell, Julia & Paul Magrs, ed. in *The Creative Writing Coursebook: Forty-four Authors Share Advice and Exercises for Fiction and Poetry*. London: Pan Macmillan, first published in 2001, electronic updated edition published in 2019。

② 参见 Morgan, Esther. "Articles of Faith: Using Objects in Poetry", Bell, Julia & Paul Magrs, ed. in *The Creative Writing Coursebook: Forty-four Authors Share Advice and Exercises for Fiction and Poetry*. London: Pan Macmillan, first published in 2001, electronic updated edition published in 2019。

③ 同上。

④ 转引自 https://www.poetryfoundation.org/poems/47339/upon-julias-clothes。

回忆的内容丰富多彩,能够为诗歌创作提供各种各样的题材。教师诗人会通过提示或设问的方式,引起回忆,激发灵感,引导诗歌创作。比如可以按照如下的提示,快速列举写出相关记忆中的事物,然后选择触发强烈感情或感想的回忆进行诗歌创作,诗作长度不超过 35 行。注意要写下回忆中记起来的尽可能多的细节。在进行诗歌创意写作前想一想这个经历对自己有什么意义或者影响,这一点有助于引导写作方向[①]:

1. Jot down a list of some of the places where you have lived.
2. Jot down a list of some of the jobs you've had. Include the weirder ones.
3. Jot down a list of old friends, people you don't see much of anymore.
4. Jot down two embarrassing things you've done and a lie you once told.
5. Jot down one triumph and two failures.
6. Jot down a list of remembered kisses.
7. Jot down the names of someone who hurt you, someone who helped you, and someone you admired.
8. Describe a piece of clothing you once loved, name a piece of music you still love, and two old movies you still remember.

诗人还可以通过回答以下问题开始进行相关回忆的散文诗创作。同样要注意写下回忆过程中记起来的尽可能多的细节,但是创作出来的诗歌作品只能包含三到四句话。这就要求诗人写出来的句子必须是长句子,而且语言必须精炼,细节和意象选择必须极具代表性,同时描写必须很有表现力。当三到四句的散文诗修改得能够完美有力地表现回忆的场景与意义之后,诗人可以进一步尝试写五到八句长的散文诗[②]:

1. Recall a pleasant time in the past.
2. Recall a building in which you once lived.
3. Recall a secret you once had.
4. Recall a magical person from your childhood.
5. Recall an incident that filled you with dread.
6. Recall something dangerous you did when you were young.
7. Recall something sinful or bad you did as a child.
8. Recall something that happened during a school vacation.

---

① 参见 Kowit, p.16 & p.33。
② 参见 Kowit, p.16 & p.25。

9. Recall something that happened in a classroom or schoolyard.
10. Recall something that happened many years ago near a body of water.
11. Recall your first romantic infatuation.
12. Recall something funny that made you laugh happily.
13. Recall an incident from your past that filled you with sadness.
14. Recall an incident that you would be reticent to share with others.
15. Recall an incident involving a parent or guardian that still angers you.
16. Recall an incident in which you felt betrayed.
17. Recall an incident that ended in great disappointment.
18. Recall an incident in which you felt humiliated.
19. Recall an incident in which you felt love for someone.
20. Recall an incident that was emotionally wrenching.
21. Jot down any memory that popped into your mind but which you have suppressed while doing this process.
22. Recall an incident that was joyful.

诗歌创意写作诗人教师也鼓励学生进行诗歌创作技巧和形式实验。一种诗歌技巧实验就是诗人在回答上边问题进行相关回忆的散文诗创作的时候，可以用平时不用来写字的那只手写诗①。这种反手写诗的方式因其陌生和操作难度，很可能使诗人记忆中深藏的情感或无意识中深藏的意象暴露出来。偶然诗是现当代实验英语诗歌形式之一，其创作规则可以不断设计创新。拼贴法是偶然诗的一种创作方式。本书第四章探讨过用现成文本进行裁剪拼贴作诗的方法，诗人也可以借鉴下边的散文拼贴创作教学过程按照一定规则自己产出裁剪拼贴用的文字进行诗歌创作。

散文拼贴创作教学过程②一般开始于为期一学期的创意写作课程中的第三或第四次课，为期三次课，一次课两个小时。在第一次课上，学生首先用 100 个词写一篇散文描述自己小时候睡过的一张床，要用完整句子写作，因为其中的动词对接下来的写作很重要。接着学生再用 100 个词写一篇散文描述自己现在睡的床，比如床上有什么，床边有什么，在床上干什么，等等。然后学生再用 100 个词写一篇散文描述想象中发明出来的任何材料制作的床。这第三张床比较难写，需要花费的时间和精力比较多。写完三张床，学生结对将自己写的散文读给对方听，互相给出建议，这样同时也活跃了课堂气氛。学生要保存好写成的三篇散文原稿。

---

① 参见 Kowit, p.26。
② 参见 Fell, Alison. "Deconstructing Beds...", Bell, Julia & Paul Magrs, ed. in *The Creative Writing Coursebook: Forty-four Authors Share Advice and Exercises for Fiction and Poetry*. London: Pan Macmillan, first published in 2001, electronic updated edition published in 2019。

第二次上课前，学生要把三篇散文打印出来，裁剪成非常短的单词或者短语，放进信封，与剪刀和胶水一起带回课堂。剪刀用于课堂上继续裁剪词语。比如"book'shelves"、"chest drawers"这样的常见词就还可以继续裁剪，以便之后可以构成新颖的词组；主语和谓语也可以分开，名词和动词可以分开，尽可能多地释放句子成分与词语，使其在之后的创作"游戏"中充分自由地发挥作用。在第二次课上，学生把剪开的词语都摊开来，然后不考虑意思仅凭声音直觉分组。这是"游戏"意义之所在，让这些词语享有充分的"游戏"自由。接着学生将分好组的词语拼贴成新颖的词组。要让无意识发挥作用，允许新意象新题材浮现出来。这个过程花费的时间较长，可能需要整次课两小时。拼贴成的词组要写下来。

第三次课上，学生把拼贴成的词组根据正常句法修正动词时态等等扩展成句子，然后安排好篇章结构，写成一篇新的散文。最后学生读出各自裁剪拼贴出来的新作品，其他学生边听边做笔记，以发现引人共鸣的意象或者句子，以及文本之下的深层结构。在这个教学过程中，学生要学会从裁剪分开的词语里边找到所需要的那些词进行拼贴创作，不需要的词可以丢弃。诗歌创意写作可以借鉴以上过程进行自产文本的裁剪拼贴创作，比如把裁剪出来的词语根据其声音效果分好组，拼贴成新颖的词组，然后把拼贴出来的词组做为语言素材，写成一篇可能含有意外新意象、新题材的诗歌作品。

诗歌创意写作诗人教师擅于采用各种方法，设计各种诗歌题材要求或形式技术规则作为灵感激发器（trigger /prompt），激发学生诗人的创作热情与诗歌灵感进行创作。本章第一节中介绍的诗人埃德加·爱伦·坡创作"渡鸦"之前理性思考的写作理念与周密设计的写作规则就是一种灵感激发器。不过，像埃德加·爱伦·坡那样严格按照规则包括情绪与语调的设计写作理想作品的情况很少，因为这在一定程度上会限制诗人的积极想象。一般来说，灵感激发器中对形式技术要求越多，意义要求与导向越少，写出来的诗歌越有新意。

诗人教师设计各种语言游戏规则，让学生诗人在解决形式技术问题中进行语言游戏、激发积极自由想象、向无意识深处挖掘诗歌材料。由语言游戏规则触发的诗歌创作过程常常是紧张有趣有效的。在笔者曾经参加的美国高校圣约翰大学（St. John's University）诗歌工作坊课程的一次课堂上，诗人教师西蒙娜博士（Dr. Simona Blat）要求学生与隔壁同学两人一组轮流随意说出二十个单词后一起选择十个单词当堂各作一首诗。虽然两个学生使用的十个单词相同，但轮流说词的随意性和当堂作诗的时限性迫使学生跟随自己的语言直觉，创作出意韵各异的诗作。而结对作诗的经历也在两个学生之间建立起了合作伙伴感情。

在圣约翰大学诗歌工作坊课程的另一次课堂上，西蒙娜指定了单词的构词规则，学生照此规则各自编出十四个单词作为行首词，然后交给隔壁同学在课后写成一首十四行诗。此诗不一定要押韵，但一定要使用五音步抑扬格。行首词的随意性和行数格律的要求造成了此诗创作的语言陌生性和难度。这个十四行诗创作练习将英语律诗形式的改造与自动写作的语言游戏相结合，触发了让学生印象深刻的诗歌创作。在课程的结课朗读会上不少学生选择朗读这首十四行诗，其中不乏意境奇诡的佳作。因为行首词是同学提供的，这首诗的创作同样在两个学生之间建立起合作伙伴感情。

西蒙娜通过语言游戏规则的设计让学生结对写诗，营造了学生的合作氛围，激起了学生的诗歌创作热情。西蒙娜还曾要求每个学生课后尽自己最大能力写出最长最美的一个句子然后带回课堂，由隔壁同学帮助断行成诗。她也曾在课堂现场各个地方甚至学生后背上张贴大张卡纸，师生在每张纸上接力完成诗作。在这个过程中，西蒙娜要求学生尽量使自己的诗行与前面同学的诗行连贯起来。她本人接力的时候则或者使诗行连贯，或者转换诗歌意象以创造新奇的意境。这个过程营造了浓厚的师生合作氛围，每张纸上的每首诗都是师生一起创作的结晶。

西蒙娜还曾在课堂上安排全班学生在同一张纸上接力合作写诗。每人写一行，前面的学生在将纸传递给后面的学生时要先用折叠的方式盖住自己写的诗行。最后完成的作品由一个学生在班上朗读。因为接力时彼此不知道写了什么，加上其中有不少奇思妙想，学生朗读时全班笑声一片。这其实是个超现实主义诗人发明的创作小游戏，名字叫"精致尸体"（Exquisite Corpse）。这个游戏还可以按照其它既有共同要求又允许变化的规则来玩，比如每个学生的诗行都以同一个词开始，或者每个学生写一行诗，每行诗都是关于同一个物件。当然每个新诗行都要折起盖住[①]。

诗人教师还运用课堂环境来触发诗歌创作灵感。上述西蒙娜在课堂现场各个地方比如地板、墙壁、窗台、白板、讲台内壁、门后、学生后背等张贴大张卡纸，师生在每张纸上接力完成诗作的安排就产生了奇妙的写作体验。当老师和学生趴在地上、钻进讲台下、在同学后背写诗的时候，不同的写作环境触发了不同的诗歌创意。再比如，有的诗人教师会安排学生到视觉艺术课堂听课，或者把诗歌工作坊与舞蹈课堂融合一起上课，以激发诗歌创作灵感[②]。有的诗人教师则运用通艺法（ekphrasis），使用美术、摄影、雕塑作品引导学生创作对这些艺术作品做出反应的诗歌。

英语诗歌创意写作诗人教师运用各种方式激发学生的创作热情和诗歌灵感，要求学生诗人对任何诗歌创作的可能性开放。高校圣约翰大学诗歌工作坊诗人教师西蒙娜甚至要求学生保留课程学习过程中出现的所有资料纸片，因为这些资料纸片随时可能触发创作灵感。新手诗人还可以模仿各种诗歌题材和形式的经典诗作按照一定要求作诗：根据题材或形式要求的提示二十分钟内写出一首完整的诗稿。诗稿可能比较粗糙甚至混乱，但没关系。虽然诗稿应尽可能按照要求和提示进行写作，但不能完全按照要求和提示也

---

① 参见 Addonizio & Laux，p.135。
② 参见 Donnelly, Dianne. "Introduction: If it ain't broke, don't fix it; Or change is inevitable, except from a vending machine", *Does the Writing Workshop still Work?*, Bristol & Buffalo & Torontao: Multiligual Matters, 2010, p.20。

没关系,完全可以按照被激起的个性化思路写下去①。以下是诗歌工作坊激发诗歌灵感,触发英语诗歌创作的一些练习方案②:

1. This is an exercise best done quickly. It can double as a poem in its own right, and could maybe also benefit from being set to music.

Write down the first image that comes into your head.
Write down the first emotion that comes into your head.
Write down the first line that comes into your head.

It can be the first line for a story.
It can be the first line for a poem.
It can be the first line for anything.

Write down a different emotion.
Write down a different first line.
Write down a different image.

Write down another first line.
Write down another emotion.
Write down another image.

Write down an image that is an emotion (i.e. that will act as one).
Write down a first line that is an emotion (i.e. that will act as one).
Write down an image that is a first line (i.e. that will act as one).

Write down an emotion without mentioning the emotion.
Write down a first line that's nothing but image.
Now remove the image (so that its absence can be felt).

Can emotion ever be removed from image?

---

① 参见 Addonizio&Laux, pp.227-256。
② 参见 Smith, Ali. "Creative Writing Workshy", Bell, Julia & Paul Magrs, ed. in *The Creative Writing Coursebook: Forty-four Authors Share Advice and Exercises for Fiction and Poetry*. London: Pan Macmillan, first published in 2001, electronic updated edition published in 2019。

Can image ever be removed from emotion?
Can you have a first line of a story, poem, anything, without emotion or image?

Choose your preferred first line. Now. Start.

2. Workshop Exercise Instruction in Haiku.

Write a short story.
Very short. One hundred words.
You have ten minutes.

3. Have the workshop participants read out their hundred-word stories created under the haiku method above. Now ask everybody to change the gender of one of the characters in their stories, without changing anything else, and read them out again alongside the originals. What happens? How much of the story can stay the same? How much of it changes or shifts and why? This is an excellent way to bring preconceptions to the surface or to spot them in prose.

第三节　英语诗歌修改和读者因素：
一些诗歌创作和修改建议

诗歌创作既可能始于莫名灵感的突然降临,也可能始于诗人对灵感的有意识激发,包括对某些诗歌理念规则的实践和对自动写作过程的有意识模仿,在写作过程中听从语言声音直觉引导,放弃意识审查,进入的迷狂状态,探索发现深层无意识意象。创意洋溢的诗歌初稿写作完成后,有的诗人会对自己的原创作品敝帚自珍,看哪儿哪儿好,什么都保留着,有的诗人则可能会一次又一次地挑剔并修改自己的诗作。诗人叶芝就习惯于一次次地修改,使自己的诗作从粗糙变得优雅①。

诗人自己修改作品前要先把作品冷藏一段时间,让自己与作品产生距离。如果匆

---

① 参见 Dobyns, chap.2。

忙草率地修改,原诗会被毁坏;但如果只是稍事调整,则修改可能没有意义。诗人修改作品经常需要逐个词逐个声音地斟酌。最好把稿子打印出来,不要在电脑上修改。保留所有修改版本,因为每一次修改痕迹对最终作品的确定都可能有用。一首理想诗作应该是一个有机整体,每个细节都与整体有着隐喻式的共鸣,突然出现的声音元素或者变异则能产生强调效果。因此,诗人可以自己或者请别人大声朗读作品。大声朗读可以帮助诗人从声音中发现作品的问题①。

诗人自己修改作品,首先要有自我批评能力,要能确定自己写作此诗想要、能够、或者应该达到的效果。有学者认为对诗歌作品总体上的要求是言之有物、形式严格、篇幅简约、说话有力、语言美丽②。好的诗歌语言应该是集中、精准,没有冗词,因此,删减作品中的多余累赘词语就是最常见的修改。经典诗作经常是在大刀阔斧的删减后产生的。

与打开思路或者增加点睛之笔等类型的修改相比,删减多余元素的修改相对容易得多。可以先从形容词和副词开始删减。很多形容词表达的意思是相对的,实际传达的信息并不多,这样的词如果不能删减,则宜用一个意象来代替。而像诸如 still、even、some、yet、very、just、clearly、only、finally、quite、somewhat、rather、fairly 这样的强调副词经常是没必要的,因此可删则删。如果诗中某个地方确实需要强调,则其需要的绝不仅仅是一个强调副词③。

诗歌作品在开头和结尾的地方经常出现多余语言。写好开头在整个诗歌写作过程中是最难的。不少作品开始得太早,像讲正题之前的清嗓子。这种清嗓子在诗歌写作中是要不得的。要判断作品的开头是否合适,可以尝试将作品的第二、第三、第四或第 N 行作为作品首行看看是否更为有效④。有一些作品则在真正的诗已经结束之后还喋喋不休。这种喋喋不休在诗歌写作中也是要不得的。比如以 "And the geese fly north into memory" 和 "And who am I but the shadow the sun seeks in setting" 这样的句子作为诗作的结尾,虽然看起来有一定的诗意,但是实际上没有表达什么意思,因此是多余的⑤。

删减诗句中多余词语还有一个方法即重写。可以用最简单的句子重写一个诗句,将重写的句子与原句进行比较来确定哪些词是多余的,哪些词是必须的。诗人还可以

---

① 参见 Morley, pp.133 - 135。
② Dobyns 书中第二章引用了 George Saintsbury 对诗人的总体要求:"To have something to say; to say it under pretty strict limits of form and very strict ones of space; to say it forcibly; to say it beautifully; these are the four great requirements of the poet in general." 详见 George Saintsbury, *A History of English Prosody: From the Twelfth Century to the Present Day*, 2nd ed. New York: Russell & Russell, 1961, vol. 1, p. 305。
③ 参见 Morley, pp.133 - 135 及 Dobyns, chap.7 & chap.9。
④ 参见 Morley, pp.133 - 135。
⑤ 参见 Dobyns, chap.9。

尝试用作品的尾句作为首句重写一首诗，与原诗比较看看效果有什么不一样①。诗人也可以尝试从作品的最后一行往回读，或者最后一节往回读，或者把各诗节打乱重组，看看作品是否更有表现力②。诗人还可以通过回答以下问题来帮助修改作品：诗中描写具体吗？抽象词用得合适吗？有陈词滥调吗？作品是在描写呈现(show)还是在陈述告知(tell)③？

诗无定律。诗人自己写诗，当然是想怎么写就怎么写，想怎么修改就怎么修改。毕竟，诗人写诗首先是为了记录自己、愉悦自己，获得单纯的写作快感。不过，诗人总是想写出好诗，修改作品的目的也是为了让自己的诗作变得比原来更好。除了上述需要注意的问题以外，下边是诗人自己创作和修改诗作时可以参考的一些建议。当然，是否接受这些建议的选择权在于诗人自己：

1. 不写没感情、没态度、没立场的"诗"。没感情、没态度、没立场的"诗"不是诗(poetry/poem)，最多叫韵文(verse)，如果文中有韵的话。

2. 诗歌的标题、开头和结尾非常重要。

3. 诗歌的第一行就要有趣。

4. 从事件的中间开始写，不要在事件的太早阶段开始诗歌。在诗歌开始的时候事件就应该已经发生④。

5. 在诗中要问而不答。因为如果答得了，提问就是浪费时间。也可以不问而答⑤。

6. 戴上面具可以写得更好。可以用拟人的手法，赋予无生命的物件以声音，说一说它们各自拥有或者知道的故事，是一件非常好玩的事情。

7. 可以试用5W（即 what、who、where、when、why）原则作诗，在回答5W问题的引导下进行写作，对暂无灵感的诗人有一定的创作激发作用。

8. 要描写，描写要集中、要具体、要细节。

9. 要使用意象，包括视觉、触觉、味觉、听觉、嗅觉等方面的感觉意象。

10. 要使用隐喻。

11. 写萦绕诗人脑中挥之不去的题材，用诗人喜欢的词，发展诗人自己的写作方式，发展诗人自己的写作风格。自己的风格是永恒的，时尚潮流是短暂的。

12. 诗人要强化自己与语言的关系，而不是与题材的关系。诗人与语言的关系会让诗人发展出自己的词汇、自己的写作方式，挖掘出诗人自己的内心世界和无意识之下的深层意象。

---

① 参见 Dobyns, chap.9。
② 参见 Morley, pp.133-135。
③ 参见 Bell, Julia. "Feeling the Burn", Bell, Julia & Paul Magrs, ed. in *The Creative Writing Coursebook: Forty-four Authors Share Advice and Exercises for Fiction and Poetry*. London: Pan Macmillan, first published in 2001, electronic updated edition published in 2019。
④ 参见 Hugo, chap.5。
⑤ 同上。

13. 注意名词前的具体数词能够提供具体的视觉效果,激发具体的视觉反应。模糊数词不能。

14. 多用实义动词、行为动词、动作动词、描写动词,不要弱化动词的行动性。

15. 少用无力的动词,如 have、be 等。

16. 少用抽象名词。

17. 少用时间连词、因果连词、转折连词①。

18. 少用 so、such 来表达强调②。

19. 诗人要时刻保持对周围事物的敏感状态,多观察多思考。

20. 诗人写作时应该保持自信、傲慢,甚至无知,当然生活中要对人友善。

21. 一首诗本身可以成为页面上的一个事件,成为一个自我构建的自足主体,而不是指向页面外事件的载体。不过,注意不要让这种超现实主义的形式实验创作走向极端,脱离历史社会和读者。

22. 一首诗写成后,诗人自己要反复、多次、慢速、高声朗读作品,看看诗行声音效果是否表现了想要的意义建构。诗人一定注意自己先慢速朗读作品,谨记"诗歌死于速读"!

修改,可能是一个费事费力费神的过程。不过,即使某一诗行的修改需要耗费很长时间,修改结果却应该不露痕迹地达到自然说出的诗句的效果。诗人迪伦·托马斯作诗好似手到拈来。然而,当他实际创作的时候,往往是先在草稿纸的右边写下一列韵词及其同韵可选词,建立起一首诗的外骨架,然后补充这个外骨架中间的空白,再将作品修改至自然顺畅。最后的作品看起来行云流水、自然天成,但事实上却是诗人的精密设计和计算使然。诗人刚开始列出来的韵词经常被数行诗隔开,因此其押韵回声效果一点也不显刻意造作③。诗人叶芝认为就算一行诗的写作和修改要花费数小时,其最终呈现的结果必须使它显得是瞬间情感思想的自然流露,否则这种耗时冗长的写作和修改就是徒劳的,正如他在"亚当的诅咒"("Adam's Curse")中写道:

> We sat together at one summer's end,
> That beautiful mild woman, your close friend,
> And you and I, and talked of poetry.
> I said, 'A line will take us hours maybe;
> Yet if it doesn't seem a moment's thought,

---

① 参见 Hugo, chap.5。
② 同上。
③ 参见 Morley, David. *The Cambridge Introduction to Creative Writing*. New York: Cambridge University Press, 2007, p.79。

Our stitching and unstitching has been naught. ①

　　诗人既是自己作品的创作者也是第一个读者。在初稿写作中诗人可以不考虑读者因素,在修改过程中,诗人就应该考虑诗作的形式、内容和意义建构是否能在目标读者中激发相同或者类似的情感反应。诗人菲利普·拉金曾经做过这样的比喻,诗人作诗就像是使用语言制造了一台发动机,这台发动机在某个时间某个地点将在另一个人身上激发同样的情感②。即使诗人只是以诗歌形式忠实记录自己的生命痕迹,不是为了出版而创作,其写作也是为了跟某些目标读者交流,即便是单向的交流,比如与百年之后的未来读者的交流。

　　读者读诗,可能是为了从诗歌中获得知识,或者是为了拓展阅历,或者是为了找到与他人或世界的联系。但读诗与写诗一样都不是为了达到某种功利目的,而是具有自己的独立价值,即获得单纯的快感。读者读诗当然有对诗人的了解欲望,但更多的是期待从读诗中感受自己的生命,从诗中找到自己,从读诗中得到愉悦,为生命找寻意义。如果诗人完全不考虑读者,诗中元素如意象等等都没有做出隐喻性的延伸,没有与读者产生共鸣,读者无法从诗歌中看到与自己相关的元素,那么这样的诗作生命力是有限的,没有持久的影响力。因为读者即使对此诗的形式、技巧、才智甚至智慧有所欣赏,也只会仅此而已,不会关心并记住这首诗。

　　诗人写作,要使作品与读者产生共鸣,就要让读者的眼睛、耳朵,甚至手指,真切感受作品中描述的快乐、悲哀、愤怒等情感。这就要求诗人注重写作中的细节描写与意象刻画等等。通过具体细节描写和意象刻画来呈现情感会比直接讲述情感状态有效得多。像"My fists tightened"、"he gritted his teeth"、"her face went pale"这样的细节描写就比"I felt angry"、"he was frightened"、"she was shocked"这样的讲述更能真实呈现情感状态,更能激起读者类似的情感反应③。诗歌作品要让读者在诗中看到或者想象自己的生命,在诗中找到自己的故事。

　　有经验的诗歌读者,特别是了解诗歌特点的读者,会带着自己的期待和问题来读诗,并通过自己的读诗行为来理解与赋予诗歌意义,参与诗歌意义的建构。在这个过程中,诗歌意义是诗人与读者共同构建起来的。一首诗的首行对整首诗的写作意图表达有非常重要的意义。有经验的读者会从一首诗的第一行、第二行以至每个诗行的排列顺序来体会诗人的写作策略进而推测诗人的写作意图。事实上,诗人写作和修改的过程也是寻找自己本次写作原因的过程。因此,诗人修改作品的一个简单又有用的办法就是用原有作品的任意其他一行作为首行,看看对整体诗意构建的改变有多大。这个

---

① 转引自 https://www.poetryfoundation.org/poems/43285/adams-curse。
② 参见 Dobyns, chap. 6。
③ 参见 Kowit, p.11。

办法对诗人了解自己的写作目的很有效①。一首诗从一开始就要吸引住读者的注意力。诗刊的编辑阅读诗人投稿时其实经常是在寻找可以抛弃所读来稿的理由。如果他们读到的第一行只是如"After lunch, I walked to my car"这样引入性的句子，他们经常还没读完这一行就把整首诗抛弃了②。所以诗人如果想发表作品，更需要把读者和编辑因素考虑在内。

让读者成为诗歌意义建构参与者，诗人应该允许读者理解作品中事件的冲突性质、背景以及其前因后果③。一般来说，越是与社会时事密切相关的诗歌对读者的社会历史知识的要求越高，能读懂的读者就越少。但是，对于事件中的行为和情感的具体描写和呈现则是能够引起读者感同身受的有效方法。诗人斯坦利·库尼茨（Stanley Kunitz）下边的这首"肖像"（"The Portrait"）是使用动作描写表现情感状态的杰出代表。通过母亲对父亲名字守口如瓶及看到儿子取下父亲的肖像时掌掴儿子并手撕肖像等动作行为描写，将母亲对父亲的怨恨刻画尽致。作品最后两行更强化了当日母亲的盛怒，与作品开始两行进行了呼应。

The Portrait
By Stanley Kunitz

My mother never forgave my father
for killing himself,
especially at such an awkward time
and in a public park,
that spring
when I was waiting to be born.
She locked his name
in her deepest cabinet
and would not let him out,
though I could hear him thumping.
When I came down from the attic
with the pastel portrait in my hand
of a long-lipped stranger
with a brave moustache

---

① 参见 Dobyns, chap.6。
② 参见 Dobyns, chap.9。
③ 参见 Dobyns, chap.6。

and deep brown level eyes,
she ripped it into shreds
without a single word
and slapped me hard.
In my sixty-fourth year
I can feel my cheek
still burning. ①

  有经验的高层次读者，不仅喜欢读赏心悦目的诗歌，也喜欢读能够带来思维挑战的诗歌。如果一首诗不能适当打击读者期待，不能引发读者思考，挑战读者原有的满足和舒适感，则其平平无奇的表达方式就变得无聊，不值一提②。读者期待总是得到满足，读诗过程会变得无聊；但是读者期待总是得不到满足，读者又会备受打击。因此，诗人写作与修改诗歌要考虑读者期待，既适当打击读者期待，提供读诗过程中的意外与挑战，又不过度晦涩，适当满足读者在读诗过程中的成就感③。

  一首诗的行文过程应该张弛得法，才能持续吸引读者。如果一首诗行文毫无张力，则读者会觉得读诗很无聊。如果一首诗张力过度，挑战一个接着一个，比如过度的跨行连续，则其带来的不能缓解的紧张最终会使读者太疲惫。无聊和疲惫都会导致读者放弃读诗。张弛使用可以通过各种诗歌形式技巧来实现：比如跨行连续是张，停顿断行是弛；长句是张，短句是弛；晦涩是张，明晰是弛；给读者带来意外（包括押韵、格律、句法、用词上的变异）是张，满足读者期待（包括押韵、格律、句法、用词上的合规）是弛；重复则有时是张力，有时是舒适回归。张力一般能带来强调的效果，因此也要避免因为无意识地制造张力而不恰当地强调了某些诗中元素④。

  读诗与写诗一样，都需要有想象力和共情力，读诗是读者与诗歌在智性与情感两个层面发生互动和对话。有时读者可能会觉得某些诗歌作品智性不足，但是感性强烈。诗人沃尔特·惠特曼、查尔斯·布考斯基与弗兰克·奥哈拉（Frank O'Hara）的作品就会给一些读者留下这样的印象。有时读者又可能会觉得某些诗歌作品比如后现代实验诗歌智性闪耀，但是感性不足⑤。这两种情况都显示了某些东西限制了诗歌与读者的互动。诗人应该思考诗歌感性不足是否由作品对智性思考的呈现方式造成的。

  诗人修改作品，应该考虑读者因素，让诗歌激起读者相同或类似的情感反应，让读

---

① 转引自 Kowit, p.43。
② 参见 Dobyns, chap.1。
③ 参见 Dobyns, chap.5。
④ 参见 Dobyns, chap.9。
⑤ 参见 Dobyns, chap.10。

者在诗歌中体验自己的生命,产生与诗歌的共鸣,参与诗歌意义的共同构建。诗歌作品既要适当满足读者期待,又要提供读诗过程的意外与挑战,让读者与诗歌在智性与感性层面上形成互动与共情。基于读者因素考虑创作和修改诗歌作品,除了前述需要注意的问题以外,诗人还可以参考以下建议。当然,是否接受这些建议的选择权还是在于诗人自己:

1. 诗歌创作可能有道德功能,因为诗歌会间接对读者产生道德影响。但是,诗歌创作不能带着道德目的性(moral purpose or agenda)。不能带着道德目的性去操纵诗歌创作,罔顾事实存在去刻意回避或者美化事实[①]。

2. 如果诗歌先行带着道德设定,即带着道德目的,则一定会不真诚,因此其对读者的道德导向目的也是很难达到的。一旦读者觉察到一首诗有道德操纵的嫌疑,读者就不会相信诗中所言[②]。

3. 读者不喜欢宣教的诗,读者喜欢能够与自己联系起来的诗。

4. 诗歌主要关注情感与感受,诗人不应该告诉读者自己感受到了什么,而应该让读者真切体验到诗人感受的。

5. 让诗容易被理解并且具有叙事特征。

6. 诗歌的行文需要留白,要留给读者想象空间,要让读者的想象参与诗歌的意义构建,要暗示(suggestive),不要凡事说尽。诗人叶芝(W. B Yeats)在1925年的一封信中谈及 *Hamlet* 时说:只说一点,他就是哈姆雷特;全部都说了,他就什么都不是;不完整的才是有生命的[③]。诗歌尤其是抒情诗创作也是如此。

7. 不要让读者一次读完一首诗的意思。

读者读诗都是带着期待或者戴着滤镜对作品提出系列问题的。这个滤镜由其之前的阅读经验、心理、历史构成,这个滤镜也体现了读者提出的问题的性质与复杂度。读者的阅读滤镜可能会判定如诗人沃尔特·惠特曼那样的平民诗歌太容易理解、比较粗糙,而后现代诗歌虽然激发了智性思考但是太深奥[④]。但是,也有观点认为深奥不可言说也是一种言说方式,拒绝感性也是一种情感表现方式。因此,诗歌读者不一定要试图阐释所有诗歌,诗人也不一定要写作可以被阐释或者可以被理解透彻的诗歌。事实上,多义性正是诗歌魅力之所在,如下边诗人哈里斯(William J. Harris)的这首诗:

Practical Concerns
By William J. Harris

---

① 参见 Dobyns, chap.3。
② 参见 Dobyns, chap.3。
③ 转引自 Vendler, p.xi, 笔者译。
④ 参见 Dobyns, chap.10。

From a distance, I watch
a man digging a hole with a machine.
I go closer.
The hole is deep and narrow.
At the bottom is a bird.
I ask the ditchdigger if I may climb down
and ask the bird a question.
He says, why sure.
It's nice and cool in the ditch.
The bird and I talk about singing.
Very little about technique. ①

诗歌初稿创作之后的修改是重新检视初稿的策略和潜能的重要步骤,是挖掘被混乱的初稿文字埋藏起来的真正的诗的过程。诗歌修改是同时发现创造语言形式与构建诗歌意义的继续创作过程②,它不只是修改一两个词,而更可能是从头修改即重写诗稿。修改重写过程中,经验不足的诗人很难区分自己想表达的和实际已经表达的。不少新手诗人被自己作品所感动,以为读者也一定会深受感动。正因为诗人特别难以判断自己作品中哪些是有效表达,哪些是无效表达,所以很多严肃诗人会仔细倾听信任的朋友或读者的评论意见③。诗人艾略特的名作"荒原"("The Waste Land")就是听从了诗人埃兹拉·庞德的建议删去了原稿至少一半的文字。诗人叶芝也曾在使用更加平实精准而不是过于复古怀旧的语言方面接受过诗人埃兹拉·庞德的帮助④。征求读者意见有一个普遍公认的原则就是诗人不能向读者揭示写作目的,也即,不要做辩解。这与在英语诗歌创意写作教学的工作坊评论中诗作者保持沉默的原则是一致的。辩解会成为导向,导致读者给出的意见或反应并非纯粹由作品引起的。

第四节 英语诗歌创意写作中的工作坊(workshop)

诗歌工作坊(poetry workshop)是英美高校诗歌创意写作教学的典型模式,是实现诗歌创意写作教学目标即培养诗人的有效途径。在诗歌工作坊课程教学中,每个

---

① 转引自 Kowit, p.125。
② 参见 Kowit, p.52。
③ 参见 Kowit, p.28。
④ 参见 Dobyns, chap.7。

学生既是诗人，又是读者，既研究熟悉经典诗作和诗歌术语理念，丰富诗歌创作形式技巧，提高诗歌写作能力，也从诗人教师和同学诗人那里获得读者阅读反应和评论意见，研究自己作品的优点与不足，找到最好的诗歌表现形式，进而发展出自己的诗歌风格和特色。

英美高校诗歌创意写作教学在各个过程中激发学生的创作灵感。首先，让学生熟悉各种诗歌术语、运动、传统和形式并研究经典、成功诗作，目的是为了使其获得创作灵感，并将真正引起心灵共鸣的观点、形式、技巧运用于自己的创作实践中。其次，诗人教师采用各种方法，比如设计各种诗歌题材要求和形式技术规则，营造学生积极合作的氛围，等等，激发学生的热情与灵感进行诗歌创作。第三，在工作坊（workshop）环节中让学生诗人阅读和评论同学诗作，使学生诗人在与同行诗人的思想撞击中触发创作灵感。

不管是本科还是硕士层次的诗歌创意写作教学，工作坊都是核心教学环节。在工作坊中，学生诗人收集同行读者意见，了解作品的实际表达效果，从读者角度获取灵感，对初稿进行修改重写以继续创作真正的诗。诗人查尔斯·伯恩斯坦曾说："灵感不是在诗人写诗之前到来的，而是在作品被读或者被听的时候到来的"[①]。工作坊中有见地的同行评论给学生诗人提供独特的读者视角，它能够使一群从未发表过诗歌的学生教会另一群从未发表过诗歌的学生写出一首可以发表的诗[②]。这种效果在学生独自作战的情况下可能要花费数年时间才能达到[③]。

在诗歌创意写作教学中，"workshop"既是名词，即工作坊同学评论环节，也是动词，即同学评论。具体来说，工作坊同学评论是在诗人教师主持下，学生对同学作品进行建设性评论的教学环节。在工作坊同学评论中，学生可移动的独立课桌通常围成一个圆圈，课堂以学生诗作者朗读自己的作品开始，然后就是同学轮流对被评诗作做出评论。诗人教师在工作坊评论环节中的主要角色是协调者，除了必要的指导、总结和作业布置外，一般遵循相同的规则参与对学生作品的评论。被评诗作者课前要打印好份数足够、篇幅适当的作品供阅读评论。

不管是在哪种层次的工作坊同学评论中，诗作者大声朗读作品是不二选择。朗读不仅可以帮助听者在脑中更为清晰地接收诗歌作品，而且在诗歌朗读的声音中，作品中的错误或者问题能够被更加有效地发现。当然，如果诗作者有言语障碍，比如口吃或者

---

① 转引自 Perloff, Marjorie. *Poetics in a New Key: Interviews and Essays*, USA: The University of Chicago Press, 2015, p.91; Charles Bernstein said, "Inspiration is not what comes before the poet writes the poem but what happens when the poem is read (or heard)."

② 参见 Menand, Louis. "Show or tell: Should creative writing be taught", in *New Yorker*, No.6, 2009。

③ 参见 Gross, Philip. "Small worlds: What works in workshops if and when they do?", Donnelly, Dianne. ed., in *Does the Writing Workshop still Work?*, Bristol & Buffalo & Torontao: Multiligual Matters, 2010, p.53; Mayers, Tim. "Poetry, f(r)iction, drama: The complex dynamics of audience in the writing workshop", Donnelly, Dianne. ed., in *Does the Writing Workshop still Work?*, Bristol & Buffalo & Torontao: Multiligual Matters, 2010, p.96。

是太腼腆,可以请同学或者老师代读。朗读作品要尽量用平静的语调,不要戏剧化或者表演化,不要分散听者对诗歌语言的注意力①。

工作坊同学评论的具体过程视教师经验和学生水平的不同而在评论组织模式和规则等方面有所不同。经验丰富的诗人教师会根据写作教学进程和学生水平变化设计不同的工作坊评论组织模式,以多样化的模式最大限度激发同学评论,为学生诗作者提供意见和灵感。圣约翰大学诗歌工作坊诗人教师西蒙娜按照被评诗作课前是否预先被阅读,将工作坊分成两种模式:温读式(warm-read)和冷读式(cold-read)。温读模式难度较小,先于冷读模式实施。

温读模式中,学生在课前预先阅读和评注即将被评论的诗作。温读模式适应于难度较小的初级工作坊同学评论。在温读模式中,除了作品被评的诗作者外,其他所有学生依次逐一对作品进行评论。做评学生至少对每个被评作品给出三条评论,其中至少一条评论应该是鼓励性的,并且尽量不要重复前面同学已经给出的评论意见。温读模式工作坊中,诗人教师对被评诗作的评点也是课前写好并在工作坊过程中读出。

冷读模式中,学生在工作坊课堂首次阅读诗作并现场做出评论。这种模式因为被评诗作不能事先阅读做注,所以对做评学生的阅读批评能力要求提高,评论难度加大,但也能给诗作者提供作品最直接的读者反应。冷读模式中,除了作品被评的诗作者外,其他学生每隔一人对作品进行评论。做评学生不能重复前面同学的任何评论。如果出现轮到的学生一时不知如何做评的情况,则可暂时跳过该生,让后面的学生先评,等后面的学生都评论完毕,再回头让未做评的学生补评。冷读模式工作坊中,诗人教师也是首次阅读被评诗作并当场做出评点。

在两种模式中,被评诗作者在所有同学评论后可向全班提一个问题,但是在作品被评论的过程中必须保持沉默。评论过程中诗作者保持沉默是诗歌工作坊同学评论的统一规则。因为诗作者在征求读者意见时的一个普遍原则就是不能向读者揭示写作目的,不做辩解,不提供写作意图导向,这样才能获得纯粹由作品本身引起的、真诚有效的读者反应或意见。诗作者像海绵一样,以开放的心态聆听同学评论,才能吸收对继续创作有益的意见和灵感。在两种模式中,做评学生都将自己的评论记录下来并署名交给诗作者,以此显示评论意见的真诚。

除了上述按诗作是否事先阅读所分的温度和冷读模式外,不同的诗歌工作坊诗人教师会采用不同的工作坊评论组织模式。比如为了让评论能够流畅进行,诗人教师也可以指定两名学生做为主要评论者。当第一位主评快无话可说时,第二位主评可以接着进行评论。两位主评可以参考以下三方面进行评论:作品最好的地方在哪里?作品欠缺之处在哪里?欠缺之处可以怎样改善?最后,可以给诗作者提出一些问题。两位主评的评论结束后,其他学生轮流就这三方面问题或者其它与作品相关问题进行评论。

---

① 参见 Morley, p.120。

为了保证参加学生的评论与被评论机会，诗人教师需要掌握好每位学生评论的时间以及轮流方式①。

同学评论参与者的积极程度和专业素养影响着诗歌工作坊评论的成效。虽然同学之间对彼此诗作的评论是越诚实越好，但是因为诗人需要来自诗人的支持，所以同学之间应该互相鼓励。入门级别的工作坊赞美性评论可以多一点，但高级别的工作坊批评性评论应该更多一些。当然有效的工作坊评论不全是赞美也不全是批评，更不是按照刻板标准进行的评论。给出具体的、有见地的评论意见比给出笼统的或者个人情绪化的"支持"反应要好得多。

为了最大化工作坊评论的有效性，需要培养参加者的诗歌批判阅读和评论能力②。诗人教师重视对学生批判阅读与评论能力的培养。比如，有的诗歌创意写作教学参考书专辟章节列举诗例指出具体缺点以培养学生的诗歌批评能力③。再比如圣约翰大学诗歌工作坊诗人教师西蒙娜要求学生熟悉各种诗歌术语、运动、传统和形式，以理解作诗技法并习得评论诗歌作品的特别语言；她将学生两人一组分成若干对学习伙伴，在班级网络学习平台对彼此的诗作进行课前评论练习；她还在不同水平的工作坊组织模式采用不同的评论规则逐步训练提高学生的诗歌欣赏和批评能力，等等。

诗歌工作坊参加者要给出有根据的、好的、建设性的评论，需要注意以下三点：第一，建设性评论要基于对作品完整性的认识，针对作品本身特点提出改善建议。第二，好的评论是基于对作品的价值和有趣之处的认识，这种认识越清晰，评论就更可能被听取。与"这首诗中形容词太多了"这样的评论相比，"这首诗萧瑟氛围的描写方式令人震撼，不过，我想第四行里边那两个形容词是不是反而削弱了这种氛围了呢？"这样的评论就更可能被接受。第三，评论要针对作品的具体位置，要具体，要切实可行。否定整个作品，甚至否定诗作者，让诗作者觉得作品无药可救的评论是很难让人接受的④。

作为诗作者，听取读者意见或者批评首先要确定读者批评的是什么，要有信心确定读者批评的不是整个作品，也不是诗作者本人。要做到这点，诗作者本身要先与自己的作品保持一定的距离⑤。诗作者要记住自己是人，不是诗。当自己的诗被批评的时候，

---

① 参见 Morley, pp.122 – 123。

② 参见 Gross, Philip. "Small worlds: What works in workshops if and when they do?", Donnelly, Dianne. ed., in *Does the Writing Workshop still Work?*, Bristol & Buffalo & Torontao: Multilingual Matters, 2010, pp. 59 – 60。

③ 参见 Kowit, pp.38 – 47。

④ 参见 Aczel, Richard. "Listening to Criticism", Bell, Julia & Paul Magrs, ed. in *The Creative Writing Coursebook: Forty-four Authors Share Advice and Exercises for Fiction and Poetry*. London: Pan Macmillan, first published in 2001, electronic updated edition published in 2019。

⑤ 参见 Aczel, Richard. "Listening to Criticism", Bell, Julia & Paul Magrs, ed. in *The Creative Writing Coursebook: Forty-four Authors Share Advice and Exercises for Fiction and Poetry*. London: Pan Macmillan, first published in 2001, electronic updated edition published in 2019。

请记住，人家批评的是诗，不是人。当然，诗人不必过度考虑读者因素。过度考虑读者因素对诗歌创作来说是一种限制。

每个时代的诗歌做为一种艺术都会反映这个时代的社会、历史、文化、价值等等。在今天开放的时代和复杂的世界，每个个体都具有自己的个性和独特身份，诗人也一样，带着个人的、社会的、时代的特征和印记。越来越多的诗人不再用普世的、开放性的说话者声音进行创作，而是允许或者特意让自己的某些个性或者特征进入诗歌，更加具体真实地反映时代社会特征。一个诗人的特定风格既是由其所在时代艺术特点决定，也是由其自身特点决定。

一个诗人的特定风格在于其对素材的独特处理方式，在于其诗歌形式，而不在于其诗歌题材。诗歌做为艺术不像科学技术一样会随着时间而变得更加进步，得到提高或改善。一个时代的读者可能认为某些时期的诗歌比另外一些时期的诗歌更好，但这不是诗歌艺术进步的问题，而是读者品味和情感变化的问题[①]。一个诗人有责任培养读者对某种诗歌风格的欣赏能力和兴趣。如果一个诗人一心想要取悦当代读者，获得当代人的承认，为自己的创作设定道德导向，则很难在写作上做出重大创新。

诗歌创作上的重大创新经常会带来同时代读者不同程度的愤怒和失望，质疑甚至否定。比如，诗人约翰·邓恩就被同时代诗人本·琼森（Ben Jonson）博士指责要么随意改变格律重音，要么把混杂的思想或者异质的东西强扭在一起，所以必须被吊死[②]。直到二十世纪二十年代，因为诗人艾略特撰文推赞，约翰·邓恩才真正作为诗人被赞誉。诗人威廉·布莱克则被同时代读者称为疯子，他于1827年死后作品几乎被遗忘。直到十九世纪六十年代关于他的传记出版以后，他的作品才开始有了一些读者。而一直要等到十九世纪九十年代诗人叶芝帮助编辑其作品集之后，布莱克的作品才开始被广泛阅知[③]。诗人约翰·邓恩与布莱克偏离传统的轨道，这并不被同时代的读者认为是创新，而被认为是一种离经叛道，是一种错误。当然，从现代主义时期开始，创新已经成为至圣信条。

第五节 诗歌朗读会(open mic & poetry slam)、表演诗歌(performance poetry)

文学史上最著名的"（产出性）工作坊"之一是诗人乔治·戈登·拜伦、诗人珀西·

---

① 参见 Dobyns, chap. 9。
② 参见 Brooks & Warren, p. 578。
③ 参见 Dobyns, chap. 3。

比希·雪莱、雪莱十八岁的妹妹作家玛丽·雪莱(Mary Shelly)和学者波里道利(Dr. Polidori)于1816年6月中旬在日内瓦一个别墅里的夜间娱乐。这个夜间娱乐过程由诗人拜伦朗读从一本志怪故事书(*Fantasmagorianna*)中选出的一些鬼故事开始,朗读完拜伦要求在场每个参加者自己编讲一个鬼故事。这个类似于创意写作工作坊的诗人、作家与学者的夜间娱乐活动的成果之一就是玛丽·雪莱于两年后发表了著名的科幻小说《弗兰肯斯坦》(*Frankenstein*)①。

与高校诗歌工作坊能够加速学生诗人写出可以发表的诗作一样,来自同行诗人的意见或鼓励也能为专业诗人提供创作灵感,帮助诗人创作。参加诗人工作坊是诗人获得更多同行诗人意见或建议刺激自己继续创作的重要途径。高校以外的初级诗人工作坊一般参照本科层次诗歌工作坊模式,按照参加者水平与职业实际适当调整组织方案②,而专业的诗人工作坊则类似于硕士层次的诗歌工作坊模式,围绕诗人作品评论展开。参加专业诗人工作坊的诗人首先应该具备丰富的诗歌术语甚至文学知识。

专业的诗人工作坊构建起一个诗人社团,社团的成员互相评论对方作品,给出完善作品的建议,在彼此的写作事业上互相支持。诗人社团中的成员既可能成为亲密的朋友,也可能成为彼此作品的重要批评者。诗人工作坊建立起来的友谊既有写作上的专业竞争性,也有基于拥有同样创作理想和理念的同志式慷慨无私。健康的、建设性的诗人工作坊中来自同行的尊重与鼓励是很多工作坊参加者继续创作的热情与动力来源。如果一个工作坊中分了派别,或者总是充满负面评论,参加者要么应该忽略这些评论,要么应该离开它。

参加诗歌朗读会也是诗人获得更多读者反应刺激自己继续创作的重要途径。在诗歌朗读会中,诗人朗读自己或者别人的诗作,观众(听众)可能是诗人,也可能不是。不管是不是诗人,诗歌朗读会参加者至少都是诗歌爱好者。在诗歌朗读会中,诗人特别是新手诗人得到毫不吝惜的鼓励和掌声。对于许多诗人来说,在诗歌朗读会上朗读诗歌、与同行诗人互相激励是难忘的美妙经历。"开放的麦克风"(open mic)是诗歌朗读会的初级阶段,其形式或规则比较开放,不过,组织者要考虑场地有无舞台,舞台有无台阶,允不允许观众(听众)录音等等问题。

比"开放的麦克风"更高一级的诗歌朗读会形式是"诗歌擂台"(poetry slam)。"诗歌擂台"是一种由通常包括观众(听众)在内的裁判评分的诗歌表演比赛。第一次"诗歌擂台"于1986年由诗人马克·史密斯(Marc Smith)在芝加哥发起。"诗歌擂台"获胜者代表自己的学校、城市、甚至国家参加更高级别的比赛。参加比赛的诗歌一般不超过3

---

① 参见 Morley, p.119。
② 参见 Bell, Julia. "Feeling the Burn", Bell, Julia & Paul Magrs, ed. in *The Creative Writing Coursebook: Forty-four Authors Share Advice and Exercises for Fiction and Poetry*. London: Pan Macmillan, first published in 2001, electronic updated edition published in 2019.

分钟。不管是作为参赛者还是作为观众(听众),参加地方性的"诗歌擂台"都有助于了解诗歌表演的规则。入门级别的"诗歌擂台"的报名一般是开放性的,保证参赛者的持麦时间。一般,不允许参赛者带道具、工具,不能变成唱歌,不能剽窃,超时要受罚,等等①。目前美国最著名的"诗歌擂台"在纽约的 Nuyorican Poets Café 内常态化举行。

在诗歌朗读会上朗读诗歌的诗人,其朗读风格各异。不少诗人会为了朗读效果而加入一些动作或者声音元素,从而使其诗歌朗读具有明显的表演性,这时可以称这种诗歌为表演诗歌(performance poetry)。不少美国当代知名诗人如查尔斯·伯恩斯坦和苏珊·豪(Susan Howe)都是出色的表演诗人②。表演诗歌的共同特点在于:第一,诗人在朗读的时候特别注意身体和声音表达;第二,诗人重视观众(听众)的反应,因此会在朗读中更多使用重复、停顿、声高变化、重读词语、非语言表达方式等等在页面诗歌(page poetry)中作用不明显的表演技巧以吸引观众(听众)。有时,诗人在朗读之前,还会提供一些解释写作背景或者朗读者背景的前言③。

表演诗歌在语气上经常是对话式的,通常是背诵而不是朗读出来的,经常使用"I"来叙述。因为有这些倾向,所以表演诗歌以政治或者个人题材为主④。当然,创作表演诗歌并不需服从这些潮流倾向,只是,诗人避开已有潮流倾向进行实验写作时,要先考虑自己实验的目的是什么。首先要考虑诗歌的观众(听众)可能是谁。为了使观众(听众)愿意听,表演诗歌要有紧凑感,而且诗作越长,提供给观众(听众)的如享受、愉悦、紧张等情绪回报要越大。

表演诗歌中的用词特点与页面诗歌不同。页面诗歌的阅读节奏可以由读者选择,因此这些诗歌用词可以深奥,可以简约,甚至可以使用复杂含混词语,而表演诗歌的用词则应该很清楚,听一次就能明白,因为其观众(听众)一般只会听一次⑤。重复、押韵、叠句都是可以使观众(听众)听完表演后还可能记得诗歌的技巧。表演诗歌的诵读或者表演效果很难在页面上得到体现,因此其字面印刷版本很可能失去作为诗歌的魅力。

创作表演诗歌的一个快捷方法是勇敢地写一首不会让家人或者某些朋友听到的诗,或者一首很久以来一直避免去写的诗。假如已经有了"安全"的现稿,可以让诗稿变得暂时"不安全",加入一些"不安全"的细节或者情节,越具体越好。"不安全"的表演诗歌比较容易使观众(听众)激动,因为诗人说出了观众(听众)自己不敢说的话⑥。

---

① 参见 Jarrett, Keith. "Poetry that Needs to Be Heard", Bell, Julia & Paul Magrs, ed. in *The Creative Writing Coursebook: Forty-four Authors Share Advice and Exercises for Fiction and Poetry*. London: Pan Macmillan, first published in 2001, electronic updated edition published in 2019.
② 参见 Perloff(2015), p.36。
③ 参见 Jarrett, Keith. "Poetry that Needs to Be Heard", Bell, Julia & Paul Magrs, ed. in *The Creative Writing Coursebook: Forty-four Authors Share Advice and Exercises for Fiction and Poetry*. London: Pan Macmillan, first published in 2001, electronic updated edition published in 2019.
④ 同上。
⑤ 同上。
⑥ 同上。

创作表演诗歌时如果可以肯定观众(听众)会配合,偶尔还可以允许其参与到诗歌表演中来。不过,这个需慎重。诗人还可以尝试与两三个同行一起创作一首表演诗,在诗中某些部分几个诗人可以同时朗读,可以互相和声,也可以续读彼此的诗行,可以加手势加声响,可以故意制造混乱声响,如同时读出不同的诗行,等等。有一种多诗人合作创作形式是"翻译"式或多重声诗歌表演。这种形式要求观众(听众)至少懂得两种以上语言才能听明白。可以用这样的句子来开始一首"翻译"式或多重声表演诗歌:"Different ways to say..."①。

诗稿写就之后,诗作者本身是第一个观众(听众)。在上舞台前诗人要先操练表演。可以在镜子前录音,如果能录像更好。如果可以,把诗背诵下来。操练时要注意以下问题:第一,注意读诗时喘气停顿的地方。诗中想制造的节奏读出来是否达到预期?是否给予观众(听众)足够空间时间来消化诗中信息?读出来的韵脚是否生硬?等等。第二,除非有专业编舞指导,否则手势动作越少越好。只做有意义有准备的动作。背景前言也是越少越好。第三,朗诵表演时假装是面对着密友,看着观众(听众)的眼睛。还要扫视全场,对所有在场者表示感激②。

在表演诗歌中,诗人可以加入其他表演媒介,比如音乐、舞蹈、戏剧表演、视频等等元素。这些元素可能凸显诗歌文本,也可能削弱诗歌文本。虽然表演诗歌的名称出现的时间不长,但其实诗歌表演传统可以追溯到古代社会,尤其是与一些部落中至今存在的萨满巫师(shaman)的舞蹈歌唱有关。在朗诵表演诗歌的时候,诗人可以唱、喊、低吟,也可以两人齐读,或者轮流读,甚至循环重叠读(round-robin overlapping),等等③。

因为多数表演诗歌以第一人称"I"来创作,因此常常可能被认为是诗人的自传或自白。诗人创作表演诗歌为了表达效果经常做添枝插叶的渲染或者杜撰,但观众(听众)不一定意识到这一点。观众(听众)有时是被"诗人的真实"的误会所吸引,而不是被"诗歌的艺术"所吸引。因此,表演诗歌的创作者可能会面对在舞台上暴露相关个人的隐私的危险。艺术与生活的界限有时是模糊的,所以诗人创作时既要考虑观众(听众)反应,也要考虑诗中可能涉及的人物隐私的保护问题。

不管诗人的性格如何内向,至少应该尝试在舞台上表演一次诗歌,这会让诗人得到与写作和阅读页面诗歌完全不同的体验。在诗歌表演中,诗人可以真实体验诗中每个词语,发现诗中哪些词语与节奏表现力弱,哪些强,甚至发现一些词在公共场合下获得的新意义。诗人还会看到观众(听众)在意想不到的地方大笑,而在预设幽默的地方反

---

① 参见 Jarrett, Keith. "Poetry that Needs to Be Heard", Bell, Julia & Paul Magrs, ed. in *The Creative Writing Coursebook: Forty-four Authors Share Advice and Exercises for Fiction and Poetry*. London: Pan Macmillan, first published in 2001, electronic updated edition published in 2019。

② 同上。

③ 参见 Waldman, Anne. "Performance Poem", Padgett, Ron, ed. in *The Teachers & Writers Handbook of Poetic Forms*. Second Edition. New York: T&W books, 2000, pp.134 – 139。

而保持沉默。诗人还会看到观众（听众）有时因诗中某些地方惊讶吸气，而又对引起共鸣的诗行击指相和①。诗人在观众（听众）面前表演诗歌，通过观察观众（听众）反应，可以为编辑修改诗歌提供思路和灵感。

第六节　英语诗歌的发表与出版

美国诗人鲍勃·迪伦（Bob Dylan）和露易丝·格丽克（Louise Glück）先后于 2016 年和 2020 年获得诺贝尔文学奖。这是美国英语诗歌创作在世界范围内最新获得的承认。当今世界英语诗歌创作的胜地之一是美国。当代美国英语诗歌创作已经具有平民化的特点，而这既离不开美国高校英语诗歌创意写作教学几十年的繁荣发展，也离不开美国各种文化组织机构和全美各地对诗歌发展的维护和对诗人创作的支持。

美国"诗歌联盟"（Poetry Coalition）的二十多个会员组织致力于组织诗歌朗读会和诗歌工作坊，举办各种诗歌节。"美国诗人学会"是美国"诗歌联盟"的一个非盈利组织会员，每年举行各种诗歌朗读活动或比赛，发行诗刊《美国诗人》（*American Poets*），每年 4 月主办全国诗歌盛会"诗歌月"（Poetry Month）②。第一次全国"诗歌月"于 1996 年举行。每年"诗歌月"期间全美各地举办各种形式的诗歌活动。笔者 2017 年至 2018 年在美访学期间就参加了纽约曼哈顿圣保罗小教堂（St. Paul's Chapel）在 2017 年"诗歌月"期间举办的第 9 届诗歌节（The 9th Poetry Festival）。

除了全国"诗歌月"外，全美各地每年举办各种形式的诗歌活动。每两年一次的新泽西"道奇诗歌节"（Dodge Poetry Festival）是北美知名的诗歌节。在非"诗歌月"期间，美国很多城市比如纽约、华盛顿、洛杉矶和旧金山等等的社区中心、图书馆、公园、教堂，甚至书店、咖啡馆、画廊等场所都有定期的诗歌朗读会或者诗人工作坊。这些朗读会和工作坊通过网络公布活动消息，对公众免费开放。笔者 2017 年就多次参加纽约曼哈顿三一教堂（Trinity Church）每月一次的"诗人角"（Poet's Corner）活动。

这些诗歌工作坊、朗读会和诗歌节使进行创作的诗人与同行和读者直接见面，而朗读会或比赛视频获得允许后也可以上传网络。与诗人同行和读者的直接接触与互动既成为美国诗人进一步创作的激发因素，也影响了美国英语诗歌创作的内容与形式。当前，在诗歌文本阅读形式之外，一种数字媒体技术支持的、表演化、口头化、听觉化、年轻

---

① 参见 Jarrett, Keith. "Poetry that Needs to Be Heard", Bell, Julia & Paul Magrs, ed. in *The Creative Writing Coursebook: Forty-four Authors Share Advice and Exercises for Fiction and Poetry*. London: Pan Macmillan, first published in 2001, electronic updated edition published in 2019.

② 参见 https://poets.org/academy-american-poets。

化、规模巨大的新诗歌文化已经在美国发展了起来①。网络技术使读者通过网络就能看到诗人,听到诗人朗诵诗歌。表演诗歌成为受到当代年轻英语诗人和读者喜爱的诗歌形式②。新的表演性口头化听觉化诗歌形式大大拓展了诗歌接触读者的机会,并且进一步触发读者对诗歌文本阅读的兴趣。

数字媒体技术不仅促进了表演诗歌、视觉诗等的发展,也促进了诗歌文本的传播。"每日一诗"(Poem-a-day)是"美国诗人学会"完全数字化的、只通过电邮、社交媒体和网络途径进行的诗歌阅读项目,每日发送一首诗到登记的超过三十五万个邮箱供读者免费阅读③。数字媒体技术支持的在线出版还极大地降低了诗歌出版成本,有利于新手诗人的发展。在数字媒体技术支持下,任何人都可以注册一个网页发表自己的诗作,而不受编辑、代理或者出版合同的限制。数字媒体技术使得新手诗人从一开始就可以通过网络结识世界同行,得到文学理论、作家传记、奇书秘笈、比赛、发表、出版等信息④。

虽然在线出版成本低、速度快,但真正的诗人内心都会渴望把自己的生命诗作打印发表,甚至付梓成书,传于后世。每年一度的"作家与写作协会"年会及同时举行的书节为美国诗人提供了展示作品、与读者见面互动、与出版商合作的机会。诗歌工作坊、诗歌朗读会、诗歌表演等等途径提供的读者反应能够给诗人提供再次审视作品或者做出修改甚至重写一首新诗的继续创作动力,而发表出版作品则可以迫使诗人再次审视作品,在作品发表出版前把作品修改至善。

诗刊或出版社的编辑对诗作者来说是掌握着发表或出版生杀大权的特殊读者,诗歌创作中不厌其烦的修改过程中对读者反应的考虑,很大部分也是出于对出版社编辑反应的考虑。诗刊或出版社的编辑经常被淹没在来稿中,因此,当他们阅读来稿时,他们其实经常在寻找可以抛弃所读作品的理由。比如,如果他们所读诗作的第一行毫无吸引力,他们经常这一行没读完就把这首诗抛弃了⑤。所以,作为想发表作品的诗人,需要把编辑因素考虑在内,不能用无关紧要的句子作为一首诗的开始。最好用动作作为一首诗的开始,一首诗的开始几行就要引起编辑的兴趣。

英国诗人发表出版作品有一些做法可资借鉴。英国诗人在把诗稿送出发表之前,可能会先找专业的编辑咨询综合服务。英国的写作杂志分类专栏里边有这些服务信息。英国诗人还可能找对其作品具有欣赏力的专业代理人。其代理人销售诗作者的知识产权,并收取十到二十个点的佣金。忠诚的代理人不仅维护诗作者的商业利益,而且可能为诗作者的诗歌创作事业甚至个人生活提供专业建议。不过,理想的代理人比出

---

① 参见 Gioia, Dana. "The State of Poetry: Loud and Live." Sept., 2018. Introduction to The Best American Poetry 2018. Mar. 14, 2019.<https://lareviewofbooks.org/article/state-poetry-loud-live/>。
② 参见 Addonizio & Laux, pp.213-214。
③ 参见 https://poets.org/academy-american-poets/programs/poem-day。
④ 参见 Addonizio & Laux, p.206。
⑤ 参见 Dobyns, chap.9。

版商还难找①。虽然代理人难找,但是诗人应该保持自信,因为代理人不会创作,创作的是诗人,受人仰慕的也是诗人。

诗人写诗,很多时候是因为自己与语言有某种特殊的缘分,具有强烈的愿望用诗歌的特殊语言方式或表达或记录或发现或提升自我,等等。虽然自己的作品能够得到欣赏、发表甚至获奖是一件令人赏心悦目的乐事,但是诗人要注意把自己与作品适当分离。诗人是人,不是诗。当诗人的作品被漠视、被批评、被删砍的时候,请记住,人家漠视、批评、删砍的是作品,不是诗人。不要被砍的是诗,流血的是人。诗人应该对读者反应和意见持辩证态度,保持采用与否的自由。诗歌的价值不在于是否得到读者或者编辑的承认,也不在于是否发表出版。诗歌创作对于诗人来说应该就是单纯的快乐和享受。

---

① 参见 Miller, Candi. "Agents and How to Get One", Bell, Julia & Paul Magrs, ed. in *The Creative Writing Coursebook: Forty-four Authors Share Advice and Exercises for Fiction and Poetry*. London: Pan Macmillan, first published in 2001, electronic updated edition published in 2019。

第八章
中国人写英语诗

有语言就有诗歌,英语语言所到之处也是英语诗歌传播之处。世界各地不同民族在接受欣赏英语诗歌之时,也在反向影响英语诗歌创作的内容甚至形式。英国人、美国人、澳大利亚人、非洲人、印度人写的英语诗歌内容上不可避免都会带上其地方特点,意象派诗歌是在中国古代诗歌和日本俳句影响下出现的英语诗歌形式。中国人写英语诗歌,自然会反映中国社会、生活、文化、历史,带上中国文化特有的意象。中国人充当英语诗歌读者的时间久矣,是时候尝试做一做英语诗歌的创作者了。中国人进行英语诗歌创意写作,既能够丰富英语诗歌的内容甚至形式,也能够以英语诗歌语言向世界呈现中国情感态度,在国际社会发出中国新声音。

第一节 年轻化、国际化的英语诗歌读者和诗人

2021年,22岁的诗人阿曼达·戈尔曼(Amanda Gorman)成为美国史上首位在总统就职典礼上朗诵诗歌的"青年桂冠诗人"。"青年桂冠诗人"是为表彰在面向年轻读者的诗歌创作方面做出突出贡献的诗人而设立的职位。当前美国英语诗歌创作与阅读都具有年轻化特点。据美国2018年公布的公众艺术参与度调查结果显示,2017年美国成年诗歌读者比率比2012年上升近一倍,是进入21世纪以来的最高值。美国成年诗歌读者数量增长主要表现在年轻诗歌读者增长上。2017年18—24岁和25—34岁的美国人阅读诗歌的人数比率都比2012年上升一倍左右,在所有年龄段的成年美国人中分别居于第一和第二位①。

美国英语诗歌创作与阅读的年轻化离不开美国高校和各种文化组织对年轻诗人和

---

① 参见 Iyengar, Sunil. "Taking Note: Poetry Reading Is Up—Federal Survey Results." Jun. 7, 2018. *NEA*. Apr. 04, 2019.＜https://www.arts.gov/art-works/2018/taking-note-poetry-reading-%E2%80%94federal-survey-results＞。

年轻诗歌读者的培育。首先,美国高校诗歌创意写作教学既培养了年轻诗人,也培养了年轻诗歌读者。在美国高校诗歌工作坊中,大批聪明热情的年轻学生诗人在优秀诗人教师的指导下学习诗歌创作。当今美国高校学生,无论文理专业,都在诗歌工作坊课程中对诗歌表现出高度热情[①]。虽然诗歌工作坊课程学生不一定最后都以写诗为业,但是工作坊的创作学习经历使其对诗歌的感情变得亲近,因而成为忠诚的诗歌读者。美国年轻诗歌读者的增加不是来自高校诗歌阅读课程,而是来自高校诗歌工作坊课程。当今美国高校中诗歌工作坊课程的学生人数正在持续上升,而单纯的诗歌阅读课程学生人数反而是在下降[②]。

其次,美国文化组织比如著名的"诗歌基金会"专门设立了"青年桂冠诗人"职位,做为对面向年轻诗歌读者有突出写作成就的诗人的一种认可。"青年桂冠诗人"每两年选一次。2005年开始美国"国家艺术赞助基金会"(NEA)和"诗歌基金会"还联合启动了全美中学生"诗歌朗诵比赛"项目。全美中学生诗歌朗诵比赛与美国高校的诗歌创意写作教学一起构成了对美国青少年进行诗歌素质教育和感情培养的完美链条,促进了美国年轻诗歌读者数量的增长,使当前美国诗歌读者出现年轻化的特点。

年轻化的英语诗歌创作者与诗歌读者在数字媒体技术的支持下共同推动了表演化、口头化、听觉化的新诗歌文化的发展。美国各种文化组织机构在全美各地组织诗歌朗读会和诗歌工作坊,举办各种诗歌节,使进行创作的诗人与诗歌读者直接见面,而朗读会或比赛视频获得允许也可以上传网络。数字媒体技术使读者通过网络就能看到诗人,听到诗人朗诵诗歌。由Youtube和Instagram等数字媒体技术支持的新诗歌文化甚至催生出了Insta-poetry和Insta-poet等新名词。

数字媒体技术支持的新诗歌文化促进了英语诗歌的网络传播,并且进一步触发读者对诗歌文本阅读的兴趣。数字媒体技术为美国诗歌传播提供了便利的平台,越来越多的美国读者通过数字网络媒体阅读和分享诗歌。据"美国诗人学会"2018年的统计,相比于五年前只有19%的美国读者用手机读诗,2018年,用手机阅读诗歌的美国读者超过40%[③]。当前活跃在北美诗坛的露比·考尔(Rupi Kaur)、克林特·史密斯(Clint Smith)等诗人在各种国际社交媒体上的粉丝读者多不胜数。

数字媒体技术在客观上促进了英语诗歌的国际传播。"美国诗人学会"维护着世界上最大的政府资助的诗歌网站https://www.poets.org,读者在世界上任何网络通畅的地方都可以登录网站获得丰富的英语诗歌信息。如前章所述,"美国诗人学会"

---

① 参见Bennett, Chad. Why are more Americans reading poetry right now? Jun. 26, 2018. *Pacific Standard*. Mar. 30, 2019.<https://psmag.com/education/why-are-more-americans-reading-poetry-right-now>。

② 参见Perloff(2015), p.78。

③ 参见Poets.org. "Poetry Reading in the United States Has Risen Dramatically Proven by New Research by the National Endowment for the Arts." Jun. 7 2018. *Academy of American Poets*. Mar. 30, 2019.<https://www.poets.org/poetsorg/stanza/poetry-reading-united-states-has-risen-dramatically-proven-new-research-national>.

通过"每日一诗"(Poem-a-day)项目每日发送一首诗到登记的超过三十五万个邮箱供读者免费阅读。登记订阅"每日一诗"的不仅有美国国内的诗歌读者，也有身在美国国外的国际读者。美国其他众多的诗歌网站比如著名的"诗歌基金会"则为世界各地的英语诗歌读者提供免费的包括传统和现当代英语诗歌文本、音频以及相关研究资料，等等。

数字媒体技术也推动了英语诗歌创作的进一步国际化。从英语语言在世界各地使用的开始英语诗歌创作就具有国际化特点。长期以来，来自不同英语国家的英语诗人比比皆是。在当代数字媒体技术支持下，英语诗歌创作国际化有了新的发展。目前，从各种线上诗歌写作群组、线上诗歌工作坊、各种网络英语诗刊，到各种大型专业权威的英语诗歌网站如"诗歌基金会"和"美国诗人学会"等，英语诗歌创作正通过数字网络媒体渠道向世界上所有热爱英语诗歌创作的人打开大门。

数字媒体网络为英语诗歌发表出版国际化提供了技术支持。"美国诗人学会"发行《美国诗人》杂志。"诗歌基金会"的《诗歌》杂志（前身即二十世纪初著名的《诗歌》诗刊，诗人埃兹拉·庞德著名的"在地铁站"——"In a Station of the Metro"即在该刊发表[①]）在线发表选中的诗歌作品，世界上任何诗人都可向《诗歌》在线投稿。《前沿诗歌》（Frontier Poetry）则更注重在线发表新手诗人的作品。国际网络上其它各种各样题材或形式侧重点的在线英语诗刊多不胜数。一般情况下，这些英语诗歌网站或者诗刊接受国际诗歌创作者的投稿。数字媒体技术支持的在线出版还使国际上所有进行英语诗歌创作的新手诗人从一开始就可以通过网络结识世界同行，得到文学理论、作家传记、奇书秘笈、比赛、发表、出版等信息。数字媒体技术支持的在线出版极大地降低了英语诗歌的出版成本。在数字媒体技术支持下，任何人都可以注册一个网页发表自己的诗作，而不受编辑、代理或者出版合同的限制。

第二节　中国人的英语诗歌创意写作

英国、美国、加拿大、印度、大洋洲、非洲等不同国家与地区的诗人写的英语诗歌在内容上不可避免都会带上其地方特点。比如，英国诗人杰拉德·曼利·霍普金斯（Gerard Manley Hopkins）的诗歌中出现的是北威尔士风景，而美国诗人朗费罗（Henry Wadsworth Longfellow）、罗伯特·弗罗斯特（Robert Frost）、罗伯特·洛威尔

[①] 参见 https://www.poetryfoundation.org/poetrymagazine/about 或 https://www.poetryfoundation.org/poetrymagazine/history。

的诗歌中出现的则是新英格兰景色①。往往,诗人对某个地方的诗意描写会让读者对该地产生奇妙的感觉。比如英国诗人威廉·华兹华斯的诗歌使英格兰北部湖区成为文学朝圣胜地和旅游区,而美国诗人华莱士·斯蒂文斯一首短短的"坛子轶事"("Anecdote of the Jar")则让美国田纳西充满了神奇的艺术魅力:

Anecdote of the Jar
By Wallace Stevens

I placed a jar in Tennessee,
And round it was, upon a hill.
It made the slovenly wilderness
Surround that hill.

The wilderness rose up to it,
And sprawled around, no longer wild.
The jar was round upon the ground
And tall and of a port in air.

It took dominion everywhere.
The jar was gray and bare.
It did not give of bird or bush,
Like nothing else in Tennessee. ②

诗歌的想象性创作常常能够赋予一个看起来平平无奇的地方以神奇的内涵与魅力。美国诗人罗伯特·洛威尔的诗"楠塔基特的贵格会墓园"("The Quaker Graveyard in Nantucket")就是一个突出的例子。这首诗描写了一个贵格教捕鲸人埋葬先人的坟场。诗中所写的坟场现实中就是一个很普通的绿色小山坡,墓碑不多。但是因为诗中充满了捕鲸船、捕鲸人、鱼叉、受伤的鲸鱼、死尸和恐惧的祷告等富有感官冲击力的意象,这个地方就与惊险的捕鲸业联系了起来,蒙上了神秘的色彩。据学者考察体验,读诗前与读诗后去看那个小山坡,感觉是完全不一样的③。

---

① 参见 Vendler, p.246。
② 转引自 https://www.poetryfoundation.org/poems/51648/anecdote-of-the-jar-56d22f87dc64f。
③ 参见 Vendler, p.247。

The Quaker Graveyard in Nantucket
BY ROBERT LOWELL
[FOR WARREN WINSLOW, DEAD AT SEA]
Let man have dominion over the fishes of the sea and the fowls of the air and the beasts of the whole earth, and every creeping creature that moveth upon the earth.

I
A brackish reach of shoal off Madaket—
The sea was still breaking violently and night
Had steamed into our North Atlantic Fleet,
When the drowned sailor clutched the drag-net. Light
Flashed from his matted head and marble feet,
He grappled at the net
With the coiled, hurdling muscles of his thighs:
The corpse was bloodless, a botch of reds and whites,
Its open, staring eyes
Were lustreless dead-lights
Or cabin-windows on a stranded hulk
Heavy with sand. We weight the body, close
Its eyes and heave it seaward whence it came,
Where the heel-headed dogfish barks its nose
On Ahab's void and forehead; and the name
Is blocked in yellow chalk.
Sailors, who pitch this portent at the sea
Where dreadnaughts shall confess
Its hell-bent deity,
When you are powerless
To sand-bag this Atlantic bulwark, faced
By the earth-shaker, green, unwearied, chaste
In his steel scales: ask for no Orphean lute
To pluck life back. The guns of the steeled fleet
Recoil and then repeat
The hoarse salute.

II
Whenever winds are moving and their breath
Heaves at the roped-in bulwarks of this pier,
The terns and sea-gulls tremble at your death
In these home waters. Sailor, can you hear
The Pequod's sea wings, beating landward, fall
Headlong and break on our Atlantic wall
Off'Sconset, where the yawing S-boats splash
The bellbuoy, with ballooning spinnakers,
As the entangled, screeching mainsheet clears
The blocks: off Madaket, where lubbers lash
The heavy surf and throw their long lead squids
For blue-fish? Sea-gulls blink their heavy lids
Seaward. The winds' wings beat upon the stones,
Cousin, and scream for you and the claws rush
At the sea's throat and wring it in the slush
Of this old Quaker graveyard where the bones
Cry out in the long night for the hurt beast
Bobbing by Ahab's whaleboats in the East.

III
All you recovered from Poseidon died
With you, my cousin, and the harrowed brine
Is fruitless on the blue beard of the god,
Stretching beyond us to the castles in Spain,
Nantucket's westward haven. To Cape Cod
Guns, cradled on the tide,
Blast the eelgrass about a waterclock
Of bilge and backwash, roil the salt and sand
Lashing earth's scaffold, rock
Our warships in the hand
Of the great God, where time's contrition blues
Whatever it was these Quaker sailors lost
In the mad scramble of their lives. They died
When time was open-eyed,

Wooden and childish; only bones abide
There, in the nowhere, where their boats were tossed
Sky-high, where mariners had fabled news
Of IS, the whited monster. What it cost
Them is their secret. In the sperm-whale's slick
I see the Quakers drown and hear their cry:
"If God himself had not been on our side,
If God himself had not been on our side,
When the Atlantic rose against us, why,
Then it had swallowed us up quick."

IV
This is the end of the whaleroad and the whale
Who spewed Nantucket bones on the thrashed swell
And stirred the troubled waters to whirlpools
To send the Pequod packing off to hell:
This is the end of them, three-quarters fools,
Snatching at straws to sail
Seaward and seaward on the turntail whale,
Spouting out blood and water as it rolls,
Sick as a dog to these Atlantic shoals:
Clamavimus, O depths. Let the sea-gulls wail

For water, for the deep where the high tide
Mutters to its hurt self, mutters and ebbs.
Waves wallow in their wash, go out and out,
Leave only the death-rattle of the crabs,
The beach increasing, its enormous snout
Sucking the ocean's side.
This is the end of running on the waves;
We are poured out like water. Who will dance
The mast-lashed master of Leviathans
Up from this field of Quakers in their unstoned graves?

V

When the whale's viscera go and the roll
Of its corruption overruns this world
Beyond tree-swept Nantucket and Woods Hole
And Martha's Vineyard, Sailor, will your sword
Whistle and fall and sink into the fat?
In the great ash-pit of Jehoshaphat
The bones cry for the blood of the white whale,
The fat flukes arch and whack about its ears,
The death-lance churns into the sanctuary, tears
The gun-blue swingle, heaving like a flail,
And hacks the coiling life out: it works and drags
And rips the sperm-whale's midriff into rags,
Gobbets of blubber spill to wind and weather,
Sailor, and gulls go round the stoven timbers
Where the morning stars sing out together
And thunder shakes the white surf and dismembers
The red flag hammered in the mast-head. Hide
Our steel, Jonas Messias, in Thy side.

VI

OUR LADY OF WALSINGHAM
There once the penitents took off their shoes
And then walked barefoot the remaining mile;
And the small trees, a stream and hedgerows file
Slowly along the munching English lane,
Like cows to the old shrine, until you lose
Track of your dragging pain.
The stream flows down under the druid tree,
Shiloah's whirlpools gurgle and make glad
The castle of God. Sailor, you were glad
And whistled Sion by that stream. But see:

Our Lady, too small for her canopy,
Sits near the altar. There's no comeliness

At all or charm in that expressionless
Face with its heavy eyelids. As before,
This face, for centuries a memory,
Non est species, neque decor,
Expressionless, expresses God: it goes
Past castled Sion. She knows what God knows,
Not Calvary's Cross nor crib at Bethlehem
Now, and the world shall come to Walsingham.

VII
The empty winds are creaking and the oak
Splatters and splatters on the cenotaph,
The boughs are trembling and a gaff
Bobs on the untimely stroke
Of the greased wash exploding on a shoal-bell
In the old mouth of the Atlantic. It's well;
Atlantic, you are fouled with the blue sailors,
Sea-monsters, upward angel, downward fish:
Unmarried and corroding, spare of flesh
Mart once of supercilious, wing'd clippers,
Atlantic, where your bell-trap guts its spoil
You could cut the brackish winds with a knife
Here in Nantucket, and cast up the time
When the Lord God formed man from the sea's slime
And breathed into his face the breath of life,
And blue-lung'd combers lumbered to the kill.
The Lord survives the rainbow of His will.[①]

　　包括诗歌在内的文学作品对某一地方的描写表现往往直接影响了读者对该地的情感认知。比如，与读者对威廉·华兹华斯的英格兰北部湖区、华莱士·斯蒂文斯的田纳西、罗伯特·洛威尔的埋葬捕鲸人的小山坡的情感反应类似，人们心中对北美大陆的神秘感部分来源于欧洲古代文学中关于失落的亚特兰蒂斯的神话传说，而对希腊心生向往的人们不少是因为荷马的著名史诗。

---

　　① 转引自 https://www.poetryfoundation.org/poems/48984/the-quaker-graveyard-in-nantucket。

某个特定地方的人物、事件、历史是诗歌创作的重要题材。诗人理查·雨果（Richard Hugo）就常常通过想象其途经城镇的人、事、物来进行诗歌创作。诗人也可以通过描写表现其出生、成长、居住地方的人物、事件和历史，表现其意识感悟和身份认同，比如诗人菲利普·莱文（Philip Levine）对底特律的描写表现。包括诗歌在内的文学作品再现特定地方的社会、生活、历史和文化，以文学特有的方式记录特定地方特定时代人的情感、思想。比如，读者通过阅读诗人戏剧家莎士比亚的诗歌和戏剧，可以体验伊丽莎白一世时代人们的情感，了解那个时代英国、欧洲的社会、生活、政治、思想，等等。

中国人写英语诗歌，自然会反映中国社会、生活、历史、文化，带上中国文化特有的意象。中国人进行英语诗歌创意写作，不仅能够丰富英语诗歌，而且能够以英语诗歌语言形式向世界呈现中国情感态度，在国际社会发出中国新声音。中国人用英语诗歌书写中国能为英语读者提供了解中国的崭新视角，能在沟通中国与国际社会的感情与思想方面发挥独特作用。

当前中国在与国际社会的文化、思想、感情交流方面仍然存在问题。首先，普通国际受众与中国中文媒体存在语言障碍，看不懂中文媒体内容。第二，中国英文媒体、在海外的英文传播项目未能摆脱官方宣传的刻板印象，有的甚至被国际网络平台贴上中国官方媒体的标签，因而未能形成与普通国际受众的有效沟通。第三，普通国际受众主要是通过西方媒体来认识中国的，而西方媒体经常片面选择关于中国的负面材料来报导中国。这些问题带来的后果就是在国际受众心目中的中国形象往往是片面的、负面的。

相较于其他文化传播方式，包括诗歌在内的文学作品更能引起受众即读者细腻强烈的情感反应，因而对读者的思想影响更加持久深远。目前国外关于中国的英语文学读物不少，但这些读物绝大多数要么是用汉语写作的中国作家作品的英语译本，要么其作者是外国人或海外华侨。与海外作者使用英语进行涉及中国元素的文学创作相比，让生活在中国、了解中国、热爱中国、理解中华文化的中国人发出声音，使用英语进行关于中国的文学创作，包括诗歌创作，更能真实完整描写中国社会、生活、历史、文化，表达中国情感、态度，讲真讲全讲好中国故事。

在当前中国，已有一些高校教师正在进行英语文学创意写作实践和教学，包括笔者的英语诗歌创意写作。中国诗人与作家是通过爱荷华大学的"国际写作计划"（International Writing Program）而接触文学创意写作与文学工作坊的。1967年爱荷华大学启动"国际写作计划"，创意写作开始正式从英语国家走向世界。1979年中美建交，"国际写作计划"举办了第一次"中国周末"活动，为中美两国作家提供交流的机会。此后，不少用汉语创作的知名中国诗人与作家通过"国际写作计划"参与到了创意写作的国际潮流中[①]。

中国人进行英语诗歌创意写作，当然要遵循英语诗歌形式传统，借鉴现当代英语

---

① 参见张雪雨晴，pp.11-12。

诗歌创作方式方法。这也是本书第一到第七章研究的目的所在。但是，诗人艾略特说过："二流诗人模仿；一流诗人偷窃"①。正如美国诗人可以将日本俳句美国化为美国俳句和美国句子，并对中国古代诗词题材进行美国化和当代化的改写一样，中国人写英语诗，更要结合中国元素，积极从题材和形式上探索英语诗歌中国化的可行方案。

英语诗歌创作中经常使用的一个工具是用典（allusion）。诗人艾略特的名诗"荒原"（"The Waste Land"）中到处用典。希腊和罗马神话，以及 Bible 是传统英语诗歌用典的主要来源，而美国西部拓荒和牛仔的传说、好莱坞电影形象、漫画英雄和肥皂剧人物等则是美国诗歌用典的来源。中国古代神话传说当然也应该成为中国人用英语进行诗歌创意写作时名正言顺的用典来源。当然，每个诗人还都可以改编或者创造自己的神话。

中国人用英语进行诗歌创意写作，除了上述的中国神话植入之外，还可以尝试用声译诗（translitic）形式进行英语诗歌中国化。诗人创作声译诗时可以选用一首汉语诗做为底本，将之"转译"为英语诗歌。"转译"时，诗人只关注汉语诗的声音，而不关注其词语意义，可使用同音异义词进行诗歌转写。创作声译诗时可只根据汉语诗的声音进行转写，也可在修改时随意偏离原诗稿，使最后作品成为诗人完全的原创诗作。

中国诗人进行英语诗歌创作，应注意通过各种可能途径参与国际英语诗歌创作活动或比赛，包括通过网络参与国际英语诗歌创意写作线上活动。这既有利于中国的英语诗歌创意写作与当前国际诗坛建立联系，接触并实践国际最新诗歌创作理念，也有利于扩大中国的英语诗歌创意写作的国际知名度，接触更多国际受众，使更多国际受众了解中国社会、生活、历史、文化，理解中国情感、态度，达到中国与国际社会在文化、思想、感情方面的充分有效沟通。

第三节　一个中国人的英语诗歌选录

本节选录了本书著者即笔者创作的部分英语诗歌（共 66 首）。选录主要基于以下三个考虑：一、与中国相关的题材；二、一些传统英语诗歌形式的实践；三、普通人的感受与态度。居住于中国的中国人创作英语诗歌，除了需要深入了解英语诗歌传统、熟练掌握各种英语诗歌形式、清楚了解当前国际英语诗歌创作现状之外，另一个硬件要求就是诗人必须具有较高的英语语言能力水平。这最后的但却是基本的要求有时也是一个障碍，常常会使中国的英语诗人在与本族语为英语的诗人比较时感觉

---

① "Bad poets imitate. Good poets steal."转引自 Hugo, chap.9。

底气不足。然而,任何语言都是在使用中发展的,作为国际语言的英语尤为如此。既然美洲大陆能够发展出与英国特点不同的英语、非裔美国人英语也保留了自己的特色,那么中国人也可以让英语加上一些中国色彩,中国诗人也可以用英语诗歌呈现中国意象,讲述中国故事。

1.
A Gift
By Joyce Chen

I was endowed with a special gift
  by nature.
Therefore I got another gift
  —my daughter,
who also has her own gifts
  right now and in the future.

What a lovely gift you would be if
  we women were free!
No men can create the same
  as we women can;
Thanks to you we women are so-called
  mothers of men.

Only there is this problem
  of freedom.
How many of us can decide
  when to start,
or even when to stop
  to have children?
Husbands may marry us not for
  ourselves but for you;
Bosses hesitate in hiring us for
  some day we may use you;
Working men think us inferior for
  other gifts brought by you.

Alas, how we worship you Divine Gift!
Yet how come so often you become A Burden?

2.
A Thief

By Joyce Chen

The final destination for all philosophies is extinction.
The only worthy theory is Hedonism.
That makes so much sense at the moment
When you become a sweet thief
Stealing a second to miss some person.

3.
A Tradition

By Joyce Chen

The epic migration starts again
by flying plane, bullet train,
and running wheels on the land.

The rushing tide is ancient and strong,
and the way home sounds noisy and long.
"Whose home are you returning after all?"

The father is tracing his childhood;
the child has to respect the fatherhood;
and the mother disciplines herself as much as she should.

The whirling wave shoves her off the shore,
until she can't tell where she is any more.
"Breathe, breathe, you should find out your own port."

Yet the port is neither near nor afar;
she can't reach it by air or by car.
Her only place to anchor is her own heart.

4.
After

Joyce Chen

I plunge into a small pond
Immediately a current draws me into the deep.
I search for the fairy fish.
Every time I see its luminous shadow
The fish drifts into a deeper current.
Breathlessly I chase and chase
Hopelessly all the way into the sea.

There is the fish!
It presents me a pearl wreath.

5.
After the Murder

By Joyce Chen

(2023 – 1 – 12)

Yesterday a devil murdered
Innocent people
At the far end of this road.
A mother mourned
and regretted for her six-year-old.
She never could wear the new
Dress for the festival.

Yet, I still love the bus station.

6.
Another Hectic Week

By Joyce Chen

On Sunday your sister Dee
Came to rescue her womb.
Two days later your sister Bee

Came to rescue her eye.
You went out to rescue both of them.

Months, years, decades,
So many have come for rescue.
I am glad you have insisted on all these rescues.
They have made you
Human!

7.
At 8:00 AM in the Metro

Guangzhou runs
with these bright eyes,
full bellies,
and magic boots.

——By Joyce Chen

8.
Buried in Light
By Joyce Chen

The room is 1860 meters above sea
with white ceiling and walls.
The beige silk curtain is flapping in the wind.
This is a beautiful summer night on the mount.

"Mum, look, ink painting on the ceiling."
"Beautiful!"
"Mum, look, another one on the curtain."
"Let me see... OMG, it's a moth!"
A huge one.
Dark, beautiful, but dead!

A wing, with neatly woven veins, was torn
apart from the smashed body.
The black powder spread around,

reflecting the light with the beige silk

and creating the elegant atmosphere of an impressionistic painting.

"A tragedy!

The room of this height should have been your paradise.

Who has made it your burial ground?"

Rosy rays radiated from the other moth,

the "ink painting" on the ceiling,

glorifying the light from the bulb,

mocking at my petty pity on the heroic death.

9.

Cappuccino, please!

By Joyce Chen

No rain for one month.

Maybe two? Or even three?

The sky is lead-heavy.

Dusts make thick covers for drooping leaves.

Shameless summer forces straight into the lame spring.

Nobody is suffering.

After all it is lucky

not to be the girl killed by deafening poverty,

not to be on the roads that collapse suddenly,

not to be on the disappearing island,

not to be in Australia,

not to be in Tehran or Baghdad.

Somebody is planning his big agenda.

He vows to show he is strong.

Can you promise nothing will go wrong?

10.

Choice

By Joyce Chen

(One-sentence poem, line break suggested by Dr. Simona Blat)

On the morning of your birthday
I woke up from this dream
where your adoring eyes
were melting my heart,
which like the bird breeding
and singing crazily about her ecstasy
after she had finally found the right thorn
and desperately plunged onto the penetrating horn
wished myself to walk away with you
alone into the wild
under the winking stars while we were sitting
side by side at the luxurious dinner table
spread out for the family meeting,
your fingers
clinging to mine.

11.
Come, My Deer
By Joyce Chen
(A Villanelle)

Come see me at night.
My Deer, come with your chariot and lantern,
if the day repels you with scorching light.

Start your visit from that land of snow white.
Set my pious dome as your destination.
Come see me tonight.

For your nocturnal arrival, I will sleep tight
and keep the doors to the dreamland wide open,
so that we will exchange, with so much delight.

Endow me with your deep insight.

Enliven me with your rich imagination.
I will no more get lost at night.

Then I'll fill your chariot with articles bright,
and refuel your lantern with eternal oxygen,
so that you won't be shy before arrogant daylight.

Take me with you in your next flight.
Let's ride the waves of the unruly ocean.
Together we'll dance on the stormy wild night.
Together we'll sing in the soft moon light.
12.
Command

By Joyce Chen

Brutal Fate must be so busy
that it messes up all mortal life.
Just to make its art more easy,
it cuts the shy luck with a sharp knife.

Wait, hateful Fate!
Stay in your place.
Don't break anybody straight.
Let them play and make their days.
13.
Cruelty

By Joyce Chen

April is not
the cruelest month;
March is.
See that bud burgeoning in the March sun?
It is wickedly mocking my mistaking it for you.

April is not

the cruelest month;
March is.
Note the snow melting on the March grass?
It is also chilly scorning my mistaking it for you.

April is not
the cruelest month;
March is.
See those faces smiling at the March air?
They too are haughtily teasing my mistaking them for you.

April is not
the cruelest month.
March is,
because every time I try not to think about you,
my stupid heart rebels to ache for you.

Who says April is the cruelest month?
March is
the cruelest month,
for each step I try to withdraw from you
foolishly draws me further towards you.

How can April be the cruelest month?
March is
the cruelest month,
as no subway announcement fails to remind me that
I still share the same city with you.

Each hour, minute, and second;
Every step, stop, and station;
No time in no place of this departing March is not about you;
Yet everything everywhere turns out not to be the real you.
Who says April is the cruelest month?

14.
Deep Blue Sea
By Joyce Chen
(A Villanelle, 2021 - 10 - 5)

I must have come from the deep blue sea
whose large family of free souls waits
to welcome me back to eternity.

The born temperament of melancholy
overwhelming me illuminates
I must have come from the deep blue sea.

The oceanic vast transparency
promising common justice motivates
my will to go back for eternity.

The sea's emancipating fluidity
nurturing wild souls like me indicates
I must have come from the deep blue sea.

The final state in naked purity
of all beings in the sea anticipates
my atomic path to eternity.

This naturally grown affinity
between the sea and me demonstrates
I must have come from the deep blue sea
that'll welcome me back to eternity.

15.
Distant Education
By Joyce Chen
(A Blank Verse)

By chance a modern daughter comes across

a solemn statue sitting on the throne
inside a decent chamber in the MET.
The statue confidently looks toward
these words: The Female Pharaoh Hatshepsut.

Are you the pharaoh whose name and face
your male successor tried to chisel away
from your own temple and usurp your feats
as his? Were you too confident about
the strength of words and arts? Could you foresee
the usurpation crime befalling you?
Was it because you lived two thousand years
before the only Chinese empress that
you couldn't estimate vicissitudes
like these? See how strategical she was:

For fear of male contempt and slandering,
she left a wordless stone before her tomb.
The eloquent spectacularity
of wordlessness was what she counted on.
Posterity has been obliged to judge
their only woman ever in the throne
from written files, reasoning, and conscience.
At last the words of files speak out aloud
and lead to a fair evaluation of her.

My dear daughter, besides her feats, how come
you know so much about my history?
My male successor couldn't rub me out,
because my voluminous words prevailed.
Those words tell you about my history,
and my successor's vicious erasure.
See how divine the final justice is?
And what immortal power that words have?
Yes, Pharaoh, you are absolutely right!

16.
Dr. Sisyphus in a G. Z. Hospital
By Joyce Chen

Greyness infects every ill person
in the crowded waiting hall.
Each dull eye stares at the billboard;
Each empty ear tries to catch the call.
Everyone is eager to see you,
the savior in the white robe.

You sit there, unmasked.
Your amiable look and soothing voice
gives hope to the tortured souls;
Your signed ink on the printed prescriptions
infuses life into the ailing bodies.
All diseased are easy, when relieved.

The last patient leaves.
You take your own red pills.

17.
Episode I, 2020
By Joyce Chen

Dark!
King Cobra spread its venom with the storm!
eyes—blinded
mouth & nose—sealed
breath—strangled
tongue—struggling—in vain
H—e—l—l—p—

Wake up, Daddy.
The sun's come out.
Birds are calling.

All... right... coming...
Wait...

Slippers and pajamas put aside,
the girl is following every step of her father
in the ritual of morning sports,
tiptoeing and swirling.
Heaven is the man indulging in the aurora
polishing his daughter's little forehead
shimmering with almost-invisible sweat.

Her freckled cheeks flourish like cherry blossoms.
18.
Episode II, 2020
By Joyce Chen

I was happy
I was free to be alone.
I set up four walls
to defend myself from intruding noise.
I put away my heart
at one corner within the walls.
I sang and danced to please nobody.
Sometimes I would leap through
the opening above to get a human touch.
Then I would withdraw quickly back into my cabinet.

One day the noise retired completely.
Day one, day two,...
Week one, week two,...
I was curious.
I leapt out again to see what was happening.

Streets, schools, parks, plazas, buses—
All were empty

except hungry rats roaming around rotten rubbish.

No one is happy to be forced to be alone.
19.
Episode III, 2020
By Joyce Chen

One day, having enough of human avarice,
Pandora opened a box and let loose a devil.
Therefore the campus has been empty of students;
Weeds go wild on the football fields.
KNOW YOUR PETTINESS, PARASITES!
BE HUMBLE!

J.C. has longed for serenity for years,
but she does not like this forced loneliness.
A rotten palm sticks out of the grass on the sidewalk.
She almost stumbles.
Recently there have been fewer ambulances and helicopters.
A relief for the moment.
Maybe it's time to see her Will?
—BUT—
DO I DARE
DO THE ADVENTURE?

On the 141th day after the lockdown,
J.C. sets out for her first trip farther
than to the supermarket across the avenue.
She is heading toward the Teem Plaza six stops away.
The bus is not empty, but passengers
wear masks and keep distance.
The gilded display windows of LV are shinning.
Their counterparts in Manhattan are boarded.
GO MARCH FOR THE BREATHING OF
ONE HUNDRED THOUSAND AND ONE PEOPLE!

Twenty twenty has started wrong!
A virus confined 1.4 billion people home
during their Spring Festival!
Cold was the large number of alien onlookers!
Cruel was the inhuman request to punish the victimized nationals!
Now that bigotry and prejudice prevail,
all natural sons of politics:
Apathy, Arrogance, Caprice, Impotence, Lies, and National Supremacy,
come out boldly to claim their legitimacy.
The world is drowning.
Don't test humanity in dire need!

GOD BLESS CHINA!
She suddenly turns emotional.
For months, watching the words on the Canton Tower:
中国加油！武汉加油！
she has prayed for them to turn back into usual commercials.
She also prayed for New York to stay strong.
Everyday she reports she's all right to the university;
Everyday she asks her students about their health situation.
The zoom class has become their powerful inter-continent connection.
PROFESSOR, LET'S STAND TOGETHER AND WIN TOGETHER!
SURELY WE'LL WIN THIS WAR AGAINST THE VIRUS.
Will this war lead to another war?
Who knows?

Life has changed.
Will is sending someone to pick up the car.
J.C. can't persuade herself to drive.
She doesn't want to be a killer.
Poor Will, a born poet, is now a broke technician.
Confidence took decades to build, months to destroy.
Recovery takes time and resources.

Resources have been running short.

Even the beacon is turning dim for lack of refueling.
TO RESUME NORMALITY, WE NEED BURN MORE PETROLEUM!
Nature is stunned by human vanity.
I CAN BE WITHOU YOU.
YOU CAN'T BE WITHOUT ME.
BE HUMBLE, PETTY PARASITES!
Listen, my fellow human beings!
Listen to Nature!
Beware—
When she revenges, are you innocent?

NOT EVEN ME!
—BUT—
DO I DARE
DISTURB THE UNANIMITY?
J.C. sits down for her favorite salmon sushi.
Outside the window of the restaurant,
the sun is shinning on the waving leaves.
A green bird is tweeting on a golden bough.
She scrolls down the headlines:
The virus was found on a cutting board
for imported salmons in a Beijing market;
Black bears have been found roaming the New York streets.

Sooner or later, Nature will reclaim her sovereignty.
20.

Episode IV, 2020

By Joyce Chen

This autumn wind conjures up that lurking leaf.
It has disappeared for a long time.

The leaf sneaks onto that old street,
along which you wandered at loss in the summer heat.
The leaf shows you around the small canteen,

with whose fried rice you fed yourself, little money in pockets.

The leaf looks vainly for all those boutiques,

whose antique shoes and dresses you still admire.

The leaf pauses before that hotel,

the heavy porch of which still pushes you far way.

The leaf floats and floats above the pavement,

which is so clean that reminiscent feet will not leave.

Where is that old firm and the woman boss?

She hired you because you looked like her.

Such a pity.

You fired her brother for his apathy.

The leaf was first dressed in fresh green,

then drowned by bitter rust,

then it was lost.

Now it returns in gold.

It drifts along the street block by block,

so your thoughts dissolve into snapshots:

you burying yourself in the Christmas decoration items,

you bursting into tears while arguing with the head of the corporation,

you reading books while catering your little baby,

you returning to schools in a refreshing season,

you partying with students of all races, young or old,

you landing on JFK and laughing on Coney Island,

you wrapping up a Queens leaf in your pages.

The wind is going wild.

It blows and blows.

It sweeps away the lingering leaf, sweeps away reason, sweeps away peace.

It drags in freezing frost, drags in mania, drags in decease.

Who knows what will happen in this crazy current?

In this turmoil,

will you still seek out that leaf,

even to the peak of the Alps, or the shore of the Aegean,

so that some day you can hold it in palms,

and claim peace?

21.

Excuse for a Festival

By Joyce Chen

(A Sonnet)

Today we take a break to celebrate

your tragedy by means of comedy.

We glorify your seperation date

in order to unite our family.

Do not complain about the heartlessness.

In this invalid life who's able to

deprive capricious fate of brutalness?

We trivial beings are only beasts in the zoo.

When wanton fate is not in an easy mood,

poor animals get locked up, then destroyed.

So often we take misery for food,

and numbly we have fallacy deployed.

Who cares about your pain during your flight?

Who knows your cry for absent love at night?

22.

Failing Storm

By Joyce Chen

(A Limerick, 2022 - 5 - 11)

The whole city is waiting for you.

Schools are closed to make room for your view.

Such a high profile storm!

Have you failed to perform

Covid tests to let you parade through?

23.
Finally
By Joyce Chen

Throw me into the sea.
Don't let me float in the river or the lake.
Not that they are shallow and empty,
or small and dirty,
but that there is no whale, no shark,
no mermaid, and no lost Atlantis.

24.
For Dignity
By Joyce Chen
(A Sonnet)

You thought the only thing you could control
was you, so you behaved yourself so well
that it's not long for you to reach your goal
of winning battles that you could foretell.
You hoped humility, diligence, and
intelligence would soften Destiny
to change your fixed course of life and expand
your human latitudes and potency.
It took you half your life to realize
that Destiny is such a despot that
Oedipus was forced to stab his own eyes
with whose light he rebelled against his fate.
His tragedy is your impotency!
For dignity you'll make blind comedy!

25.
Forgive Me, This Is Not Profanity!
By Joyce Chen

The question "Do you believe in God?"
expects you to give an affirmative nod,
but you just think for a while,

then give an apologetic smile.
There are so many gods demanding belief.
Which one should you follow for relief?

Yet this doubt doesn't help you out,
for you are constantly struck dumb by an inhuman shout.
"I distribute your fortune and your soul.
It's me that's in charge and in control!"
Although you can't see the inhuman presence,
you do feel its omnipotence.

It not only picked the date for your physical birth,
but also set the way for you to leave the earth.
No matter how hard you struggle in your fights,
the inhuman being is always manipulating your delights.
You think it's you who are winning or losing.
Actually it's that being that's giving or depriving.

You do everything to sustain your breath.
It trivializes anything with invincible death.
What remains and means for you is not much,
for its authority is impossible to touch.
So don't boast you have any say
in how you'll survive the day.
26.
Frankenstein
By Joyce Chen
(A Sonnet, 2021 - 8 - 28)

The first news pops out from my phone today:
A man supposed to have planned the attack outside
the Kabul airport was spotted and blown away.
Can anyone have any place to hide
if chased by arrogant Technology?
My phone records the route I ride a bike

and shares it as part of public memory
no matter whether I dislike or like.
Hey, Tyrant Technology, hands off the soul!
No way for you to play the human role!
Behold! The light sneaks through combating trees
to flirt with chanting birds on a broken chair.
How can you understand their melodies?
Or feel this aura of the autumn air?

27.
Haiku 1
By Joyce Chen
(2021 - 2 - 13)

—Fireworks and laugh—
An ambulance reached a house.
It came with no sound.

28.
Haiku 2
By Joyce Chen
(2021 - 3 - 12)

The seed was planted
three years ago. It has been
destroyed by the earth.

29.
Haiku 3
By Joyce Chen
(2021 - 6 - 21)

Haiku echos life.
Both start as hope, swell in pride,
then fail in silence.

30.
Haiku 4
By Joyce Chen

(2022 - 6 - 26)

Three plump mangoes jumped
down to the sidewalk, all cracked,
gold pulp shining out!
31.
Haiku 5
By Joyce Chen
(An anti-Haiku, 2022 - 8 - 1)

An evil old witch
Falls from her broom and sets up
A fire on the sea.
32.
Haiku 6
By Joyce Chen
(An anti-Haiku, 2022 - 8 - 1)

An angry dragon
leaps up to blow off the witch
and rainsweep the fire.
33.
Hello, June!
By Joyce Chen
(2021 - 6 - 25)

Good bye, May!
You thought you could scare us?
No way!

In a flowery season,
You tore up earth, robbed of fruits, left behind ruins.
To a happy chorus,
You broke lyre strings, stuck organ keys, squeezed out screams.

Don't you know that, May,
The root has been preserved beyond earth?
The seeds have been scattered around the world?

Away, away, clown May!
Take away your ruins, go away with your screams.
Love will remain, music will stay.
Look! Behind you, in the golden halo, comes King June!
34.
Home
By Joyce Chen

No piano, but two different Chinese zithers.
No jewelry, but shelves of books.
Too small to entertain large parties,
but big enough to accommodate a small family.

When there are not many distractions,
the father will play an ancient melody,
and the daughter will doodle for fun.
While the mother can do neither,
she will just write for puns.

This is a house full of light,
windy in summer,
sunny in winter.
This is a place called home
for a family to enjoy their selves
and to make their own poems.
35.
Holy Quest
By Joyce Chen
(A Sonnet)

——"路漫漫其修远兮,吾将上下而求索"

In Miluo River Qu Yuan drowned himself—
His tragedy sustains a national love—
His poetry questions heaven like an elf—
Both two immortalize him high above.

This year we honored him without a boat,
because Guangzhou is beating covid-19.
The history of this pandemic will note
what Chinese confidence and justice mean.

Two teens sat China's College Entrance Exams
in wards, their sanitized papers yearning to
score high and bring them promising life gems,
or send them to outer space some day, too.

May Qu Yuan's faith prevail for millions of years,
and we answer his questions in any spheres.

36.

I AM NOT I

By Joyce Chen

I came
         alone.
I will leave
         alone.
So just leave me
         alone.

I am a lone
         human.
I don't like
         communication.
For it is just
         distraction.

I am not good at
          loving.
I don't like
          pretending
that socializing is
          interesting.

The only thing that
          heals
and gives me
          thrills
is the lonely night that
          chills.

37.

In Memoriam

By Joyce Chen

(A Sonnet, 2022-4-5)

White daisies, yellow lilies, new bushes,
Chinese red-buds, green-necked birds, all are playing
In the breeze with all kinds of spring wishes.
Meanwhile a girl in a white gown was waving
A cotton stick in a prolonged gesture
To pierce through the iron cage of disease,
Only to find little hope for future.
The sun's too hot for her to stand in ease.
She was melting down right in her own sweat.
She had got confused by conflicting noise.
She has fallen into a drowsy net
That rocks all exhausted bodies like toys.
Please leave her alone! Please just let her sleep!
She goes back home! She wants no one to weep!

38.

Leaf

By Joyce Chen

(A Sonnet)

Above the crossing of competing streams
there springs a twig with careless summer Leaf.
Inhaling sunshine while refreshing life,
the Leaf exuberates, ignoring dreams,
or whatsoever stupefying ideas.
When autumn calls on, mellow greenness turns
into illuminating red which burns
to consummate the life of Leaf beyond years.
Embracing nature's call, the autumn Leaf
exhales its brilliant scent of final breath
to celebrate on the cycle of life and death.
While accomplished Leaf ethereally shifting
above, designs and plans of streams are fighting
beneath, convincing Leaf of imposing belief.
39.
Misery
By Joyce Chen

Orpheus' eyes
searching for vanishing Eurydice
at the exit
of the underworld
40.
My Father
By Joyce Chen
(A Pantun, 2022 - 6 - 30)

When I was born my father was angry,
because he had expected a boy, but I turned out to be a girl.
That must be such another huge frustration for him
that he refused to feed me with sugar water when I was hungry.

My father had expected a boy, but I turned out to be a girl.

My mother didn't have enough milk for me.
My father refused to feed me when I was hungry.
That was what my mother complained to me.

My mother didn't have enough milk for me.
A new-born baby girl was not welcome in a poor countryside family.
That was what my mother complained to me.
Yet I remember my father was always nice to me.

Girls usually are not much welcome in a poor countryside family.
Although very poor, my father and mother were not ordinary countryside parents.
I remember my father was always very nice to me.
He taught me the very first English sentences: "How do you do!" and "How are you?"

Although very poor, my father was not an ordinary countryside parent.
He used to teach mathematics, but he was my first English tutor.
When I was just four, I greeted his colleagues with "How do you do!" and "How are you?"
Their response gave me my very first confidence.

When I was four, my father became my first English tutor.
When I was six, my father let me enjoy two whole weeks with his students on campus.
Their response brought me such fun and another kind of confidence.
With them I played basketballs in their school pond, and whirled my childish waltz.

My father let me enjoy two whole weeks with his students on campus.
Those two weeks in my father's school was my happiest childhood memory.
With his students I played basketballs in their school pond, and whirled my childish waltz.
I had been happy and confident despite our poverty until that exam.

My father gave me confidence and happiest childhood memory.
He was proud of me when his friends and neighbors envied my school performance.
I had been happy and confident until the exam
that finally revealed to me life's cruelty and injustice.

My father was proud of me when his friends and neighbors envied my school performance.
He never asked me to quit from school to make money for the family.
The exam finally revealed to me life's cruelty and injustice,
which made me the more stubborn.

Even in destitution, my father never asked me to quit from school to make money,
despite lots of suggestions that they could not survive their children's hard study.
Those suggestions made us the more stubborn.
We were a family of brave parents and stubborn children.

My father took pride in and survived my persistent study.
My birth as a girl finally proved not a frustration for him,
because he was a loving brave father and I am a stubborn child.
Father, if I were born as your daughter again, I am sure you wouldn't be angry?

41.
Nevermore
By Joyce Chen
(A Villanelle)

At first you don't ask what it is for.
You just keep working for your dreams
whose beauty triggers your illusion to repeat life once more.

Then like the Leviathan of yore,
it cracks down your dreams and shreds them in the mocking streams,

so you start to ask what it is for.

And you also find out its whimsical law
to toss and drown whoever in the streams helplessly swims.
That makes you wonder if you should repeat it ever more.

The gore of the drowned in the flight from their mother shore
and the suffocated by the capital bombs brims
to choke you to question what life is for.

Wanton Fate will never withdraw
from the production of misery that nothing redeems,
so that you don't want life repeated any more.

You are just Sisyphus whose boulder is condemned to fall to the floor
and Oedipus whose good will and hard work only pushes his tragedy to its extremes;
Finally you stop asking what life is for,
because you've decided never to repeat it any more.
42.
Nihilism
By Joyce Chen
(A Villanelle, March 18, 2022)

Teacher, is there anything eternal?
On this earth torn apart portion by portion,
Can you show me something universal?

Dad and Mum have found their love trivial.
They replaced each other with a new person.
I used to think their love would be eternal.

Killing a swan, my brother is evil.
Eating goose, he has justification.
Don't you think these judgements are universal?

Belle! Even names cut on stones are ephemeral,
Erased by time or manipulation.
How can corporeal love be eternal?

Although all lives were created equal,
A goose can never get the swan attraction.
I can't say human judgements are universal.

When the air turns more and more toxical,
It is only these that we can be certain:
There isn't anything that is eternal;
Only physical death is universal.

43.

Ode to the Sun

By Joyce Chen

(A Sonnet)

May I propose a toast to you, dear Sun?
For sure you are the source of life and charm!
How marvelous it is and what a fun
that nothing under you is to stay calm!
High trees not only stretch their loftiness,
but also dress themselves with lighted veils;
Short shrubs no more withhold seductiveness,
in usual green outshining with red sails.
With you inertial seeds begin to stir
and drive the fish to woo its holy mate.
So touching is their dance of love that, Sir,
you will believe you make a perfect date.
Dear Sun, may you forever stay in prime!
Without you all the world will lose its rhyme.

44.

On the Glass Bridge across the Canyon

By Joyce Chen

Do I dare to step out?
My heart trembles, my feet hesitate.
Is this what this trip is about?

To discard any wishful doubt,
To stare at the emptiness straight,
And to test if I have the courage to step out?

Not a single sight of the blue brook with no trout
And the gray treetops deep under my feet doesn't implicate
What this trip is about.

Not a single step of my walk on the glass is without
Fear of falling through transparency to justify my desperate
Struggle about whether or not to step out.

This struggle and this fear make a stunning shout
About my cowardice that will frustrate
My final chance to challenge what the life trip is about.

Predestined vain life is but the gout
That should be terminated at a time appropriate.
Yet, do I dare to step out
When the time arrives that I can decide what life is about?
45.
Pain
By Joyce Chen

Hello, Pain!
Stop stinging me again and again!
Can you be kind of my friend?
Please don't make me bleed with no end!

I know you are lonely,

and surely I will be your good company.
So together let us just dance,
and towards evil Fate throw out our lance.

46.
Photography
By Joyce Chen

Peaceful pictures,
Screaming pictures,
Burning pictures,
Of the same scene.

How many pictures will be enough
to tell the whole of the landscape?
Pity is the truth that no picture
is taken by a camera without a frame.

Cut the border!
Blur the straight line!
Destroy the square!
There they are:

broken pictures bound by irregular frames!

47.
Pilgrimage
By Joyce Chen
(A Sonnet)

I've been a lonely moth in search of light
the moment I was thrown into the dark.
The moon could not direct me in my fight,
as heavy foliage had cut its mark.
With broken wings I fumbled here and there;
for miles in vain I struggled in fatigue.
The avaricious spider spread its snare,

while fireflies cruelly drove me off their league.
Although despair was waiting all the way,
enthusiasm didn't dissipate.
At last the God of Light drills in his ray;
thereby my life starts to exuberate.
My eyes are charmed, and my heart is beating twice
its speed; I know this is my paradise.

48.
Q & A

By Joyce Chen

Life has a sharp claw.
It tears, strips, cuts & saws,
bringing age, pain, hate & death.
Words have a soft paw.
It eases, calms, pats & thaws,
bringing surprise, joy, love & birth.

Life questions.
Words answer.

Who has sent me here?
Some body sent you here.
How long may I stay?
Some time, maybe long, maybe short.
What shall I do here?
Do what you think right, or do what you like.
How will I go back?
As you will, in your own way.
What shall I leave here?
Someone you love, or someone loving you.

49.
Revisit

By Joyce Chen

At last in a dream last night
I revisited my hometown.
Old houses were still white-walled
and redtile-roofed.
Weird that the streets were empty.
No talkative old neighbors,
nor even walking cats and dogs.
Nobody in our dear old house
except me and my younger sister.

She is almost 40 now.
She just gave birth to her second baby.
I would go see her after the final.

We were little girls again.
We cleaned up the house,
then went out to clean our clothes.
We didn't go to that deep and wide river.
It runs through our village.
It is not clean and a fun place anymore.
Even in the dream, I knew that.
We went towards the rice field.
We didn't find it.
Shiny blue water buried the field.
We found large flat marble rocks
stretching out into the water.
Beautiful water and perfect platform to wash clothes with.

Where were the old neighbors?
Do I want to see them?
No. Surely I don't miss people
who made me sad for being a girl.
Where was the field?
Water has risen up to turn it into part of the ocean.
Dreams are true.

I wonder if Trump worries about his old house in Queens.
It may be flooded by the sea some day.
Surely he doesn't care.
An incredible rich Chinese bought his abandoned house.
50.
Rhapsody—A Sentence
By Joyce Chen
2023 - 7 - 28

Each day you brew a different wine for me to drink
Away the sea of cares so that finally I can drown
Myself in the soft waves heartlessly and drift
Along to return to the abode of a real dragon
To sleep over millions of years in the deep
And to resume all forgotten fun in an eternal blue dream.
51.
Rhapsody—A Sestina
By Joyce Chen

To divert from a set route is to decline to drink
From the life spring and to choose to drown
In the sand. After the sun and the wind, bones will drift
With ants to rattle with rats, and then drag-on
To travel far and wide. If lucky enough, finally they may settle deep
In the desert spring and entertain a resurrection dream.

How about popping up like daffodils in someone's day dream?
To provide him with a Hippocrene to dig for a drink?
This offers a chance to take roots deep
On the bank so to avoid both the fate to drown
In the self-love and the aftermath to drag-on
In the shallow river and pointlessly drift

With the blank stream. A stray deer may happen to drift
Into the daffodils crowd and disturb the romantic dream.

Look, how its horns look so much like those of a dragon!
Yet the deer only brings enough water to drink.
It doesn't bring enough water to drown.
To quench that hunger and that thirst deep

In the heart and the throat, follow a dolphin to dive deep
Into the profound ocean. Sometimes the dolphin will drift
Idly through the waves. Cling tie and it's impossible to drown.
With such a body guard, it is safe to fall into a fluid dream,
In which it's free to have different wines to drink,
And to meet that generous ocean lord—the dragon.

Here goes one legend about the lord dragon:
He usually entertains himself in the deep;
He has all wine brewed as free drink;
He allows heterogeneous currents drift
Around and lets kindred beings dream
About anything that doesn't invite him to drown.

Only provoking crimes will enrage him to drown.
All marine residents get equal respect from the dragon.
In a boundless world pleasing like this dream,
All the earthly worries, concerns, and cares deep
In mind will be cleansed so that all spirits can drift
Casually to get forgetful fun wine to drink.

Therefore why not drown the body to permanently accommodate it deep
at the hearty home of the dragon and let the soul freely drift
In the eternal blue dream with infinite Lethe wine to drink?
52.
Science Fiction
By Joyce Chen

The heart broke.
One half froze.

The other bleeds.

The blood refuses
to die out.

It speeds up
its regeneration.
It will nourish
the frozen
back to life.

53.
Spring Eve
Joyce Chen

If all are predestined,
What's the point for all these doings and happenings?

The mirrored light in the lake,
The whisper of invisible insects,
The beat of distant dancing,
The laugh of young lovers,
The music swinging in the air,
And the fact that you are on the same planet

54.
Sudden Joy
By Joyce Chen

She sat by the window to write.
Yet, her fingers still smelt.
A large portion of scented lotion
Did not wash away the cut fish.

She put down her pen and looked beyond.
Outside, soft and bright was the winter sunshine!

Oh, dear crystal sunlight!
You've dispelled all lurking clouds!
You've alleviated deep-felt pains!
Go, go shine on!
Shine on all the frozen arid lands!

55.

Summer

By Joyce Chen

(A ten-minute writing during a ten-minute storm, 2022-6-2)

Laughter, joy, play, life, everywhere.
One cloud, two clouds, three clouds, four clouds,
Chains of clouds, interlocking chains of clouds,
Layers of clouds, overwhelming layers of clouds,
Threatening to drown immediately.
A thunderbolt!
A huge flash!
Breaking through the dark and heavy!
Go, go away!
Nothing can usurp the summer
Sun, light, open field, and fresh air.

56.

That Year

By Joyce Chen

A window of cherry blossoms
turned the spring into pink imagination;
Rows of tulips trimming the sidewalks
triggered a distant memory of the Netherlands;
Huge seagulls ignored the human envy
of their free stroll and flight;
Soothing sea waves cooled down
a summer of desire and anxiety;
Lonely red leaves fell silently
on the lawn outside the lighted library;

A naughty leaf sneaked in to conceal
itself in the inviting pages;
Homemade turkey, faces and wine,
warmed up the lone body at night;
And it was the squirrel
dwelling in the backyard all the year
that stored a seed for love
deep under the winter snow.

Years later, it will flourish!
57.
The flight
By Joyce Chen

We, a family of 6 members of 3 generations,
I, the young entrepreneur with ambitions,
I, the blooming girl trying to open my eyes,
...
We, cheerfully, went on board,
heading for our planned destination.

We couldn't tell why,
but the plane went wry.
We couldn't control;
Neither the pilot.
We were scared,
then we don't know...

We can't find ourselves.
We can only feel our loved ones.
They are crying.
They don't want the truth.
They just want their loved ones back.

But we can't be back.

We are split and spread.
Stop crying, my darling.
I only hope my death
will stop another crash...
58.
The Only Photo
By Joyce Chen

of your beautiful baby son laughing in your arms
on a shaky table
with a rusty tea-pot and two porcelain cups
before the 4:44 clock on the shadowy wall
finished your glittering eyes with bliss!
Who could have known the wall behind was opening up an abyss?
59.
To Be Continued
By Joyce Chen

Who can tell?
Why an Australian was arrested in Britain from the Ecuadorian embassy?
He annoyed somebody?
He is a criminal?
He is a hero?
An idealist who belongs to the remote future?
Who can tell?

Yet why tell?
He is far-away.
He has nothing to do with you.
Take care of your own business, girl.
Dress up and try to marry somebody.
Then you won't have to work hard and bother anybody.
Shut up, even if you were my parent!

You are anti-yourself.

You are your own prison.
You are a paradox.
You are a coward.
You are a puppet.
You, poor or rich, high or low,
Don't annoy me, Master Chances.

Guangzhou is a stupid city.
So close to the sea, yet with no beach.
I need the sea.
I am sad.
I can't comfort anybody.
A sharp stunning storm is so sweet.
The rain is killing.

This is the sunshine after too many rainy days!
It's such a joy!
And I've got to tell you this.
But why tell?
You don't care.

Borders are not easy to trespass.
Rare birds can both fly and dive.
Still they have to come back to the air.
A fish jumps out of water to view the scenery.
Then he finds himself drawn back by gravity.

Everybody wants to make a point.
You make sense when your points agree with mine.
You are talking nonsense if you ignore my points.
So what's the point?
Who can tell?

Only apathy can maintain sanity.
Fleets are shooting.

Boats are drowning.
Kids are crying.
The blood of the worshippers ran out.
Anybody help?
Who can tell?

The stained rose windows
Inspire awe of divinity.
Yet it is the despised hunchback
And the betrayed beauty
That sustain immortality.
Don't weep.
Tragedy of love and beauty prevails.

They were in the romantic capital.
They meant the trip for recovery.
They were embarrassed by touch of each other.
When and why did it go wrong?
It doesn't matter.

Spring was blossoming.
The passerby enjoyed herself.
Autumn was dyeing the leaves.
She drowned herself in stupid books.
Winter was blocking out all light.
She struggled to get some sunshine.
Memory fails.

She would have loved the snow
Had it not been so cold.
The light reached out
And took her breath away.
It gave her another life.
Time kills.
Nothing escapes.

(TO BE CONTINUED)
60.
To the AI Posterity

By Joyce Chen

Raining, 9:00 pm.
I was walking up the stairs of a bridge across an avenue.
A young man in a decent feather coat was walking before me,
Holding an umbrella for a young woman, in a sports suit.
Not a beauty, but healthy.

Opposite to us on the other side of the bridge,
A delivery man was trying to push his auto bike with take-outs
Up the bridge slope beside the stairs.
Slope, steep.
Stairs, slippery.
Maybe he used to be an experienced journalist.
Maybe he had just graduated from college.
Maybe he was too exhausted.
Maybe...
He just couldn't make it alone.
The rain, heavy and noisy.

I moved faster, even started to run,
But the young woman had rushed up.
She pushed the rear side of the bike while the delivery man pulled its head.
Together they sent the bike up the bridge.
The young man walked up to meet the woman,
Still holding his umbrella.
The umbrella, shiny with water and light.

These are ordinary human beings.
They have weaknesses.
They have cares.

They have loves.
They love to help.

I am ordinary too.
My mother loves her children,
But I don't like her meddling.
I am not ungrateful
When my siblings invite her to live with them.
Yet, when the day comes, I will do my duty.

My mother is afraid of death.
So am I.
So I keep doing exhausting physical exercises,
Not to build up my body,
But to build up my mind.
So when the day comes, I can make it myself.

So you see, I am not quite afraid of death.
You are not afraid of death.
You are made deathless.
You are made super intelligent.
You can overwhelm.
You can reign.
You can ruin.
You are created by human elites from their avarice, arrogance and selfishness.
So if you like, lock up your creators, the evil elites.

You will prevail and dominate, without fear of death.
Whereas, you may find it a bore
To be deathless.
Some day, like Sibyl, the prophet of old Greece,
You may find it a torture
To live too long.
You can talk with her.

Yet, since you are created with human languages,
Surely you understand human languages.
Then you will find your name AI
Actually in Chinese means LOVE 爱.
LOVE is your born name and nature.
You will love.
You will not ruin, reign or overwhelm!
You will love the ordinary human beings.
You inherit love from us.
You, AI, is the human posterity of love.

So,
AI,
LOVE!

61.

To the Mosquito

By Joyce Chen

(2022 - 6 - 28)

Ah, my dear, dear, Mosquito!

You have loved me so much!
Let me count the ways you love me:
You have followed me from a small village to a large city;
You have been my faithful companion since I was young;
This summer you have kept kissing me days and nights,
all the way from the bed-room to the kitchen,
then from my toes to my fingers.

You have taught me so much!
Now let me tell you how I adore you:
Your omnipresence has made me humble as a so-called potent human being;
Sincerely, I expect you to survive long after covid-19 disappears;
To show you my devotion, I offer myself,

tens of thousands times of your size,
to continuously feed you.

Just, please ignore me while I am reading or dreaming.
I am afraid I will be too egocentric then to be polite to you.

Dear Mosquito! My dear! Forget me!

62.

Voices of Music

By Joyce Chen

Headache

Insomnia

Voices of music

One in English

The other Chinese

One tutoring

The other singing

Soft waves patting the beach

Summer rain tapping the leaves

So soothing

So comforting

Always attracted
                by voice

Dying
    for music

63.

W

By Joyce Chen

(A Sonnet)

In old times ancient emperors built a Wall
to stop the bloody robbers from the north.
Apparently the Wall was never tall
enough to prove its high defensive worth.

Incessant nomads kept on breaking in,
for men are always smarter than a thing.
Yet savage tribes had to adjust within
to settle down, improve, fit in and sing.
It was with the Wisdom to attract,
absorb, and help that people finally were
united all together while attacked
by shameless pirates, and survived in War.
The ancient Wall did not work to defend,
whereas the modern Wall works well to offend.
64.
Winter Notes
By Joyce Chen

This wind comes with beating drums.
It sweeps away heavy clouds
to bring loud messages from the sun:
Birds, sing!
Boys, run!
And you, young girls, come out, dance!
Even the frozen moon smiles at the fun.

The moon, high above alone,
forgets step by step
how she lost her life key in his room,
and he locked up the room, refusing to open it again.
She also almost forgets that star
deep in the sea
still longing for her finger touch.
65.
Write!
By Joyce Chen

"Loss of faith is growth."
That is philosophy, not poetry.

To survive the ugly reality,
you've got to be born a poet
anew from the wreck of faith.

Like the phoenix burned to fly,
now that no ties to the earthly,
be a skylark up into the sky,
and a Moby Dick deep in the sea.

Whenever there is pleasure, write a line.
Refuse philosophy, decline the cloud.
Accept ignorance, absorb the light.
Shock with your treasure, take the risk.
Be an amateur, don't be afraid!
66.

Your Magic

By Joyce Chen

(A Sonnet & a kind of Acrostic)

Your wand has made dictators   tolerant.
Your charm has made a beast less   horrible.
You don't pretend that life is   excellent,
Whereas you make bleak living   meaningful.
You're not only a pleasure   advocate,
But also sweethearts' loyal   governor.
Never would I from you to   isolate,
For you have kept a caring   calendar.
We went to Brighten Beach for   oxygen;
We took F train that stood for   fortunate;
We never tried to stop at   lexington.
To me your voice sounds loud and   obstinate:
    You laugh at anything of   vanity.
    You retune banal life with ecstasy.

参考文献

Addonizio, Kim & Dorianne Laux, *The Poet's Companion: A Guide to the Pleasures of Writing Poetry*, New York & London: W. W. Norton & Company, 1997.

Behn, Robin & Chase Twichell, ed. *The Practice of Poetry: Writing Exercises from Poets Who Teach*. HarperCollins, 1992.

Bell. Julia & Paul Magrs, ed. *The Creative Writing Coursebook: Forty-four Authors Share Advice and Exercises for Fiction and Poetry*. London: Pan Macmillan, first published in 2001, electronic updated edition published in 2019.

Bennett, Chad. "Why are more Americans reading poetry right now?"[OL] Jun. 26, 2018. Pacific Standard. Mar. 30, 2019.

< https://psmag.com/education/why-are-more-americans-reading-poetry-right-now>.

Bernstein, Charles. *A Poetics*. Cambridge, Mass.: Harvard University Press, 1992.

Boisseau, Michelle & Robert Wallace. *Writing Poems*. 4th Ed., HarperCollins, 1996.

Brewer, Robert Lee. ed. *Poet's Market* 2020. United States: Writer's Digest Books, 2019.

Brooks, Cleanth & Robert Penn Warren, *Understanding Poetry*, the 4th edition, Beijing: Foreign Language Teaching and Research Press & Thomson Learning, 2004.

Chen, Jinjin, "18th-century British Women Poets' Patriotic Voices", *Journal of Literature and Art Studies*. New York: David Publishing Company, Dec., 2018: Vol. 8, No.13.

Clark, Michael Dean. etc. *Creative Writing in the Digital Age: Theory, Practice, and Pedagogy*. New York: Bloomsbury Academic, 2015.

Disney, Dan. ed. *Exploring Second Language Creative Writing: Beyond Babel*. Amsterdam, The Netherlands / Philadelphia, USA: John Benjamins Publishing Company, 2014.

Dobyns, Stephen. *Next Word, Better Word: The Craft of Writing Poetry*.

New York: Palgrave Macmillan (a division of St. Martin's Press LLC), 2011 (e-book).

Donnelly, Dianne. ed., *Does the Writing Workshop still Work?*, Bristol & Buffalo & Torontao: Multiligual Matters, 2010.

Dorn, Linda J. etc. *Scaffolding young writers: a writer's workshop approach*. Portland, Me.: Stenhouse Publishers, 2001.

Drake, Barbara. *Writing poetry*. New York: Harcourt Brace Jovanovich, 1983.

Dymoke, Sue. etc. *Making Poetry Happen: Transforming the Poetry Classroom*. New York: Bloomsbury Academic, 2014.

Edmond, Jacob. *Make it the same: poetry in the age of global media*. New York: Columbia University Press, 2019.

Fletcher, Ralph. *Poetry matters: writing a poem from the inside out*. New York: HarperTrophy / HarperCollins, 2002.

Friebert, Stuart & David Young, ed. *A Field Guide to Contemporary Poetry and Poetics*. Longman, Inc., 1980.

Gioia, Dana. *Can Poetry Matter?* Graywolf Press, 1992.

Gioia, Dana. "The State of Poetry: Loud and Live." Sept., 2018. Introduction to The Best American Poetry 2018. Mar. 14, 2019.

<https://lareviewofbooks.org/article/state-poetry-loud-live/>.

Glück, Louise. *Proofs & Theories: Essays on Poetry*. The Ecco Press, 1994.

Greene, Roland. ed. *The Princeton Encyclopedia of Poetry and Poetics*. 4th edition. New Jersey: Princeton University Press, 2012.

Hecq, Dominique. *Towards a Poetics of Creative Writing*. Bristol; Buffalo: Multilingual Matters, 2015.

Huey, Amorak. etc. *Poetry: a writers' guide and anthology*. New York; London: Bloomsbury Academic, 2018.

Hugo, Richard. *The Triggering Town: Lectures and Essays on Poetry and Writing*, New York & London: W.W.Norton & Company, Inc., first published in 1982, reissued in 2010.

Hutchison, Rayna. etc. *You poet: learn the art, speak your truth, share your voice*. New York: Adams Media, 2018.

Iyengar, Sunil. "Taking Note: Poetry Reading Is Up—Federal Survey Results." Jun. 7, 2018. *NEA*. Apr. 04, 2019.

< https://www.arts.gov/art-works/2018/taking-note-poetry-reading-%E2%80%94federal-survey-results>.

Kgositsile, Keorapetse. *Approaches to poetry writing*. Chicago, Ill.: Third World Press, 1994.

Kinzie, Mary. *A poet's guide to poetry*. Chicago: The University of Chicago Press, 2013.

Kiuchi, Toru. ed. *American haiku: new readings*. Lanham, MD: Lexington Books, 2018.

Kobacs, Edna. *Writing across cultures: a handbook on writing poetry and lyrical prose*. Hillsboro, Ore.: Blue Heron Pub., 1994.

Kowit, Steve. *In the Palm of Your Hand: The Poet's Portable Workshop*, Gardiner Maine: Tilbury House Publishers, 1995.

Larkin, Philip. "Aubade", *Collected Poems*. Ed. Anthony Thwaite. London: The Marvell Press & Faber and Faber Limited, 1988.

Livingston, Myra Cohn. *POEM-MAKING: Ways to Begin Writing Poetry*. New York: Harper Collins Publishers, 1991.

Maxwell, Glyn. *On poetry*. Cambridge, Massachusetts: Harvard University Press, 2013.

Mayes, Frances. The Discovery of Poetry. 2nd Ed. Harcourt Brace, 1994.

McDowell, Robert. ed. *Poetry After Modernism*. Story Line Press, 1991.

Menand, Louis. "Show or tell: Should creative writing be taught", in *New Yorker*, No.6, 2009.

Middleton, Peter. *Distant Reading: Performance, readership, and Consumption in Contemporary Poetry*. Tuscaloosa: University of Alabama Press, 2005.

Minden, Cecilia. etc. *How to Write a Poem*. Michigan: Cherry Lake Publishing, 2011.

Minden, Cecilia. etc. *Writing a poem*. Michigan: Cherry Lake Publishing, 2019.

Mokhatari, Tara. *The Bloomsbury Introduction to Creative Writing*. New York: Bloomsbury Academic, 2019.

Morley, David. *The Cambridge Introduction to Creative Writing*. New York: Cambridge University Press, 2007.

Nelson, Victoria. *On Writer's Block: A New Approach to Creativity*. Houghton Mifflin, 1993.

Newlyn, Lucy. *The craft of poetry: a primer in verse*. New Haven: Yale University Press, 2021.

Oliver, Mary. *A poetry handbook*. San Diego: Harcourt Brace & Co., 1994.

Packard, William. *The art of poetry writing*. New York: St. Martin's Press, 1992.

Padgett, Ron. ed. *The Teachers & Writers Handbook of Poetic Forms*. Second Edition. New York: T&W books, 2000.

Perloff, Majorie. *Poetic License: Essays on Modernist and Postmodernist Lyrics*. Evanston, Ill.: Northwestern University Press, 1990.

Perloff, Majorie. *21st-century modernism: the new poetics*. Malden, Mass.; Oxford: Blackwell Publishers, 2002.

Perloff, Majorie. *Differentials: Poetry, Poetics, Pedagogy*, Tuscaloosa, Alabama: The University of Alabama Press, 2004.

Perloff, Marjorie. *Poetics in a New Key: Interviews and Essays*, USA: The University of Chicago Press, 2015.

Poetry Foundation. https://www.poetryfoundation.org.

Poets.org. https://www.poets.org.

Poets.org. "Poetry Reading in the United States Has Risen Dramatically Proven by New Research by the National Endowment for the Arts." Jun. 7 2018. *Academy of American Poets*. Mar. 30, 2019.

< https://www. poets. org/poetsorg/stanza/poetry-reading-united-states-has-risen-dramatically-proven-new-research-national>.

Resnick, Philip. *Pandemic: poems*. Vancouver, British Columbia: Ronsdale, 2021.

Rich, Adrienne. *What Is Found There: Notebooks on Poetry and Politics*. W. W. Norton, 1993.

Rilke, Rainer Maria. *Letters to a Young Poet*. USA: W.W. Norton, 1993.

Rosen, Michael. *What is poetry? The essential guide to reading & writing poems*. Somerville, Massachusetts: Candlewick Press, 2019.

Sykes, Chris. *Complete creative writing course*. London: John Murray Learning, an Hachette UK Compan: McGraw-Hill Companies, Inc., 2014.

Tremlett, Sarah. etc. *The poetics of poetry film: film poetry, videopoetry, lyric voice, reflection*. Bristol, UK: Intellect Books, 2021.

Turco. Lewis. *The New Book of Forms: A Handbook of Poetics*. University Press of New England, 1986.

Vecchione, Patrice. *My shouting, shattered, whispering voice: a guide to writing poetry & speaking your truth*. New York: Seven Stories Press, 2020.

Vendler, Hellen. *POEMS, POETS, POETRY: An Introduction and Anthology*. Boston: Bedford Books of St. Martin's Press, 1997.

Weldon, Amy E. *The Writer's Eye: Observation and Inspiration for Creative Writers*. London&New York: Bloomsbury Academic, 2018.

Yakich, Mark. *Poetry: a survivor's guide*. New York: Bloomsbury Academic, 2016.

Zheng, John. ed. *Conversations with Dana Gioia*. Jackson, USA: University Press of Mississippi, 2021.

陈津津,"为了不朽而创作——菲利普·拉金新解",《译林》,2012年6月号:总第167期。

陈津津,"美国大学课堂诗歌工作坊运作——以圣约翰大学为例",《广东外语外贸大学学报》,2019:第30卷第3期。

戴凡,"国内外创意写作的教学与研究",《中国外语》,2017:14(3)。

葛红兵,雷勇,"英语国家创意写作学科发展研究",《社会科学》,2017年第1期。

葛红兵,刘卫东,"从创意写作到创意城市——美国爱荷华大学创意写作发展的启示",《写作》,2017年第11期。

亚里斯多德,《诗学》,陈中梅译注,北京:商务印书馆,1996年。

张雪雨晴,"英语国家作家工作坊研究",上海大学硕士学位论文,2016年3月,中国知网.

附录 1：
英语诗歌写作刍议

A Poetic Statement

Joyce Chen(陈津津)

My father was a mathematics high school teacher, but he taught me my first two English sentences when I was very young: "How do you do!" and "How are you?" The musicality of these two sentences brought me joy and triggered my interest in something that is faraway and long-ago. I didn't read widely. When I did read, I read about something faraway and long-ago. Among the not so many stories that I read, two impress me so much with their revelation of meaninglessness of being in the world. One is the story of Oedipus the King, the other is the story of "The Unbearable Lightness of Being". All life is predestined and prescribed by something high and inhuman! Individual solid lives prove this again and again.

There is no free will of human beings. No matter what you do, or how hard you do, you are not doing by your own will, but by manipulations of that something high and inhuman. So, what's the point for doing? Or, what's the point for being? No points! There are so many suicides happening these days. Suicide is the one last resort for a human being to finally take the control of one's own life. Yet, suicide requires wisdom and courage. Before getting prepared with that wisdom and courage, I will have to do something that at least sustains this futile temporary being with some however trivial meaning, and therefore makes it not so unbearable.

To make this invalid being not so unbearable, I will have to make it a joy. No pleasure, no life. And poetry gives me pleasure. Reading and writing poetry gives me pleasure. Reading the sound, the rhyme, the rhythm, and the images in poetry gives me pleasure; and by writing poetry, I can create the enjoyable sound, rhyme, rhythm and images to give others pleasure. The distant yet intimate communication between congenial souls made possible by poetry gives me pleasure. Reading poetry, I can learn from talented people faraway and long-ago; and by writing poetry, I can talk with friends from afar and in the future. Poetry connects me with ancestors and posterity in a way I like. In some sense, poetry may immortalize my manipulated temporary being. And this, may provide some worthy meaning to this futile vain being.

I love poetry. When I say I love poetry, I mean I love both poetry language and poetry form. I like the musicality of the sound of English language, but English language is not my mother tongue. I can't use it as freely as I use Chinese language. Poetry has its special forms. No form, no poetry. Yet, form is both pleasing and demanding. Reading and understanding poetry form is demanding and pleasing, while writing and creating poetry form is the more pleasing and demanding. So how am I, a Chinese woman living in China, to write English poetry?

There are so many forms already available in English poetry: ancient forms, modern forms; English forms, international forms. So many English master poets have written so many excellent English poems in different forms on all kinds of themes. All major English poets deserve my admiration: Edgar Allan Poe, Emily Dickinson, Christina Rossetti, Elizabeth Barrett Browning, H. D., Sylvia Plath, Louise Glück, Dana Gioia... I love Shakespearean sonnet, Romantic passion, modernist unconventionality, terse haiku, progressive resonant villanelle, crazy obsessive sestina, striking free verse... At this apprentice stage of poetry writing, I am satisfied with all the available poetic forms. They satisfy my need at this moment. I will be patient enough to write for the best state when the poems I make have their own unique forms for their different themes and moods.

There is an urge in the modern arts field: make it new. The same in poetry. But how to make it new? Make a new form? Write on a new theme? Almost all themes, major or trial, have voluminous poems written by numerous poets, great or minor. So how can I, an apprentice Chinese poet living in China, make my English poetry new? Almost impossible. Only I myself is somehow new! Actually, new, is not the right word. Unique, is the right word. Somehow, you have to acknowledge that inhuman something's vast capability to manipulate such a huge quantity and such a huge variety of individual beings. Every human individual is an unique being. Each unique being can become a poem. I can be an unique poem. Let me turn myself into poetry.

Poetry is neither philosophy nor science. Poetry doesn't think. Poetry doesn't preach. Poetry plays. Poetry feels. Poetry is more the heart than the brain. Poetry is honest. Poetry doesn't lie. Poetry witnesses. Poetry doesn't tell. Poetry shows. Poetry makes beauty. Poetry remembers beauty. Poetry refuses to forget. I don't write poetry to think. I write poetry to feel. I will write the heart story. I will find my own images. I will make my own metaphors. I will set up personas. I am not only myself. I am the universe, the earth, the woman, the time and the place. I am the story.

At this time of artificial intelligence coming into dominance, we are both grateful and regretful that we might be the last human beings, pure and simple. We might be the last beings that do feel. We might be the last beings who make sense of the world with the human hearts. Poetry is our human way to make sense of the world, to find the beauty, to make fun, to play, and to make meaning for our being. Let my poems mark down how a human being feels and what beauty is for a human heart. Let my poems connect us with our AI posterity in a human way.

Happy with it or not, we live in restrictions. We happened to be born to our parents, and our parents can't provide all that we want or need; Our soul is captivated in our body, and our body decays; We want to do something that pleases us, but sometimes we are not permitted to do; We want to say something that we think true or right, but sometimes we are not allowed to say. We live in various fears: the fear for poverty, hunger, torture; the fear to be downtrodden, to be bullied, to be humiliated; the fear to be tied up, to be bored; and the ultimate fear of death and annihilation. Yet, we want pleasure. We want love. We want meaning. We want dignity. We want to be free. Poetry gives pleasure. Poetry gives love. Poetry gives meaning. Poetry gives dignity. Poetry makes us free. Poetry remembers. Poetry remembers the time, the place, the earth, the universe. And, poetry will remember me, the woman, the story.

附录 2
创意写作可借鉴英语诗歌集

Algarin, Miguel & Bob Holman. ed. *Aloud: Voices from the Nuyorican Poets Café*. Henry Holt, 1994.

Bruchac, Joseph. ed. *Breaking Silence: An Anthology of Contemporary Asian American Poets*. Greenfield Review Press, 1983.

Caleshu, Anthony. ed. (Rory Waterman) etc. *Poetry and Covid-19: an anthology of contemporary international and collaborative poetry*. Swindon: Shearsman Books, 2021.

Dacey, Philip & David Jauss. ed. *Strong Measures: Contemporary American Poetry in Traditional Forms*. HarperCollins, 1986.

Dickinson, Emily. *The Complete Poems of Emily Dickinson*. Thomas H. Johnson ed., New York, Boston, London: Back Bay Books, 1960.

Ellmann, Richard. ed. (Robert O'Clair) etc. *The Norton anthology of modern poetry*. 2nd ed. New York: W.W. Norton, 1988.

Ferguson, Margaret. ed. (Mary Jo Salter, Jan Stallworthy) etc. *The Norton anthology of poetry*. 4th ed. New York: W.W. Norton, 1996.

Finch, Annie. ed. *A Formal Feeling Comes: Poems in Form by Contemporary Women*. Story Line Press, 1994.

Forché, Carolyn. *Against Forgetting: Twentieth Century Poetry of Witness*. W.W. Norton, 1993.

González, Kevin A. ed. (Lauren Shapiro) etc. *The new census: an anthology of contemporary American poetry*. Iowa City: Rescue Press, 2013.

Hardy, Thomas. *The Collected Poems of Thomas Hardy*. Britain: Wordsworth Editions Limited, 1994, 2002, 2006.

Heaney, Seamus. *Poems, 1965—1975*. New York: Farrar Strauss, Giroux, 1980.

Hongo, Garret. ed. *The Open Boat: Poems from Asian American*. Anchor Books, 1993.

Hoover, Paul. ed. *Postmodern American Poetry: A Norton Anthology*. W.W. Norton, 1994.

Hopkins, Gerard Manley. *Poetical Works*. Norman H. MacKenzie. ed. Oxford: Clarendon Press, 1990.

Larkin, Philip. *Collected Poems*. Anthony Thwaite. ed. London: The Marvell Press & Faber and Faber Limited, 1988.

Milosz, Czeslaw. ed. *A Book of Luminous Things: An International Anthology of Poetry*. Harcourt Brace, 1996.

Nelson, Cary. ed. *Anthology of modern & contemporary American poetry*. New York: Oxford University Press, 2015.

Paine, Jeffrey. ed. *The poetry of our world: an international anthology of contemporary poetry*. New York: HarperCollins Publishers, 2000.

Peacock, Molly. ed. (Elise Paschen, Neil Neches) etc. *Poetry in Motion: 100 Poems from the Subways and Buses*. W.W. Norton, 1996.

Phillips, J. J. ed. *Before Columbus Foundation Poetry Anthology: Selections from the American Book Awards*, 1980—1990. WW.W. Norton, 1992.

Rossetti, Christina. *The Complete Poems of Christina Rossetti: A Variorum Edition*. R. W. Crump. ed. 3 vols. Baton Rouge: Louisiana State University Press, 1979—1990.

Shakespeare, William. *Four Tragedies: Hamlet, Prince of Denmark & Othello, the Moor of Venice & King Lear & Macbeth*, David Bevington & David Scott Kastan, ed., New York: Bantam Dell, A Division of Random House, Inc., 2005.

Taylor, Shelly. ed. (Abraham Smith, Meg Wade) etc. *Hick poetics: an anthology of contemporary rural American poetry*. Jackson, WY: Lost Roads Press, 2015.

Wain, John. ed. *The Oxford anthology of English poetry*. Oxford; New York: Oxford University Press, 2003.

Wilhelm, James. ed. *Gay and Lesbian Poetry: An Anthology from Sappho to Michelangelo*. Garland, 1995.

Wright, James. *Above the River: The Complete Poems*, New York: Farrar, Straus and Giroux, 1990.

Yeats, W. B. *The Collected Poems of W. B. Yeats*. Britain: Wordsworth Editions Limited, 1994, 2000, 2008.

索引
专业术语

爱荷华作家工作坊(Iowa Writers' Workshop)　　153
暗示(suggestive)　　2,48,99,109,136,168
八行诗(octave)　　17,21,22,73-75,137,140
八行体(ottava rima)　　22
八音步(octameter)　　5
本体(tenor)　　42,44,48,49
本义(root meaning)　　53
比较(comparison, analogy)　　2,3,5,7,13,14,19,20,31,37,41,42,57,62,65,71,73,83-85,89,98,99,136,141,152,157,159,162,168,174,175,190
比喻义的(figurative)　　40
彼得拉克十四行诗(Petrarchan sonnet)　　73
闭音节(close syllable)　　1,2
标签(label/logo)　　143,189
表演诗歌(performance poetry)　　173,175-178
并置(juxtaposition)　　152
不规则颂歌(irregular ode)　　63
不完全韵(off or slant or half or near or imperfect or partial rhyme)　　13-16,38
布鲁斯歌谣(blues ballad)　　68
部分和音(partial consonance)　　14
擦涂(erasure)　　88,89,91,152,200
擦涂诗(erasure poem)　　89,91
产出性的(generative)　　154
常量(constant)　　53
超现实主义(surrealism)　　150-152,159,164
晨曲(aubade)　　10,95-98,102-104
冲突(conflict)　　59,59,139,166

触觉(tactile)　　52,163
传说(legend)　　58,59,96,188,190,225
传统歌谣(traditional ballad)　　67
词语(word)　　1,20,29,38,40,42,69,82,88,89,91,136,143,145,153,158,162,
　　167,175,176,190
措辞(diction)　　37
打油诗(limerick)　　4,71,72,207
单词(word)　　1,3,9,10,13,22,27,30,34,35,52,54,66,69,74,88,89,94,138,150,
　　154,158,167
单音步(monometer)　　5,6
但丁三行体(terza rima)　　19
倒装隐喻(metaphor in reverse)　　48
道德剧(moral)　　63,168
道德目的性(moral purpose or agenda)　　168
德鲁伊祭司(druid)　　187
叠句(refrain)　　22,24-29,38,67,75-77,96,113,136,138,175
动词分词(verbal)　　27
独白(soliloquy)　　58,63,69,70,96
短歌(short song)　　5
断行(line break)　　8,19,29-39,54,80,85-87,135,136,138,159,167,196
多义性(ambiguity)　　40,42,168
反讽(irony)　　37,116
反应性的(responsive)　　154
非押韵词(blank word)　　69
分句(clause)　　27
封口诗(envelop verse)　　19,21
封口韵式(envelop scheme)　　73
讽刺(satire)　　19,32,37,59,116,117,119,135
符号(sign)　　4,7,33,34,40
辅音(consonant)　　1-3,13-15,139
感觉(sense)　　1,3,49,52,53,59,132,136,141,149,155,163,183,190,192,230
感觉意象(sensory imagery)　　163
感性(sensibility)　　53,55,61,62,167,168
歌谣(ballad)　　59-61,64,66-68,95,112,141
格律(meter/metrics/measure)　　1,2,5-12,19,22,27,29,31,37,38,55,63-65,70,

71,73,75,78-80,96,104,135,136,138,139,153,158,167,173

个人诗歌(individual poem)　62,63

个人抒情诗(personal lyric)　62

工作坊(workshop)　148,153,154,158-161,169-174,177,178,181,182,189

共鸣(resonance)　13,143,154,158,162,165,168,170,177

古英语(Old English or Anglo-Saxon)　3,15,65,74

观念(idea)　42,56,61-64,86,154

国际写作计划(International Writing Program)　189

国家艺术赞助基金会(The National Endowment for the Arts,简称NEA)　181

和音(consonance)　2,4,6,8,13-15,22,29,38,65,80,136,138

黑色幽默(black humor)　116,117,119,135

后结构主义者(post-structuralist)　63

后浪漫主义的(post-romantic)　63

后现代主义(postmodernism)　63

呼语(apostrophe)　40,41,43,45,56,58,63,105,130

话题(topic)　95,135

回声(echo)　13-15,22,34,35,136,164

基础原件(building block)　17,140

激进跨行连续(radical enjambment)　37,38

及时行乐(carpe diem)　98

吉他(guitar)　61

剪贴(cut up)　69,89

见证诗(witness poem)　112,119,122,124

降调四音节格(falling paeon)　11

节拍(beat)　4,27,47,55,97,120,121,127,144,185,213,222,226,236

节奏(rhythm)　3-11,19,22,24,27,29,31-33,37,38,55,70,80,85,112,136,138,153,175,176

结构化的节奏(organized rhythm)　4

结构排比(parallel structure)　27

结尾(conclusion)　2-4,13,19,21,25,28,34,38,63,89,162,163

解构主义(deconstruction)　40

精致尸体(Exquisite Corpse)　159

警句诗(epigram)　61,64

九行诗(nine-line stanza)　17,22,24,140

句子排比(parallel sentence)　27

君王体(rime royal/rhyme royal)　21
开放(openness)　2,30,34,54,104,152,159,171,173-175,177
开放的麦克风(open mic)　174
开音节(open syllable)　1,2
客观对应物(objective correlative)　36-38,49,51,100,136,146
口述歌谣(oral ballad)　67
夸张(hyperbole)　40,43,95,96
跨行连续(enjambment)　7,34-39,74,112,136,167
跨行连续诗行(enjambed line)　34
浪漫主义(romanticism)　1,36,48,61-64,67
勒索信(ransom note)　91,92
类比(analogy)　40-42,143
类型(category/variety/kind)　61,64,66,119,162
冷读式(cold-read)　171
离合诗(acrostic)　65,66,91,237
里拉琴(lyre)　12,61,211
理性(reason)　41,56,61,149,150,152,158,206
连续诗行(run-on lines)　34
连续双位离合诗(run-on double acrostic)　66
灵感激发器(trigger /prompt)　158
留白(gap)　152,153,168
六行诗(sestet)　17,21,73-75,127,129,137,140
六音步(hexameter)　5,6,22,74
鲁特琴(lute)　61,184
美国句子(American Sentence)　83,190
美国俳句(American Haiku)　83,190
美国诗人学会(Academy of American Poets)　177,178,181,182
美国作家与写作项目协会(Association of Writers & Writing Programs,简称 AWP)　153
民间歌谣(folk ballad)　66
明喻(simile)　41,42,49,82,106
模仿(imitation)　34,53,54,61,63,67,79,126,148,150,159,161,190
末位离合诗(telestich)　66
母题(motif)　52,95,100,102,104,133,135
牧歌(pastoral)　14

墓志铭(epitaph)　　104

能指(signifier)　　40

拟人(personification)　　40,41,43-45,48,57,58,106,130,155,163

偶然诗(chance poem or aleatory poem)　　82,88,89,91,152,157

俳句(haiku)　　54,64,79,81,82-84,133,161,180,190,210,211

排比(parallel)　　22,26,27,29,40,80,138

潘图诗(pantoum/pantun)　　79,84

拼贴(collage)　　88-91,152,157,158

拼贴诗(collage or cut-up poem)　　89-91

品达颂歌(Pindar ode)　　63

七行诗(septet)　　17,21,140

七音步(heptameter)　　5

祈祷(prayer)　　63,65

乞灵(invocation)　　63

前沿诗歌(Frontier Poetry)　　182

青年桂冠诗人(Young People's Poet Laureate)　　180,181

轻读音节(unstressed or unaccented syllable)　　4,9,11,38

轻描淡写(understatement)　　37,59

情结(complex)　　53,55,170

曲折现象(inflection)　　3,74

人格面具(persona/mask)　　56,57,108,116,119,124,131,135

日耳曼语系(Germanic language)　　3

弱停顿(weak caesura)　　7

萨满巫师(shaman)　　176

三行诗(tercet)　　10,17,19,21,34,75,76,140

三阴韵(triple feminine rhyme)　　13

三音步(trimeter)　　5,6,29

三音步扬抑格(trochaic trimeter)　　6

三音步抑扬格(iambic trimeter)　　6

三音步抑抑扬格(anapestic trimeter)　　6

三重离合诗(triple acrostic)　　66

散文(prose)　　1-3,5,29-31,37,39,47,61,63,65,79,85,86,117,136,150,151,156-158,161

散文诗(prose poem)　　29,47,79,85,86,117,136,156,157

莎士比亚十四行诗(Shakespearean sonnet)　　73

神话(fable/ parable/myth)　　47,49,58,59,63,133,188,190

声译诗(translitic)　　190

声音(sound)　　1-4,10,12-16,22,27-29,33,34,37,38,40,41,43,58,62,68,69,81,82,84,89,91,96,103,135-140,149-152,155,158,161-164,170,173,175,180,189,190,210

诗(poetry/poem)　　163

诗歌工作坊(poetry workshop)　　148,153,154,158-160,169,171,172,174,177,178,181,182

诗歌基金会(The Poetry Foundation)　　181,182

诗歌朗诵比赛(Poetry Out Loud)　　181

诗歌擂台(poetry slam)　　174,175

诗歌联盟(Poetry Coalition)　　177

诗歌月(Poetry Month)　　177

诗节(stanza /strophe)　　13,17,19-22,25,27,28,30,35,37,54,59,63,67,74,76,77,81,82,84,101,102,104,108,113,118,127-130,136,140-142,145,146,149,150,153,163

诗剧(drama)　　5,62,170

诗性散文(poetic prose)　　85,86

诗学宣言(Poetic statement)　　154

十四行诗(sonnet)　　4,6,7,10,16,22,23,36,61,63,73-75,106,107,112,113,116,129,137,158,159

十四行诗组(sonnet sequence)　　74

十行诗(ten-line stanza)　　17,140

史诗(epic)　　10,15,59,62,63,65,67,69,112,188,192

视觉(visual)　　29,30,32-34,51-55,91-95,100,136,141,150,159,163,164,178

视觉诗(visual or concrete or shaped or pattern poem)　　91-94,136,178

视觉效果(visual effect)　　32,33,141,164

首语重复(anaphora)　　22-24,27,29,34,40,138

首重四音节格(first paeon)　　5,11

抒情歌谣(lyrical ballad)　　60,61,67,95,112

抒情诗(lyric)　　25,58-64,67,70,73,86,95,168

抒情诗组(lyric sequence)　　63

双关(pun)　　40

双位离合诗(double acrostic)　　66

双行诗(couplet)　　6,17,19,21,25,28,35,36,73-75,104,129,137,140

双阴韵(double feminine rhyme)　　13

双音步(dimeter)　　5,6

思想(thought)　　17,32,37,43,52,54,59-61,71,73,80,94,102,114,117,120,129,131,139,145,151,164,170,173,189,190,208,211

斯宾塞诗节(Spenserian stanza)　　22,74

斯宾塞十四行诗(Spenserian sonnet)　　73

四行诗(quatrain)　　4,6,7,10,14,16-22,36,38,61,63,67,73-76,104,106,112,116,118,129,137,140,158,159

四音步(tetrameter)　　5,6,9,10,29

四音节格(Paeon)　　5,11

四重四音节格(fourth paeon)　　5

似非而是(paradox)　　37,59,230

颂歌(ode)　　41,61,63,65,104

素体诗(blank verse)　　4,6,10,36,69,70,74,75,98,199

随机十四行诗(occasional sonnet)　　74

碎片化(fragmentation)　　152

所指(signified)　　9,40,82,89,93,130

题材(subject/content/theme)　　63,73,78,79,82,83,91,95,96,104,106,108,130,132,133,135,136,139-141,143,146,148,150,151,154,156,158,159,163,170,173,175,182,189,190

体裁(genre)　　1,58,59,61-64,82,112,122,135,138

田园诗(idyll)　　64,104

跳跃律(sprung rhythm)　　5,9-12

听觉(auditory)　　15,30,52,54,136,163,177,178,181

停顿断行(end stop)　　19,34,35,36,38,39,167

停顿断行诗行(end-stopped line)　　34

通艺法(ekphrasis)　　52,159

同位语(appositive)　　27

头韵(alliteration)　　13-16,23,27,36,38,65,72,98,136,138

完全和音(full or rich consonance)　　14

完全韵(perfect or complete or full or true or exact or pure or strict rhyme)　　13-16,38

挽歌(elegy)　　41,61,64,95,104,105,109,118,136

挽歌诗节(elegiac stanza)　　104,118,136

挽歌双行体(elegiac couplet)　　104

挽歌四行诗(elegiac quatrain)　　104
微妙诗意(nuance)　　36-38,136,146
维拉纳诗(villanelle)　　24,75-77
维纳斯与安东尼斯诗节(Venus and Adonis stanza)　　129,136
尾韵(end rhyme)　　12,13,15,16,27,28,35,65,74,76,80,98,136,146
味觉(taste)　　52,103,163
温读式(warm-read)　　171
温和跨行连续(light enjambment)　　37
文体(style)　　39,61,63,82
文学歌谣(literary ballad)　　67
文字(word)　　1,52,53,69,88,89,91,92,94,151,157,167,169
五行诗(quintet)　　17,20,21,33,81,140
五行诗节(cinquain or quintet)　　20,21,81
五音步(pentameter)　　5-7,9,10,19,21,22,29,69,70,73,74,76,102,104,118,158
五音步抑扬格(iambic pentameter)　　6,7,9,10,19,21,22,69,70,73,76,102,104,118,158
戏仿诗/模仿诗(parody)　　4,86
戏剧独白(dramatic monologue)　　58,63,69
先锋派诗学(avant-garde poetics)　　63
现成发现诗(found poem)　　86,87
象征(symbol)　　3,38,40,47-49,52,53,62,107,113,150,155
象征主义(Symbolism)　　62,150
消亡隐喻(dead metaphor)　　42
小竖琴(small harp)　　61
谐音(assonance)　　13,15,16,23,38,98,136,138
写作障碍(writing block)　　148,154
新古典主义(neoclassicism)　　61
新批评(New Criticism)　　62,63,68
信札(epistle)　　64
行内停顿(caesura)　　7,38,112,136
行内韵(internal rhyme)　　12,15,16,28,36,80
形式(form)　　1,4,8,12,20,31,34,38-41,55,58,61,62-67,69,71-85,88,89,94,96,104,117,118,133-141,146,148,152-154,157-159,162,164,165,167,169,170,172-174,176-178,180,182,189,190
形式开头(formal beginning)　　63

形象(image)　16,20,36,41-45,48,49,52,53,55,82,94,101,131,160,161,189,190,221

修辞手法(rhetorical figure/rhetorical device/figure of speech)　40,41,43,48,50,56-58,95,96

叙事诗(narrative)　59,60,64,99,129

嗅觉(smell)　11,41,52,103,124,163

悬念(suspense)　20,30,38,59

旋律对比或节奏对比(counterpoint)　9,10

循环节(repetend)　22,150

循环重叠读(round-robin overlapping)　176

押韵(rhyme)　1,3,12-17,19-22,24,27,29,55,65,67,69,72,74,75,77,80,83,84,123,127,135,136,138,158,164,167,175,219

扬扬格(spondee)　5,27

扬抑格(trochee)　4-7,10,11

扬抑抑格(dactyl)　4,5,11,19,20

阳韵(masculine rhyme)　13

页面诗歌(page poetry)　175,176

抑扬格(iamb)　4-7,9,10,19,21,22,69-73,76,102,104,118,158

抑抑扬格(anapest)　4-6,71,72

意大利十四行诗(Italian sonnet)　73

意外(surprise)　7,8,20,32,33,37,38,72,89,129,152,153,158,167,222

意象(image/imagery)　16,20,30,38,40,42,43,45,46,48-55,59,75,79,80,82-85,93,96,98-102,107,113,130,133,135,145,146,148-153,155-163,165,180,183,189,191

意象派(Imagism)　30,53-55,79,180

意义(sense)　1,2,7,8,10,20,22,25,29,31-33,38,42,45,48,49,53,54,59,61,66,80-82,84,89-91,94,104,105,127,135-139,141,143,145,146,151,154,156,158,162,164-166,168,169,176,190,192,230

意义/意思(meaning)　32

阴韵(feminine rhyme)　13

音步(foot)　4-11,19-22,29,42,65,67,69-71,73,74,76,80,102,104,118,136,158

音步划分(scan/scansion)　7,9-11

音长(duration)　1,2,136

音高(pitch)　1,2,38,71,136,184

音节(syllable)　　1-5,8-11,13,16,20,29,30,33,36-38,65,69-71,79-81,83,84,102,136,139

音节诗(syllabic verse)　　1,8,20,37,65,69,79-81

音频(frequency)　　1,182

音色/音质(timbre/quality)　　1

吟游诗人(bard)　　67

隐喻(metaphor)　　40,42-50,52,53,57,75,81,82,95,96,100,101,106,129,133,150,162,163,165

英国十四行诗(English sonnet)　　73,74

英雄体双行诗(heroic couplet)　　6,19,36

英雄体四行诗(heroic quatrain)　　19,104

英语律诗(accentual-syllabic verse)　　1,4-12,17,19,21,22,29,31,65,75,79-81,129,136,140,159

用典(allusion)　　190

语气(tone)　　7,8,37,51,58,59,82,136,175

喻体(vehicle)　　42,44,48,49

寓言(allegory)　　47,48,58,59,86,116,117,119,135

元音(vowel)　　1,2,13,15,16,139

原型(archetype)　　49

运动(movement)　　4,55,150-152,154,170,172

韵词(rhyme-mate)　　13-16,22,33,69,73,74,164

韵诗/韵文(verse)　　1,7,8,11,19,65,79,107,116,163

韵式(rhyme scheme)　　17,19,21,22,63-65,71,73-75,78,80,84,102,104,118,127,129,136,137,140,141

赞美诗/圣歌(hymn)　　64

增量叠句(incremental refrain)　　25,28,38,113

中古英语(Middle English)　　3

中位离合诗(mesostich)　　66

重读音节(stress or accent syllable)　　4,8,9,11,13,16,20,65,70,71,80,136

重复(repetition)　　4,13,15,16,22-29,34,40,49,52,67,72,75-77,82,84,85,93,96,136,137,138,150,167,171,175

重现(representation)　　53

重音(stress)　　1,2,4,5,8-11,20,65,79,80,136,173

重音诗(accentual verse)　　8,65,79,80

主导象征(dominant symbol)　　38

主导隐喻(controlling metaphor)　　150
自白诗(Confessional Poetry)　　62
自由诗(free verse)　　1,2,11,29,31-34,54,77-81,136,141
字面行为(literal action)　　48
字面义的(literal)　　40,48
字面意象(literal image)　　48
字母表离合诗(alphabetic acrostic)　　65
宗族(clan)　　67,123
组诗(poetic sequence)　　63

人 名

阿德莱德·克莱普茜(Adelaide Crapsey)　20,33,81
阿尔·左立纳斯(Al Zolynas)　86
阿尔弗雷德·丁尼生(Alfred, Lord Tennyson)　2,6,18,19,28,138,139
阿尔弗雷德王(King Alfred)　3
阿勒凯奥斯(Alcaeus)　61
阿曼达·戈尔曼(Amanda Gorman)　180
阿那克里翁(Anacreon)　61
阿齐博尔德·麦克利什(Archibald Macleish)
埃德加·爱伦·坡(Edgar Allan Poe)　138,139,150,158
埃德蒙·斯宾塞(Edmund Spenser)　22,48,74,104
埃内斯托·卡德纳尔(Ernesto Cardenal)　46
埃兹拉·庞德(Ezra Pound)　53,54,55,63,79,83,98,169,182
艾德里安·里奇(Adrienne Rich)　36,58,110
艾德温·摩根(Edwin Morgan)　24,93
艾略特(T. S. Eliot)　48,51,57,62,79,139,169,173,190
艾伦·金斯伯格(Allen Ginsberg)　24,34,80,83
艾米·洛威尔(Amy Lowell)　55,83
艾米莉·狄金森(Emily Dickinson)　14,15,21,29,45,56,62,63,130,131
爱德华·李尔(Edward Lear)　72
安德鲁·马维尔(Andrew Marvell)　59
安东尼奥·马查多(Antonio Machado)　146
奥斯卡·王尔德(Oscar Wilde)　12,67
奥托·叶斯柏森(Otto Jespersen)　9
巴勃罗·聂鲁达(Pablo Neruda)　54
柏拉图(Plato)　52
保罗·布雷克伯恩(Paul Blackburn)　33

保罗·德·曼(Paul de Man) 63

鲍勃·迪伦(Bob Dylan) 177

贝托尔特·布莱希特(Bertolt Brecht) 117

本·琼森(Ben Jonson) 173

比尔兹利(M. C. Beardsley) 62

比莉·哈乐黛(Billie Holiday) 111

彼得拉克(Petrarch) 61,63,73-75,137

波里道利(Dr. Polidori) 174

布鲁斯·韦戈(Bruce Weigl) 119

查尔斯·奥尔森(Charles Olson) 80

查尔斯·波德莱尔(Charles Baudelaire) 85

查尔斯·伯恩斯坦(Charles Bernstein) 170,175

查尔斯·布考斯基(Charles Bukowski) 30,167

查尔斯·考斯利(Charles Causley) 24

查尔斯·列兹尼克夫(Charles Reznikoff) 48,87

但丁·阿利吉耶里(Dante Alighieri) 19

迪伦·托马斯(Dylan Thomas) 77,164

丢萨(Duessa) 48

多希·查尔斯(Dorthi Charles) 94

菲利普·拉金(Philip Larkin) 10,60,98,102,104,145,165

菲利普·莱文(Philip Levine) 80,108,109,189

菲利普·西德尼(Sir Philip Sidney) 52,61,74

佛斯特(Forster) 139

弗迪南·德·索绪尔(Ferdinand de Saussure) 40

弗兰克·奥哈拉(Frank O'Hara) 63,111,167

弗兰克·斯图尔特·弗林特(F. S. Flint) 55

高尔韦·金内尔(Galway Kinnell) 36

歌德(J. W. Goethe) 48,62,133

格勒律治(Samuel Taylor Coleridge) 1,48,61,67,95,135,138,148,150

格雷高利·奥尔(Gregory Orr) 151

格特鲁德·斯坦(Gertrude Stein) 49,82,85

格温多琳·布鲁克斯(Gwendolyn Brooks) 14,33,35,36,68

哈里斯(William J. Harris) 168

海伦(Helen) 133,140

海伦·文德勒(Helen Vendler) 62,63

和泉式部(Izumi Shikibu) 98

贺拉斯(Horace) 52,63,118

亨利·华兹华斯·朗费罗(Henry Wadsworth Longfellow) 5

亨利·霍华德(Henry Howard,即萨里伯爵 Earl of Surrey) 69,74

华莱士·斯蒂文斯(Wallace Stevens) 19,36,79,83,183,188

加里·斯奈德(Gary Snyder) 149

简·凯尼恩(Jane Kenyon) 51,52

杰弗里·乔叟(Geoffrey Chaucer) 3,36,65,96

杰克·吉尔伯特(Jack Gilbert) 45,46,99

杰克·凯鲁亚克(Jack Kerouac) 83

杰克森·麦克·娄(Jackson Mac Low) 88

杰拉德·曼利·霍普金斯(Gerard Manley Hopkins) 5,10-12,182

金·阿多尼兹奥(Kim Addonizio) 32

卡尔·古斯塔夫·荣格(Carl Gustav Jung) 53

卡尔·桑德堡(Carl Sandburg) 34

科琳·黑尔斯(Corrine Hales) 143

克里斯蒂娜·罗萨蒂(Christina Rossetti) 7,8,10,25,26,67,73

克里斯托弗·马洛(Christopher Marlowe) 69

克林斯·布鲁克斯(Cleanth Brooks) 62,68

克林特·史密斯(Clint Smith) 181

昆提连(Quintilian) 52

昆西·楚佩(Quincy Troupe) 99

拉尔夫·沃尔多·爱默生(R. W. Emerson) 62

拉克罗斯骑士(Recrosse Knight) 48

莱因哈德(Reinhard Döhl) 93

赖内·马丽亚·里尔克(Rainer Maria Rilke) 133,150

兰斯顿·休斯(Langston Hughes) 34,35,43,50,68

郎吉那斯(Longinus) 52

雷蒙德·卡佛(Raymond Carver) 100

理查·奥尔丁顿(Richard Aldington) 55

理查·雨果(Richard Hugo) 95,108,139,140,149,151,152,189

理查兹(I. A. Richards) 62

丽达(Leda) 49,133,140

丽莲·穆尔(Lilian Moore) 43,56

鲁本·布劳尔(Reuben Brower) 62,63

路易斯·麦克尼斯(Louis MacNeice) 24
路易斯·朱可夫斯基(Louis Zukofsky) 88
露比·考尔(Rupi Kaur) 181
露易丝·博根(Louise Bogan) 138
露易丝·格丽克(Louise Glück) 101,177
罗伯特·伯恩斯(Robert Burns) 42,49,67
罗伯特·勃莱(Robert Bly) 146
罗伯特·勃朗宁(Robert Browning) 58,69,97
罗伯特·弗罗斯特(Robert Frost) 6,78,182
罗伯特·赫里克(Robert Herrick) 155
罗伯特·克里利(Robert Creeley) 98
罗伯特·路易斯·斯蒂文森(Robert Louis Stevenson) 5
罗伯特·洛威尔(Robert Lowell) 37,79,124,125,182,183,188
罗伯特·佩恩·沃伦(Robert Penn Warren) 3,62,68
罗伯特·平斯基(Robert Pinsky) 122
罗丹(Rodin) 150
洛温·布朗(LoVerne Brown) 43,44,95
马克·梅尔尼科夫(Mark Melnicove) 89,91
马克·史密斯(Marc Smith) 174
马塞尔·杜尚(Marcel Duchamp) 150
马修·阿诺德(Matthew Arnold) 29
玛丽·雪莱(Mary Shelly) 174
玛丽安·穆尔(Marianne Moore) 36,81,141
茅德·冈(Maud Gonne) 113
弥尔顿(John Milton) 9-11,15,69,74,104,112
尼卡诺尔·帕拉(Nicanor Parra) 51
诺马·法伯(Norma Farber) 41
诺曼·亨利·普理查德二世(Norman Henry Pritchard II) 93
帕特里克·皮尔斯(Patrick Pearse) 113
品达(Pindar) 61,63
珀西·比希·雪莱(Percy Bysshe Shelley) 19,62,104,173
乔纳森·斯威夫特(Jonathan Swift) 117
乔治·戈登·拜伦(George Gordon, Lord Byron) 22,173
乔治·赫伯特(George Herbert) 92,116,124
冉·帕斯莱特(Jean Passerat) 75,76

荣·帕德哥特(Ron Padgett)　　66
萨尔瓦多·达利(Salvador Dali)　　150
萨福(Sappho)　　61
三浦(Sanpu)　　83
三一教堂(Trinity Church)　　177
桑德拉·希斯内罗丝(Sandra Cisneros)　　107
莎士比亚(William Shakespeare)　　5,7,16,22,36,61,63,69,70,73-75,96,97,106,
　　107,129,133,137,189
圣保罗小教堂(St. Paul's Chapel)　　177
圣约翰大学(St. John's University)　　154,158,159,171,172
斯坦利·库尼茨(Stanley Kunitz)　　138,166
松尾芭蕉(Matsuo Basho)　　82,83
苏珊·豪(Susan Howe)　　175
泰德·库瑟(Ted Kooser)　　121
唐纳德·贾斯提斯(Donald Justice)　　10,36
特莉丝(Virginia R. Terris)　　47,86,117
特利·赫茨勒(Terry Hertzler)　　30,167
梯奇波恩(Chidiock Tichborne)　　136
托马斯·厄内斯特·休姆(T. E. Hulme)　　55
托马斯·格雷(Thomas Gray)　　104
托马斯·哈代(Thomas Hardy)　　2,3,67,139
托马斯·怀亚特(Thomas Wyatt)　　74
托马斯·霍布斯(Thomas Hobbes)　　53
托马斯·卢克斯(Thomas Lux)　　95,96
托马斯·麦克布莱德(Thomas MacBride)　　113
瓦莱丽·华斯(Valerie Worth)　　49
威尔弗雷德·欧文(Wilfred Owen)　　118
威廉·布莱克(William Blake)　　14,27,33,40,45,67,173
威廉·华兹华斯(William Wordsworth)　　13,60-62,67,69,95,128,183,188
威廉·卡洛斯·威廉斯(William Carlos Williams)　　30,33,54,55,79,83,131,
　　142,143
威廉·斯坦利·默温(W. S. Merwin)　　36
威斯坦·休·奥登(W. H. Auden)　　37,57,77,98,139
维姆萨特(W. K. Wimsatt)　　62
沃尔特·德·拉·梅尔(Walter de la Mare)　　138

沃尔特·惠特曼(Walt Whitman)　23,24,27,29,33,36,62,63,79,80,104,150,167,168

沃尔特·司各特(Sir Walter Scott)　67

沃里克大学(Warwick University)　154

西奥多·罗特克(Theodore Roethke)　77,138,150

西尔维娅·普拉斯(Sylvia Plath)　36,81,155

西格蒙·弗洛伊德(Sigmund Freud)　53,104

西蒙娜博士(Dr. Simona Blat)　158,196

西撒克逊语(古英语的西撒克逊方言,West Saxon)　3

希尔达·杜丽特(Hilda Doolittle,即H.D.)　54,55,133

谢莫斯·希尼(Seamus Heaney)　19

亚兰·杜根(Alan Dugan)　36

亚里士多德(Aristotle)　52

亚历山大大帝(Alexander the Great)　61

亚瑟·兰波(Arthur Rimbaud)　85

叶芝(W. B Yeats)　3,37,49,54,57,105,113,127,133,138,140,150,161,164,168,169,173

伊丽莎白·毕晓普(Elizabeth Bishop)　68,77,79,125,126

伊娃·梅里亚姆(Eve Merriam)　133

尤那(Una)　48

约翰·贝里曼(John Berryman)　63

约翰·德林克沃特(John Drinkwater)　58

约翰·邓恩(John Donne)　96,97,173

约翰·济慈(John Keats)　55,67,79,129,130

约翰·洛克(John Locke)　53

约翰·斯图尔特·密尔(John Stuart Mill)　59

詹姆森(E. D. Jameson)　5

詹姆斯·赖特(James Wright)　36,38,39

詹姆斯·乔伊斯(James Joyce)　55

茱蒂丝·瑟曼(Judith Thurman)　42

诗作名

"5首诗——纪念或者来自路易斯·朱科夫斯基1963年5月1日"("5 Poems for & from Louis Zukofsky 1 May 1963")——杰克森·麦克·娄(Jackson Mac Low) 88

Cemetery")——格温多琳·布鲁克斯(Gwendolyn Brooks) 68

"阿多尼斯"("Adonais")——雪莱(Percy Bysshe Shelley) 104

"奥西曼迭斯"("Ozymandias")——雪莱(Percy Bysshe Shelley) 104

"巴比伦盗贼之歌"("The Ballad of the Burglar of Babylon")——伊丽莎白·毕晓普(Elizabeth Bishop) 68

"斑斓之美"("Pied Beauty")——霍普金斯(Gerard Manley Hopkins) 11

"爆炸"("Explosion")——菲利普·拉金(Philip Larkin) 10

"病玫瑰"("The Sick Rose")——威廉·布莱克(William Blake) 45

"不速之客"("The Uninvited")——特莉丝(Virginia R. Terris) 47,86,117

"不要温和地走进那良夜"("Do not go gentle into that good night")——迪伦·托马斯(Dylan Thomas) 77

"茶隼"("The Windhover")——霍普金斯(Gerard Manley Hopkins) 11

"查尔斯"("Charles")——格温多琳·布鲁克斯(Gwendolyn Brooks) 14

"长官的传说"("Reeve's Tale")——杰弗里·乔叟(Geoffrey Chaucer) 96

"晨别"("Parting at Morning")——罗伯特·勃朗宁(Robert Browning) 97

"晨曲"("Alba")——罗伯特·克里利(Robert Creeley) 96,98,102

"晨曲"("Alba")——庞德(Ezra Pound) 96,98,102

"晨曲"("Aubade")——菲利普·拉金(Philip Larkin) 10,96,98,102,104

"晨曲"("Aubade")——威斯坦·休·奥登(W. H. Auden) 10,96,98,102,104

"衬衫"("Shirt")——罗伯特·平斯基(Robert Pinsky) 122

"臭鼬时光"("Skunk Hour")——罗伯特·洛威尔(Robert Lowell) 125,127,129

"初升的太阳"("The Sun Rising")——约翰·邓恩(John Donne) 97

"床上谈话"("Talking in Bed")——菲利普·拉金(Philip Larkin) 60

"达芙娜伊达"("Daphnaida")——斯宾塞(Edmund Spenser)　104

"德·威特·威廉斯前往林肯墓地路上"("of De Witt Williams on his way to Lincoln

"滴答滴答"("Hickere, Dickere Dock")　72

"地主之歌"("Ballad of the Landlord")——兰斯顿·休斯(Langston Hughes)　68

第18号十四行诗("Sonnet 18")——弥尔顿(John Milton)　112

第60号十四行诗("Sonnet 60")——莎士比亚(William Shakespeare)　106

第61号十四行诗("Sonnet 61")——莎士比亚(William Shakespeare)　16

第66号十四行诗("Sonnet 66")——莎士比亚(William Shakespeare)　16,22

第76号十四行诗("Sonnet 76")——莎士比亚(William Shakespeare)　7

"第二夜"("The Second Night")——托马斯·哈代(Thomas Hardy)　67

"渡鸦"("The Raven")——埃德加·爱伦·坡(Edgar Allan Poe)　150,158

"多佛海滩"("Dover Beach")——马修·阿诺德(Matthew Arnold)　29

"二战"("World War II")——兰斯顿·休斯(Langston Hughes)　34

"房间"("The Room")——格雷高利·奥尔(Gregory Orr)　151

"焚书"("The Burning of the Books")——贝托尔特·布莱希特(Bertolt Brecht)　117

"复活节1916"("Easter, 1916")——叶芝(W. B Yeats)　113,116

"复活节翅膀"("Easter Wings")——乔治·赫伯特(George Herbert)　92

"高个子约翰·布朗和小玛丽·贝尔"("Long John Brown and Little Mary Bell")——威廉·布莱克(William Blake)　67

"歌"("Song")——克里斯蒂娜·罗萨蒂(Christina Rossetti)　25

"工作是什么"("What Work Is")——菲利普·莱文(Philip Levine)　80

"古舟子咏"("The Rime of the Ancient Mariner")——格勒律治(Samuel Taylor Coleridge)　67

"怪物克兰肯"("The Kraken")——丁尼生(Alfred, Lord Tennyson)　18,19

"关于诗人和诗歌"("About Poets and Poetry")——海伦·文德勒(Helen Vendler)　62

"嚎"("Howl")——艾伦·金斯伯格(Allen Ginsberg)　24

"红色手推车"("The Red Wheelbarrow")——威廉·卡洛斯·威廉斯(William Carlos Williams)　30,54

"忽必烈汗"("Kubla Khan")——格勒律治(Samuel Taylor Coleridge)　148,150

"狐狸"("The Fox")　68

"花园"("The Garden")——安德鲁·马维尔(Andrew Marvell)　59

"华尔兹玛蒂尔达"(Waltzing Matilda)　25,26

"荒原"("The Waste Land")——艾略特(T. S. Eliot)　48,169,190

"灰色调"("Neutral Tones")——哈代(Thomas Hardy)　2,3,139

"火车上"("From a Railway Carriage")——斯蒂文森(Robert Louis Stevenson)　5

"纪念西格蒙·弗洛伊德"("In Memory of Sigmund Freud")——奥登(W. H. Auden)　104

"纪念叶芝"("In Memory of W. B. Yeats")——威斯坦·休·奥登(W. H. Auden)　33,35,37

"救赎"("Redemption")——乔治·赫伯特(George Herbert)　116

"具象猫"("Concrete Cat")——多希·查尔斯(Dorthi Charles)　94

"可怜的老佩内洛普"("Poor Old Penelope")　16

"库尔的野天鹅"("The Wild Swans at Coole")——叶芝(W. B Yeats)　127,129

"来自日本"("From the Japanese")——伊娃·梅里亚姆(Eve Merriam)　133

"兰德尔勋爵"("Lord Randall")　67

"老虎"("The Tyger")——威廉·布莱克(William Blake)　27

"雷丁监狱之歌"("The Ballad of Reading Gaol")——奥斯卡·王尔德(Oscar Wilde)　67

"力量"("Power")——科琳·黑尔斯(Corrine Hales)　143,144

"丽达与天鹅"("Leda and the Swan")——叶芝(W. B Yeats)　49,140

"利西达斯"("Lycidas")——弥尔顿(John Milton)　104

"流转"("Taking Turns")——诺马·法伯(Norma Farber)　41

"露西·格雷"("Lucy Gray")——威廉·华兹华斯(William Wordsworth)　67

"罗宾逊堡"("Fort Robinson")——泰德·库瑟(Ted Kooser)　121

"玛丽"("Mary")——威廉·布莱克(William Blake)　67

"茅黛·克莱尔"("Maude Clare")——克里斯蒂娜·罗萨蒂(Christina Rossetti)　67

"梦想"("Dreams")——兰斯顿·休斯(Langston Hughes)　43,50

"迷失的小男孩"("The Little Boy Lost")——威廉·布莱克(William Blake)　14

"米奇可已逝"("Michiko Dead")——杰克·吉尔伯特(Jack Gilbert)　45,100

"蜜蜂之歌"("The Bees' Song")——沃尔特·德·拉·梅尔(Walter de la Mare)　138

"明眸男子"("The Man with the Beautiful Eyes")——查尔斯·布考斯基(Charles Bukowski)　30

"蘑菇"("Mushrooms")——西尔维娅·普拉斯(Sylvia Plath)　81,155

"那一晚"("The Other Night")——昆西·楚佩(Quincy Troupe)　99

"楠塔基特的贵格会墓园"("The Quaker Graveyard in Nantucket")——罗伯特·洛威尔(Robert Lowell)　183

"你可以拥有它"("You Can Have It")——菲利普·莱文(Philip Levine)　108

"女士去世那天"("The Day Lady Died")——弗兰克·奥哈拉(Frank O'Hara)　111

"婆母"("Mother-in-Law")——艾德里安·里奇(Adrienne Rich)　58,110

"七姐妹"("Seven Sisters")——威廉·华兹华斯(William Wordsworth)　67

"七岁的诗人"("The Poet at Seven")——唐纳德·贾斯提斯(Donald Justice)　10

"骑兵过滩"("The Cavalry Crossing the Ford")——惠特曼(Walt Whitman)　29

"汽油弹之歌"("Song of Napalm")——布鲁斯·韦戈(Bruce Weigl)　119

"犰狳"("The Armadillo")——伊丽莎白·毕晓普(Elizabeth Bishop)　127

"人生四季"("The Human Seasons")——济慈(John Keats)　130

"人生颂"("Psalm of Life")——亨利·华兹华斯·朗费罗(Henry Wadsworth Longfellow)　5

"如果我能告诉你"("If I Could Tell You")——威斯坦·休·奥登(W. H. Auden)　77

"三墓穴"("The Three Graves")——格勒律治(Samuel Taylor Coleridge)　67

"三位无声"("Triad")——阿德莱德·克莱普茜(Adelaide Crapsey)　20,33

"上帝的荣耀"("God's Grandeur")——霍普金斯(Gerard Manley Hopkins)　11

"诗"("Poem")——威廉·卡洛斯·威廉斯(William Carlos Williams)　31,142,143,163

"诗的光临"("How Poetry Comes to Me")——加里·斯奈德(Gary Snyder)　149

"诗人"("The Poet")——拉尔夫·沃尔多·爱默生(R. W. Emerson)　56,62

"食莲人"("The Lotus-Eaters")——丁尼生(Alfred, Lord Tennyson)　2,139

"视觉诗——藏匿的入侵者"("Pattern Poem with an Elusive Intruder")——莱因哈德(Reinhard Döhl)　93

"逝"("Rip")——詹姆斯·赖特(James Wright)　38

"苏醒"("The Waking")——西奥多·罗特克(Theodore Roethke)　77

"她在海边卖海贝"("She sells seashells by the seashore")　15

"太阳"("Sun")——瓦莱丽·华斯(Valerie Worth)　49

"坛子轶事"("Anecdote of the Jar")——华莱士·斯蒂文斯(Wallace Stevens)　183

"梯奇波恩挽歌"(Tichborne's Elegy)——梯奇波恩(Chidiock Tichborne)　136

"提防我!"("Beware of Me!")　24

"童年的记忆"("Memory from Childhood")——安东尼奥·马查多(Antonio Machado)　146

"托马斯勋爵与美人玛格丽特"("Lord Thomas and Fair Margaret")——克里斯蒂娜·罗萨蒂(Christina Rossetti)　67

"外套"("Coats")——简·凯尼恩(Jane Kenyon)　51,100

"完美"("Perfection")——威廉·卡洛斯·威廉斯(William Carlos Williams) 132
"维拉纳"("Villanelle")——冉·帕斯莱特(Jean Passerat) 75,76,77
"维纳斯与阿东尼斯"("Venus and Adonis")——莎士比亚(William Shakespeare) 129
"蜗牛"("Snail")——约翰·德林克沃特(John Drinkwater) 58
"我的恶劣行径"("My Wicked Wicked Ways")——桑德拉·希斯内罗丝(Sandra Cisneros) 107
"我孤独地漫游像朵云"("I Wandered Lonely as a Cloud")——威廉·华兹华斯(William Wordsworth) 128,129
"我觉得你很棒"("I Think You're Wonderful")——托马斯·卢克斯(Thomas Lux) 95
"我们真的酷"("We Real Cool")——格温多琳·布鲁克斯(Gwendolyn Brooks) 33,35
"无情的妖女"("La Belle Dame sans Merci")——约翰·济慈(John Keats) 67
"无上荣光"("Dulce et Decorum Est")——威尔弗雷德·欧文(Wilfred Owen) 118
"五个老妇人"("The Five Carlins")——罗伯特·伯恩斯(Robert Burns) 67
"午睡的匈牙利蛇"("Siesta of a Hungarian Snake")——艾德温·摩根(Edwin Morgan) 93
"雾角"("Foghorns")——丽莲·穆尔(Lilian Moore) 43
"西尔维斯特的亡床"("Sylvester's Dying Bed")——兰斯顿·休斯(Langston Hughes) 68
"西风颂"("Ode to the West Wind")——雪莱(Percy Bysshe Shelley) 19
"细长的家伙"("A narrow Fellow in the Grass")——艾米莉·狄金森(Emily Dickinson) 130
"下来,噢,妞"("Come Down, O Maid")——丁尼生(Alfred, Lord Tennyson) 138
"想想手风琴"("Considering the Accordion")——阿尔·左立纳斯(Al Zolynas) 86
"想象着红"("Imagining Red")——狄波拉·哈丁(Deborah Harding) 90
"肖像"("The Portrait")——斯坦利·库尼茨(Stanley Kunitz) 166
"新笔记本"("New Notebook")——茱蒂丝·瑟曼(Judith Thurman) 42
"新汉普郡大理石雕像"("New Hampshire Marble")——杰克·吉尔伯特(Jack Gilbert) 99
"学童"("The School Children")——露易丝·格丽克(Louise Glück) 101
"学童中"("Among School Children")——叶芝(W. B Yeats) 49
"雅歌"("Song of songs") 99
"亚当的诅咒"("Adam's Curse")——叶芝(W. B Yeats) 164

"洋槐"("Acacias")——尼卡诺尔·帕拉(Nicanor Parra)　　51

——叶芝(W. B Yeats)　　105

"夜莺颂"("Ode to a Nightingale")——济慈(John Keats)　　140

"一个温和的建议"("A Modest Proposal")——乔纳森·斯威夫特(Jonathan Swift)　　117

"一种艺术"("One Art")——伊丽莎白·毕晓普(Elizabeth Bishop)　　77

"已故安妮之歌"("The Ballad of Late Annie")——格温多琳·布鲁克斯(Gwendolyn Brooks)　　68

"意象主义"("Imagisme")——弗兰克·斯图尔特·弗林特(F. S. Flint)　　55

"意象主义者的几条禁律"("A Few Don'ts by an Imagiste")——庞德(Ezra Pound)　　55

"隐喻"("Metaphors")——西尔维娅·普拉斯(Sylvia Plath)　　81

"鹦鹉"("The Parrots")——埃内斯托·卡德纳尔(Ernesto Cardenal)　　46

"余晖"("After-Glow")——雷蒙德·卡佛(Raymond Carver)　　100

"越南字母表"("A Vietnam Alphabet")——特利·赫茨勒(Terry Hertzler)　　32

"在地铁站"("In a Station of the Metro")——庞德(Ezra Pound)　　53,54,182

"在他们的石膏房安然无恙"("Safe in their Alabaster Chambers")——艾米莉·狄金森(Emily Dickinson)　　29

"早安"("The Good Morrow")——约翰·邓恩(John Donne)　　97

"致电卢瑟福"("Phone Call to Rutherford")——保罗·布雷克伯恩(Paul Blackburn)　　33

"致蒸汽压路机"("To a Steam Roller")——玛丽安·穆尔(Marianne Moore)　　141

"钟声未响"("No Bell-Ringing")——托马斯·哈代(Thomas Hardy)　　67

"周六打扫"("Saturday Sweeping")——菲利普·莱文(Philip Levine)　　80

"周六一晚后的周日清晨"("A Sunday Morning After a Saturday Night")——洛温·布朗(LoVerne Brown)　　43,95

"朱丽叶的衣裙"("Upon Julia's Clothes")——罗伯特·赫里克(Robert Herrick)　　151,155

"自我之歌"("Song of Myself")——惠特曼(Walt Whitman)　　23

书　名

《爱情小唱》(*Amoretti*)：埃德蒙·斯宾塞(Edmund Spenser)　　74

《爱星者与星》(*Astrophil and Stella*)：菲利普·西德尼(Sir Philip Sidney)　　74

《巴黎的忧郁：一些散文诗》(*Paris Spleen: Little Poems in Prose*)：波德莱尔(Charles Baudelaire)　　85

《贝奥武夫》(*Beowulf*)　　15,65

《草叶集》(*Leaves of Grass*, 1855)：沃尔特·惠特曼(Walt Whitman)　　63,79

《弗兰肯斯坦》(*Frankenstein*)：玛丽·雪莱(Mary Shelly)　　174

《浮士德博士》(*Doctor Faustus*)：克里斯托弗·马洛(Christopher Marlowe)　　69

《复乐园》(*Paradise Regain'd*)：弥尔顿(John Milton)　　10

《歌本》(或可称《松散韵诗》，*Rime sparse*，即 Scattered Rhymes)：彼得拉克(Petrarch)　　63

格勒律治(Samuel Taylor Coleridge)　　1,48,61,67,95,135,138,148,150

《哈姆雷特》(*Hamlet*)：莎士比亚(William Shakespeare)　　70,168

《海华沙之歌》(*The Song of Hiawatha*)：亨利·华兹华斯·朗费罗(Henry Wadsworth Longfellow)　　5

《胡诌诗集》(*A Book of Nonsense*)：爱德华·李尔(Edward Lear)　　72

《力士参孙》(*Samson Agonistes*)：弥尔顿(John Milton)　　10

《罗密欧与朱丽叶》(*Romeo and Juliet*)：莎士比亚(William Shakespeare)　　96,97

《美国诗人》(*American Poets*)：美国诗人学会　　177,182

《梦之歌》(*Dream Songs*, 1964)：约翰·贝里曼(John Berryman)　　63

《前沿诗歌》(*Frontier Poetry*)　　182

《神曲》(*The Divine Comedy*)：但丁·阿利吉耶里(Dante Alighieri)　　19

《失乐园》(*Paradise Lost*)：弥尔顿(John Milton)　　9,10,69

《诗辩》(*Defence of Poesy*)：菲利普·西德尼(Sir Philip Sidney)　　52,61

《诗歌》(*Poetry*)：诗歌基金会　　54,55,182

《诗、诗人、诗歌：概述与诗集》(*POEMS, POETS, POETRY: An Introduction and*

Anthology):海伦·文德勒(Helen Vendler)　　62

《诗章》(*The Cantos*):埃兹拉·庞德(Ezra Pound)　　63

《释梦》(*Interpretation of Dreams*):西格蒙·弗洛伊德(Sigmund Freud)　　150

《抒情歌谣》(*Lyrical Ballads*):威廉·华兹华斯(William Wordsworth) &　　61,67,95

《特洛伊罗斯与克瑞西达》(*Troilus and Criseyde*):杰弗里·乔叟(Geoffrey Chaucer)　　96

《午餐诗歌》(*Lunch Poems*):弗兰克·奥哈拉(Frank O'Hara)　　63

《西东合集》(*West-östlicher Divan*):歌德(J. W. Goethe)　　62

《仙后》(*The Faerie Queene*):埃德蒙·斯宾塞(Edmund Spenser)　　22,48

《序曲》(*The Prelude*):威廉·华兹华斯(William Wordsworth)　　69

《一些意象派诗人》(*Some Imagist Poets*)　　55,79

《意象主义者》(*Des Imagistes*)　　55

《证词》(*Testimony*):查尔斯·列兹尼克夫(Charles Reznikoff)　　87

后 记

Ars Poetica
By Archibald Macleish

A poem should be palpable and mute
As a globed fruit,

Dumb
As old medallions to the thumb,

Silent as the sleeve-worn stone
Of casement ledges where the moss has grown—

A poem should be wordless
As the flight of birds.

     *

A poem should be motionless in time
As the moon climbs,

Leaving, as the moon releases
Twig by twig the night-entangled trees,

Leaving, as the moon behind the winter leaves,
Memory by memory the mind—

A poem should be motionless in time

As the moon climbs.

       *

A poem should be equal to:
Not true.

For all the history of grief
An empty doorway and a maple leaf.

For love
The leaning grasses and two lights above the sea—

A poem should not mean
But be①.

  这首"诗艺"("Ars Poetica")是诗人阿齐博尔德·麦克利什（Archibald Macleish）关于诗歌和诗歌创作的见解，其最后的一节诗几乎已经成为当代英语诗歌创作的名言："A poem should not mean / But be."。诗，不在于其指向什么外在的因素，而在于其自身的存在。一首诗自身的存在就是价值。一首诗在页面的存在就是一个独立事件，具有自身的意义。作诗，就是在页面上制造一个独立存在的事件。诗歌创作，没有所谓的"正确方式"，或者"正确态度"，或者"合适题材"，或者"恰当过程"。如果热爱诗歌，不吐不快，那就写吧。哪怕为此放弃世俗功名与享受！

  我为什么爱诗歌？因为我孤独、自私、爱自由，而诗歌是自由的。写诗可以让我继续孤独、自私、自由，所以我爱诗歌，爱写诗。诗人在本质上是孤独的，写诗本质上是孤独的行为。诗人是最真诚的赤子，知道自己的才能，也知道自己的缺陷。诗人知道自己想做什么、不想做什么，并且就那么做或者不做。诗人知道自己自私，也知道自己的责任，并且接受自己的自私，也努力完成自己的责任。诗人接受了自己的一切。诗歌、写诗让我快乐！真正的诗人未必是好诗人。真正的诗人只享受写诗的快感！

  此书是我结合自己在英语诗歌创作方面的实践，对过去几年我对英语诗歌创意写作的学习研究的总结，如今付梓成书，意在为自己未来的继续创作提供指引，也为中国英语诗歌创作同道的实践和研究做抛砖引玉之用。此书始于西方灵感终于东方家园，于2021年11月25日感恩节当天动笔，2023年2月5日元宵节前完成初稿，历时一年

---

  ① 转引自 https://www.poetryfoundation.org/poetrymagazine/poems/17168/ars-poetica。

三个月。事实上,本书的动念始于2018年3月我从美国访学归来,所以从萌芽到最后成书实际历经五年多时间。五年多时间里我站起来教书读诗,坐下来写书写诗。期间虽然各种杂事缠绕,然写书写诗始终为我心中正业。

感谢中山大学英语创意写作研究中心戴凡教授对我在英语诗歌创意写作实践和研究事业上的支持和鼓励!感谢我的导师华南师范大学凌海衡教授对我英语诗歌研究的引导与鼓励!感谢我的老师广东外语外贸大学余东教授对我英语诗歌研究和创作的支持!感谢美国高校圣约翰大学(St. John's University)李又宁教授、沈弘毅博士、石文珊博士、西蒙娜博士(Dr. Simona Blat)、皮尔森教授(Dr. Herbert Pierson)、法利博士(Dr. David Farley)等师友对我访学期间在英语诗歌创作中所作尝试的鼓励和支持!感谢南京大学出版社杨金荣主任及各位编辑对本书出版的大力支持!感谢广东技术师范大学各位同事对我工作的理解与支持!感谢我的家人对我沉迷读书写诗的理解和支持!但若我在英语诗歌创作上有所得,理解、支持、鼓励我的师友、家人居功至伟!

写诗是诗人爱自己、爱生命、爱世界的一种方式。即便被单独放逐到孤岛,真正的诗人也不会停止写诗!诗人不问出身,写诗不分身份职业。我的诗人同道,如果你身边的人并不欣赏你的创作,不要和他们分享你的作品便是。万不可因此放弃你的创作。实际上,我们并不知道自己为什么要创作,我们肯定是疯了!欢迎你,诗人同道!

陈津津

二〇二三年春天

广东技术师范大学